SUPER SPREADER

FORREST MAREADY

Published in the United States by
Feels Like Fire, an imprint of Feels Like Fire.
Wilmington, N.C.

Non-fiction books by Forrest Maready:
The Moth in the Iron Lung: A Biography of Polio
Red Pill Gospel: Christianity, before it was ruined by Christians,
The Tribal Instinct: The Sacred Desire for People & Place
The Autism Vaccine: The Story of Modern Medicine's Greatest Tragedy
Crooked:Man-made Disease Explained
Unvaccinated

ISBN 979-8365725997
Printed in the United States of America

The cataloging-in-publication data is on file with the Library of Congress.

30 29 28 27 26 25 24 23 22 21

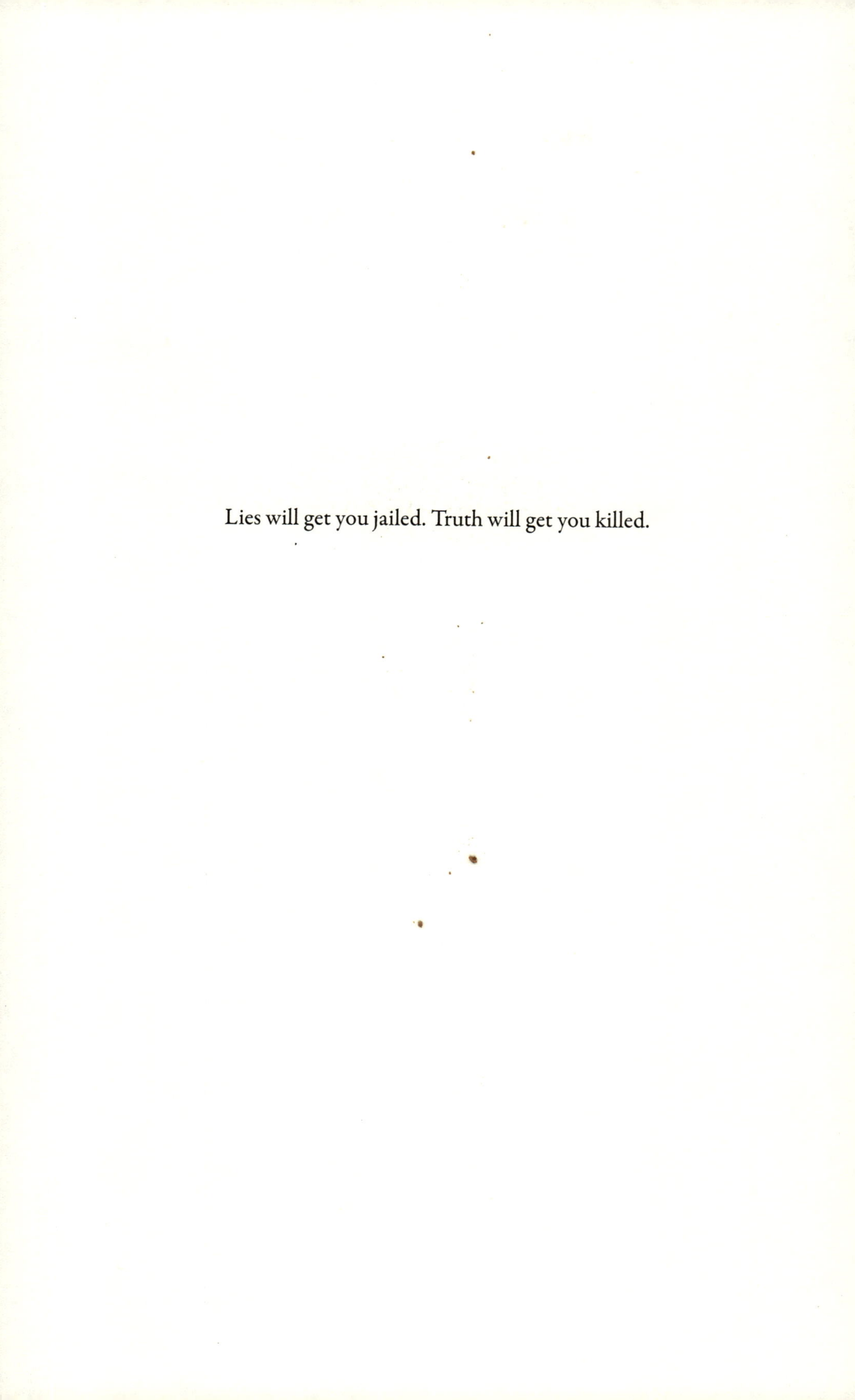

Lies will get you jailed. Truth will get you killed.

CHAPTER 1

It was winter, but deep within Washington, D.C.'s National Cathedral was a brewing tempest. There was a small chamber, a chapel where believers might entreat God more privately. It was early, and the sun was still low enough to cast splintered rays of amber and rose-colored light into the room, illuminating millions of dust particles swirling in the air—a reminder, for some in attendance, of the aerosolized threats surrounding them.

People were, in large part, gathered on one side of the aisle. Numbering over a dozen, they were mostly scientists with a few religious leaders sprinkled amongst them. The other side of the room was nearly empty. Two episcopal priests. A scientist. A former public health official. A pastor made famous by his best-selling books.

Ye of little faith, Yuval Naftali thought to himself as he waited impatiently.

The morning's demonstration was a last-minute addition, a joint request from high-ranking clergy, fearful of being humiliated in view of the largest media event the world had ever witnessed. Yuval initially refused, but without proof, the Bishop of Rome threatened to return to Italy—a rejection that would have undoubtedly cascaded onto other important dignitaries.

Yuval clicked his tongue as he checked his watch.

"Just a few more minutes and we'll begin," he said, forcing a crooked smile across his bony face.

The chapel had been transformed into something of a laboratory. The front pews were pushed back. Two large monitors stood on either side of the altar. Cables ran everywhere, connecting a group of ornate antennas to everything else.

The door to the chapel opened, and security personnel walked in, their eyes darting about the room. One of them led a dog spiraling through the pews, stopping to sniff everyone.

"Please," Yuval said in embarrassment. "We are all friends here, are we not?"

The men ignored the startled reactions they created and eventually settled into the corners, their arms resting atop submachine guns jutting out from beneath their coats. A number of high-ranking clergy, clothed in brilliant ruby vestments, walked in and took their seats.

"Ah! Here we are," Yuval said as he gestured towards the door.

A man in a motorized wheelchair rolled into the room, its joystick pressed forward by his gnarled hand. A priest dressed in a flowing red and white robe followed him to the front.

"The Archbishop of Asunción," Yuval announced with reverence, as if applause were expected.

"Which one is he?" one of the scientists joked, his shorts and sandals a marked contrast to the spectacle of liturgical clothing in the room.

"Please, gentlemen," Yuval pleaded with them. "We are all friends here."

The world was set to enter its second decade since the microbe known as MALKA-6 had been officially recognized. Almost ten years earlier, stories emerged of a killer virus in China that had people dropping dead in the streets. Within months, nearly the entire planet was consumed with panic.

Tensions ran high because there was another group of people who responded differently. Some of them were deeply religious, others not. They were bound by their refusal to be afraid. Rather than fear, they had responded with a distinct lack of concern. They had carried on with their lives as if nothing had changed. And for that, there was resentment.

As head of the World Health Alliance, Dr. Yuval Naftali felt some responsibility for bringing these two groups together, a meeting most said would never happen. He took a few deep breaths to gather himself and motioned for the man slumped in his wheelchair to turn towards those in attendance.

"Thank you all for being here today. I appreciate your putting aside your differences for a few hours—a sacrifice, I think, that will benefit the world."

Several of those seated looked across the aisle at their sworn enemies, skeptical reconciliation would ever be possible.

"You all know why we're here," Yuval said. "You've heard of discoveries that have been made over the past few months. I was hoping for everyone to witness this miracle firsthand tonight—along with the rest of the world. But there are doubters amongst you. As someone who once wrestled with my faith, a struggle I can certainly understand."

A member of the security team walked to the doorway and peered outside before returning to his post.

"And so, it seemed a small demonstration was in order. Cardinal Gordillo," Yuval said, gesturing toward the priest, his plump fingers resting on the shoulders of the crippled man. "On behalf of the Pope, Cardinal Gordillo has requested a demonstration. I trust you will talk to no one else about what you are about to see?"

The Cardinal nodded his head in agreement.

Yuval looked at the others in the room. "Everyone else?"

They affirmed their promise.

"Very well," Yuval said, removing his jacket. "Cardinal, how long have you known Mr. Maduro here?"

"Twenty-seven years," the Cardinal responded, his baritone accent booming. "He was my very first *bautismo*, an honor I will never forget."

"It was a beautiful christening, I'm sure."

Yuval paused again, this time purely for dramatic effect. "We're also honored to have Dr. Luis Yamamoto here today—his studies of motor neuron disease familiar, no doubt, to some of you."

One of the scientists bowed his head and waved his hand in acknowledgement.

"You have had just a short time with Mr. Maduro this morning, Dr. Yamamoto. Are you able to make a diagnosis of his condition?"

Dr. Yamamoto stood. "His condition is consistent with late-stage amyotrophic lateral sclerosis."

"ALS," Yuval said. "Or Lou Gehrig's disease, for those of you unfamiliar with medical terminology. Muscle weakness. Respiratory failure. No cure. Most dead within two to ten years."

Many in attendance looked uncomfortably towards Mr. Maduro, his eyes locked on the floor.

"Did you have a chance to look at his electromyography charts?"

"I did," Dr. Yamamoto said.

"And?"

"Consistent with late-stage amyotrophic lateral sclerosis."

"Very well," Yuval said, turning towards the Cardinal.

"Cardinal Gordillo, are you able to recall Mr. Maduro before this condition?"

"Yes, of course. He was the star of his school football team. An average student, but athletically gifted."

"Did you and your congregation ever pray for this man?"

"We have lifted him up in prayer for over eight years."

"Has his condition improved in that time?"

"He is still alive, a blessing for which we are eternally grateful."

Yuval nodded his head in agreement. "Yes, we are grateful for that blessing," a trace of mockery slipping through his teeth.

"Dr. Yamamoto, you are one of the world's preeminent neurologists. What do you say to Mr. Maduro? What cures can you offer him?"

"None," he replied quickly, without a trace of emotion.

"What medicines?"

"Riluzole and edaravone. Neither work as well as we'd like."

"Can either of them return this man's ability to speak clearly?"

"Unlikely," Dr. Yamamoto replied.

"Would they allow him to walk again one day?"

"Never," he said. "It'd take a miracle."

"A miracle?" Yuval asked playfully. "Wouldn't that be something? A miracle? Just like we read about as children?"

The distant strains of an orchestra and choir drifted through the entire building, a haunting tune of pure reverberation.

A rehearsal for this evening, Yuval thought. *So many moving parts, finally coming together.*

This was his rehearsal. Here, beneath the great sanctuary above, he could practice the timing. The pauses. The phrases—all of them carefully planned out weeks ago. Tonight, he would get one chance to execute the program flawlessly as the entire world watched.

"Where did miracles go?" he asked slowly. "What happened to them?"

Yuval's dramatic delivery, intended for the millions that would be watching later that evening, began to wear thin on those in the room.

"Gentlemen," he asked, "is there anyone here who doubts the condition of Mr. Maduro?"

Silence filled the room. Cardinal Gordillo wiped some spittle from the man's mouth onto a bib tied around his neck.

"Then we seem to be at an impasse, do we not? Science claims to have all the answers, but, as Dr. Yamamoto has just admitted, it's clear there are none. Mr. Maduro would seem to have no hope of ever getting better."

Yuval glanced towards the wheelchair. "My apologies, Mr. Maduro—if only temporarily."

"Our religious faith makes the same claim. God loves his children greater than we love our own, does he not, Cardinal Gordillo? He has infinite power at his disposal and yet—despite years of prayer—he is silent. He does nothing."

Yuval's tone reached another register as darkness enveloped the room.

"What hope, then, do we have for Mr. Maduro? If science cannot save him, and spiritual powers cannot either, what hope does he have?"

Yuval relaxed as he leaned against the altar, a pose he'd practiced hundreds of times. He looked around the room, making eye contact with everyone there.

"It turns out," he whispered, as if to share a precious secret, "it turns out, there is hope. Not through science alone. And not through faith alone. But through their *union*. Through their *marriage*. A blending of the two we have only just begun to understand."

A metallic crash reverberated from outside, followed by someone yelling in anger, breaking the spell Yuval had cast.

"Could someone close the doors?" he asked, perturbed by the disturbance.

One of the Cardinal's security detail left his corner post and silently shut the doors.

Union. Marriage. Where was I?

"A blending of the two," Yuval continued, "we have only just begun to understand."

Yuval switched on the monitors and rolled some of the equipment around the man in the wheelchair.

"Do you believe?" Yuval asked Mr. Maduro, pulling his head upright. "Do you believe in the power of this union?"

Despite years of ALS, the man still had limited movement. He shook his head up and down as best he could.

"Is that a yes?" Yuval asked again, his voice rising in tone. "You do believe?"

The man continued to nod.

"Cardinal Gordillo, could you ask some of your brethren up here? We're going to pray for this man."

Gordillo appeared shocked at the request, unsure if he was being mocked or not.

"Go ahead," Yuval said, as he continued to manipulate some of the equipment surrounding the altar. "Get your best men up here. Pastor, you, too."

Some of the scientists grew uncomfortable with their choice of seats, subconsciously sliding away from the center aisle as a few of the clergy walked toward the front.

Yuval sensed their unease. "Scientists, your work is already done. You can just sit back and enjoy the show—unless you feel like joining us in prayer."

Yuval kneeled directly beside the crippled man, their eyes level with each other. "Is your family here with you today?" he asked.

Mr. Maduro struggled to shake his head no.

"Why isn't your family here with you?"

Mr. Maduro pressed his knuckles against the screen attached to his wheelchair, typing a response.

"You're my family," a computerized voice prompted as the man slapped his chest and tried to point at Yuval, his eyes filling with tears.

"So touching. The man has no family."

Yuval gestured to his right. "Our best scientists." To his left. "Our best men of faith."

He held both arms up in the air. "Yet Mr. Maduro is left with nothing—not even a family to take care of him. But he believes in what you—what all of us—might accomplish."

Four men encircled the wheelchair. Yuval grabbed the Cardinal's hand in solidarity.

"Pastors and priests. Scientists and researchers. You will never forget about you are about to witness," he said, his voice booming louder than ever as he turned one of the monitors inwards. "The union of science and faith will be sealed forever!"

* * *

Outside the chapel, Natalie Connolly couldn't make sense as to what was going on within. She'd been looking for her father—lately always within an arm's length of Yuval—when she heard someone close the wooden doors. Through stained glass windows, she could vaguely see a group of men surrounding something, their hands outstretched in fervent prayer. She craned her neck, trying to find a better pane of glass through which to see. Although she couldn't hear what they were saying, the way their shoulders shook made it look as though they were weeping.

Suddenly, something made her feel as though a lightning bolt struck her chest. In the center of the room, barely visible, was a wheelchair—laying on its side.

It was empty.

CHAPTER 2

Some ninety miles away, in the crags of northern West Virginia, Thomas Finch listened intently as he hugged the cold mountainside. There were few sounds in winter but, nevertheless, he'd grown accustomed to cataloging everything he heard. Right now, the list included gurgling water, a diesel engine in the distance, and the snapping of a twig. Cracking wood wasn't normally a cause for alarm, but the silence that followed had his pulse thumping in his ear. About 40bpm too high, he guessed.

Animals don't care about making noise, he thought to himself. *Not unless they're hunting something.*

Located at the bottom of a dead-end gravel road that twisted for a half-mile down the side of a mountain, he was less than a hundred feet from a hunting cabin he had recently commandeered when he heard the snap and froze. Finch scanned the terrain, looking for any sign of movement. He hadn't had a shower in days, but if his hands were any indication, his face would have been nearly indistinguishable from the fauna surrounding him. Years earlier, in better health, he would have taken a chance and made a run for it.

"You're built for speed, Finch. Not endurance."

He could hear the words of his cross-country coach echoing through his head, polite words meant to steer him into another sport—a suggestion he refused. Now he couldn't take any chances—not even a sprint. His heart was falling apart—he could tell. It was only a matter of time.

He can't see me if I don't move. Unless he's already seen me. In which case I'm already dead.

It was early morning and leaves were still covered in frost. At least they'd keep silent. He looked up the mountain above him and could see nothing but tree trunks breaking through the last bit of fog. Just below, a creek cut along the small pasture the cabin occupied, its banks encrusted with shards of ice.

Trying to slow his heart, Finch opened his mouth wide and began taking deep breaths.

Shit.

Several men emerged from the mist above him. Three of them, possibly four, just a few hundred feet away. Rifles. Full tactical gear. Even their faces were covered. He slid his canvas bag above him in hopes it might offer camouflage as they made their descent.

Finch began to shimmy down the mountain, pulling his bag with him.

Shit.

To his left, another team of men began to scramble their way down. He glanced to his right. Four hundred feet away, a third team had nearly reached the creek below him.

A shot split the air in half. Finch instinctively closed his eyes and clenched his bag in hopes the folded canvas might offer some protection. Another shot, then another, echoed across the mountainside. Men began to yell directions to each other.

He stole a glance above him. One of the men dragged another behind a tree. Two others lay in a twisted pile on the ground.

What the?

Finch looked around, and the other teams had disappeared into the trees.

Where'd they go?

He grabbed his bag and clambered down the mountain, expecting another shot would ring out at any moment, ending his life. The creek was too wide to jump. He stomped on the edges, breaking the ice apart, the resulting noise giving his position away for anyone who cared to listen.

Slow is steady. Steady is fast. The words of his least-favorite drill instructor ran through his mind.

He stepped into the creek, and his legs seared with pain.

Slow is steady. Steady is fast.

Finch held his bag above the water and forced himself across, flinging each leg forward through the frigid current. He slammed his elbow down upon the ice lining the bank, again and again, until he had a clear path.

Why'd they stop shooting?

His heart was pounding, but there was nothing he could do as he flung his bag onto the rocks. The ice caught his pockets and tore through his leg as he tried to claw his way out. He was stuck.

Cargo pants.

He looked up the mountain above him. The two figures remained where they had fallen. The others were either gone or hiding. Finch backed down into the water and smashed a bigger opening within the ice. His fingers were too numb to grasp nearly anything.

Another crack of gunfire split the air.

I'm going to be killed by fucking cargo pants.

Finch scissor-kicked his legs furiously. He rose out of the water high enough to grab a low-hanging branch. It bent down into the water, and by grasping hand-over-hand, he pulled himself onto the shore.

It was only thirty feet to the cabin, but there was no cover—he'd be totally exposed. Finch grabbed his bag and tried to run but immediately stumbled to the ground, his legs frozen stiff. Instinctively, he raised his hands in the air and stumbled backward toward the cabin.

"I surrender," he said out loud. "I surrender."

Finch reached the porch and tried to throw the sliding glass door open. It wouldn't budge.

Huh?

He hobbled around to the door on the side. It was also locked.

What the?

He'd just left the cabin to look for something—anything—to eat and felt sure he'd left the doors unlocked. He held his bag against the windowpane and slammed it with the heel of his hand, a wild punch which did nothing. He tried his elbow. Again, nothing.

What I'd give for a hammer.

He collapsed on the porch and tried to slow his breathing. One hundred and forty beats per minute. One-twenty was supposed to be his max—any more was too risky. Twisting sideways, he peered around the corner, looking for signs of men crossing the creek. A digital tone played from within his bag.

Why is my phone still on? he thought to himself. *No wonder they found me.*

Just days on the run and they'd already traced the burner he'd stolen from a local gas station. He fumbled through the bag and held the phone up to his face.

What I'd give for a hammer—and some reading glasses.

Finch squinted his eyes, still unable to decipher what the message read. He made an okay sign with his hand, curling his finger so only a sliver of light could pass through—makeshift readers he'd come to rely on.

Shit.

It was a message from Natalie—his ex-wife.

They did it, the text read.

He had just texted her an hour earlier—the first time in forever.

She had replied.

I just saw it. They can heal her.

Finch clutched his chest as his heart skipped hard.

CHAPTER 3

John Brinkley stood outside the bedroom door, praying for strength. Beside him waited two of his deputies and a priest—all of them more anxious than he. At 52, Brinkley was a beast of a man—heavier than he would have liked, but with a frame that still carried his weight with ease. *Brinks* they called him. An armored truck.

He put his elbow against the door and paused.

Maybe I'm getting too old for this.

At this point in his life, he thought nothing could genuinely frighten him.

He was wrong.

When he heard the call come in—a frantic mother screaming for her child—it chilled his entire body. Once he arrived at the scene, the parents were so hysterical he'd been forced to escort them outside.

"You boys ready?" he asked.

They all nodded solemnly.

The door jamb had already been split open along two deadbolts set above the knob. He cracked the door and peaked inside. He could see nothing but floor, smeared with blood.

"We're going to need some shoe covers."

Both deputies turned back down the hall.

"Monroe," Brinkley barked. "Stay here." The deputy reluctantly turned around and stood behind the priest.

Brinkley pushed the door open with his elbow, giving a full view inside the room. It was clearly a young girl's bedroom, once decorated with care. Blue walls. Stuffed animals. A tiny chandelier over the bed.

But things were out of place. Sheets were torn from the bed. The mattress was set at an angle across the box springs. Toys were strewn about the room. Swirls of blood across the floor gave clear indication of struggle.

At least she put up a fight.

The girl's body lay on her stomach, as if she were looking at something under the bed.

"Where's her head?" Monroe asked in horror.

Brinkley doubled over as he fought the urge to vomit. A barb of pink spinal column protruded from the bloody stump of what had been her neck, the flesh completely shredded.

"Dear God," the priest said, instinctively covering his face with his hands.

In twenty-four years of law enforcement, Brinkley had never seen anything like it. Crime scenes, particularly involving children, were still difficult for him to process. This was something entirely different.

He peered around the perimeter of the room, looking for her head. The hysterical phone call made sense now, his subconscious already removing the mother from a list of suspects.

"Monroe, go get those shoe covers and tell Garcia to get friendly with the dad."

A breeze picked up outside, knocking something against the house. The priest tapped Brinkley on the shoulder and pointed to a bloody window beside the bed. A chill coursed through his body as he realized the killer might still be in the room. Instinctively, he grabbed for his pistol, but it wasn't there—forgotten by his bed in his haste to leave.

I AM too old for this.

Monroe returned and handed the covers to Brinkley.

"Give me your gun," he said as he slipped the plastic sleeves over his shoes. "I forgot mine."

Brinkley stepped into the room and nearly retched as his feet begin to slide and stick with every step. He peeked under the bed and saw that it was clear. Monroe pointed at the closet door as Brinkley made his way around the edge of the room. The muffled voices of Garcia and the sobbing parents could be heard coming through the window, resting slightly ajar.

Brinkley yanked the closet door open, peering in from the side. Normally, he would have boomed a thunderous command to intimidate whomever might be hiding into submission, but for some reason, his voice faltered. He tried to project but couldn't.

"Clear," he said, his voice cracking with anxiety. Even though the closet was uninhabited, he couldn't shake the creepy feeling the whole scene generated.

"No head?" Monroe asked.

"I don't see it anywhere," Brinkley replied, taking a closer look at the body. "Did the parents say anything to you? What the locks were for?"

"I can probably answer that," the priest chimed in. "They were having trouble controlling her. They said she was trying to hurt them, trying to hurt herself—totally out of control. Thought I might be able to help."

"How long you been here?" Brinkley asked.

"I don't know. 15 minutes before she called you."

"Who busted the door open?"

"Must have been the dad. I was with the mother."

Brinkley looked around the room again. Drawings. Pictures of friends. Swimming in a lake. Riding a horse.

"How old was she?"

"Six or seven, I think."

"And you're their priest?"

"No," he replied, beginning to sense an accusation. "I don't know them. I was the first person they came across with experience in dealing with... supernatural things, I guess you would say."

Now we're starting to make some sense.

"She was possessed?" Deputy Monroe asked.

"Well, she was obviously disturbed—that's all I can say. I never even saw her until just now."

"Did they *suggest* to you she was possessed?" Brinkley asked, his detective engine firing on all cylinders.

"No. They don't seem like the superstitious type."

This would make anyone superstitious.

Brinkley snapped on a latex glove and took a closer look at the body. Her hands were covered in blood, the fingernails encrusted with some unlucky person's flesh.

I've never seen a kid put up such a fight.

"Supposedly, people who are possessed can show superhuman strength," Monroe offered. "Whoever did this ran into the wrong girl."

Brinkley looked around and mentally processed the room again.

What am I missing?

Her bed had been moved—marks in the floor made it obvious. The stuffed animals—their heads, torn off. An empty bowl sat on the floor beside the bed. The lamp on the nightstand was still on, a few children's books and a bottle of Pepto-Bismol, its only contents.

A blood-curdling scream floated in from outside, the same haunting voice from the 911 call. Brinkley ran to the window and looked outside. The father was holding the mother, who had collapsed into his arms. Garcia's back was toward the parents, his arms outstretched as if shielding them from something.

Brinkley threw the window open, blood dripping from the sash. "What is it? Garcia! What's going on?"

Garcia looked back and said something to the father, who dragged the mother away. Once they had moved far enough, Garcia pointed down emphatically toward the ground then toward his temple.

"What's he saying, Brinks?" Monroe asked.

"I think we found our head."

"Out there? What's it doing out there?"

Brinkley looked around the room again, tracing the swirls of blood. Something began to click.

Dear God.

He looked around the window and poked his head outside for a moment. He turned back and looked at the body again. The hands. The fingernails.

This can't be possible.

"Who could do something like this?" the priest asked.

"A monster," Monroe said, as nausea turned to anger.

The priest crossed himself and began reciting a whispered prayer.

Brinkley grabbed the muzzle of his gun and handed it back to Monroe.

"I don't think this was murder," Brinkley said, his mind filled with dread. "I think it was suicide."

CHAPTER 4

Dr. Albert Connolly stormed towards the cathedral, looking for Yuval Naftali. Something unexpected had happened, something for which Connolly was furious.

I cannot believe he did this, he thought to himself as he flashed a security badge to the men guarding the entrance.

Word of Mr. Maduro's miraculous recovery spread quickly, despite Yuval's insistence those in the room say nothing of what they had witnessed. As head of the National Institutes of Health, Connolly had insisted things remain a secret until later that day, a necessary step to ensure the maximum media coverage possible. No one but a few had seen Yuval's discovery in action—not even Connolly. The fact others had seen it first—common people who had spent nothing, risked nothing, and dreamed nothing to make it possible—had him fuming. The fact the premature reveal had been specifically at Yuval's request guaranteed there would be fireworks.

The evening's event was billed as something dramatic—the most important advance in the history of science. But there was a twist, a wrinkle that had nearly everyone on the planet intent on watching. The advance wasn't *just* scientific—it was also *spiritual.* It was the culmination a lifetime of work of Albert Connolly, a man who had felt the presence of God within the lab as much as any church sanctuary. For him, the Psalms and Proverbs offered solace and comfort, but so, too, did the journals of Linnaeus and Mendel. Bach and Handel were glorious—the polio vaccines of Salk and Sabin, even more so.

The sanctuary was still being prepared for the event. Workers were everywhere. Risers for media were set in the back. Cables snaked down the sides, connecting cameras and microphones to the enormous production trucks parked outside. At around 7pm, velvet pipe and drape would direct the scientists, clergy, politicians, and celebrities along the red carpet from their vehicles into the narthex, cheered by the thousands of spectators already gathered outside the chain-link fencing surrounding the building.

That was just ten hours away.

The guest list was impressive. A bevy of stars ensured news of the event would reach the common man. Cosmologists would attend. Molecular biologists would be there. The academic world was buzzing with news of their discovery and several particle physicists were thrilled to have received an invitation. But without the appearance of esteemed men of faith, their followers would likely never believe what would be reported. And so, the Catholic and Orthodox churches were to be represented by their highest ranking officials. The Grand Ayatollah and Grand Imam were expected, as were a few prominent Hindu priests and Buddhist monks. Connolly had pulled every string, every favor he was ever owed—whatever it took—to guarantee their presence.

For the aging doctor, the event could not have come soon enough. At 78 years old, the mental acuity that had so effectively powered his spiritual and scientific exploration was fading. His six-and-a-half-foot frame, once an imposing presence throughout the halls in Bethesda, was beginning to feel less so. Through his jovial attitude and frequent charity events, he was the vision of eternal youth imbued. But tension from years of MALKA-6—not to mention the strain of his attempts to bridge two sides of the enormous conflict it caused—had taken its toll.

Connolly appeared to have aged ten years since he received the call, just weeks before.

"It works," Yuval told him. "It's confirmed."

It had taken two decades of secretive research and development, a long series of incremental advances that made this final call seem all but inevitable. But it had finally happened.

It works, Connolly thought to himself, shaking his head in disbelief. *I can't believe we did it.*

* * *

The unlikely bond Dr. Connolly and the mercurial Yuval Naftali developed during the previous decade was legendary. Connolly was the highest-ranking health official in the United States, an elder statesman within the scientific community, the religious themes he attempted to weave throughout his work a constant source of ridicule—scorn he was willing to bear. Yuval, once an up-and-coming phenom whose research amazed the world, had recently extended his influence into social and economic arenas as he took over the World Health Alliance. Connolly signed off on nearly every grant—billions in funding. Yuval and his team tore through every dollar. Through incredible tension, they both remained laser-focused on the mission. Other personalities came and went, but Connolly and Yuval had somehow been able to shelve their egos in hopes of serving the greater good—no matter their differences on what *greater good* actually meant.

The tenuous affinity they shared with each other seemed to evaporate the morning after the call.

"We should pray," an exuberant Connolly said after rushing to the laboratory. "Don't you think? We should give God thanks for this incredible gift."

Yuval froze. He was stunned, unsure what to say.

"It's only fitting," Connolly said. "We should consecrate this breakthrough. Dedicate it to the service of God."

"Which god?" Yuval asked, straining to conjure a smile from his face.

"Oh come now, we both serve the same *Yahweh*, don't we?"

"Dr. Connolly, I'm concerned at how the religious community might receive our work." Yuval was clearly headed in another direction. "The union of science and faith is not something they're going to accept. Not readily."

"You'll have some wonderful papers, I'm sure. The journals will kill each other to publish them."

"Priests don't read scientific papers."

"Some do," Connolly chimed.

"Most do not. Rabbis don't. Imams don't. The Hindus and the Buddhists—I don't imagine they do either."

"What do you propose?"

Yuval breathed deeply, his eyes wandering to another place or time. "We should do a demonstration. A public demonstration."

"The auditorium at the NIH—it can seat two hundred people."

"No," Yuval shot back. "A *very* public demonstration. On their turf. In their space. In a setting they're used to seeing. In a language they're used to hearing."

Connolly's mind began to swirl.

"It can't be seen as a science event," Yuval continued. "It's got to feel like a very special religious occasion. That must come first."

"The National Cathedral," Connolly muttered.

"Yes," Yuval replied, his brow furrowed with intensity. "Invite everyone."

* * *

"What do you think you're doing?" Connolly screamed.

He found Yuval in the temporary office he'd seized for the week. Workers outside stopped as Connolly slammed the 8-foot door behind him, sending a concussive boom rolling through the halls.

"Careful," Yuval said. "We're in a house of God here."

Connolly walked around the conference table to confront him directly, his nose whistling with air as he tried to control his breathing. "We agreed. Absolute secrecy. No leaks! No nothing!"

Yuval backed away.

"We agreed!" Connolly screamed, grabbing Yuval by the shirt. "What are you doing?"

Yuval took Connolly's hand and tried to calm him. "It was just a few people."

"Everyone out there is talking about it! We've taken everybody's cell phones, but it'll get out. It'll be over every newsfeed within an hour!"

"We were about to lose the Cardinals," Yuval countered. "If they don't come...."

"You should have let me handle that!"

He is taking over, Connolly thought to himself. *He is taking over, and there is nothing I can do to stop it.*

Connolly walked away, trying to gather himself.

Just a few more hours and my life's work will be complete. Just a few more hours and he won't be a threat anymore.

"You have a darkness," Connolly stated matter-of-factly. "Has anyone ever told you that?"

Yuval appeared unmoved.

"I wasn't always high church," Connolly continued. "I had a Pentecostal phase. Do you know what that is—Pentecostals? They're wild. They dance. They speak in tongues. All the crazies are Pentecostals. I was one of them. I outgrew it, eventually. But one thing stuck with me—auras. Almost like a smell you can see."

"And I suppose you can smell me?" Yuval sneered.

"I can see a smell. I hadn't noticed it before. I can see it now. It's a darkness. Something's changed."

"You're positive your devotion to science survived this Pentecostal phase?"

"What the hell is that supposed to mean?"

"Auras, Connolly? Darkness. I suppose next I can expect to be labelled a demon?"

"I know about your research," Connolly said. "Technion Institute, Transcriptomic Laboratory: Myth, Magic, and the Teoma Gene. By Hans Ylimäki et. al. That ring a bell?"

"I have no idea what you're talking about."

"I know your aliases, Yuval. I didn't grant you all that money without looking into things."

Yuval pretended not to be shocked Connolly knew his secret identity. "I was a rebellious post-doc who should've never been given a lab and a microphone. I said crazy things. I was speaking in tongues, like you."

"We replicated your paper, *Hans*."

Yuval looked stunned. "What are you talking about?"

"We replicated your research. We used twins and everything. You know that almost never happens. We did it twice, just to make sure. And it worked both times."

"I don't even remember half of that study."

He's lying, Connolly thought. *He's hiding something.*

Something dark.

"You think I'm not being honest with you?" Yuval asked.

"I think you're up to something. I think that stunt you pulled this morning was just the first part of something else."

"Okay," Yuval said, pulling away and gathering himself. "I'll be upfront with you. We have an unannounced person making an appearance tonight. I wanted it to be a surprise."

"Who?"

"Your son-in-law."

"Finch?"

Yuval smiled broadly. "Yes."

"You know where he is? Not sure if you've heard, but he's missing. He escaped. Days ago. He's vanished."

"We found him."

"And he's coming? Tonight?"

"Yes."

Connolly was stunned. "Why? No one on our guest list will come if he's here."

"Thus, the secret."

"He's the most hated man on the planet."

"Not by everyone," Yuval countered. "You live in a bubble here in D.C. and your conferences and galas. Out there, people love him."

"How is that possible? After what he did?"

"They think he did the world a favor. He's a hero in their eyes."

Traitor. Murderer.

Connolly paged through years of anger he normally kept squirreled away. "I just don't see it."

"Tonight represents the union of science and faith. Don't think of it like a marriage. Think of it like a reconciliation. What better moment will there ever be to show the world reconciliation is possible? Finch, making a public apology, confessing his sins before the world, surrounded—in forgiveness—by those very people he so wronged. It will be beautiful."

"He's rejected science. He has no spiritual faith. He's a murderer who has nothing to do with anything we're doing here."

"He will atone for his sin. I can assure you of that."

"They'll arrest him the moment they see him."

"I've made arrangements to ensure that won't happen—at least, not tonight."

Connolly was still unconvinced. "How are you planning on getting him here? You know how petulant he is—he'll never agree to doing any of this."

"Oh, I think he will," Yuval said. "They should be putting him on a helicopter right about now."

CHAPTER 5

In Bethesda, Maryland, Natalie Connolly raced over the cobblestoned courtyard of the mansion they called home for the week. It was a wonder someone had enough wealth to loan a house like this to others—an enormous French Colonial with wine cellars, two pools, and a world-class library. But, her father had many friends—friends who owed him favors. The space was a perfect location to entertain—and in some cases, house—the seemingly endless collection of celebrities and dignitaries that needed coddling and assurance their presence was appreciated.

* * *

"Is this the Biltmore Mansion?" her daughter had asked when they arrived, days earlier.

"No, but it's a close second."

"We really get to live here?"

"For a while, Eva. Not long—just a week or two."

"Can you take me on a tour? Like at the Smithsonian?"

"I will do my best."

The cobblestones were rough, but once Natalie moved Eva inside, the gurney she was confined to—along with all the ancillary equipment stored beneath—rolled more easily.

"Here," Natalie said, adjusting the incline of the bed. "Sit up a little bit more so you can see better."

"It's loud in here."

Needs more paintings, Natalie nearly said before stopping herself.

"That's because there's no carpet. This is the Grand Foyer. This is where all the distinguished guests will come in and receive a warm welcome from Papa."

"And us, too?" Eva asked.

"Papa will be happy to see us, too."

"No—I mean, will we get to welcome the distinguished guests?"

Pain shot through Natalie's heart. Then anger, always following close behind.

It was too much for her to bear. The best medical care in the world, her father the most well-known celebrity in public health. Her only child, unable to even move her arms to shake someone's hand.

Why didn't he just kill her?

Natalie couldn't believe the thoughts that flashed through her brain. Unlike her father, her faith in God was non-existent. She'd spent her entire education in parochial schools—typically a guarantee of spiritual rebellion—but had somehow emerged apparently unharmed. It was much later, after her daughter's accident, that the prayer and silent reflection stopped.

Her marriage in shambles, her father consumed by work, she withdrew into herself and resolved to a lifetime of bitter nihilism.

* * *

Natalie bounded up the spiral staircase and into her daughter's bedroom, cicadas piping through the open windows. Eva was asleep, the clicking and whirring of machines under her bed a discomforting reminder of her condition.

I can't believe this is possible. Natalie had been whispering it to herself the entire ride from the cathedral. *I can't believe it.*

"Eva," Natalie said, rocking her gently. "Eva, baby. Wake up."

The young girl stirred as Natalie wiped beads of sweat from her tiny nose. "Wake up, honey."

She opened her eyes and looked around for a moment, confused. "What is it?"

"Remember your paintings? Remember the paintings you used to make for me?" They were Natalie's most treasured possessions. She'd consulted with preservationists at the museum on how to care for them.

Eva was still groggy from sleep. "I think so."

I can't believe I'm saying this.

"How would you like it if you could paint again?"

CHAPTER 6

They can heal her.

He hadn't heard from Natalie in years. Or she hadn't heard from him, depending on who was telling the story. She was too angry. He was too proud. Big days came and went. Anniversaries. Birthdays.

Somehow, he'd managed to escape. He was being moved somewhere. Another prison, some said. A medical research facility, someone else suggested. Whatever the case, someone messed up. The van was unlocked, the guard distracted. Finch threw the door open and bolted for the woods.

Throwing caution to the wind, he ran for what felt like a mile. He ran until the iron-flavored tang of blood filled his mouth, his lungs pushed beyond their breaking point. Looking behind him, there was no one. There were no barking dogs. No sirens. Just the cold, crisp air of West Virginia mountains and the hope he'd never have to see the inside of a jail cell again.

Several days passed, and Finch's optimism began to fade. Food was difficult to come by. Restful sleep, impossible. He began hearing sirens wail in the distance. Dogs barking. Confident his capture was imminent, Finch texted Natalie earlier that morning.

Hey. It's me.

She wouldn't have recognized the number. He wasn't sure what to say.

I'm sorry for everything, Nat, he typed before deleting it.

It's me, Nat. How is she? another phrase he couldn't bring himself to send.

Instead, he just typed a simple phrase.

Hey. It's me.

Finch hit the send button and hoped she would reply. An hour or two later, his hideout apparently surrounded, she did.

They can heal her.

Finch guessed what Natalie meant and regretted his decision to reach out.

They better not touch her. They better not lay a single finger on her or I will kill them all. Painfully.

Furious, Finch stepped off the porch and found a fist-sized rock he could comfortably hold.

Hammer.

He slammed it into one of the door's window panes, but it twisted in his hand, glancing off the glass and across the porch.

This glass is bulletproof, he thought. *Or hammer-proof, at least.*

He rifled through his bag, looking for anything that might be useful.

Why are these doors locked?

He still couldn't understand what was going on. Finch dropped the bag and scanned the porch. Rocking chair? No. Firewood? No. An old toilet?

A porcelain toilet?

Most medical schools wouldn't take Finch, due in part to his criminal record. He had a habit of breaking into cars in high school—their tempered-glass windows no match for the porcelain spark plug fragments he always carried. He threw the toilet onto the rocks beneath the porch, shattering into several large pieces.

So much for stealth, he thought as he broke the toilet down to even smaller pieces.

Finch looked at his pants, one side torn and soaked with blood. He removed the belt from his waist and jammed a few slivers of porcelain into the canvas just beside the buckle. A modern day morning star.

He slammed the strap against the pane just above the doorknob, and the window shattered instantly.

Even my belt is more useful than these cargo pants.

Reaching through the pane, he opened the door outward, scampering inside as shards of glass crumbled underneath his boots. Finch peered outside into the woods, his ears focused on the beeping of a large vehicle backing up.

Evacuated, he thought. *The wounded at least. Maybe everyone. They'll be back.*

He checked his pulse.

130bpm.

"Twenty minutes," he said to himself as he set a timer on the kitchen counter. "Twenty minutes and you'll be at 80bpm."

Time was a luxury he seldom enjoyed. Even the remote cabin wasn't worth risking more than a day or two in before he would need to move. The tiny kitchen felt like heaven—coffee, a forbidden pleasure. Caffeine had him so wired he barely noticed the bleeding on his leg. He pulled the torn pants back and grimaced at what he saw. Finch reached into his canvas bag and pulled out a white plastic tool.

Don't make skin staplers for nothing.

His bag had little food, few tools, and even fewer medical supplies. But he did have a medical stapler, something he had saved just for such an occasion. Multiple combat tours as a special operator in the Middle East, years of residency as a physician in the ER, and he'd never treated someone for an ice wound.

He'd never stapled himself, either, but decided to save the Lidocaine for later —just in case. Staples were one thing. Appendectomies? Cardiac catheterizations? He felt sure he'd pass out if he had to try those without anesthesia.

Finch stood up, trying to get the sides of the wound to align. After pinching it closed, he squared the stapler, closed his eyes, and squeezed.

Not as bad as I thought, he lied as his eyes began to water. He inserted another staple.

Okay, much worse.

His fingers began shaking so he sat down and shot seven more staples along the wound, using both hands to steady the device. Finch looked at the timer—twelve minutes left. He checked his pulse.

113bpm.

Again, a digital tone played from within his canvas bag.

Shit.

He grabbed his phone and was about to turn it off, but froze. It was Natalie—*calling* this time. A hundred unfinished conversations ran through his head. It had been years since they'd actually spoken.

They can heal her, she had texted.

Finch knew about the research her father was funding in partnership with the World Health Alliance. He'd uncovered many things they didn't want others knowing about, knowledge which made him the enemy of very powerful people.

A news report jumped into his mind, every word perfectly remembered: *Eva Finch, granddaughter of NIH head Albert Connolly, has been diagnosed with C4 quadriplegia in yesterday's terrible incident. Loss of nearly all motion. Loss of bowel and bladder control.* Her diagnosis—all the horrible details—broadcast for the world to see. Nearly four years old at the time, her life ruined.

They did it. I just saw it. They can heal her.

But how? How could it actually be possible? Spinal cord injuries were like tearing a hundred interlocking spider webs into pieces. How could anyone ever put something so intricate—so fragile—back into its original shape? Still fuming at what they'd done to his heart, Finch trusted no one.

They will not touch her, he thought to himself. *Not if I can help it.*

His phone stopped ringing. Just days of living on the run and Finch was already making mistakes. Days of living like an animal and nothing but a pair of shredded cargo pants and a heart condition to show for it.

He held the power button down.

Shutting off, it displayed before going completely dark.

Finch grabbed his wrist and counted.

118bpm.

His pulse was going in the wrong direction.

CHAPTER 7

Cardinal Gordillo arrived at the Prince George State Hospital, a single black SUV serving as his motorcade.

"Lovely," he said mockingly to his driver as they entered the campus.

In continuous existence for over 170 years, it was the oldest public medical center in the country, a sprawling campus full of dilapidated buildings frequently rented to Hollywood productions for their unmistakable asylum aesthetic.

"Wait here," Gordillo said as they stopped under the tower of an imposing three-story Gothic building.

Layers of flowing red fabric swirled behind him as his enormous bulk hobbled inside, his entrance much different than the theatrics of the chapel. No security detail. No bomb-sniffing dogs. No wheelchair-bound Mr. Maduro.

Within, Gordillo was met with the distinct aroma of institutional health, a smell impossible to replicate without decades of linoleum and vomit. There was no receptionist. No nurses on duty. Just a long hallway with two very anxious parents waiting at the end.

"Cardinal! Cardinal!" They began calling the moment they could see him. "We thought you'd never get here."

"I am here! Not to worry. I am here."

The mother's face showed concern. "Where are all the nurses? The staff?"

"Have they left you all alone?" Gordillo laughed, his brows turned down in feigned sadness.

"It's just that we..." the father said before he stopped. "We're not used to having such little care."

"He's in such a fragile state—from all the travel," the mother added.

"Not to say we're not extremely thankful for this opportunity, of course."

"Yes, yes," Gordillo said, his eyes darting back towards the entrance. "An incredible opportunity, of course. So very exciting. Is the boy inside?"

* * *

When Albert Connolly and Yuval first discussed who the star of the evening's show would be, the mother and father's son—a boy called Mongchai—was the obvious choice. Through an incredible sequence of events, he'd become a global celebrity at just six years old. Trapped for weeks within a flooded cave, he and several other children were assumed to be dead. Attempts were made to recover their bodies, but navigating the narrow channels proved impossible for even the smallest divers who tried.

Nearing starvation, Mongchai resolved to find a way out—by diving through tunnels of pitch black water. He made four tries, each unsuccessful attempt an agonizing process of discovery as the confined passageways meant he was unable to turn around, each return trip a maddening swim backwards in complete darkness. Realizing even if he were to make it out, the larger kids would likely be unable to, he fashioned a rope out of shoe strings, torn fabric, and anything else the children could salvage.

"If I pull three times, that means I'm through," he told them before making what he thought would be his last trip. "If I pull more, that means I need help."

Mongchai almost made it. He was just 10 feet from the cave entrance when divers found him nearly lifeless. He was airlifted to a hospital, where, incredibly, he survived. The makeshift rope tied to his ankle was used to ferry food and messages back to the others, the entire world shocked to learn the children were still alive. Eventually, all were rescued, unharmed despite their incredible ordeal.

The boy who saved them did not fare as well. Mongchai's brain was not working. He was unresponsive—alive, but little more. *Persistent vegetative state*, the doctors called it. In a moving tribute for him and his family, the children he saved gathered in his hospital room to cast their Buddhist prayers in hopes of his recovery. With news cameras rolling, their interlocked hands forming a circle around him, something remarkable happened. He squeezed his mother's finger—three times.

Months passed, and others who came to visit Mongchai experienced the same phenomenon. Sometimes it was faint, other times distinct. He hadn't spoken. He had barely moved. Regardless, the boy's resilience and fight to survive captivated the world.

* * *

"He's been vegetative for over a year," Connolly said to Yuval as they discussed who the event might feature. "You know that, right? It seems risky. You're sure it will work on someone like him?"

"Ye of little faith," Yuval chided.

"*Me* of little faith? You're the one who won't even pray."

"I expect it will work just as well as the others."

Connolly still had trouble wrapping his head around what they had done. Healing. Miracles—straight from the Bible days. Just like Jesus. They needed to reveal their discovery to the world in a way no one would be left doubting.

Yuval sensed some reluctance. "You're not convinced."

"They're Buddhist, Yuval. I believe in the technology, but it seems like a more Christian story might resonate better with our Western audience."

"Who's more well known than him?"

"No one."

"Who would people want to see healed more than him?

"No one I can think of."

"Who's more *deserving* of being healed than him?"

Eva.

Connolly immediately thought of his granddaughter. Perfectly innocent. Pure light. Unbridled joy.

Yuval continued. "Who has more life in front of them, once they're healed, to spread the gospel—*our* gospel of science and faith?"

My only grandchild.

Connolly thought back to a game he played with Eva. He could see her head roll back, her hands covering her face in rapturous laughter. Stiff as a board, she would fall backwards off the couch into his arms, again and again, completely trusting he would catch her.

"Connolly," Yuval said.

The belief of a child. He longed for such faith.

"Connolly! It has to be him. There is no other choice."

* * *

"Let me have just a moment with Mongchai," Cardinal Gordillo told the parents, resting his hand on the mother's arm with assurance. "Let me pray with him to make sure he has a clean spirit. These things can go wrong sometimes. There will be millions watching tonight. We have to be careful."

Gordillo opened the door to the room. Beneath a large window was an old radiator. The walls had started to peel long ago, leaving the wooden floor covered in flakes of paint. An old sink was attached to the wall. Beside it, a metal-framed bed with no mattress. Lying directly on top was the tiny body of their son, wrapped in what appeared to be his father's jacket.

The Cardinal stepped inside and closed the door behind him.

CHAPTER 8

Brinkley and his two deputies left the priest to comfort the parents and left for their office to get an evidence kit and cleaning supplies. With no back seat, Garcia's truck made for an intimate conversation.

"Suicide?" Agent Monroe asked Brinkley for the fifth time. "Seven-year-old girl rips her own head off and throws it out the window?"

Brinkley had worked hundreds of cases over the years, many of them murders made to appear as suicide. He'd seen one or two where someone killed themself and tried to stage a murder, a pitiful attempt to spare their families one final bit of guilt or shame.

He'd never seen anything like this.

"Let's just assume she was...possessed," Brinkley said.

"Head spinning around?" Garcia asked. "Climbing on the ceiling?"

"No, dummy. Not possessed—disturbed. Assume she was really *disturbed* and had the strength of six men. Could she physically do what we just saw?"

"What about the pain?" Monroe, himself a father of two young children, asked. "Who could suffer through that?"

"You see how bad her arms were? The priest said she'd been scraping herself—I think we can assume she had no sensation of pain at all."

Monroe stared into the air, pondering for a moment. "She'd have to do it quick—before she ran out of blood."

"Exactly," Brinkley said. "It'd have to be quick."

"But how do you get the head outside?" Garcia asked. "She's dead. You can't open a window then throw your own head outside."

"Did you see the window?"

"Covered in blood," Garcia replied.

"Everything was covered in blood," Monroe added.

"No, not everything," Brinkley interjected. "There was nothing on the closet, where she might hide. Nothing under the bed, where she might try and hide. Nothing on the back of the door, the natural escape route."

"What's that supposed to mean?" Garcia asked. "She was over-powered by someone who wanted to kill her."

"She didn't try to hide or escape. Not through the door, not in the closet, or under the bed."

Garcia and Monroe grew silent, unsure what to make of his suggestion.

"She had enough flesh on her fingernails to kill a grown man, and yet, no blood outside the room, and none that I could see outside the house—besides the head?"

Brinkley paused, letting the implications sink in.

"The window had blood all over it," Monroe said. "Maybe she tried to escape that way."

"Maybe," Brinkley replied. "Or maybe death was her escape. Maybe she didn't want to leave the house. Maybe she wanted to leave this world."

"Through a window?" Monroe asked, still confused.

"Through a guillotine." Brinkley replied.

"Strength of six men," Garcia chimed in.

Monroe nearly broke down. The image of the girl's body and the thought of the window slamming down on one of his children's necks was too much.

"Maybe she'd already done half the work herself," Brinkley said. "The window just finished her off."

Suddenly, the scene began to make sense. The swirls of blood on the floor. The mangled neck. The angle of the body as it fell away from the window.

Garcia spoke up, then paused. "No one could do that who wasn't actually...."

Brinkley tried to ignore the chill that ran down his spine as he finished the sentence in his mind.

"I don't believe in all that," Monroe said.

"Me neither," Garcia added.

Brinkley clasped his hands together. "Well then, you boys have got a murder to solve."

Garcia tried to defend a possible murder hypothesis. "The mother said she thought someone tried to break-in to their house a few days ago. You think that's significant?"

"We cleared the scene, didn't we?" Brinkley replied. "You think we missed him hiding in the laundry chute?"

"No."

"Behind the wood pile? In the basement?" Brinkley was chiding him now.

"No, Brinks. We checked everywhere," Garcia said. "I'm sure of it."

Garcia's phone flashed an alert from the dispatcher.

Call for service. 4300 Windhaven Drive.
Domestic. Homicide/possible attempted suicide.
Caller is hysterical. Not making sense.
Ambulance en route.
NOTE: Cabin access is off-road. Will need 4WD.

As Garcia read the call out loud, Monroe's chest collapsed with dread.

Brinkley handed a folder containing his notes to Garcia. "Y'all better get right with God... while you still can. Something evil's on the loose."

CHAPTER 9

Albert Connolly marched through the cathedral towards the southern transept where a vehicle waited to take him and his assistant to the mansion where they were staying. It was obvious to him news of miracles and healing had already begun to spread. People stared. Conversations stopped mid sentence as he walked by.

A security detail stopped him at the door before he could go outside and handed him a thick blue vest.

"Will this fit?" an officer asked.

"A bulletproof vest?" Connolly asked, confused. "What's going on?"

"They're getting rowdy out there. We didn't plan on this many people."

"I'm just walking to our car."

"We haven't been able to maintain the perimeter for at least an hour. I have no idea who's out there and what they might be carrying."

The officer opened the vest to help Connolly put it on. "Please."

"Where's Brooke? Has she already gone out?"

"She's in the car, waiting for you."

Why do they hate me? Connolly thought to himself.

As conflict had grown, Connolly worked tirelessly to maintain peace. It did not matter. As head of the NIH, he was seen as a crucial proponent of official pandemic policy. A *pharma shill*, they called him, second in their mind only to Walter Faucett, the man they felt was responsible for both the virus *and* the vaccines that followed. When Faucett died, Connolly hoped their thirst for revenge would subside. Instead, their hatred had doubled. Even tripled.

Reluctantly, Connolly donned the vest.

"Would you like a mask?" the officer asked. "It might help."

"I'm not going to hide like an animal," Connolly snapped. "Just open the door. Let's get on with it."

* * *

Outside the cathedral, the crowd had swelled to hundreds. Two news helicopters hovered overheard, broadcasting a live feed of the growing masses to the world. Security barriers were installed days before, a move many thought to be in bad taste for such a promising event. It was clear more would be needed.

A black limousine was parked in the street, engine running, waiting for Connolly to depart. Beyond was a sea of people, shouting behind temporary fencing.

"Oh my God," Connolly muttered to himself as he set his eyes on the clamoring mob of humanity. Suddenly, he was glad for the vest.

Signs were everywhere. *Pray for Mongchai*, many of them read, hopeful the heroic boy might finally be healed. *Connolly = Faucett. Faucett = Murderer*, another read. *Keep your science off my faith* was a popular one, as was its sibling, *Keep your faith off my science.*

"Let's go," the officer yelled as he pulled Connolly toward the car, the doctor's unmistakable frame doubling over to fit within the doorway. Inside, his assistant closed her laptop and made room.

Connolly moved to shut the door but the officer climbed in after him.

"You're coming with us?" he asked.

"I'm going to be your sidekick," the officer said, patting Connolly on the thigh. "Doctor's orders."

"What doctor?"

"Dr. Naftali," the officer responded. "Let's go, driver."

The hulking vehicle, loaded with three inch-thick layers of glass, lumbered towards the exit. Once they neared Wisconsin Avenue, Connolly was able to more clearly grasp the size of the crowd as hundreds of others milled about, happy to make use of all the publicity the news cameras provided.

Just as the limousine made the turn, it screeched to a halt, the windshield covered by a man who had jumped onto the hood of the car, blocking their view forward.

"What should I do?" the driver asked.

The officer scrambled towards the front seat. "Floor it!"

"No!" Connolly shouted. "There's cameras everywhere. Don't do it."

People began to surround the vehicle, banging on the windows outside, their shouting impossible to decipher through the bullet-proof glass. Others laid down in front and behind, blocking them from moving.

"Who are they?" Brooke asked.

"Freaks," the officer said.

"Just wait let them say their piece," Connolly said, imploring the driver for calm. "They know the cameras will be on us."

The man climbed onto the roof of their car, unfurling a banner behind him.

"What is it?" Brooke asked. "What's he doing?"

"Can't you electrocute him or something?" the officer asked.

"Just the door handles," the driver responded. "I've got five hundred horsepower under my right foot. That will fix a world of problems."

"No!" Connolly screamed. "Just wait."

The protestors tightened the slack in the banner as helicopters above zeroed in on Connolly's limousine, completely immobilized amidst the hundred bodies laying around it.

The officer peered upward, trying to understand what was happening. "It's a sign," he said. "Some kind of banner."

From far above, the news cameras zoomed in to frame the emerging chaos. As the last corner was unfolded, the message came into clear view for anyone watching, a cryptic communication the world would notice:

FINCH SAVES.

CHAPTER 10

Natalie tried Finch's number for the third time but, still, he wouldn't answer.

I shouldn't have told him, she thought to herself. She'd been so disciplined in not reaching out to him, despite the frequent ache in her heart. He had destroyed their lives, yet somehow, she was still drawn to him, the emotional paradox a constant struggle.

With news of his recent escape, Natalie wondered if her husband might try and find her, every creak and groan of the house offering the possibility he had tracked her down and was trying to break in.

The simple message she'd received earlier that morning left her stunned.

Hey. It's me.

Somehow, she felt confident it was Finch. Unsure how to respond, she left for the cathedral to help her father when she stumbled upon the incredible scene that played out before her through the chapel doors.

They can heal her.

Again, she couldn't believe what she had said. Eva's condition was irreversible, her life ruined. There was no medicine, no surgery, no transplants, and no technology that could help. Initially, Natalie's belief they could significantly improve her daughter's quality of life was unwavering. Through her father, they had access to anyone and anything—experimental or otherwise—that might provide a constant stream of optimism. *Hopium*, Finch would have called it. A steady supply of hope, the only drug that could relieve her suffering.

Over the past few days, Natalie had become familiar with the enormous mansion, but there was seemingly always another wing or hallway waiting to be discovered. The library was her favorite—a long, wood-paneled hall, two-stories tall, with reading nooks at every window. It had become a small sanctuary where she could grab a few moments of quiet while Eva slept—or if visiting celebrities grew bothersome.

In better times, she would have immersed herself in study, picking a book at random and forcing herself to read through it, no matter the subject matter. *Ball Lightning in the Appalachians. Technics and Civilization. Storehouses of the King: The Pyramids of Egypt.* College, she had come to regard, a success—not so much because of her classwork but, instead, because of her hours of dissociative reading.

Natalie ran her finger down a shelf of books and tried her luck: *Journal of Cross-Cultural Psychology, 2010.*

Not today, she thought as she put it back on the shelf and grabbed another: *The Complete Works of Gerard Manley Hopkins.*

Definitely not.

Hopkins was a Victorian poet who converted to Catholicism, his works thought to be some of the greatest of the 19th century. Many featured themes she could not bring herself to contemplate.

"Natalie?" a voice called from the doorway. "Are you in here?"

It was Eva's nurse.

"Is something wrong?" Natalie responded, her daughter's condition a constant source of anxiety waiting to appear.

"No, it's just… have you been watching the news?"

Natalie tilted her head in mock disbelief. "Really?"

"I know… I know you don't watch. It's just that the situation at the cathedral is becoming interesting."

"Does it involve Tom?" Natalie asked. The young nurse knew not to bring him up.

Natalie's hatred for Finch ran deep—so deep she felt it was hers alone. Somehow when others piled on, when others disparaged him in the most trivial way, it hurt. To see much of the world turned against him, his face plastered across televisions and websites, was too much for her to bear.

The nurse's silence was answer enough.

"What are they saying about him?"

Natalie paused, unsure if she was prepared to hear the answer. "It's okay, you can tell me. I promise, it's okay."

"There's a huge crowd at the cathedral. Like hundreds. It's insane."

"They want to see the boy healed."

"Most of them do."

"What do you mean?" Natalie asked.

"There's a lot of protestors there. I mean a LOT."

"Of course. Freaks who hate everything."

"They don't hate your husband."

"Ex-husband," Natalie defended, a public-relations move her father had advised.

"They're trying to stop the event. They're trying to shut it down."

"Why?" Natalie asked. She felt she could never understand those who so blindly rejected the promise of science.

"They think it's another step closer. Another step towards... I don't know. People trusting science more than God?"

Natalie's chest began to constrict with anger, her breathing shallow. "Listen to me, Martta. I saw something this morning I was not supposed to see. Do you remember the man in the wheelchair from the party? The one with the Cardinal in the red robes?"

"Yes," Martta said. "I tried to introduce him to Eva, but he didn't seem interested."

"He looked pretty bad off, wouldn't you say?"

"Well, sure. I could have looked at the wheelchair alone and told you ALS."

"That man is walking right now," Natalie said, looking Martta directly in the eyes. "That man is walking right now."

The nurse was confused. "You saw him?"

"I saw people around him praying. They had their hands on him. Some of them were crying, like they were just overcome with emotion. It was completely freaky."

"And then he walked?"

"I couldn't see exactly what happened. I saw his wheelchair tip over. Everyone backed away, and the wheelchair was empty."

"Then what?"

"Someone inside noticed me looking and covered the door, so I ran away."

"So it's true?" the nurse asked. "They can heal people."

Natalie had her doubts. "I'm not sure. I think so."

"Eva!" the nurse said, her eyes beginning to water.

"Yes. Eva."

"Do you think it's possible?"

"I don't know," Natalie said, struggling to control her emotions.

"Do you *believe* it's possible?" the nurse asked, pushing Natalie further, a question she was still unwilling to answer.

CHAPTER 11

Months of atrophy had wrecked Mongchai's body. The fearless nine-year-old looked barely alive. He had once braved the pitch black tunnels of water to save his friends' lives. His face was now sunken, his muscle tone nearly gone—but his eyes were still bright beams of light, staring straight ahead.

Your battle will soon be over, the Cardinal thought to himself.

He pulled aside the jacket covering the boy's body and could barely distinguish his legs from his arms, so emaciated was his appearance.

Where is his hand? I want to feel his power.

Gordillo delicately pulled Mongchai's arm away from his side, curling the boy's fingers around his own.

"Do you know who I am, boy?" the Cardinal whispered as he looked him directly in the eye. "I am a representative from God."

He waited for movement but sensed nothing.

"There are many people who are alive today because of you. God is very pleased."

The boy might have appeared to be sleeping, had there been a sensation of breathing. As it was, with no clear signs of respiration, with not a single blink from his eyes, he just looked dead.

A door slammed far down the hallway. Hurried footsteps. Talking.

Someone knocked on the door.

"Who is it?" Gordillo asked, annoyed.

"It's Yuval," a voice outside said, the voice of his driver. "He needs to talk to you."

Yuval never called. Gordillo opened the door and grabbed the phone.

"Who is this?" he asked.

"It's me," a familiar voice replied.

The Cardinal's body stiffened with tension. "What's going on?"

"Change of plans. They missed him this morning."

"I thought you said they had him."

"They did," Yuval said.

"They were your best men?"

"They were. Something went wrong. Badly wrong. We lost four of them."

"Send more."

"It's too messy. Local police are on the way. People are asking questions."

The Cardinal was growing angry. "So what do we do? This will all be for nothing if we can't get him there."

There was a long pause on the line.

"Yuval?" Gordillo asked, thinking the line had dropped.

"Eva," Yuval said, as though stating a fact.

"What about Eva?"

"Listen, Gordillo. We need to make tonight's star someone special. Someone we know Finch will not want to miss."

"Eva?" Gordillo asked. "Connolly won't allow it. He'd never bring this upon his family. You know that."

"Unless..." Yuval proposed. "Unless he has no other choice."

"What are you talking about?" Gordillo asked. "The entire world is waiting for this boy to be healed."

Another long pause. "Have you met him yet?" Yuval asked.

"Yes, I'm here in the room with him right now."

"He looks frail does he not?"

Gordillo paused for a moment and began to connect the dots.

"Very," he said.

Gordillo ended the call and handed the phone back to his driver.

"Leave us," he said.

From the hallway, the boy's parents looked in, anxious and confused as to what was happening.

"Just a moment," he told them. "Just a moment more."

The Cardinal smiled, closed the door, and twisted the lock gently. He walked to the window and looked onto the courtyard outside. A concrete pond was set in the center, encircled by majestic oaks stripped bare for winter, their leaves swishing along the ornate brickwork that connected several other buildings together. Like the rest of the facility, it appeared nearly devoid of human life.

Gordillo returned to the bed. "Mongchai—sometimes God heals people. Sometimes in ways we can't understand."

He pulled a chair closer to the bed and groaned in discomfort as he sat.

"Sometimes, he doesn't. Sometimes God doesn't heal people."

The Cardinal stroked his chin then leaned in towards the boy's ear.

"'If I pull three times, that means I'm through'—isn't that what you told the children? Isn't that the sign you've given people?"

Gordillo delicately pulled Mongchai's arm away from his side, curling the boy's fingers around his own.

"Do you know who I am, boy?" the Cardinal whispered. "I am a representative from God."

He waited for movement but sensed nothing.

"Come on, boy. Give me a sign."

A surge of adrenaline shot through Gordillo's body before he could even tell what happened. Mongchai had squeezed his hand.

"Jesus," the Cardinal said in fright. "That's one."

The boy squeezed again.

"Alright. Two. That's enough."

A frenzied discussion could be heard outside the room.

"Here's a sign from God," Gordillo hissed as he wrapped the sleeve of his robe around the boy's neck and squeezed. "That's one."

The knob shook as someone tried to get in.

Gordillo squeezed again, this time with slightly more pressure.

"That's two."

He stared at the boy's chest, looking for any motion. He adjusted his grip on Mongchai's neck and squeezed, this time hard.

"Three," Gordillo whispered as someone began banging violently on the door.

He placed his hand under the boy's nostrils and felt for the warm air of an exhale.

There was nothing.

"You're through," he said as he stood up and straightened his robe. "Say hello to God for me."

CHAPTER 12

Garcia's truck bounced along the winding trail that led down to the cabin. Rain had washed out parts of the gravel road, forcing him to a stop.

"You ever been around here, Brinks?" he asked as he got out of the truck and locked the hubs on his front axle.

"Never," Brinkley replied.

"Me either," Monroe said.

Garcia shifted the truck into four-wheel drive and inched backward, listening for the wheels to catch.

"Bet there's a lot of gas," Garcia said as they started to move forward. Mineral rights were one of the few perks of the area, wells of natural gas utilities would mine and pay land owners a royalty for.

"Free heat all winter," Monroe said. "I could deal with that."

"All your chit-chat isn't helping, is it?" Brinks asked. "You boys are scared shitless."

Brinks was right. The small talk was doing little to comfort them, their apprehension growing with each minute. The image of the girl's body was still fresh in their minds. Garcia fared worse—he'd seen her head. The presence of the priest, with his crucifix and rosary beads, only served to heighten the feeling they were living within a horror film.

They crawled down the mountainside, a painfully slow descent as they switched back around hairpin turns every few hundred feet.

"Hope this guy is okay," Monroe said.

"Me too," Garcia replied. "That call was twenty-three minutes ago."

"These folks know that," Brinkley said. "They don't live back here on accident. They know help is miles away."

"Hope we can help him," Monroe said, skeptical their arrival would change anything.

They rounded a bend and could see the cabin in the distance, across a glistening stream of water flowing beside it. Ahead, the trail was partially blocked by a large vehicle.

"Is that our EMTs?" Garcia asked.

"Must be stuck," Monroe said.

They pulled up behind and could see it was a white and green ambulance.

"That's Hardy County Rescue," Monroe said. "What're they doing all the way over here?"

The huge vehicle was turned at an odd angle, its back wheels lodged into a channel of road washed out by summer rains.

"Anyone in it?"

"Go take a look, Monroe," Brinks said.

Monroe paused.

"They're our guys, Monroe. Just take a look. Time's wasting."

Brinks pushed him out of the door.

Monroe peered into the back window of the ambulance and shrugged his shoulders.

"Check the cab," Brinks yelled out to him.

Monroe walked around towards the front, his right hand resting on his holster.

"Hardy County's got four-wheel drive," Garcia realized. "We don't. That's why they sent it."

"Ten thousand pounds and completely uselessness," Brinks said to Garcia. "They'll never fit a wrecker down here. Can you get around it?"

"I can try."

Monroe peered around the cab, ducking his head just enough to see what was inside. Satisfied it was clear, he opened the door to confirm.

"Empty," he called out. "No one here."

"We'd probably be faster walking," Garcia said as he crawled forward along the edge of the road.

"Too far," Brinkley shot back. "Those EMTs are young. They don't mind walking."

Monroe backed away from the ambulance to give Garcia's truck more room. It was an old 1987 Ford F250 with bench seats. Manual everything. One feature it did have: torque.

"I don't think you're gonna fit," Monroe said. "You might slide off a little."

"I don't care," Garcia said. "Just watch my mirror."

After several attempts, Garcia was able to squeeze the truck around the ambulance. Monroe got back in the truck and they continued down, crossing the small wooden bridge that led to the cabin.

The rickety structure appeared abandoned. No cars. No signs of life.

"What's that?" Monroe asked, pointing towards the edge of the clearing.

"Where?" Brinkley asked.

A dark green shape was barely visible among the rocks.

"That's a body," Garcia replied.

"I can't see anything," Brinks said.

They pulled closer. Monroe could discern an orange stripe running along the green clothing. "I think that's our EMT."

"Shit," Brinkley said, pushing Monroe out of his way. "Let me out."

He walked towards the other side of the clearing and bent down as he drew closer. It was the lifeless body of a paramedic, her green shirt still glistening with blood.

Something is watching me.

Brinkley felt it right away—the hairs on his neck never lied.

"Go back," he said to the men in the truck. "Back up slowly."

"What's he talking about?" Garcia asked Monroe.

"Get away from here," Brinkley said again, this time shouting.

"Back up," Monroe said. "Just back up."

Garcia slammed the truck into reverse and spun his tires as he moved away.

He has no idea we're law enforcement, Brinkley thought to himself. *I'm not a threat. I don't have a gun.*

Brinkley stood straight and pulled his shirt up, showing his waist.

See? No gun.

"What's he doing?" Monroe asked.

"Where's the other EMT?" Garcia asked. "They're always in pairs."

Monroe called out to Brinkley. "Is he dead, Brinks?"

"*She* is dead. Now shut up and listen to me. Back up to the wood pile over there and put some of it in the back of your truck."

"What the hell?" Garcia said under his breath.

"Just do it!" Brinkley yelled before calming his voice. "Leave your radios in the car. Don't come towards the house. Wait for me to come to you."

Garcia backed his truck closer to the creek where unsplit wood had been thrown into a large pile. Monroe got out and opened the tailgate, trying not to stare at Brinkley.

There's another dead EMT somewhere around here. Maybe they made it inside.

Brinkley forced a smile onto his face and slowly walked toward the cabin.

"Hey neighbor," he said, waving his hand in the air. "Hey neighbor. Mind if we grab some firewood?"

The door on the side was partially open, glass scattered along the floor within.

Are you outside or inside?

Without turning his head, he scanned as far as his eyes would allow, looking for any sign of life.

"Hey neighbor," he said through the doorway. "Mind if we grab some of your firewood?"

He opened the door with his elbow and stepped inside.

Garcia opened the truck door and rolled his ankle on something as he stepped down. He picked it up to examine it more closely—a large white chunk of something.

"Looks like porcelain," he said to himself.

"This is an active crime scene," Monroe reminded him. "Don't touch the evidence."

Garcia looked around and saw bigger pieces—enough to puzzle together what it was.

"Just a toilet," he said. "Doubt it's a murder weapon."

Brinkley stepped into the kitchen and continued scanning.

Coffee.

He held his hand towards the pot. *Still warm. Dispatch said caller was hysterical.*

Drops of blood were speckled across the floor. He touched one to his finger. Slightly tacky.

Twenty minutes old, he guessed.

"Did you hear that?" Monroe whispered.

"Yeah, I heard it." Garcia stood motionless. Something was moving through the woods. Hearing was sometimes a much better tool than sight. It worked in every direction, no matter which way your head was pointed. Optical illusions could betray you in ways your ears never would.

"I'm calling for backup."

"Who'll come out here? It'll take them half an hour anyway."

"Should we go check on Brinks?"

"He said to wait here. I've got no problem with that."

"Hey neighbor."

Brinkley opened the lone door within the cabin to a steep flight of stairs leading down into darkness.

Root cellar, he guessed from the foul smell.

"Hey neighbor," Brinkley called again. "We're grabbing some firewood."

Just as he turned away, he felt something very odd. His shirt constricted around his chest so tightly his collar choked him. Someone had grabbed him from behind. Despite his 230 pound frame, he was lifted into the air and thrown down into the root cellar, landing hard on his back.

Looking up the stairs, Brinkley watched as the silhouette of a man limped by the opening, a hunting rifle in his hands.

Monroe, he thought. *Garcia*. He attempted to scream out in warning to them, but pain shot through his rib cage with the slightest inhalation of air.

Gunfire exploded within the cabin, followed by the sound of the man racking the bolt on his rifle. Another crack split the air as the man fired again. Brinkley gasped in horror as he rolled over onto his side and realized he was laying on top of someone else. Through the darkness, he could discern green canvas with an orange stripe.

EMT, he realized. *Dead.*

"All gone!" the man screamed out loud, laughing maniacally.

Brinkley could hear the floor creaking as the man returned to the door.

Meth, Brinkley thought. His right foot was bent sideways, his ankle clearly broken. Doubled over in pain, his face covered in sores, the man couldn't have weighed more than 130 pounds.

"I shot them all!" he screamed as he took a step down the stairs. "They were coming for me. I knew they would. But I wasn't going to let them."

Brinkley gathered enough air to whisper a question. "Who's coming for you?"

"I don't want anymore!" the man screamed, the tendons in his neck bulging with fear.

"Who's coming for you?" Brinkley asked, trying to calm the man. "I can help."

"Can you hear them? How can they whisper so loud?"

Brinkley's head filled with a hundred questions.

"Those were EMTs. They came to help."

The man jumped down the stairs and smashed the butt of his rifle into Brinkley's side, sending bolts of pain shooting through his body.

"They're all in on it!" the crazed man screamed again. "They're not helping."

"Who are you talking about?"

The man got right in Brinkley's face, his cheeks oozing with blood. "Soldiers," he whispered. "From the NIH."

"NIH doesn't have soldiers."

"Really," the man laughed. "You don't think so? You really don't think so?"

He hobbled back up the stairs and flicked the light switch, blinding Brinkley for a moment.

"Look around you. What do you see?"

Brinkley raised himself just enough to focus on the room around him.

"Jesus," he said out loud.

He couldn't believe his eyes.

CHAPTER 13

From across the creek, Finch stared at the hunting cabin as gunfire continued to erupt from within. When he had seen the sheriff approaching, he had crawled out the side door and trudged back across the water. Now, with some sort of gun battle raging within, it was clear he hadn't been the only person in the cabin.

I slept in there for the past two nights, he thought. *Someone was in there with me.*

He could have been killed at any time while he slept. He realized that earlier, as he ran from the soldiers, the gunfire must have never been directed at him.

Who is it? Why did he save me?

As the subject of a nationwide manhunt, Finch redefined the term "wanted man." For years he'd been the most popular physician on the internet, the ruggedly handsome son-in-law of Albert Connolly, his frequent videos on health and disease insightful commentary unlikely to be found through traditional channels.

When the pandemic hit, everything changed. As pressure grew to relay certain viewpoints on the nature of the disease—and the vaccines that soon followed—Finch found himself beginning to question what others were saying. When he began receiving financial offers to say things that were patently untrue, he really began to doubt.

Intensely curious, and with his father-in-law's connections, Finch was able to gain access to nearly all preprint research on the planet—the *real* science according to him, the science before it was sanitized by peer review or blocked from publication. His videos began to take on a different quality, a conspiratorial tone that often put NIH lead Walter Faucett squarely within his crosshairs.

"Who funded this research?" he asked in one popular video with a picture of Faucett in the background. "Who was funding the research to create this virus, long before China ever had anything to do with it?"

"At the beginning of the pandemic," he said in another, "there were more American scientists, health officials, and government authorities that knew about malkavirus than Chinese. Ask yourself why that is. Ask yourself why a university in North Carolina was essentially weaponizing this thing ten years ago."

For months, his very public relationship as Albert Connolly's son-in-law bought him leeway from the censors. Eventually, the videos took a darker turn, a direction that forced Connolly to disavow him.

"The virus is not the point," Finch suggested in his final video before it got pulled. "The virus is not the point," he said again. "The virus was to make people get the vaccine. The vaccine was the point. Your immune system is too good for biological weapons to have mass effect. If you really want to affect the global population, you have to bypass your immune system. Vaccines are the only way to do that. And they did it. They got what they wanted. We can never roll it back."

The video, watched tens of millions of times, had many people asking the same question: *What were the vaccines for?* If not to stem the harm or spread of malkavirus, then what purpose did they serve? Finch's disappearance soon after only served to heighten wild theories that emerged around the intentions of the global, frequently mandated, immunization campaigns—speculation that rarely involved malkavirus itself.

The media turned squarely against him, an organized crusade that pitted the once beloved doctor against the entire medical establishment. Videos of aggressive outbursts from his military enlistment were leaked, a personality trait Finch worked hard to shield from public view. College papers with questionable beliefs made him the source of mockery and ridicule among the academic establishment.

None of that would compare to the damage caused by a tragic accident several months later. Walter Faucett, the man whose unwavering confidence and scientific integrity had given much of the world their only source of hope through years of lockdowns and fear, was dead. On the approach to a bridge, the vehicle he was in was driven off the road into the river below.

Finch was apprehended within hours, his car clearly damaged from the incident. Footage of his arrest aired on news channels throughout the world, the stunned doctor in handcuffs looking much different than the last time he'd been seen, months earlier.

"Do you know who was in that car?" a reporter asked as he was being led into a police car.

"Satan," Finch replied without emotion as he sat in the backseat.

"He wasn't alone. Did you know that?" the reporter asked. "We're hearing rumors your wife and daughter were riding with him. Were you aware of that?"

The police car door slammed on Finch as he stared at the reporter, his face frozen in shock.

CHAPTER 14

The black limousine Albert Connolly and his assistant rode in sped away from the National Cathedral towards the mansion in Bethesda, the "Finch Saves" banner flapping behind them until it finally broke free.

Connolly removed the bulletproof vest and tossed it onto the floor, straightening his silver hair as he inhaled deeply. He couldn't believe what his life had become. Forty years of service in public health, ascending to the highest rank that existed, about to reveal the most momentous discovery of his lifetime and yet, here he was with more enemies than ever, cowering from crowds behind bulletproof glass. Even his family was ruined—his granddaughter forever crippled at the hands of his son-in-law, a wanted man adored by the enemies of science.

These things shall pass.

The aging doctor played a mental recording of the Johnny Cash song in his head, a frequent reset he employed to push through difficult times. This was not how he imagined his career ending—one final event that might set right all that was wrong. A chance to align a world split in two.

A marriage of faith and science.

Yuval was right. Despite their differences, Connolly felt the man at least understood the significance of the event. The possibility for reconciliation—the *likelihood* of it, in fact, gave him great hope.

Eva.

She can be healed. He still couldn't believe it could happen. Faith in the impossible was never his strong suit. Faith in the possible? For some reason, that was even more difficult—at least when it was so personal. It was the cloud that hung over their relationship that troubled him. Something dark. Connolly detested superstition, but couldn't shake the feeling something terrible was going to happen.

"Dr. Connolly?" His assistant tried to get his attention. "Dr. Connolly?"

"Yes, I'm sorry. What is it?"

"I thought you might want to see this," she said, pointing to her laptop.

Connolly leaned over to look at the nearly blank document open on her screen.

We need to speak privately. Now.

She typed another line.

Can you ask the officer to move to the front?

Connolly looked at her, baffled.

"Isn't that interesting?" Brooke asked, her attempt to be inconspicuous confusing Connolly even further.

She highlighted the second line of text, then made it uppercase and larger.

CAN YOU ASK THE OFFICER TO MOVE TO THE FRONT?

Connolly finally caught on to her messaging. "That *is* interesting."

He turned toward the officer, whose gaze was locked on the road ahead.

"Officer?" Connolly asked as he tapped him on the leg. "I need to have a private discussion with my assistant. Would you mind moving up to the front?"

The officer looked at him, clearly perturbed. "I've been assigned to protect many other officials. I probably know more secrets than you do."

"I understand, but I'd be breaking the law if I let you overhear this conversation."

Connolly gestured to the opening that separated the back of the limousine from the front. "If you don't mind."

The officer bounced his knee for a few moments, struggling with anxiety as he stalled for time. "Okay, I'll move. But the privacy screen stays down."

"That will be fine," Connolly said as the officer clambered into the front of the vehicle.

"What in God's name is going on?" Connolly whispered, confident they couldn't be heard.

"I thought this was probably a cause for concern. Early this morning a girl was found with her head torn off. Officer on the scene thinks it was suicide."

Connolly was used to gruesome accounts of suffering and took the news with calm.

"Parents think she was possessed. Priest called in. The works."

"These things do happen sometimes," Connolly said.

"Yes, well there was another emergency call this morning. Not quite the same, but enough to get flagged."

"How close?"

"About twelve miles."

She looked at Connolly to gauge his reaction.

"What happened there?" he asked.

"I can't tell. Call for service from paranoid schizophrenic. Speaking incoherently. Some sort of state agency took over the call and coded it out, so I can't see what's going on."

"Can you show me the map? The one from the last couple of weeks?"

His assistant pulled up an image of Northern Virginia. Several markers dotted the area.

"And where are these two from today?" Connolly asked.

Brooke pointed towards the very left, just inside the West Virginia border. "Here, and here, give or take."

Connolly scratched his head in thought.

"Isolated clusters?" he asked, rhetorically. "Or vectors?"

Epidemiology had never been his focus, but he knew enough to be troubled.

"Related," she offered.

"Yes, I would agree. Definitely related."

"You think Yuval knows?"

Connolly cycled through his conversations with Dr. Naftali, searching for clues. The brilliant young researcher had always focused on the scientific aspects of the spiritual world—the very thing that had initially led Connolly to support his work. But it was dangerous. He knew Yuval was playing with fire, a $4 billion super-collider of spirit rather than body. Something about these recent events had Yuval's thumbprints all over them. He couldn't place it exactly, but instinctively, Connolly felt there was a connection.

Brooke lowered her voice further. "Something else concerns me more at the moment."

She glanced towards the officer sitting up front. "I had a friend run his name and couldn't find it anywhere. Not in D.C. Metro, not in Capitol Police. It's nowhere."

"Did you ask him his name?"

"I saw it on his badge."

"How much do we pay you?"

"Not enough," she said. "But this guy's a ghost, as far as the local blue are concerned."

"One of Yuval's guys?" Connolly asked.

"Yeah, I'm guessing so."

Connolly noticed the limousine slow as it took an offramp from the interstate.

"This isn't our exit," he said.

The limousine took a left, crossed the overpass, then slowly turned left again, back on to the interstate.

"We just made a U-turn," the assistant said.

"Driver," Connolly called out loudly. "Why did you just turn around?"

He was answered by silence.

"Driver, why are we turning around? Where are we going?"

He moved toward the front seat to ask the driver directly, but someone rolled the privacy screen up, shutting them tightly within the back.

CHAPTER 15

"What is that noise?" Natalie asked her daughter's nurse.

What started as a rumble had grown into a roar that shook the windows. Leaves swirled outside the library windows that looked out onto the front lawn.

Martta ran to the other side of the room and peered out towards the back of the property.

"It's a helicopter," she said. "It's landing."

The mansion shook as an olive green helicopter settled onto the ground. Landscaping rippled under waves of pressure that sent furniture by the pool tumbling into the water.

"It's huge," Martta said. "Like from the army or something."

Natalie approached the window, its glass panes shuddering so hard they seemed they might shatter. "So much for Eva's nap."

"I'd better go check on her."

Martta left the library, headed towards Eva's room. After a few moments, the whine of the aircraft's engines spooled down. Railings and steps extended from the backside of a door that swung down to the ground. Two men in uniform got out and walked toward the house. Behind them strode a rail-thin Dr. Naftali, ducking low beneath the helicopter's spinning blades.

He's coming to talk to me.

They last spoke several months before, an interaction that left Yuval humiliated. Natalie couldn't explain why, but for some reason, she sensed the winds had changed. The military helicopter landing in the middle of their backyard did nothing to lessen her apprehension.

She started towards the middle of the house to meet him but stopped herself short. A large book was sitting on the table of one of the reading nooks. She sat down, grabbed the volume, and pretended to absorb herself in study.

Distant conversations reverberated across the stone walls. Footsteps. More talking, then a lone pair of footsteps.

"Ah, there you are," Yuval said as he entered the room, a strained smile across his face.

"Oh, Dr. Naftali, hello. I didn't hear you...." Natalie stood and stopped talking given the absurdity of what she was about to say.

"You weren't expecting me, were you? I hope my vehicle didn't scare you and your lovely daughter."

"No, of course not. There are lots of... We have lots of visitors here." Natalie was stumbling. Words would not come as easily as she would have preferred. Their last interaction had gone poorly.

"They arrive in cars, I assume?"

"Yes, most of them. A few limos. A bus or two."

"No helicopters?"

"No, no helicopters. You're the first."

Yuval glanced at the book she held in her hands. "I hear this library is amazing. What have you found?"

Natalie closed the book and read the cover out loud. "*Metamorphosis: On the Development of Affect, Perception, Attention, and Memory.*"

"Oh, Ernest Schachtel," Yuval said, apparently familiar with the book's author. "Never was a big Freud fan myself, but he certainly was."

"I had just picked it up."

"Make sure you put that back where you found it."

"Of course. I suppose some of your works are here?"

"I would guess so, yes. Your father's as well."

"Why are you here, Dr. Naftali? Why the helicopter?"

"Yes, the helicopter. The crowds at the Cathedral have grown larger than we expected. Getting in and out is proving to be difficult. With cars, at least."

"So you snap your fingers and poof? A helicopter appears?"

Yuval smiled and bowed his head, a failed attempt to portray deference. "Something like that, yes."

"You've spent a lot of my father's money. More than anyone ever has. I hope it's not paying for joy rides."

"No, this is from a different budget altogether. Not to worry—other people's money. Other people with different concerns than your father's."

Natalie knew Yuval had loyalty to others, murky relationships she'd never fully understood. Organizations with ambitious goals that extended to nearly every aspect of human suffering and woe. Poverty. Hunger. Education. Global warming. Crime. Inequality. The list went on and on, their objectives far beyond anything science alone might be able to accomplish.

"So, why are you here?"

Yuval gestured to the chairs. "May we sit?"

Natalie pointed toward the hallway. "I need to check on my daughter."

"Of course. I will make this brief. You're aware of the boy named Mongchai, the boy who was to be our featured guest tonight?"

"Yes. What happened? Why do you say *was*?"

"He has died. I just got word this morning. He was frail, hanging on to life by a thread."

A chill ran through Natalie's body.

"No one but a few know this yet. Given the nature of our event, his death will be a humiliating loss, to say the least. Do you understand?"

Natalie instinctively wanted to leave. To hide. She never felt comfortable in the spotlight her father's celebrity status had forced her to endure. Parties. Events. Interviews. Photoshoots. Her husband's rise to fame—and tumultuous fall—was more than she could handle.

"I don't want to be involved with this," she told him. "With whatever you've got going on, I don't want to be involved."

"You understand the importance of tonight's event, do you not?"

"I believe so, yes."

"You witnessed something this morning at the chapel, did you not? With the man in the wheelchair?"

Another wave of coldness passed through her body. "How did you know that? I've told no one."

"You know what's possible. You saw it with your own eyes."

Eva.

"You know what I'm going to ask you."

They can heal her.

Natalie felt as if the room had tilted. The ceiling grew higher as shelf upon shelf extended into the air, curving around her in circles, trapping her within Yuval's reach, beneath thousands and thousands of books she could not understand.

"We need Eva," Yuval continued. "For tonight. I can't ask you more plainly than that. We need her. There is no one else. The event will be nothing without her."

Natalie collapsed into the chair, unable to hold herself up any longer. Yuval sat down across from her, staring directly at her, waiting patiently for her to speak.

"You believe we can heal her, I assume? After what you saw this morning?"

She gathered herself and looked directly back at Yuval. "He will kill you before that happens."

Yuval laughed out loud, a chortle that went uncomfortably long.

"You're talking about your husband? You defend him so. The man who ruined you and your daughter's lives, and look how you defend him."

"Ex-husband. And I defend no one," she said. "I'm just stating a fact. He will kill you if you make a spectacle of our daughter."

"You see how I travel. I'm surrounded by security. I don't think he will be able to lift a finger against me."

"I'm warning you—as a friend."

Yuval twitched. "You know where he is?"

Natalie considered her answer before speaking. "He's close enough, I'm guessing. He'll figure out a way to stop you, no matter where he is."

"I'm hoping he shows up. In fact, I'm counting on him showing up. I want him to speak. I'll give the microphone to him and let him defend himself or anything else—for the entire world to see."

"You're lying," Natalie said.

"I assure you, I'm not."

"I'm warning you. He'll kill you if you make a spectacle of our daughter."

"I'm terrified."

"You underestimate him. He's not the man you've seen portrayed."

"A twisted soul who nearly killed his entire family, crippling his daughter for life? I don't think I could think any less of him."

"He's much worse than that. You have no idea. For those he hates, he'll stop at nothing, no matter the cost."

"Even if it means sacrificing you or your daughter?"

"For sure. A thousand percent yes."

Yuval pulled a book from a shelf and pretended to read. "Is there goodness in him? Somewhere?"

"Yes. He loves. But it's nothing compared to his hate."

"Do you think he hates me?"

"I'm would guess so."

"Good," Yuval said, putting the book down. "Have you spoken to him recently?"

Natalie thought of her text to Finch from earlier in the morning. *Why hasn't he replied?*

"Not in years."

"Do you have any way of getting in touch with him?"

"I don't. I've tried in the past. But he's never answered."

"Do you consider your husband a religious man?"

"No."

"Do you think your husband prays for Eva? Do you think he prays that she'd be healed?"

Natalie was thrown. "I have no idea."

"Do you think he has hope she might be healed?"

Yuval was really beginning to bother her.

"What are you even talking about?"

Natalie hated Finch with the entirety of her being, yet felt resentment when others stole any of that animosity from her.

"Do you think he loves her?"

"Of course he loves her. He's a deeply troubled man, we all know that. He never meant to harm her."

"Natalie...."

"Where is my father? Why isn't he asking me this?"

"Natalie, I am...*we* are offering you the opportunity for your daughter to be healed from an incurable injury. For her to get her life back fully. Grandchildren for you. Hope for everyone. Reconciliation between you and your husband. Reconciliation between the world and Mr. Finch."

"Why can't this be later?"

"I need you to help me get Finch there. Tonight."

"What does Tom have to do with anything? Why does it have to be tonight?"

Yuval finally snapped. "It's tonight or never! You get one chance. That is all."

Natalie moved away from the chair so that Yuval no longer stood between her and the door. He paused a moment to gather himself.

"Natalie, we lost the dear boy who was to be healed tonight. He was so close. He'd been through so much and was so close to having his life back. A few hours earlier, and he might still be with us."

Natalie's head swirled with emotion.

"Do you consider your daughter to be stable?" Yuval asked.

"You're scaring me, Dr. Naftali."

"It would be shameful if you were to prolong her suffering another day."

"I need to speak with my father."

"I'm done playing games with you, Natalie. You need to speak with *me*!"

Natalie made a move for the door. Yuval grabbed her arm, but she twisted away and bolted down the hall that led to the other wings of the house. Unfamiliar faces filled the main living room—men in uniforms. She looked behind her but saw no sign of Yuval.

Eva, she thought to herself. *I just need to get to Eva.*

Natalie raced through another hallway and up the stairs to a landing where the childrens' rooms were located. At the top, she could see that Eva's door was closed. A man stood outside the door.

A man with a gun—standing between her and her daughter.

CHAPTER 16

The Cardinal pulled Mongchai's coat over his tiny frame, his eyes frozen open. He scanned around the room, looking for options. The window appeared to be painted shut. A conical mouthpiece extended from a decrepit pipe that ran into the ceiling, an acoustical intercom that allowed communication long before the building had electricity. A small metal box labeled "Nurse" was screwed into the wall. Tiny holes drilled into a circular pattern on the front made it obvious it had served as an electrical intercom at some point. Gordillo pressed the black button on it several times.

Probably a kilometer away, he thought to himself.

He listened for footsteps down the hall but heard nothing. Gordillo continued to scan the room and noticed a red fire alarm by the door.

In case of fire, break glass. Press button.

The glass was already broken, the hammer removed from the chain from where it once hung. He pressed the button anyway, listening for any sign of a response.

Gordillo noticed an old matchbook in a drawer beside a Bible, realizing the mouthpiece from the old intercom offered him an opportunity. He tore out some sheets and began stuffing them into the pipe on the wall. After about twenty pages of Proverbs, he lit the match and dropped it into the hole. As smoke began to rise out of the pipe, he placed the Bible back into the drawer and drew the sleeve of his robe over his mouth.

Dark gray smoke began to fill the ceiling, inching downwards by the second. The Cardinal waited until it was churning at eye level before he cried out for aid.

"Fire!" he yelled. "Help us! Fire!"

Someone outside tried the door, but it was locked.

"Help us!" he cried again. "The building is on fire!"

"Open the door!" Mongchai's mother called from outside. "Unlock the door!"

Smoke began whirling underneath the door into the hallway. Someone threw themselves against the door, trying to break it down. Gordillo got on the floor and started coughing wildly. He crawled toward the hallway, twisted the lock, and opened the door.

The enormous Cardinal collapsed onto the floor outside as Mongchai's parents ran inside the room to rescue him. Grabbing the side of the door, Gordillo pulled himself up to his feet and stumbled towards the entrance.

"Get out," he yelled to the nurses running past him. "Get out of here. The whole place is on fire."

Just fifteen yards behind him, smoke was billowing out into the hallway, filling the massive corridor with darkness. Once outside, Gordillo spotted his car, its engine already running.

"Let's go," he said as he opened the back door and climbed in. "Get out of here now."

The SUV surged away from the building as Mongchai's parents ran outside, the father carrying his son's tiny body in his arms. The driver slammed on the brakes when he spotted them.

"Go," Gordillo shouted at him. "Go now. We don't have time."

Sirens sounded in the distance as fire trucks began to near. The SUV pulled away and rounded a curve that led back towards the entrance.

"Not too fast," Gordillo told the driver.

They hurried around the enormous hospital campus as emergency vehicles drove past. Before they could exit, they approached a security guardhouse that controlled access to the entire site with a sliding gate.

"We're locked down," the officer told them. "I can't let you leave until everyone's been accounted for."

Emergency vehicles continued to arrive through a gate on the other side, their sirens piercing the air with painful shrieks.

"We'll be safer if we leave," the driver told him.

"Yeah, I know. It's their dumb rule. Should only be a few minutes. What are your names?"

Gordillo had tried to slide low enough in the seat to avoid detection but it was clear he'd been seen.

"Roll up the window," he said to his driver. "Don't answer him, and roll up the window."

Much to the confusion of the security guard manning the gate, the driver closed his window. Inside the tiny building, the guard grabbed a walkie talkie and began making a call to someone.

The Cardinal tried to calm himself. "If we stay here, they're going to start asking questions. And I don't have time for complications."

"What should I do?" the driver asked.

"Can we just drive straight through?"

"I'm guessing we can. Whether this vehicle will be drivable or not is a whole other story."

"How about the other gate? Can you cut across the next time it opens?"

"Too many bollards in the way." The area between the entrance and exit was covered with stout vertical posts meant to protect both pedestrians and the campus itself from wayward drivers.

Still on the walkie, the guard left the structure and began to walk behind their vehicle.

"Back up!" Gordillo shouted. "Don't let him get our plates."

The driver threw the SUV into reverse and hit the gas, slamming into a vehicle that had pulled behind them, their dashboard splattered with white airbags.

"Shit," the driver said. "Just got complicated."

With sirens blaring, an ambulance stopped at the entrance. The sentry ran into the guardhouse and opened the gate for them to enter.

"There's our opening!"

"Not enough room. I can't cut across."

"Well back up some more."

The driver looked in his mirror and saw a person beside their car, looking at the damage he had done. The ambulance passed by, its sirens deafening.

"Do it!" Gordillo shouted.

The man slammed the gas, ramming hard into the car behind him, pushing it back ten feet. He spun the wheel left and shot across the median that divided the entrance from the exit.

"Go! Go! It's closing!"

The SUV bounced off the median, onto the pavement and through the entrance, tearing the gate from its tracks as it scraped down the side. After a few turns, they pulled onto the interstate and merged into heavy traffic.

"Where to?" the driver asked.

"Hotel."

"I'm sure they'll get our plates from the security cameras."

Gordillo considered their options, a list growing shorter by the minute.

The driver continued his concern. "They've probably got calls out for us already."

"Get me Yuval."

The driver tried the call as their SUV hurtled around the Washington D.C. beltway. Behind them, the Cardinal scanned closely, looking for anyone who might be following.

"He's not answering," the driver said.

"Just give it to me."

Gordillo grabbed the phone and dialed a different number, nervously fingering the ornate necklace he wore as he waited for a connection.

Finally, someone picked up.

"Hello. This is Cardinal Gordillo, Archbishop of Asunción. I have an urgent diplomatic request."

CHAPTER 17

Natalie was fuming as she approached the soldier standing outside her daughter's bedroom. She reached for the door handle, but he blocked her attempt.

"Who are you? My daughter is in there. I need to see her."

"The nurse is with your daughter. She is well taken care of."

"What nurse? Martta? Eva's nurse? Or someone you brought with you?"

Natalie looked down the stairs, expecting Yuval any moment.

"She is well taken care of," the soldier said.

"Do you know who I am? Do you know who my father is?"

"You're Natalie Finch. Your husband is Thomas Finch."

"I'm not your enemy," Natalie pleaded. "I'm on your side. Do you realize that?"

The soldier remained stoic.

"I'm calling the police," she said as she fumbled through her pockets, realizing her phone was in the bedroom.

"They've already been called."

"For what?"

"Child endangerment."

"What?" Natalie asked. "What is happening?"

She reached for the door again, but the soldier pushed her away.

"I suggest you wait down stairs for the police to arrive before you do something dumb."

Natalie's head spun in anger.

"Martta!" Natalie screamed. "Martta! Let me in!"

She lunged at the door in desperation, hoping it might stir Eva's nurse into action. The soldier grabbed Natalie and threw her to the ground, falling directly on top of her.

"This is your last warning," he said, twisting her arm until her shoulder stung with pain.

Think, Natalie. What would Tom do?

"Okay. I'll stop. I'll stop."

The soldier removed his grip and returned to the door. Natalie walked across the landing and opened another bedroom door.

"I don't feel well. I'm going to lay down. Is that allowed?"

The soldier squeezed a button on his shirt and said something quietly into his radio.

Natalie entered the bedroom across the hall and closed the door behind her. She'd already discovered a hidden passageway in Eva's room—a bookcase that swung on silent hinges—and guessed she'd find a similar escape that led to the secret play area all the children's rooms adjoined.

The entire wing of the great mansion was every child's dream, designed by a light-hearted architect with a wild imagination. In this particular bedroom, she was completely stumped. Despite their stone interiors, the other bedrooms were more bright and airy. This one was decorated as if it were a sort of dungeon—darker, with narrow windows. None of the bookcases would move. The paneling on the walls showed no visible cracks or movement when she pressed them.

Think, Natalie. Pretend you're in a dungeon.

She scanned the room and noticed a comically large iron lever protruding from the wall.

Of course. Dungeons have trapdoors.

Standing beside it, Natalie braced herself for a drop as she pulled the lever down. A distinct metal click echoed beneath the floor but nothing happened. She pulled it again.

People don't send themselves to die in dungeons. Where is it?

Natalie scanned the floor but saw nothing amiss. Outside, the helicopter's engines began to spool back up to speed.

I need to see Eva now.

Increasingly desperate, she threw books and toys from the shelf, covering the floor with debris. Natalie pulled the lever and saw a section of the floor dip from the weight upon it. Before its contents could slide off, she jumped for the trapdoor and rolled into foam that lined the tiny room below.

The trapdoor shut above, plunging her into near darkness—except for a faint shaft of light coming from where a ladder led into the children's playroom—a tower that rose above the rest of the mansion. She raced up the wooden rungs and peered from high above into the backyard. The tower began to shake as the helicopter blades gained speed. A soldier inside the helicopter lowered handrails on the steps and flipped the door closed.

Natalie raced down another ladder that led to Eva's room.

"Eva," she said, pushing the hidden bookcase open from behind. "Mommy's here."

There was no answer. The room was empty.

CHAPTER 18

Brinks found himself in a small, earthen basement, the walls lined with wooden shelves. The floor was covered with mangled bodies. Most of them were identically dressed, covered from head to toe in tactical gear. One of them was an EMT.

"Jesus," he said to himself.

"Don't say that!" the man screamed. "Don't say that!"

"Who are they?"

"Demons." A sorrowful pout turned across his face. "But now they're angels in heaven."

He put the barrel of his rifle on the shoulder of one of the dead and pulled the trigger, pulverizing the arm into pieces.

"See," he said with a grin. "I saved them—with my own injection!"

Brinkley realized the man was growing unstable by the minute.

"Brinks!" someone yelled from just outside the cabin. "Brinks, you alright?"

"Get out of here, Garcia!" With a cracked rib, Brinkley's voice faltered.

The man smiled at Brinkley and held a finger to his lips as he turned off the light. "Shhh," he said, barely able to control his laughter. "We'll surprise him."

"He'll kill you, Garcia! Get out now!"

Filled with anger, the man's eyes widened at Brinkley's betrayal. "Mr. Garcia!" he yelled, spit flying from his mouth. "We're down here."

Gunfire erupted from within the cabin, sending wood splinters from the doorframe flying into the air.

"That wasn't nice, Mr. Garcia," the man said, ducking for cover. "That wasn't nice at all."

He pulled a few rounds from his pocket and pressed them into his rifle. "Don't go anywhere," he said to Brinkley. "Be right back."

Once the man had left, Brinkley looked amongst the bodies for a firearm but saw nothing. Wincing in pain, he dragged himself up the stairs and peeked into the cabin. The sliding glass door had shattered, littering the floor with glass. Outside the cabin, he spotted the man in Garcia's truck, trying to drive it away.

Stick shift, he thought to himself as the vehicle lurched forward and stalled.

With no understanding of how to drive a manual transmission, the man gave up, got out of the truck, and pushed it into the creek.

Partially submerged in water, he slipped on the hood and clambered over the roof of the vehicle into the bed. Completely unaffected by the frigid water, he climbed on the back of the truck gate and jumped across to the other side, climbing up the mountainside towards the road.

Brinkley left the cabin and walked around the edge of the clearing towards the wood pile. He was hoping to find Garcia but instead found Monroe, lying on the ground—his coat soaked in blood. Bending to the ground, Brinkley put his hand on Monroe's artery but felt nothing.

Dear God.

Brinkley immediately thought of Monroe's wife and children.

We're at war.

He'd already lost count of the bodies he'd seen that morning. And now Monroe.

Why am I not dead?

The veteran officer couldn't understand why the man hadn't killed him while he had the chance. Whether on drugs or something else, it wasn't clear. For some reason, Brinkley's life had been spared.

Garcia came running out of the woods, a gun in his hand. He kneeled beside Monroe. "I saw him drop when he got hit. Is he dead?"

"I'm afraid so."

"What should we do?"

"Our guy's running up the road. Either we chase him on foot, or we get your truck out and ride."

"Can you see him?" Garcia asked, scanning the mountainside above them. "We're going to need to call in some help."

"I tried already. My radio's not working. You?"

"No signal back in these woods. How about your cell?"

Brinkley glanced at his phone.

"Not a single bar. Maybe there's a phone inside. Try and get your truck out before it floods."

Brinkley ran inside the cabin and found what he was looking for—a landline. He picked up the handset and was relieved to hear a dial tone. For the first time in his life, he dialed 911.

A dispatcher answered. "911. Is this an emergency?"

"Tamara, it's Brinkley. We're at the mountain call. Monroe is down. The EMTs are down. Suspect is armed and on the loose. We need everybody here now."

The phone went silent for a moment. Brinkley could hear the dispatcher talking with someone in the background.

"Tamara!"

"Hold please."

"Tamara what are you doing? I've got dead bodies everywhere. We're being shot at. We need help."

"I'm sorry, Brinks," she said. "I'm going to have to transfer you. Somebody from..."

The line clicked dead.

CHAPTER 19

Finch was relieved the ambulance was unlocked. He opened the back door and climbed inside.

Supplies, he thought to himself. After days on the run, food had become a problem. But a defibrillator? Nitroglycerin? Fibrinolytics? Those were worth more than any meal he could think of.

Within the ambulance, he grabbed the biggest plastic bag he could find and began throwing anything he might need into it. After a minute of scavenging, the bag was close to bursting. Finch was ecstatic as he grabbed another bag and placed it around the first. Managing his heart had frequently hindered his movement. With what he was able to collect, he had more confidence he could push himself harder.

Suddenly, the ambulance shifted. Without any warning, the back of the ambulance slid sideways, sending Finch stumbling. The door on the back swung around as the vehicle rocked.

"What the..." Finch caught himself from falling, grabbing onto the shelves that lined the inside of the vehicle.

Again the vehicle shifted, this time even more dramatically. Finch slammed against the side of the compartment as pieces of equipment rolled against him.

Someone opened the driver-side door. His view partially obstructed, Finch ducked behind the window that separated him from the cabin as the engine of the ambulance sprang to life. The vehicle started beeping and began moving backwards, up the mountain road behind them.

I can jump out, Finch thought to himself.

The ambulance reversed slowly, rounding each bend with just inches to spare on either side of the road. Finch checked his pulse, knowing he would have to dive out of the way of the enormous vehicle before it ran him over.

148. Too high.

Finch lifted the bag of supplies, judging its weight. If the road had been wider, he might have taken a chance and jumped but, as things stood, there wasn't enough room. The vehicle rounded another hairpin turn then slowed to a stop. Through the front window, Finch could see a white truck approach, still dripping with water. The driver of the ambulance lifted a hunting rifle to the windshield and fired, tearing a three-inch hole in the glass.

CHAPTER 20

"What are they doing?" Albert Connolly asked his assistant, Brooke.

Once their limo made a U-turn, it picked up speed, driving on the right shoulder of the road to bypass slower traffic. The privacy screen was still up and despite their banging, the officer who sat in the front would not lower it.

Brooke looked for something that might allow them to break a window. "We're totally shut in back here."

"He's not stopping because he's afraid we'll jump out."

"Which means they can't lock the doors from up there."

Connolly considered her thoughts. "I think you're right. This is an executive limo. They would have given control to the people riding in the back."

"Why can't we roll down the screen then?"

"He must have disabled it somehow."

Brooke unlocked her phone. "We should call the police."

She dialed an emergency number, but the call wouldn't connect.

"No service, I'm guessing?" Connolly said.

"No service. No data. Nothing."

"They're jamming us somehow. EMF shielding? Who knows?"

"Yours, too?"

Connolly glanced at his phone. "Yep. Mine, too."

The NIH director tried to piece together what was happening. There had always been a power struggle between him and Yuval, a battle that had become more pronounced since the momentous discovery was confirmed. If they were being kidnapped in some way, this was an entirely new level—a bold move he felt even the volatile doctor was incapable of carrying out.

Why now? Connolly thought to himself. *Why, on the eve of our greatest collaboration?*

Connolly wasn't set to feature prominently during the evening's event. He had purposefully requested a small role—almost as a sideshow, a tiny part in a much bigger play. He had ceded control of nearly everything to Yuval, and yet, it seemed like it wasn't enough.

Brooke interrupted his thoughts. "What were you screaming at Dr. Naftali for? We could hear you from upstairs."

"He did something he wasn't supposed to do. I can't say anything more." Connolly's commitment to secrecy was thorough—he had protected even his faithful assistant from knowing what they were planning on unveiling.

"You obviously ticked him off."

"Yeah, well he ticked me off, too."

"You think that's what this is about? He's angry?"

"I *hope* that's what this is about."

All things considered, Connolly was afraid of Yuval. He'd never projected it publicly, but knew the man lacked the moral compass he would have preferred. Yuval was more like Faucett in that way—driven, ambitious, determined to achieve their goals, no matter the cost or political fallout. The frequent collaboration between the two during the pandemic bothered him, a troubling relationship given their callous natures and narcissistic tendencies.

In fact, when Faucett was killed, Connolly initially felt certain Yuval was behind it. Not because he believed Finch incapable but instead, because he felt the similar natures of Faucett and Yuval had gotten the better of them. As the darling of the global community, Yuval had access to enough money and political influence he could snap his fingers and have anyone killed. An entire family, if he wanted. Perhaps he snapped his fingers and paid Finch enough money to kill Faucett, purely as a display of his power.

Once Faucett was gone, Connolly knew he was essentially a dead man walking; the last of the old dinosaurs left to run the country's failing health institutions. He would hold on to the bitter end—a retirement that couldn't come soon enough. The next generation would come along, and a new set of ideas and hopes would fill the halls of Bethesda and Atlanta once again, ideas that would, no doubt, annoy and offend the old-timers.

Yuval represented that new generation. Younger, more charismatic, better connected, and certainly smarter—he possessed the skills necessary to transform Connolly's national role into a true global health czar. And it was happening. Not only was it happening, it had accelerated, and there was little Connolly could do. Tonight was to be the culmination of a lifetime of work and public service, and he had essentially handed the mic to a man he feared might kill him at any time.

The limo slowed for a line of protestors attempting to block the road in front of them.

"These people are everywhere," Brooke said.

A group of twenty had gathered beneath an overpass, their fabric signs hanging down from the bridge above.

"More cameras equals more demonstrations."

"Where are the cameras?"

Connolly pointed up. "My guess is they followed us from the cathedral."

Darkness enveloped the vehicle as they stopped beneath the bridge. The protestors were handcuffed together, making their removal more difficult for the police.

"We should get out. Make a run for it now," Brooke said.

"I don't think they'll treat us very well."

"The cameras won't see us."

"I'm not worried about the cameras."

Several of the protestors began beating on their vehicle, one of them smashing his flagpole into a window, trying to break the thick glass. The driver gunned the engine and smashed through the column of people. One of their handcuffs caught on the mirror, dragging the screaming line along the asphalt until it snapped off.

The limo smashed over something, hurling Connolly and his assistant into the ceiling before they fell back down into their seats. Behind them, a jumbled mess of bodies and signs lay tangled behind them.

"Stop!" Brooke yelled, beating on the privacy screen. "They're hurt!"

Undeterred, the driver accelerated onto an exit from the highway.

Connolly recognized the location. "This is the hotel exit. They're taking us to the convention."

CHAPTER 21

Cardinal Gordillo's SUV continued to weave through traffic as it raced toward the hotel. Two unmarked cruisers had taken up behind them, shadowing their every move.

"Why aren't they stopping us?" the driver asked.

"They can't. At least for now. They can follow us all they want, but that's all."

Until recently, Gordillo never questioned Yuval's plans. The details were too complex, too obscure for him to fully grasp. But he had tremendous power and influence, something the priest desperately needed.

As one of a handful of Cardinals being considered to replace the aging Pope, winning the ultimate prize in all of Christianity required more than luck—it took a willingness to engage many players far outside the church's natural domain, a sometimes brutal game in which Gordillo was more than happy to engage. For anyone seeking the throne of Christendom, earning the favor of Yuval was close to the ultimate prize, an endorsement likely to guarantee Gordillo's ascent.

Yuval sought one thing—the attendance of the Pope and his retinue at the event at the Cathedral. Despite his impressive network, Connolly had been unable to gain the trust of the Catholics. Calls went unanswered, messages unreturned, and it became clear the Holy Father would not attend. Through Gordillo, Yuval at least found an inroad to several other Cardinals—papal counsel he'd otherwise been unable to attain.

And so, Gordillo agreed to an uneasy partnership with Yuval. Publicly, they could not be seen together. Conversations took place within private meetings at obscure locations. Emails and text messages were forbidden. Phone calls, prohibited—a rule Yuval had just broken when he called Gordillo in the hospital. The relationship had been put to the test just hours earlier when the Pope's aides threatened to leave the event and return to Italy without some proof of Yuval's discovery, a precarious situation the Cardinal had been able to address.

Gordillo had done his job. He had delivered the guest list Yuval had asked for, humiliating himself in the process. The phone call from Yuval, however, gave him serious doubts the most important person on that list would attend.

Like everyone, Gordillo knew Thomas Finch hated the globalists, a group who counted Yuval as their chief evangelist. Finch's videos and writings depicted their goals as the most pressing existential threat to humanity the world had ever known. He might have insisted they were simply misguided humanitarian ideals but, instead, had convinced the millions who followed him they were demonic.

They had become his sworn enemy, and he theirs. Yet Yuval, the hot-tempered mess had somehow found within himself the desire to make peace. To reconcile himself to Finch in front of the world. The Asian boy, Mongchai, seemed like the perfect draw for the event, but ever since Finch's escape, Yuval had grown increasingly desperate.

"You did that back there, didn't you?" the driver asked. "You started that fire."

"Shut up. I need to think."

"I know you started that fire. You killed him, didn't you?"

"You are starting to ask the wrong kind of questions."

"I've had enough of this. I want out. I agreed to your show this morning and that was it. This is too much."

"Oh, you're already in it now."

"I am not in it. I am done. I'll take you to the hotel, but that's it."

Gordillo rubbed the back of his neck. Mongchai was dead, a situation which would cause its own set of complications. And now this. A new impediment. Betrayal from the man he'd baptized as a child.

The Cardinal's phone rang.

"What is it?" he asked.

"I have some news I thought you might be interested in," a voice responded.

"Go ahead."

"Cardinal Vallcorba and Olevnik are going to participate in some protests this afternoon."

"What for?"

"A show of solidarity or something like that. They're concerned about the optics of attending tonight."

"What's this have to do with me?"

"They're going to march with the protestors. Down Wisconsin Avenue, right past the Cathedral."

"And?"

"It's growing chaotic down there. Security will likely be difficult."

Gordillo paused to consider the implications.

"It's around 4pm. I just thought you might want to know," the voice said.

Without another word, the Cardinal ended the call. The two men most actively challenging his claim to the throne of Christendom would be together and with minimal security—an opportunity he wouldn't have even dared to pray for.

Gordillo began to tremble with anxiety at the possibility this chance might provide. His hands clutched together, he closed his hands and bowed his head.

Give me this, Father. Show me a way. Allow me to serve you.

The Cardinal ran through different scenarios in his mind, trying to figure out the best way to accomplish his mission. The morning's events had affected him deeply—particularly the ease with which he and his guest had been able to bypass security. Out of the blue, a thought occurred to him.

"Where'd you put the wheelchair?" he asked the driver. "You can be done, but I'm going to need one more favor from you. One more appearance from Mr. Maduro. No miracles this time."

CHAPTER 22

Natalie sprinted across the hall, down the stairs, and through the main living area to the large glass doors that led into the backyard. The roar of the helicopter was deafening, even from within the mansion. Debris spiraled into the air, waves of pressure that made opening the door nearly impossible.

With the weight of her entire body, Natalie threw herself against the opening, cracking it just enough to catch the wind like a sail and fling it open wide. She ran outside, stumbling under the blades of the giant aircraft as their thrust pushed her to the ground.

"Eva!" she screamed, her cries inaudible above the din of engine and air. "Eva! Don't leave me!"

The helicopter began to rise into the air. Natalie reached for the recessed door handle but there was nothing her fingers could take hold of. She hurled her body onto one of its wheels but spun from it onto the grass below.

The pressure of air doubled in intensity as the propeller blades bit into the air. Natalie covered her ears as the enormous helicopter rose into the sky, turned, then flew away.

* * *

Minutes passed and Natalie still lay sobbing in the grass. Alone.

Finch.

The man was her single thought. Her daughter had just been taken from her, but she could think of only one thing.

Finch.

She hated the man for who he was. She hated him for what he had done. She hated him for the very reasons so many loved him. But for now, she hated the same people he did. She hated those same *things* he did. Those things which drove him. And that alignment—that union of loathing—felt enough for her to forgive.

They want Finch? I'll get them Finch.

Natalie stood up and brushed the grass from her dress.

I'll get them Finch, and they'll find out what hate really is.

She felt in her pockets for her phone, but it was gone. Leaves and torn landscape fabric littered the grounds, making it impossible to spot.

Think, Natalie.

She replayed the previous hour of her life. Running down the stairs, into the backyard. Climbing into the tower. Speaking with Yuval in the library.

Bedroom.

She didn't like taking her phone into the library and had left it in the bedroom. She was sure of it. Natalie ran back into the house, her heart ripped apart at the sight of the empty room where Eva's rolling bed should have been. The nightstand, where she normally kept her phone, was bare, a disconnected charging cable strewn across the floor.

The nightstand contained nothing meaningful, as did the bathroom counter.

They took it, she realized. *Of course they took my phone.*

Running out of options, Natalie collapsed to the floor.

I have no idea what his phone number is.

Even with another phone, she had no way of contacting Finch.

Natalie froze as the sound of faint buzzing caught her ear. It was a vibration.

It's here.

She walked around quietly, waiting for it to buzz again.

Bookcase.

Natalie pulled the bookcase open. At the bottom of the ladder sat her phone, lit up with an incoming message. It was from Martta.

I'm sorry. I tried to stop them.

Natalie wept at the message from Eva's nurse. She had tried. Of course she had tried. She would have let herself be killed before she let any harm come to Eva.

How terrified they must be, she thought, riding in a helicopter with soldiers to some location unknown.

Natalie's head swirled as she called Finch. Where could they even begin to heal? What could she say that wouldn't sting? That would have to come later, she knew. For now, getting her daughter back was the priority.

"Answer, Finch."

The line continued to ring.

"Dear God, please answer."

Voicemail is full.

Of course it is. Natalie's hope of reaching Finch evaporated.

CHAPTER 23

"Back up! Back up!" Brinkley yelled to Garcia.

The blast from within the ambulance missed, but the driver was lining up another shot—this time through the hole in his windshield.

Garcia slammed the shifter into reverse and skidded backwards, his tires chattering across the gravel. The ambulance disappeared from their view as they slid around the turn.

"How many rounds do you have?" Brinkley asked.

"I've got one other mag in the glove box. This one's half empty."

"Where's *your* gun?" Garcia asked.

"I told you it's at home."

Brinkley opened the compartment and handed Garcia the magazine. "Go ahead and change it."

Garcia switched magazines and attempted to hand the gun to Brinkley. "You shoot. I drive."

"I can't see shit, you know that."

"I can't shoot left-handed."

"Alright, let me have it then."

Garcia handed the gun to Brinkley. "We should be dead right now."

"There were five or six bodies down there. Soldiers or something. The other EMT, too."

"What is this freak doing? Why were all these people here?"

"Something's going on. Tamara got called off. I asked her to send help, but someone was in the office with her and called her off."

"We're screwed," Garcia said. "He's got us trapped down here."

"No, we can make it. Let's just be careful and help will come."

"What kind of help?"

Brinkley thought. "Yeah, that part I don't know."

Hidden behind the next corner, the ambulance began beeping again.

"Okay, hear that? He's moving back again. Inch forward and let's see if I can get a clean shot."

Brinkley's phone began to ring.

"Hang on, it's dispatch." He motioned Garcia to stop and answered the call.

"Is this Tamara? We're in deep shit here, and I hope you guys have everyone coming."

"Sergeant Brinkley, this is Special Agent Vickers. Do not engage suspect. Do you understand? Do not engage the suspect."

"The hell I won't," Brinks yelled back at him. "I've got multiple fatalities, including my officer. Who is this?"

"This is a command from the Federal Government of the United States. I am ordering you to stand down. Do not engage this suspect."

"What the hell do you want me to do? Walk away?" Brinks turned on the speakerphone so Garcia could listen in.

"Sergeant, do you know who Thomas Finch is?"

"Of course."

"We have enough information to suspect he's in the area."

"Well this ain't him. I saw him, and he's not your guy."

"We believe his appearance has changed significantly. He's likely emaciated. Sickly. Difficulty with exertion."

"Yeah, like I said, this ain't your guy."

"You were close enough to see him clearly?"

"He threw me down the stairs. Got in my face with a rifle. It was clear enough."

The phone went silent for a moment.

"Are you alone, Sergeant Brinkley?"

"No, I've got Officer Garcia—the only other person the guy *who's not Thomas Finch* hasn't killed yet."

"It sounds like I'm on speakerphone. Could you turn it off?"

Brinkley looked at Garcia, confused. He switched the audio and held the phone to his ear.

"Go ahead."

"Sergeant, we've accessed your medical records. We're looking up Garcia now. I know these things aren't always accurate, so I need to ask you a question. And I need you to answer truthfully."

"Okay."

Again, the phone went silent.

"Did you get any MALKA shots?"

Brinkley looked at Garcia, unable to imagine why they might be asking that question.

CHAPTER 24

"Are you scared?" Yuval asked.

Eva's nurse, Martta, didn't answer. Like most any military aircraft, the interior of the helicopter was spartan. While comfort appeared to be last on a list of must-haves, noise must have been the first. There was nearly nothing separating them from the roar outside, the interior apparently designed in such a way as to maximize the wail of the turboshaft engine.

Eva's gurney was strapped down to the loading ramp at the rear, oversized earmuffs covering the sides of her head. Martta stood beside her, leaning into the bed for stability, caressing both of Eva's hands.

Yuval grabbed a corded headset from a hanger on the wall and handed it to Martta.

"Put this on—you can hear me better," he yelled, pointing at his own microphone.

"I don't want to hear you."

Yuval feigned sadness. "Oh, come now."

He moved to place the headset over her ears. Unwilling to let go of Eva, Martta offered no resistance. Immediately, the deafening drone of the aircraft was reduced in half, the noise-canceling technology doing its job.

"Okay, that's better, isn't it?" he asked, his voice more calm.

Martta remained stoic, unwilling to look him in the face.

"Do you know who I am?" Yuval asked.

"Someone famous," she said.

"Dr. Yuval Naftali," he sung, a melody of a title that conveyed anything but modesty. "Does that ring a bell? Dr. Naftali?"

"Maybe."

"You've seen me before? On TV?"

"At parties with Dr. Connolly. I know you work together."

"So you know you can trust me."

"You've just kidnapped me—and the six-year-old girl I'm supposed to protect—in a giant helicopter."

Yuval grimaced. "Don't say *kidnapped*."

"And you expect me to trust you?"

"Don't say kidnapped," he said again. "Think of it like a surprise party."

"For who?"

"For different people. For the world, really."

"Natalie doesn't like surprises."

"Yes, I know. But she's going to love this one."

"Is this how scientists always talk? You don't make any sense."

Yuval spent a lifetime of not making any sense. His intellect was a challenge to convey to nearly everyone, his stilted conversations always the filtered-down version of far more complex dialogues running through his head. Because of that, he constantly needed patience—a virtue that never came naturally to him, particularly in dealing with those who couldn't understand how inferior they were.

Yuval calmed himself. "I'm sorry. I speak in riddles, yes. Let me try again. Do you know what's happening tonight?"

"Not really. I know everyone's flown in from all over. Something important—a new discovery or something."

"Yes, that's right. We are showing off a new discovery."

"Something that's supposed to stop people from fighting so much."

Yuval nodded his head in agreement. "Yes, a new peace. Absolutely."

"Something to do with the Asian boy who drowned. Or nearly drowned when he saved his friends."

"That's where Eva comes in. Something terrible happened to the boy this morning. He was supposed to be the most important person at the entire event, but now he can't come."

"What happened?"

"I don't know for sure, but it sounds as though he may have died."

"And now you want Eva to take his place? In the middle of all those people?"

"Yes! Eva is going to be the most important person in the world tonight."

Martta grew angry. "Why her? After what she's been through? After what *all of them* have been through? You know they've tried to keep her out of the spotlight."

His eyes darted to the side. "Dr. Connolly asked for this. I realize Natalie may not be excited, but we felt it was the best path forward given our unfortunate circumstances."

"And so you kidnap us?"

Yuval's patience was running thin. Like most of his discoveries and research, no one understood the full significance of the evening's event. It was impossible to convey. He could see it, floating in the air before him, but no one else would be able to understand. Not Connolly, and certainly not his granddaughter's nurse, whose resistance was beginning to wear on him. They were essentially his prisoners, completely under his control. He would only need to appease them a few hours longer.

"Do you want to see Eva get better?" Yuval asked.

"Of course."

"How about healed completely?"

"That's impossible."

"Why?"

"It just is. No one recovers from injuries like hers."

"Why?"

"It just doesn't happen."

"What if it could?"

"Impossible."

"Everyone who's anyone is here in Washington, D.C. this week because they believe that maybe, just maybe, the impossible is possible. Scientists and the most important religious leaders of the world are all here to find out. This could be the most significant event in human history."

Martta was unsure what to say.

"And you think I'm going to let it be ruined because someone wants privacy for their child? Someone who doesn't even know what's going on around her?"

"She's paralyzed. That's all. She knows what's going on around her."

"Whatever."

"She can talk and think and has opinions and hopes just like all of us."

"That's very sweet. I can't think of a better person for tonight than her."

Martta took a deep breath but, for a moment, didn't exhale. "Do you have children, Dr. Naftali?"

"I do not."

"What's the closest thing to you?"

"I don't know."

"Who do you love more than anything in this world?"

"I'd have to think about that."

"Your mother or father? A wife? A lover?"

A tic juddered across Yuval's face. "I'd have to think about it."

Martta gently brushed the hair away from Eva's eyes. "I love this girl, more than anything in this world."

"I'm sure you do."

"My mother is very sweet to me, but has always been emotionally distant. My father is gone."

"I am sorry for your loss."

"I am not married. I don't have any children or a boyfriend or pets or anything."

Yuval badly misread her intent. "Perhaps we can continue to get to know each other after all of this is over."

Martta let go of Eva's hands and moved directly in front of him. "I love Eva as if she were my own daughter. I don't know if you love anyone, or even know what that feels like at all. Just know that if you mean to harm this girl, you kidnapped the wrong nurse."

CHAPTER 25

Swaying in the rear compartment, Finch braced himself as the ambulance continued backing up the side of the mountain, rounding each curve with increasing speed. Towards the front of the ambulance, two or three turns down the mountain road, the white truck continued to follow. The man driving the ambulance kept his rifle propped up on the dash, the barrel sticking through the hole in his windshield, ready to fire.

He's on my side.

Finch was certain that's why he hadn't been killed. The driver could have shot him several times over, but didn't.

Maybe he knows who I am.

It had been years since Finch allowed himself to trust anyone. The isolation was crippling—his only comfort, a precious few voicemails he'd played a thousand times.

Hi Tom. It's Natalie Connolly, just returning your call. Dad listened to your message and thought it was hilarious. Hope that's not too embarrassing. You can call me. I'll answer.

Albert Connolly's distinct New England accent was frequently lampooned by his enemies. After ignoring multiple attempts to attract her attention, Finch got her number and left her a message, his impersonation of her father picture perfect—complete with a politically incorrect joke about a future wedding with dowries and goats.

It was his favorite recording from her.

You can call me. I'll answer.

Her inflection on that last two-word sentence could have melted steel. It was feminine. It was soft. It was an invitation. It was everything he was not. Despite his public braggadocio, Finch had deep personal struggle. Natalie was beautiful. Confident. Humble—all the things every man desires. But stable, as well? It was one of Finch's many weak spots and Natalie's apparent steadiness perfectly filled that void.

* * *

Still reversing slowly, the ambulance came to a stop, snapping Finch from his daydream. Behind them, a few hundred feet away, the trail emptied onto a gravel overlook that lined the main highway. Official-looking vehicles, their windows darkly tinted, surrounded the exit. Men in uniforms—wearing the same kit as the soldiers from the morning—fanned out behind the cars.

"Not good," Finch said to himself.

Down the trail in front of them, the white truck slowed to a stop, its front barely visible from around a curve.

Trapped.

Over the past few days, he'd been able to slip out of a few difficult situations. Shoplifting at a grocery store. A clandestine visit to an ER that went wrong. Finch knew he was wanted, but this went far beyond anything he'd expected. Sheriffs. Armed soldiers. It was clear things had escalated.

We need to give up.

Finch knocked on the window that separated the cabin from the rear compartment, trying to get the driver's attention, but it didn't work. The driver scratched at his face and looked at the blood on his fingers. He pulled his rifle from the windshield, got out of the ambulance, and began walking towards Garcia's truck, the gun raised to his shoulder.

He fired once, striking the exposed corner of the white vehicle. Finch looked through the back window of the ambulance and saw soldiers advancing towards them. Unaware of their presence, the crazed man continued down the road towards the truck and fired again.

Trapped between them, Finch ducked beneath the windows as the soldiers crouched past the ambulance, weapons drawn, their faces concealed beneath tactical masks.

They don't know I'm here.

Finch slid the window open and readied himself to climb into the cabin. Realizing he was being surrounded, the man outside turned around and began firing wildly, striking the ambulance as soldiers leapt from the road for cover behind rocks and trees lining either side.

Why don't they shoot him? Finch wondered.

Full of rage, the man began to jog back toward the ambulance, firing with reckless abandon. As he got closer, the men retreated further, scampering up the road, returning to their own vehicles. Finch stuffed his bag into the front of the ambulance and crawled behind it. The man walked directly past the driver's side window, his face covered in blood.

"Hey!" Finch yelled at him, beating on the window. "Hey!"

Completely distracted, the deranged man reloaded his gun and continued to fire at the retreating soldiers, stopping at the rear of the ambulance. He opened the back door, climbed in, and closed it behind him.

Finch glanced in the side mirror and saw a large tactical vehicle turning onto the mountain road, completely blocking his escape. Again, he tried getting the man's attention.

"Hey!" he screamed through the window into the rear compartment. "Let's give up. We're surrounded. They're going to kill us."

The man turned around, a puzzled look on his gory face.

"You!" he said, his eyes glowing with anger. "You did this!"

He raised his rifle at Finch and fired.

CHAPTER 26

"Who's he shooting at?" Garcia asked.

From their vantage point, something strange had happened. Just as the man rounded the corner and was about to open fire, they saw him turn around and begin shooting at soldiers hiding behind the ambulance.

"Let's go up there and get a better view," Brinkley said, pointing to the small ridge that shielded them from the fight.

Both Garcia and Brinkley exited the driver's side door and scrambled up the line of rocks to their left. Peering over the top, they were dumbfounded at what they saw—more soldiers, crawling over the mountainside.

"Jesus," Brinkley said. "More of them."

"This *must* be Feds," Garcia replied. "Look at all of them."

An enormous black tactical vehicle inched its way down the road towards the ambulance, another group of armed men crouched behind it for safety.

"Where'd they get a JLTV?" Brinkley asked.

"Must have flown it in. You think you could take him out from here?" Garcia asked.

"Not with a pistol. Anyways, I don't know who it was that told me to stand down, but I'm standing down."

Another rifle blast disintegrated a second section of the ambulance's windshield. Immediately, it began reversing at breakneck speed, flying up the mountainside. The JLTV stopped as the ambulance accelerated towards it.

Brinkley shook his head. "He's gonna ram him."

The men behind the black vehicle dove to the side as the ambulance slammed into it, sending it skidding backwards to a stop along the gravel road. The ambulance pulled forward, its rear compartment crushed, then rammed again, turning its wheels left and right in an attempt to push the huge vehicle off the road.

"Why the hell aren't they lighting him up?" Brinkley said to Garcia.

"Shoot him for God's sake," he yelled into the air.

The ambulance pulled forward, giving itself enough runway for another attack. Trying to go on the offensive, the huge truck rolled forward and pressed into the back of the ruined rescue vehicle, its power and thousands of pounds of steel forcing the ambulance down the mountain trail. Gravel flew everywhere. The ambulance's wheels spun wildly, the vehicle unable to withstand the monstrous push from behind.

"Shit," Brinkley said. "Your truck."

Locked in battle, the two vehicles skidded down the mountain towards Garcia's truck. The officer jumped down the rocks towards the road.

"Garcia! Stop! It's too dangerous."

With no ability to steer, the ambulance shifted its transmission into drive and accelerated forward, putting space between the it and vehicle chasing it. The JLTV gained speed and rammed directly into the ambulance as it wedged itself into the side of the mountain, just short of Garcia's truck. The collision sent both vehicles bouncing into the air and onto their side, twisting off the gravel trail as they cartwheeled into the trees below.

Brinkley scampered down the rocks as soldiers emerged from the woods and ran down the road to where the vehicles had fallen. Incredibly, the man from the cabin emerged from the wreckage and was standing on top of the overturned tactical vehicle, unleashing his rifle into any opening he could find.

"Shoot him," Brinkley screamed as he steadied his pistol and began firing. Without warning, an unseen soldier emerged from behind him, wrestled his gun away and tackled Brinkley to the ground. His side exploded in pain as a rib cracked completely through.

"Do not engage, Sergeant Brinkley," a muffled voice said, his face completely obscured.

"Are you Vickers?"

"Yes."

"He's going to kill all of us! Is that what you want?"

Men with four-pronged rifles surrounded the wreckage and began firing at the crazed man. Black netting exploded from their guns, their weighted corners wrapping around his body. He screamed with effort, splitting the nylon cords that entangled him. Two more shots, then a third rang out, covering him in mesh. Again he screamed, flailing his body like a trapped animal. This time was too much—he could not break free.

"Give it up, Finch," Vickers called out to him. "It's over."

Sprawled across the top of the tactical vehicle, the man stopped moving. His face dripping with blood, he locked eyes with the soldier who called out to him.

"Thomas Finch?" he asked, his voice full of unbelief. "Is that who you're after?"

The soldiers didn't move. Brinkley rolled onto his other side to try and alleviate some of the pain racking his body.

"That was Finch?" the man asked himself as a look of sadness overcame him.

"In the ambulance with me? I tried to kill him."

Underneath the netting, the man began manipulating his rifle, pushing it outside of the netting.

"Tranquilizers!" Vickers called out. "Now!"

The soft crack of a dart being fired echoed through the woods. The man winced in pain as a blue projectile lodged into his leg.

"Stop it!" he screamed as he turned the barrel of his rifle towards his face.

"Hit him again," Vickers cried out.

Two more darts thumped into the man, his body twisting in pain. He angled the rifle into his mouth, then pulled the trigger as a mist of red drifted into the air.

"Fuck," Vickers said, turning away from the gore that coated the black vehicle.

Garcia clambered down beside Brinkley.

"Fuck," Vickers said again, pulling a phone from his pocket.

"That wasn't Finch," Brinkley said, grimacing as he tried to sit up. "I'm trying to tell you. I don't know what the hell was wrong with this guy, but he wasn't Finch. Tell him, Garcia."

"I didn't get a good look at him."

Vickers dialed someone on his phone, a look of concern on his face.

"You heard what he said, right?" Brinkley asked. "The man couldn't believe you thought he was Finch."

Vickers ended his call. "Seriously, Sergeant? You think he's somehow above lying about his identity?"

"Lying about his identity for what? So he has time to blow his head off? Does that sound like a rational explanation for what just happened?"

"My men saw him this morning."

"Then they saw somebody else."

"They confirmed it was him."

"They saw somebody else," Brinkley said again, more emphatically.

"That somebody else just blew their head off," Garcia added.

An image of the girl's headless body flashed through Brinkley's mind. The call was just a couple of hours earlier, but already it felt an eternity had passed since he woke up.

How could anyone do that to themselves? he thought. *Let alone a six-year-old girl?*

Drugs do crazy things. Brinkley knew that. He'd seen it first hand when his son battled a raging addiction, a slender 19-year-old teen that suddenly became nearly impossible to control.

Tossed like a rag doll down the stairs.

Brinkley was a large man, a defensive linebacker in college. He was used to hitting and being hit. At 230 pounds, he'd never felt someone throw him around like what the man was able to do.

He moved the ambulance.

The absurdity of what he had just witnessed began to solidify. The ambulance was abandoned, hopelessly stuck in a washed out section of the road. Somehow, the man was able to get it free—not by digging, but by *sliding* the rear of the ambulance to where it could get a better grip.

None of it made sense, a maelstrom of confusion Brinkley no longer enjoyed. Earlier in his law enforcement career, he embraced such challenges. The chaos. The seemingly unconnected clues. The riddle whose answer escaped everyone. It might take minutes, it might take months. No matter how difficult, Brinkley was the guy who wouldn't give up until he had a case solved.

Now, he regretted taking that first call earlier in the morning. The hysterical screams of the mom. His feet slipping on the bedroom floor. The thought of the window slamming down on the girl's neck. Dots were starting to form in his head, but Brinkley had little interest in connecting them. Normally, cases started out confusing. Clarity might come slowly, but at least, in general, things moved in that direction. Today's events were getting more bizarre by the hour.

Vickers reached into a pocket and pulled out a small plastic bag containing cotton Q-tips. "Sergeant Brinkley, I don't know how it's possible, but I hope to God you're right. Would you mind grabbing a few samples?"

"Why me?"

"Teeth, if you can find them."

"Why. Me."

"You're the only one who doesn't think he's Finch."

"You do it."

Vickers pulled a pair of latex gloves from another pocket and offered them to Brinkley. "Prove us wrong."

"What agency did you say you're with?"

"I didn't."

"You guys are special ops or something, right?"

"Something."

Brinkley grabbed the gloves and looked at Garcia. "Probably another three-letter agency with guns. Just what we need."

After stretching the blue latex onto his hands, Brinkley removed the Q-tips from the bag and scurried towards the overturned vehicles. Garcia moved after him.

"Not you," Vickers said as held out his arm, blocking the officer from following. "Just him."

Garcia stepped back, unsettled by the agent's forcefulness.

The rolling thunder of a helicopter approaching bounced across the dell.

"Shit," Vickers said. "He's here. Hurry up."

Brinkley looked up towards the sky. "Who's here?"

"Just hurry up."

The scene set out before Brinkley was surreal: An overturned tactical vehicle, resting amongst the wreckage of a destroyed ambulance. On top, the body of the crazed man wrapped in netting, much of his head gone. A dozen or more soldiers surrounded him, others perhaps, still concealed. An enormous military aircraft buzzed the air above them as it drew near.

Something is missing.

Brinkley scanned the area, looking for clues.

"The samples, Sergeant Brinkley!"

"Hang on. Something's wrong."

Garcia looked around and crouched to the ground as it began to shake. The roar of the helicopter was deafening as it descended nearby, its pilot scouting for a place to land safely.

"Something's missing."

"What is it?" Garcia shouted to Brinkley, struggling to be heard.

"Get me the samples, now!" Vickers screamed.

Brinkley pointed up the hill. "Your truck!"

Garcia looked and saw that it was gone.

CHAPTER 27

The helicopter touched the ground, and its engines began to slow. The huge aircraft blocked the highway where Vickers and his men had parked their cars, gathering their forces before they began their trudge along the gravel drive that wound down to the cabin.

"Where are we?" Eva asked Martta, her voice just barely audible.

"Where is this, Dr. Naftali? Why aren't we at the Cathedral? Isn't that where things are happening tonight?"

"We will go there, yes. Eventually. But, first, we are going on a little fishing trip."

Martta was unsure what he meant, a cue Yuval immediately noticed.

"We need to find Mr. Finch," he said. "We need to find him soon."

"And you think he's here? In these woods?"

"I know he's here. He's just turned up—how do you Americans say it? 'In the nick of time?'"

"How do you know it's him?"

"Oh, it's him. He's gotten careless. Left a trail we couldn't miss."

"Natalie says he'll die before he lets someone catch him. She says he's too clever."

"He's extremely clever, I'll give him that." Yuval patted Eva on the leg. "But I have a feeling he won't be able to resist our bait, isn't that right, Miss Eva?"

"I don't want to see him," Eva said.

"You don't want to see your father? How long has it been? Three years?"

"He tried to kill me."

Martta jumped in. "He didn't mean to, Eva. You know it was an accident."

"But he tried to kill that man in the car with us. That wasn't an accident."

That had been the most difficult part for Eva's mother to explain.

* * *

The night of the tragedy, Walter Faucett had asked if Natalie would drive him home, a request she reluctantly accepted. It was a huge retirement party the

National Institutes of Health held in his honor to celebrate his forty years of public service. News cameras were rolling. Speeches were made. Toasts and roasts were held. It was the biggest send-off the agency had ever conducted.

As the unofficial spokesman for the NIH, he'd seen the country—the world, in fact—through it all: AIDS. SARS. Zika. And most recently, MALKA-6. Faucett was retiring—besides her father, the last titan of the great public health officials. Together, they had enjoyed decades of unprecedented trust, their recommendations taken at face value by nearly every man and woman on the street, not to mention government authorities who ruled over them.

More recently, the public's confidence had shifted. Through years of ill-advised lockdowns, mandates, and other draconian measures, many grew to resent not only Faucett, but public health agencies in general. A growing belief the most recent vaccines had done more harm than good led to a schism among both the scientific and faith communities. One side considered Faucett and Connolly as modern-day heroes on par with Jonas Salk and Albert Sabin, the saviors of polio. The other side made wild claims about ulterior motives: Population control. Purposefully-induced mass hysteria. Genetic programming.

Scientists, doctors, pastors, and priests filled both sides of the debate and despite the relatively trivial way the virus itself had come to be regarded, their animosity towards each other continued to increase. For Natalie—her father, the most prominent public health official in the country, her husband, a board-certified doctor and the world's most infamous vaccine skeptic—managing the tension of being at the center of such an incredible storm had aged her. With an open bar and all of her normal pretense gone, Natalie was thoroughly enjoying herself for the first time in months.

Faucett approached her as the party was winding down, a few familiar faces all that were left from the ritzy gala.

"Would you, by chance, be willing to drive me home?" he asked, an odd request.

Natalie giggled in her attempt to decline. "Probably not a great idea, Sir Walter. Why would I drive you home? I'm twice your age."

Faucett smirked, but continued to press. "I don't do so well at night anymore. I really could use the favor."

"Eva's running around somewhere. Way past her bedtime."

"Albert can drive her home. We can take my car—I'll get it back tomorrow."

"You'd let *me* drive *your* car?"

Faucett's ostentatious Bentley Continental GT was a source of frequent ridicule.

"There's something I need to tell you," he said, ignoring her jest. "It may take a few minutes, and it's been so hard to find time to meet."

Natalie side-shouldered him and countered with a sly smile. "We're retired now. We've got all the time in the world."

Faucett laughed. "I guess you're right. I keep forgetting what this means."

The aging physician stepped closer and lowered his voice. "In all seriousness, Natalie, there's something I need to tell you. I know this must feel awkward, but it's serious. It involves your husband."

A wave of dread passed through her body. She had worked hard to keep her two lives separate. Strangers occasionally made jokes, but those closest to her father knew the topic was off-limits.

Natalie clenched her jaw tightly. "Why tonight?"

"It's urgent."

Albert Connolly strode up beside them. Natalie's three-year-old daughter sat on his foot, clinging to his leg as he walked.

"I suppose it's time we all head home," Connolly said.

"No!" Eva said. "I don't want to leave. Ever."

Natalie pried her daughter from her father's leg. "It's past your bedtime, baby girl."

"No!" she said, hugging Connolly's leg even tighter.

"Dr. Faucett asked me to drive him home. Would you like to ride with Papa?"

"Yay!" the girl shrieked.

"That okay with you, Dad?"

Connolly looked concerned.

Faucett tried to reassure him. "Just a few secrets, Albert, that's all—before I retire. Gotta let somebody know where the bodies are buried."

"I thought I already knew."

"Most of them," Faucett said, winking at Natalie.

"Alright," Connolly said, relaxing a bit. "Your last official charge."

He looked at Natalie. "I'll leave the porch light on if I get there first."

Natalie hugged her father. "Don't worry, Dad—I'll drive slow."

"Let's drive fast!" Eva said, leading Connolly away by the hand.

Natalie and the retiring Faucett made their way to his car on the parking deck and circled their way to the bottom. As they reached the exit, Connolly appeared with Eva in his arms and stopped them.

"Change of plans," he said as they approached.

Eva reached through the window for her mother, water pooling at the bottom of her eyes. Abandonment had been a problem since her father no longer lived with them, something Natalie was quick to recognize.

"I'm coming with you," Eva said.

Natalie looked at Faucett. "I'm sorry. It's... she gets scared."

"I understand."

"Do you have the keys?" Natalie asked her father. "Can you grab her car seat?"

"Just put her in the back," Connolly said. "She'll be fine."

"No, dad."

"There's no traffic right now. She'll lay down and be asleep in 5 minutes."

"Dad, no."

Connolly laughed. "That's how we used to do it, isn't it Walter?"

"That's how we brought them home from the hospital."

Alarms were flashing red everywhere as Natalie fought the urge to panic.

"She'll be fine," Faucett said.

Natalie's daughter scampered over the center console and began jumping in the back seat.

"Eva, honey, don't do that, please."

"See you at home," Connolly said as they drove off.

"See you," Natalie whispered, wondering what Faucett was going to tell her.

Wondering how her husband could possibly cause any more trouble.

* * *

The ramp on the back of the helicopter opened, and Yuval's men jumped out. Immediately, he didn't like what he saw. Soldiers walked up a gravel road leading towards the highway, Brinkley and Garcia following close behind.

"Well?" Yuval asked, flinging his hands into the air. "Where is he?"

Vickers stepped forward and threw a plastic bag at Yuval's feet.

"Here he is."

"What is this?"

"Remains."

Yuval's pale skin flushed red. "Remains? You were told to take him alive, no matter what."

"Yeah, well... he just blew his head off."

Yuval motioned towards someone inside the helicopter. "Would someone close this ramp? I don't want these young ladies hearing this."

He turned back towards the Vickers. "You're telling me Finch killed himself?"

"Yes."

"Today of all days is the day he decides to end his life?"

"Apparently."

Brinkley started to speak but checked himself.

"Take your gear off so I can see you."

The commander paused. "You're sure?"

"Take it off."

Vickers stepped back, unbuckled the visor that covered his entire face, and flipped it onto the top of his helmet.

"I gave instructions that no one was to even bring weapons anywhere near him. Did you receive that order?"

"I did. We only brought non-lethals. We engaged him this morning, but he started firing on us. I lost five or six men—because they had no weapons."

"Where are your fancy trucks? Surely you weren't thinking you could just walk up to him, shake his hand, and make friends?"

"We had one. And it's destroyed. Sir."

"Your fancy truck was destroyed? By Finch?"

"More or less."

"Who then killed himself, with a weapon—after destroying your truck—because you didn't have any weapons?"

"It sounds improbable. I realize that."

Garcia stepped forward. Brinkley grabbed his arm to prevent him from speaking but it came too late. "That wasn't Finch."

"I'm sorry, what?" Yuval asked.

"They're just local sheriffs," Vickers said. "Don't listen to them."

"That wasn't Finch back there," Garcia said. "That's not Finch in your plastic bags. He's gone. He stole my truck while we were distracted."

Yuval held up the bag. "Why do you think this wasn't him?"

"My sergeant here saw him up close. He's confident it wasn't."

Yuval turned to Brinkley. "You know what Finch looks like?"

Brinkley appeared reluctant to answer.

"Speak up, officer. Was that Finch who just shot himself? I'll be over the moon if he didn't, just in case it's not clear."

"I didn't get as good a look as I wanted. He was about to kill me. I'm not sure I even know what he looks like."

Garcia was baffled at Brinkley's new account. "I thought you said you were positive it was him, Brinks," he whispered.

Yuval's eyes lit up. "I have an idea. You know who knows what he looks like? His daughter. Mr. Vickers, did our mystery man have enough face left for visual identification?"

"I don't know. I didn't get close enough to see."

"How did you collect these specimens?"

"I didn't. Sergeant Brinkley here did."

Yuval glanced at Brinkley's hulking frame. "Did you give the Sergeant some form of protection?"

"Protection from what?" Brinkley asked.

"I don't think he needs any. I gave him some gloves, just in case."

"I understand. Sergeant Brinkley, did this man have enough face left for someone who knew him to identify him?"

Brinkley's stomach turned at the thought of a young girl seeing what he saw. "Probably not."

"Protection from what?" Garcia asked.

"Sergeant Brinkley, would you mind retrieving whatever is left in order that we might confirm if that was indeed Finch or not?"

"I'll take a picture and bring it back—does that work?"

"Yes, actually. That works better. You do that."

Brinkley turned to Vickers. "May we take one of your vehicles down there? It will be faster."

"Sure. Hurry up."

"Garcia, can you go grab one?" Brinkley asked. "We'll need something to get us home anyway."

The deputy took off towards the row of cars that lined the side of the highway.

Yuval turned to face the helicopter, then stopped. "Vickers—assuming these local officers are right... Is anyone on the lookout for their truck yet? He'll be long gone soon."

"I'll call in a description."

Yuval opened the side door and stopped on the steps leading into the giant aircraft. "Sergeant Brinkley—I wouldn't count on going home just yet."

"I won't."

"And bring me that picture."

He stepped inside the helicopter and shut the door behind him.

"Well he's a real piece of work, isn't he?" Brinkley said.

"You never answered my question," Vickers said.

"What question?"

"The one I asked over the phone. Did you get the shots?"

Brinkley shook his head. "War's over, Agent Vickers. I haven't heard anyone ask that in years. I thought we were done with that question."

"We were. Now we're asking again."

"What's the point? They're useless. You know that."

"I'm not here to argue their merits."

Brinkley breathed deeply, trying to control the anger that rose within him.

"You saw my medical records."

"Sergeant Brinkley, your name was flagged in our system. Probably a book or something you bought. I know what your medical records say. I was instructed to ask you directly."

Brinkley's face tightened as he considered his answer.

"I assure you I'm not here to arrest you," Vickers said. "They just want...."

"I got all of them," Brinkley interrupted. "Every one they asked for."

Vickers was stunned. "I was guessing you would say no."

"Go tell all your friends. Brinks got them all."

"I appreciate your honesty," Vickers said, lowering the gear back over his face. "You can ignore what he said. Go home. Get some rest."

"Negative. I have a dead officer down there we need to process."

"Very well. Make it quick."

Brinkley stared at the ground, his mind somewhere else.

"One more question, if you don't mind?" Vickers asked.

"What's that?"

"What color was your truck? I didn't see it."

Brinkley looked up as Garcia approached in the borrowed car.

"Blue," he said. "It's a blue Chevrolet."

CHAPTER 28

The hotel's convention center was brimming with scientists from all over the world. Connolly had seized upon the excitement around the momentous event and convened a week-long global symposium—a conference featuring presentations from the brightest minds the academic world had to offer.

Vendors filled the convention room floor, showing off their wares: Electron microscopes. Mass spectrometers. Prototypes of gear that hadn't yet been named. Lecture halls were packed, filled with raucous crowds of researchers and professors jeering and cheering the presenters, eager to make their mark on the world.

It was an impressive display of scientific might in both mind and machine unlikely to ever happen again. Connolly had played the public relations game perfectly, hinting at a discovery so significant he thought nothing short of time travel could ever top it. And so, speeches were prepared, travel funds requested, and hundreds left their universities and labs that week, promised an unforgettable week of discovery and enlightenment.

A smaller wing of the hotel was dedicated to the particulars of the evening's event—the relationship between science and faith. It was Connolly's favorite topic, a troubled alliance he had spent much of his career trying to forge. The keynote for this particular tract was titled *Miracles and Molecules: A New Understanding of Supernatural Science*, a presentation delivered by Connolly himself earlier in the week. Attendance had been less than he hoped, the scientific community's response, muted.

Outside the hotel was an entirely different story. Footage of the presentation leaked online and within hours, coordinated attacks on the event's website defaced it with a vulgar hack: *Clots, Bots, and Shots: A New Understanding of How Vaccines Fuck You Up*. Social media exploded with rage, denouncing the themes Connolly had presented. Religious leaders who had pledged to attend were pressured to pull out.

"I've treasured my relationship with Albert Connolly, but this is a bridge too far," the president of America's largest protestant denomination said in a televised interview, a devastating blow to the event's promise of unity and reconciliation.

Connolly spent the rest of the week in damage control. With hundreds of phone calls, flights abroad, and a relentless media tour, he was able to salvage much of what had been lost. Through his tireless efforts, the event would go on, with many of the world's most important religious leaders still pledging to attend.

Others would not be swayed. Through years of ineffective lockdowns and mandates—and the economic calamity that followed—their faith in public health institutions was non-existent. With Faucett dead, their unceasing hatred was now directed squarely upon the head of Connolly. Any attempt at regaining their trust was met with mockery. His audacious claims of "miracles" and "reconciliation" only served to heighten their hostility.

His *Miracles and Molecules* presentation ended up causing the opposite effect he had intended. The initial guest list he and Yuval had decided upon was in jeopardy, while thousands of protestors had now pledged to prevent the event from happening. Online rhetoric was always exaggerated, but the intensity of threats from those who opposed it—not anonymous accounts, but verified, respectable thought leaders who normally kept silent on such issues—caused serious concern.

Connolly suggested changing the venue to a less public forum, something where security could more easily be maintained. They could broadcast the event for everyone to see, a few select VIPs in attendance to bolster its authenticity—an idea Yuval was quick to dismiss.

With the event still hours away—and heightened security at the Cathedral—protestors focused their efforts at the enormous hotel where the convention was holding its final talks. Unprepared for their onslaught, the conference center was powerless to stop them. Protestors had run wild throughout the halls, destroying millions of dollars in equipment and disrupting presentations—harassing anyone who wore a conference lanyard and badge around their neck.

Attendees hid their credentials and retreated to their rooms, unsure if the event at the Cathedral was worth the risk. Satisfied the conference was thoroughly disrupted, protestors poured out of the hotel and onto the streets that surrounded it—some even making it to a nearby highway in an attempt to stop traffic.

* * *

Connolly's limousine slowed as it turned onto the boulevard that led from the highway to the hotel. Hundreds of people were running chaotically through the street, hanging from signage, flinging trash cans everywhere.

"What in the hell?" Connolly said as they moved at a crawl. "They're here too?"

"There's *more* of them here," Brooke replied. "Where are the police? Why aren't they stopping this?"

Connolly shook his head, unable to believe the uproar his presentation had caused. A trash can crashed into the side of their vehicle and bounced onto the road. People climbed onto their roof and started jumping in unison, screaming a chant, inaudible from within the limo.

Just a few more hours, he thought. *Just a few more hours and they'll see what we've done. Then they'll stop fighting. Then they won't hate me.*

"Why'd they bring us here?" Brooke asked.

The limousine came to a stop.

Brooke began to panic. "Why are we stopping?"

With the shade raised, they were unable to see what was happening in front of them. Connolly held his head to the window, trying to peer in front of them. He pressed his face to the glass, defeating the privacy the dark window tint had provided. The crowd recognized him immediately.

Outside, people began pointing towards his window, screaming his name so loud it could be heard within the vehicle.

"Connolly! Connolly! Connolly!"

Other protestors jumped onto the limousine, rocking it even more violently.

Connolly reached toward his assistant. "Brooke, give me your laptop."

"Why aren't we moving? These people want to kill us."

A mechanical chunk sounded all around them.

"They just unlocked the doors," Connolly said.

"They want these people to kill us."

"I think that's the idea."

Someone opened the passenger side door. The chants from outside, now unmuffled by the limousine's armor, split their ears. Several arms reached inside, grabbing for anything and anyone within.

Brooke screamed at the driver in fear. "Why don't you move?"

"Just give me your laptop," Albert yelled, kicking at the people trying to pull them out.

Someone stuck a flagpole inside the limo, ramming it over and over. Brooke handed her computer to Connolly, who began typing.

"How do you make it bigger?" he asked.

"What are you doing?"

"Make this as big as you can," he said, thrusting the laptop back in her face.

Connolly leaned against the seat for leverage and kicked hard at someone who had gotten nearly completely inside. Brooke clicked the trackpad a few times and threw the laptop back.

The limousine was now surrounded by a mob, unable to move. Other doors were pulled open, the furious protestors intent upon their capture.

Connolly grasped the edges of the laptop and, facing it away from him, held it towards the door, its message clearly visible to those standing outside.

FINCH SAVES.

CHAPTER 29

Finch had a growing appreciation for older trucks. No flashing lights. No dinging bells. The manual transmission was an even better sell. As far as he was concerned, the less the technology, the fewer the safety features, the better. *Just do what I say. And don't complain.* That's the kind of vehicle he preferred, a fondness that extended to people as well.

After crawling two hundred feet from the overturned ambulance, he circled back around the path to where Garcia's truck was parked. With everyone focused on the crazed man firing into the wrecked tactical vehicle, Finch had slipped into the white F250, ecstatic to see keys in the ignition.

He turned the wheel and couldn't believe his luck—even the interlock was broken. With his foot on the brake, he shifted the transmission into neutral and began silently inching his way back down the mountain, rolling away from the chaotic scene taking place in the woods.

Once he had rounded several bends, a helicopter approached, giving Finch enough confidence he could safely start the engine without being heard.

Jesus, that's loud, he thought when the truck first turned over. *Glad I waited.*

He shifted the transmission into reverse but realized gravity and judicious braking were easier than engaging and disengaging the vehicle's massive clutch. Finch cut the engine and continued coasting downwards, back towards the cabin—the only sound, the occasional vulcanized pluck of rocks popping loose from beneath his tires.

Downwards was not the direction he wanted to travel but knew the top of the road was likely being watched. As remote as the cabin was, Finch suspected hunting trails connected it to other cabins, possibly other paths of escape. They were usually only traversable by side-by-sides—essentially tiny golf-carts with four-wheel drive and camouflage. Navigating the massive Ford truck across these paths would likely be impossible, but with the prospect of being chased on foot—through the mountains, and with a heart condition—looming before him, Finch began looking for signs of a trail.

By the time he reached the cabin, he'd still not seen anything. The bodies of Monroe and the EMT still littered the meadow, lying where they fell. His physician's instinct drew him towards them. A desire to render aid. To save their lives, if possible. But he knew they were dead by now. Not even the medical supplies he had taken from the ambulance would save them.

They can heal her.

Nothing he could do would help his daughter. With the world's most talented physicians at her service, there wasn't even an experimental procedure that offered the promise of recovery. For Eva, all of his knowledge was useless. All of his bravery. His cunning. His improvisational thinking. None of it could help.

Finch entered the cabin to retrieve his canvas bag. Incredibly, he considered brewing a cup of coffee. The darkness of the morning's events cast a long shadow over the eternal optimism he had cultivated while on the run—something for which a hot mug of ground-up Arabica beans, decaf if humanly possible, felt the only possible cure. How long before they discovered their truck was missing was anyone's guess. Whether they would puzzle out he hadn't tried the natural escape route but went backwards, deeper into the mountain—that, he felt, might have bought him a few precious minutes.

Finch rifled through a few drawers in the kitchen, hoping he'd missed some decaf in his earlier rummages. Satisfied there was none, he started a pot of high-test, something for which he knew his heart would pay dearly. For now, it didn't matter. He knew his luck was running out. The events from the morning were too surreal to process, but it was clear the stakes had been raised. Ghosted by his wife for years, she'd replied to his cryptic text. That same day, helicopters. Soldiers. Tactical vehicles. Someone, somewhere was set on his capture.

The pot began to fill, and Finch drank what little was brewed.

Absolutely disgusting, he thought to himself.

Black coffee was the stuff of great men, a distinction he felt he had earned with honors—except when it came to coffee. Whatever he could add, he would. Cream. Sugar. Almond milk. The more, the better. Unfortunately, apart from the beans, the cabin had nothing but a few ketchup packets, an ingredient he'd already tried to incorporate without success.

Finch sat on the couch and placed his feet on the table in front, trying to recall what relaxing felt like. Magnified by the jolt of caffeine, his erratic inner dialogue —so helpful in times of plenty, so maddening in times of lack—sprang to life.

I could just stay here and maybe they'll never come back. Or, maybe they'll find me. What's the worst that would happen? Besides jail? Eva will never walk again. No one can change that. They would try and humiliate me, anyway. Make me recant my beliefs. Say I made up the things I had said. But, I won't. I didn't make them up. I'm just telling the truth. And truth is the most dangerous thing. To them.

Unable to sit still, Finch stood up and walked out on the porch. In the distance, the unwelcome crunch of tires on gravel reverberated across the pasture. Someone was driving towards him.

"Seriously?" he said, his shoulders slumping in disappointment. "Already?"

He returned inside and collapsed onto the couch, resigned to accept his fate—and finish his coffee.

They won't kill me. I don't think they could get away with it anymore.

That was one of the perks of his celebrity status. The little guys might suffer and no one would notice. For someone like Finch, with worldwide recognition, there was, at least, a sense of protection. With it came a lot of baggage—a lot of hatred and loathing that had eventually driven Natalie away—but regardless, at least they might think twice before killing him.

You can call me. I'll answer.

Finch didn't need to play the voicemail from Natalie anymore. He'd heard it so many times, the sound was permanently etched into his brain, instantly recalled anytime he thought of her.

I need to talk to her. Just once more before they take me. She needs to know the truth. It will help her let go.

He powered on his phone and held it up in the air, trying to get a signal. Outside, Finch could hear the sound of a car stopping on the gravel road across the creek.

"Shit," he said, unable to get a signal. He walked to the back corner of the cabin, looking for bars on his screen.

"Thomas Finch!" someone yelled from outside.

"Shit." His heart began to pound.

Just one call. Sixty seconds—that's all I need.

"We know you're in there, Finch! Don't do anything stupid."

Finch lifted the window and crawled outside, scurrying towards the woods behind the lodge.

More height. More height equals more bars.

Finch clawed his way up the ridge that ran along the rear of the cabin, checking his phone along the way. He slipped on the ice of a small creek that had frozen over, crashing his shoulder into the rocks below.

"Finch! Stop running!"

He reached the phone into the air and waited for a bar to register.

One bar. Just one bar.

No bars appeared.

"Finch! You're surrounded."

The voices grew closer as Finch clutched his chest, his heart nearing its limit.

170bpm, he guessed. *Game over.*

A notification popped up on the screen.

Another message—from Natalie.

They took her. Help us. Please.

CHAPTER 30

Albert Connolly and Brooke were able to step out of the limousine and into the crowd of protestors that surrounded them. Holding her laptop like a shield in front of him, they were able to advance slowly away from the limo.

"Traitor!" protestors screamed at him.

"Mass murderer!" others shouted.

Behind them, the front of the limo door cracked open. The officer squeezed out and attempted to follow, but it was impossible. Bodies pressed against him, flattening him into the vehicle as he attempted to make a phone call.

Connolly held the laptop aloft, trying to appease the crowd. Given the chaos of the mob which thronged around them, movement was slow, dialogue impossible. He could only show them the two words he'd seen strung from the roof of his limo just minutes earlier.

FINCH SAVES.

The protestors nearest to Connolly and Brooke formed an impromptu cordon around them—unconvinced of their profession of allegiance to Thomas Finch, yet wanting to protect them from harm should their declaration prove authentic.

"Back up!" they screamed. "Back up. Let them through!"

Water bottles and signs sailed over the human barrier that surrounded them, glancing off their backs as they ducked for cover. Connolly grabbed one of the signs that was thrown at them and handed it to Brooke.

"Hold this up," he said. "Hold it up high."

TWGYK.

"What does that even mean?"

Connolly shoved it in her face. "Just hold it up, we'll never make it out of here if you don't."

Reluctantly, Brooke took the sign and held it at her shoulder.

"Higher!" Connolly screamed at her.

Brooke raised the sign so everyone could see. A cheer went up among the crowd, ecstatic with the sense some ideological shift was taking place before their eyes. Someone shoved a *Finch Saves* T-shirt in Connolly's face.

"Please don't," Brooke said.

Connolly handed her the laptop and pulled the shirt over his jacket, prompting even more exuberant ovations from the protestors.

"When in Rome," he said.

"We'll never hear the end of this."

"At least we'll live to hear it."

Foot by foot, Connolly and Brooke made their way down the street to the grand entrance of the hotel, its valet stand and awnings destroyed.

"This place is ruined," he said. "Maybe we still have friends in there that can help us."

"Not with that shirt on."

Protestors led them inside the lobby of the hotel, its front counters abandoned, its elevators stalled. Cameras and light stands surrounded a section of the lounge, its luxurious furniture used to transform the area into the set of a professional looking talk show.

"Sit down," they said to Connolly, ushering him towards one of the plush leather seats.

"You too," one of the protestors said to Brooke, handing her back the sign she had dropped.

"What's going on?" Connolly asked. "We're not staying here. We have somewhere to be."

Someone flicked on a bright bank of lights and adjusted the angle of their direction. "This is a press conference, Dr. Connolly. It's time the world heard the truth."

CHAPTER 31

Outside the aircraft, the sounds of sirens could be heard approaching in the distance. Special Agent Vickers knocked on the helicopter door.

"They're coming," he said to Yuval. "Sounds like a lot of them."

"Who's coming?"

"I don't know. Sheriffs. State Troopers."

"I thought you called them off."

"I did."

"Why are they coming?"

"Sir, we've had choppers in and out of here all morning. There've been emergency calls. Gunfire. These people can tell when something's wrong."

"Call them off!" Yuval screamed. "I need Finch!"

"You might want to leave before they get here."

"I'm not leaving without him."

"There's going to be a lot of questions."

"I can handle the questions. Where's the rest of your men?"

"They're at the Cathedral, like you asked."

"How many do you have here?"

Vickers looked behind him and counted. "Seven. It was *twelve* when we started this morning."

"Isn't seven men enough to grab one fucking person who's probably half-starved to death?"

"Dead? Sure. Alive? It's tricky."

The sirens grew closer.

"You might want to leave," Vickers said again.

"How far do you think he's made it by now? Could we spot him from the air?"

"I don't think he ever left."

"They said he took their truck."

"No truck ever came up here. And they lied to me about what color it is."

"You think they're with him?"

"Sympathetic, at least."

"You think they're down there?"

"Possibly. Looking for him, at least."

With blue lights flashing, a silver sedan stopped several hundred feet from the helicopter. A state trooper got out and crouched behind his patrol car, waiting for support to arrive.

"Take your men—take my men, too—and get me Finch. I don't care what happens to the others."

Vickers pointed up the road, where more blue lights began to arrive. "What about these guys?"

"I'll stall for time. This is a military aircraft. I'm sure we can handle them if we need to."

Vickers and the others left the road and began jogging down the gravel drive towards the cabin.

"Alive," Yuval yelled out. "I don't care if he's on life support. As long as he's breathing—that's all I need."

CHAPTER 32

Garcia and Brinkley walked around the cabin, looking for signs of life.

"You really think he's down here?" Garcia whispered.

"How else would your truck have gotten here? Somebody drove it, and I doubt it was one of those soldiers."

The sound of sirens wailing in the distance gave Brinkley confidence help was on the way.

"Guess Tamara changed her mind," Garcia said of their emergency dispatcher.

"Yeah, she could sense something was off."

"Sounds like she sent everybody."

"Just like I asked."

Brinkley stood up and cupped his hand to his mouth. "Finch! Give it up. We've got you surrounded."

Garcia shot a confused look at Brinkley. "We've got one gun," he whispered.

"He doesn't know that."

Brinkley trained his ears towards the woods, listening for any signs of life. The wail of arriving law enforcement vehicles continued to accumulate in the background.

"Those sirens are scaring him off," Garcia said. "He's probably long gone."

Brinkley thought of a different approach.

"Finch," he called out. "I know about the Bootstrap Project."

"What are you talking about?" Garcia whispered.

"I know your theories!"

Again, Garcia was perplexed. "You do?"

"I watched your videos!"

"You did?"

"I looked into the Bootstrap Project myself, Finch!" Brinkley shouted, moving closer to the woods. "And I was amazed at what I found."

Garcia scanned the woods. A squirrel dug in the ground. A mockingbird chased a crow from its nest.

"We are not your enemy, Finch."

"Yes we are," Garcia whispered.

"There are a hundred state troopers up the road about to come down here looking for all kinds of trouble."

Brinkley moved well into the woods, leaving Garcia alone in the pasture.

"They may not be as friendly as me. I'm just a local sheriff. And I know your work. I suggest you come out now. Maybe things turn out better that way."

Brinkley's heart was racing. With no weapon, no concealment, and no bullet-proof vest, he was asking to be shot.

A feeble voice shouted a sequence of letters from beyond the clearing. "T.W.G.Y.K."

"Huh?" Garcia whispered.

"What's it mean?" the voice asked emphatically. It was a challenge. A puzzle more than a question.

Brinkley struggled to comprehend the answer. Suddenly, it came to him. It was a chant protestors had employed anytime their arch nemesis made a public appearance.

"Truth will get you killed," Brinkley said.

Satisfied with the answer, a man, covered in filth, his face nearly invisible beneath a wild mane of hair and beard, emerged from behind a stand of trees, his palms held in the air.

CHAPTER 33

The scattered chants of demonstrations wafted from outside through the broken windows lining the side of the convention center floor. Aisles and rows once neatly demarcating the vendor's displays were gone. Signage was overturned. Promotional literature was strewn everywhere. Millions of dollars in cutting edge equipment had been toppled from their stands, racks, and tables.

The fallout from Connolly's speech was immense, nowhere else more visible than the once gleaming exhibits that lined the exhibit hall. It was the greatest gathering of machines the scientific world had ever seen, photographed in all their glory like an awe-inspiring military parade. Now, they lay mostly in ruins, their creators and inventors cowering in fear in the hotel floors above.

An older man, wheezing with effort, pushed a luggage cart through the debris, picking up pieces of equipment here and there. A power conditioner. A component of an electron microscope. A tank of nitrogen. A carton of nitrile gloves.

Visually, he had the appearance of a homeless vagrant, looting what he could sell for drugs. But the careful manner in which he picked through the wrecked equipment suggested something else—someone familiar with what he saw. Someone looking for particular items. Discarding things which could not be fixed. Keeping those that possibly could.

With the cart nearly full, he weaved a path across the enormous exhibition hall towards a service elevator, the lone mechanical lift still in service. As he waited, he pulled out a piece of paper and checked a few things off his list. Of the nearly one hundred items, only a few remained—a precious few modules, ingredients that would allow him to confirm what he had begun to fear.

The doors opened, and he hauled his cart over the gap that separated the floor from the elevator, turning it around to fit inside the padded compartment. He pushed the button to the twelfth floor and closed his eyes as the doors shut.

One more trip, he thought to himself.

One more trip and we'll know for sure.

CHAPTER 34

The protestors were organized—Connolly could at least give them credit for that. The ransacked hotel and chaos outside gave the sense there was nothing but anger and madness. Here in the lobby, there was clearly some effort to portray their protests as reasonable, their demands nothing but common sense.

A camera operator adjusted his tripod so that Connolly's tall figure might fit within the frame. The young woman set to interview them turned on her own camera.

"I'm not doing this," Brooke said, backing away from the set.

"Hand him the sign, then," the interviewer said. "We don't even know who you are."

Brooke threw the sign she'd been forced to carry to the ground. "Dr. Connolly? You're seriously going to do this?"

Surrounded by protestors eager to hear Connolly recant, the set was buzzing with angry taunts.

"Mass murderer!"

"Pharma shill!"

Connolly began to take off the *Finch Saves* T-shirt, a gesture that sent the crowd wailing in displeasure.

"I don't know what choice I have," he said, sitting down in defeat.

The interviewer motioned to the man who was filming Connolly. "Start zoomed in on his shirt and then pull back to show him."

After making a few other adjustments to her camera, she started recording.

"Be quiet!" she shouted at the crowd gathered around. "They won't be able to hear."

After a few moments, she looked at the camera and began speaking.

"Good morning loyalists from all over the world, wherever you are. This is Olivia, and you are listening/watching/connecting to a special edition of the Wake-Up Report. As you know, we're broadcasting from the *once lovely* Capitol Suites Convention Center, and I'm sure they've tried to censor what's just happened outside, but we have a special guest with us—someone you won't believe—who has agreed to join us."

The video stream cut to the second camera, Connolly's wrinkled *Finch Saves* taking up the entire frame, causing the crowd to scream with delight.

"Okay, zoom out," Olivia told the cameraman.

The protestors began howling, their pitch rising in expectation as the camera pulled back to reveal Connolly, sitting uncomfortably.

"That is right," Olivia said. "Your eyes are not deceiving you. This is not a deep fake. This is not a body double—as far as I can tell. This is the real McCoy. Satan himself. Just kidding. It's Albert Connolly in all his glory, sent to us from the heavens, wearing a very strange T-shirt."

Again the crowd lit up, the protestors barely able to contain delight at seeing the man squirm.

"Tell us, Mr. Connolly," she said, skipping the doctor's title as a purposeful slight, "what do you think the outcome of tonight's event is going to be and, more importantly, what does this T-shirt you're wearing mean?"

From the corner of his eye, Connolly caught sight of an actual news broadcast on one of the televisions hanging from the ceiling in the lounge. The sound was muted, but it didn't matter—the video told the entire story.

He stood up and walked toward the screen, trying to make sense of what he saw. It was the Prince George State Hospital, surrounded by fire trucks, their hoses trained on a raging inferno that had consumed one of its buildings.

The photo of a smiling, healthy Mongchai flashed onto the screen, superimposed over the flames. Bold yellow text appeared beneath the image, a message that sent chills down Connolly's spine.

Boy Hero Dead in Fire.

Protestors Blamed.

CHAPTER 35

Natalie sat in the living room, staring at the message she had sent to Finch.

They took her. Help us. Please.

Please read this, she thought, gripping her phone in her hand. It was almost a prayer.

"God, please let him read this," she said out loud, holding the phone in the air.

There. That's a proper prayer.

"Amen."

It had been years for Natalie. Years since she'd been desperate enough to humiliate herself in that way, praying with the hospital chaplain that her daughter would survive. Begging God that he could somehow swap her place with her daughter's, a request she knew wouldn't be answered.

* * *

Like her daughter, Natalie had spent the night in surgery. A broken femur. Severely concussed. Multiple lacerations. When she awoke, she had no memory of the crash, just a sliver of a conversation with Walter Faucett in the car.

"Natalie," he said. "I need to talk to you about Tom. Your father's told me you've been separated and are trying to work things out."

When the details of her family life were made public, even if only between her father's colleagues, it bothered Natalie, a constant annoyance given the notoriety of her husband. Faucett's insistence she drive him home—on the night of his retirement party—gave her the sense something serious was going on.

"We have good reason to believe your husband may be planning an attack. Something big. Something sophisticated."

"You mean like a bombing or something?"

"Much worse. A biological attack. Something designed to kill millions of people."

"Tom's full of anger and spite and hate—we all know that by now. But terrorism? Innocent people?"

"*Millions* of innocent people," Faucett emphasized.

Natalie shook her head to keep it from spinning. "Millions of innocent people? Why are you saying this?"

"I trust you'll keep this private?"

"Of course I will. I know everything my father knows and then some. Probably more than you."

"We've discovered some infiltration into one of our research teams. Two scientists, we believe, are sympathetic to your husband."

Natalie was incredulous. "You know what they stand for, right?"

"I do."

"And you think they're going to organize some biological attack?"

"Based on the materials they've been accessing, I think they might."

He's lying, Natalie thought to herself, staring at the speedometer in front of her as another car zoomed past.

Finch once told her Faucett was "the most evil person" he'd ever met, a charge she attributed to the researcher's willingness to underwrite controversial research. Her husband insisted it was something more simple.

"He's just evil," Finch had said. "Be careful."

Faucett's lying, Natalie repeated to herself.

Why is he telling me this? Finch would never do that.

That was the last thought Natalie could recall from before the crash. She awoke to a hospital bedroom with her father asleep in the chair beside her.

"Dad?" She said. "Dad?"

Connolly stirred, exhausted from a sleepless night of phone calls, confusion, and media requests.

"What happened?" she asked. "Why am I here?"

"You were in a very bad car accident. You broke a few things. You're all patched up now. You're going to be okay."

Party.

The previous evening flooded into her head. Toasts. Speeches. Faucett asking her to drive him home.

"What happened? Was I alone? Was Dr. Faucett with me?"

His face tightened with grief, Connolly stood up. "He was. He didn't make it."

Natalie's heart fluttered. "He's dead?"

Silently, Connolly shook his head in acknowledgement.

"Was I driving?"

Connolly grabbed both of his daughter's hands. "Natalie...."

"I should have driven. I shouldn't have let him drive."

Realizing her recollection of the previous few hours was poor, Connolly clenched his fist and held it to his mouth, trying to not fall apart. "Look, Nat. You probably don't remember this, but Eva was in the car with you."

Eva.

Natalie immediately began to sob uncontrollably, her convulsing sending shockwaves of pain through her body as she pictured her three-year-old lying asleep in the backseat of the car.

"She's alive," Connolly said as he tried to calm her. "She's alive."

Nearly unable to breathe, Natalie attempted to speak. "Where is she?"

"She's here. She's still in surgery. It's bad, but they've told me they think she's going to make it."

"I want to see her."

"You can't."

"I want to see her, please."

"Nat, you can't right now. She's in the O.R. and... they're working as hard as they can."

"Where's Tom? Is he with her?"

"I'm going to get the chaplain," Connolly said. "Let's pray for Eva. She's going to need it."

CHAPTER 36

"Don't move," Brinkley shouted out to the disheveled man in the woods.

"I don't have any weapons."

"I don't know that."

"I'm laying down."

"No! Turn around and walk backwards toward me. Slowly."

With his hands over his head, Finch got on his knees and laid down sideways on the ground.

"I said walk towards me!"

"I'm about to have a heart attack. Shoot me if you want. I'm going to lie down."

Brinkley looked at Garcia, unsure how to proceed. "How long do you need to lie down for?"

"I don't know. Ten minutes. Maybe less. I'll call my pulse out to you."

"Are you Thomas Finch?" Garcia asked.

"Yes."

"Prove it."

Finch held his fingers out towards them. "Take some prints. Run them through your system. I'm sure I'm at the top of the list."

"You are," Brinkley said. "Do you know you're the most wanted man by about every three-letter agency in this country?"

"Just this country?"

"It's Finch," Brinkley said to Garcia, the man's acerbic wit clearly on display.

"How'd you know my riddle?" Finch asked.

Brinkley paused before answering. It was a topic he and Garcia never discussed, a minefield he preferred avoiding.

"Just heard it somewhere, I guess."

"Did you actually kill Faucett? Cripple your daughter? All that?" Garcia asked.

"Yes."

Brinkley cut in. "They said you were set up. They said you were framed to make it look like you did it."

"I wasn't set up. I killed him. You have my confession. Tell the world. Make your millions. Want a video?"

Brinkley couldn't believe he was staring one of the world's most wanted criminals in the face, a man barely recognizable from any of the images forensic artists had created depicting his possible appearance.

"Hands where I can see them!" Brinkley screamed at Finch, who'd pressed a finger to his carotid artery.

"I'm at 150bpm. Maybe if you shout less it will come down faster."

Brinkley scanned behind them, beyond the cabin and creek that lined the gravel drive. He moved directly beside his deputy, beyond the earshot of Finch.

"You know who that was up there in the helicopter?" Brinkley whispered to Garcia.

"No. I've seen him before."

"That was Yuval Naftali. Head of the World Health Alliance."

"Who's that?"

"One of the most powerful people in the world, according to some."

"What's he doing way out here in the middle of nowhere? Is he that interested in Finch?"

"He's not here to sight-see, I can guarantee you that."

"You sure it was him?"

"Positive."

"We better turn Finch in, then. Whatever's going on, I don't want to get involved."

"You can talk normal," Finch said. "I just didn't like the shouting. The whispering is kind of freaking me out."

"Quiet," Brinkley shouted at him. "What's your pulse?"

Again, he looked for movement through the woods beyond the cabin.

"Something's off," Brinkley said. "The way they took over our call. I don't like it."

"They've got a helicopter and mercenaries. We've got a 9mm with a mag and a half."

"I want to take him in. Run it through proper channels. Those guys will probably fly him out of the country and do terrible things."

"Yeah, there's a reason—because everyone hates him."

"Not everyone."

"Still 150bpm," Finch told them, now standing on his feet. "I think I liked your shouting better."

"Listen, Garcia. I'm going to need you to trust me on this, okay? I don't want to give him up to those guys. Something tells me they're bad news."

Garcia's face showed reluctance. Rubbing his head, he swallowed hard. "You better do something fast. They'll be down here looking for us any minute."

"And the troopers," Brinkley said.

"All of them probably."

Brinkley walked back towards Finch. An option had materialized in his mind, a course of action he couldn't believe he was considering.

"Finch, we're going to take you in, but I need you to work with us."

"What are you talking about?"

"You know who these guys are chasing you?"

"U.S. Marshals, I'm assuming?"

"I don't think so. Guess who's up there in that helicopter?"

"Santa Claus."

"Yuval Naftali."

Finch went numb, his witty comebacks completely offline.

"You know who he is, of course."

Finch remained speechless.

"Do you know why he might be so interested in your whereabouts?"

They can heal her.

They took her. Help us. Please.

Finch thought back to Natalie's messages. He'd heard that Yuval and her father were working on something special.

He knows I'll try to stop him, Finch thought to himself.

"Finch? Why's he after you like this?"

"I think he's afraid."

"Of what?"

"Something to do with my daughter."

"Like what?"

Finch shook his head in confusion as he tried to reason out a plausible scenario.

"Like they've got some new technology they're going to use on her and he knows I'll try and stop it."

Garcia's eyes widened. "Well, you're as loony as advertised."

"I don't know if technology's the right word. Maybe discovery."

Brinkley held his hand up. "Shut up, Garcia." He turned to Finch. "What kind of technology?"

"My ex-wife texted me saying *They can heal her* this morning. I hadn't heard from her in ages."

"You think she was talking about your daughter?" Garcia asked.

"Yes. She wouldn't have messaged me for anything else."

Brinkley remembered something. A significant event. "You seen the news recently?" he asked Finch.

"Not in months."

"There's a huge thing going on down in D.C.—like a big science fair or something. Only reason I know about it is because my wife follows that Asian kid that saved all the other kids from drowning. He's in town for the event, and supposedly something amazing is going to happen."

They're going to try and heal him.

Finch's anger began to boil as he thought of what kinds of demonic medicines and procedures they might attempt on the little boy.

Eva.

Suddenly, Finch's soul collapsed into nothingness as he pictured his daughter, her tiny body held in place with pins and rods, tubes running everywhere—a debilitating set of injuries that had been inflicted upon her. The ache was nearly unbearable, so disabling he never even let himself think about her. During the profound loneliness of the past few years, Natalie would frequently enter his mind. But Eva—that was something he had trained himself to avoid. Almost as if she had never existed.

They can heal her. I saw it.

But how? How was such a thing even remotely possible? Finch's life mission had become singularly focused—to bring people like Yuval Naftali to heel. To show the world how diabolical their "good intentions" actually were. The thought of the scientist's discovery healing Finch's daughter—while the world worshiped at Yuval's feet—made Finch sick to his stomach.

"Look, Finch, we need to go, but like I said, you're going to have to work with us—unless you want to take a ride in the helicopter with Dr. Naftali."

"Okay."

"You know where Monroe is?" Brinkley asked Garcia.

"Yeah, he's over there by the woodpile."

Brinkley looked at Finch, making a mental comparison in his mind. "You remember what he was wearing?"

"Just his jacket and hat. Jeans, maybe."

The sheriff pointed towards their captive. "You think they'll fit?"

CHAPTER 37

Gordillo walked toward the hotel, his body starved for oxygen. Behind him rode Mr. Maduro, trundling along the sidewalk in his motorized wheelchair. The hotel's parking garage was inaccessible, as were the neighboring blocks around it —streets and sidewalks made impassable by roving bands of protestors. Because of that, they'd parked what felt like miles away, a hike the Cardinal was physically unprepared to make.

"We're going to need to recharge your chair," Gordillo said.

"How far are we going?"

"I need one more favor from you. I'll put you on a plane back home tomorrow morning."

Mr. Maduro was reluctant. "I can't do all that again. The moaning. The drooling. It's too much."

"You don't need to. You're healed now, remember? Praise God, you're healed. So—we're going to show you off alongside the other Cardinals in a parade this afternoon."

"Why the wheelchair if I'm healed?"

"Well, you're not *totally* healed. These things take time, of course. You'd been an invalid for years. Give it some time, and you'll walk normally. For now, the wheelchair is easier."

"What do I have to do?"

"Just ride beside them in the parade. Wave to everyone. Smile."

"Then I can go home?"

"Yes."

"First class?"

"Even better. You can take my plane."

"I don't understand the reason for all of this."

"We have to have everyone here tonight—I told you that. Some of them were threatening to leave."

"They don't believe it can be done."

"Miracles? They believe in miracles, just not *our* miracles."

"Is it all fake?"

"It's not *all* fake. It works. We just needed something fast. They would have left if we didn't show them proof."

"Why didn't you just use whoever's wheelchair you stole?"

"My God—so many questions, Mr. Maduro. They didn't want to be made a spectacle of. We didn't steal it. We borrowed it. They'll get it back."

An improvised drumming circle had formed along the intersection, its musicians shaking water bottles filled with rocks while others beat on the sides of plastic trash bins. As they got closer to the hotel, the density of people around them continued to increase, something which concerned both Gordillo and his wheelchair-bound friend. Thankfully, alliances were constantly shifting, a fact many clergy had taken advantage of more recently to play both sides.

"Won't they think something is off if I show up to the parade back in the wheelchair again?"

"Here's what we'll do. When you get to them, stand up. Walk over to them—stumbling a little bit of course—and give them a hug. It will be a touching moment for all the cameras."

"So there'll be media there?"

"Probably."

"What if they ask me questions?"

"Just say these two men prayed for you this morning, and now you're healed, something that wouldn't have happened without the technology."

"You said no more miracles."

"Maybe just one more," Gordillo said. "If we're lucky."

Both men paused to let traffic pass, then proceeded through the intersection to the next block. Across the street, a small group of armed men—dressed in plain civilian clothes—continued to follow, shadowing their every move.

CHAPTER 38

Yuval peered through the window of the helicopter. It was nearly fifteen minutes since Vickers and his men ran down the gravel drive in attempt to get Finch. More state troopers had appeared, now blocking the highway—both in front of and behind the aircraft. Others continued to arrive.

"They should be back by now," Yuval said to the pilot. "Did you get a look at the terrain as we came in?"

"Just a winding road."

"Any idea how long it was?"

"I couldn't say."

The pilot pointed to a video feed on his instrument cluster. "Looks like they've officially run out of patience."

A camera pointed behind the aircraft showed troopers leaving the safety of their vehicles as they marched towards the rear of the helicopter, assault rifles at their shoulders.

"You think they checked our call sign?" Yuval asked.

"We're just a MEDEVAC as far as the F.A.A. is concerned."

"I don't think they're buying that."

"Probably not."

"Can you listen to their radio traffic?"

"I'm sure it's encrypted. I don't think they need radios, anyways. Looks like they're all here."

The troopers stopped their movement one hundred feet short of the aircraft. Yuval could see one of them raise a bullhorn to his mouth, his words imperceptible inside the helicopter.

Yuval swung the side door open. "This should be awkward."

He stepped down the stairs and onto the highway, forcing a scowl onto his face as he walked confidently towards the men stationed on the road.

"Why are you here?" Yuval asked.

"Identify yourself," the trooper announced through the bullhorn.

"You were asked specifically by the NIH and possibly other federal agencies to stand down. Why are you here?"

The trooper was left momentarily stunned.

"This is a classified operation you have completely blown."

With Yuval close enough to be heard, the trooper lowered his bullhorn. "We didn't get any orders to stand down."

"I'm quite sure you did, but someone ignored them and felt they needed to call you anyway."

"You have a military aircraft blocking a highway. You cannot do this without traffic support. I don't care what the feds say."

"Well then, support me," Yuval said. "Re-route traffic. Wave your orange batons. We will be done in less than fifteen minutes."

"That's not going to happen. Until I have a direct order from my supervisor, who would need a direct order from his supervisor—something that'd come down from the state—you are considered in violation of several laws."

The troopers turned their attention behind Yuval as Eva's nurse jumped through the helicopter doorway, stumbling onto the asphalt below. Yuval turned to run towards her, but then stopped himself.

"Not yet!" he yelled toward her. "Not yet!"

He turned back towards the troopers and shook his head. "Actors!"

"What is going on?"

"Hostage drills. She was supposed to jump off *after* the soldiers arrive with our other hostage."

Martta stood up and began running towards the troopers. "Help! We've been kidnapped. Help!"

Yuval shook his head in feigned disappointment. "One moment gentlemen, let me reset the scene."

As Martta tried to run past, Yuval grabbed her by the arm and squeezed hard.

"I will kill you right now if you don't stop this," he whispered.

Martta's face turned white at the threat. "Help," she said, this time her voice quivering with fear.

Yuval took her by both arms and began walking her back to the helicopter. Martta collapsed to the ground, forcing Yuval to attempt to drag her across the road.

The trooper held the bullhorn back to his mouth. "Freeze! Do not move."

Yuval yanked on Martta's arm as she struggled to stand, her body stiffened with anxiety.

"Stand up!" Yuval screamed at her.

Martta began to heave, her body trembling. "I can't move."

Yuval leaned into Martta's ear. "I will kill Eva, too. I will kill her first, so you can see it. Now stand up and walk back with me calmly."

The young woman rolled onto her hands and knees and pulled one foot underneath her. Just fifty feet away, the troopers began advancing towards them.

Yuval yanked Martta to her feet and dragged her behind him.

The trooper sent some of the others running after them. "Stop him!"

With Martta fighting every step, Yuval stumbled to the helicopter and pushed her through the doorway onto the floor.

"We need to leave!" he screamed to the pilot inside.

"What's going on?"

"Now!"

Yuval clambered onto the aircraft as the pilot began the startup sequence.

"How long?" he asked them.

"Three minutes."

"*I* could start this thing faster than you. Make it shorter."

Troopers appeared around the doorway, their weapons pointed directly inside. Yuval grabbed Martta and held her in front of him.

The bullhorn held to his mouth, a trooper moved in front of the aircraft, directly visible to the pilot as the whine of its three engines turned into a howl.

"Shut it down!" he yelled, slicing his finger across his neck to visually convey the message.

"He's telling us to stop," the pilot said.

"We are not stopping. We are leaving."

"You're going to need to close that door."

Yuval grabbed the handle, but with Martta in-between him and the door, couldn't find enough leverage.

"Do we have any more weapons?" Yuval asked the pilot.

"Check the locker. Whatever you're thinking is a very bad idea."

The helicopter's rotor began to turn, its enormous five blades circling above the state troopers' heads.

"How much longer?" Yuval asked.

"Ninety seconds."

Yuval pulled Martta from the door and crawled past Eva's gurney to the cargo bay. A metal storage locker ran from floor to ceiling, its doors padlocked shut.

"Where's the key to this locker?" he asked the pilot.

"Who knows?"

Yuval ripped a fire extinguisher from its mount and slammed it down against the lock. The doors bent inward but, still, they would not open.

As its rotors accelerated, the helicopter began to vibrate, oscillating so violently it made standing in place difficult. Out of the corner of his eye, Yuval saw Martta crawling towards the door. He jumped across the cargo bay and grabbed her leg just as she was about to fall through the doorway. Outside, someone grabbed her arms and began pulling on her.

"I need help," Yuval yelled to the pilot.

The pilot spun out of his chair and drew a small sidearm from its holster.

"Shoot him!" Yuval screamed.

Just beyond the opening, a trooper had his feet braced against the doorway, both of Martta's arms firmly in his grasp as he tried to pull her to safety.

"You do it." The pilot placed his firearm on the floor and grabbed Martta's other leg.

The aircraft's violent vibrations sent the pistol spinning down the floor. Yuval turned onto his side and reached for the gun. He braced himself against the side of the aircraft and put the trooper in his sights, Martta's body bobbing in and out of the way.

The trooper saw the gun aimed directly at him and let go, falling onto the pavement below. Martta and the pilot slid back away from the door as Yuval opened fire on the fallen trooper, firing multiple shots into his torso.

In an effort to close the door, Yuval snatched at the handle but gunfire immediately erupted, bouncing harmlessly off the aircraft's outer shell.

"They'll kill me if I try and close it," Yuval said as the pilot jumped back into his seat.

"I can't fly with these vibrations. They'll tear us apart."

"Just get us away from here. We can close it later."

The pilot ignored the flashing red lights across the instrument cluster and pulled on the control stick that gave them lift. The aircraft vibrated wildly, blurring the vision of everyone who rode on it. Martta stumbled to the back, covering Eva's body with hers.

The angle of the rotor blades twisted, biting into the air and picking the craft off the ground. Dirt and grit beside the highway swirled into the air as the helicopter rose, giving Yuval a full view of the scene beneath them. Hundreds of cars were backed up on either side. Dozens of state troopers stood helplessly, their weapons aimed at the sky.

He scanned the gravel drive that curved down the mountainside, looking for Vickers, but saw nothing. More importantly, there was no sign of Finch. Just a tiny white pick-up truck snaking its way up the path.

CHAPTER 39

Arvo Ikänen rolled the cart down the long hallway that led to the executive suite where he and another scientist had encamped. For two days, they had hidden, content to eat whatever food they could scavenge from the floor's vending machine.

As protests raged throughout the convention center, they worked tirelessly within their makeshift lab, their collaboration not one of passion, but of fear. With every communication channel monitored, they had planned for months to use the conference as a cover to discuss their concerns more freely. But, new information had come to light. Timelines had changed. Despite the chaos that surrounded them, they vowed they would labor to uncover a horrible truth that had, so far, remained hidden. And so, with equipment scavenged from the ruins of the exhibit halls, they had cobbled together a makeshift laboratory, a carpet-lined research facility with twin king beds, a whirlpool, and a tiny wet bar.

They had gathered not out of anxiety for the miracle technology Connolly and Yuval had promised to shock the world with, but something completely different. For years, rumors churned around the hasty rollout of the malkavirus vaccines. Clinical trials were rushed. Approvals were rubber-stamped. Despite their highly experimental nature, concerns were swept under the rug, a global push to immunize the world that left many in the scientific community scratching their heads.

Public curiosity offered no shortage of conspiracy theories: Population control through purposefully wrecking women's fertility. Race-specific variants of the shots that would target certain ethnicities. Some even attached a biblical element to their distribution—the mark of the beast mentioned in the book of Revelation. No matter their nature, no hypothesis was considered unfeasible by a public furious at being forced to take the experimental treatments.

Those in the scientific community who harbored their own doubts were kept silent. Any pushback, any questioning of whether the technology was ill-advised or not was immediately quashed. Tenures were lost. Grants were denied. Board seats revoked. Any sign of dissent from universal acceptance of the worldwide rollouts was enough for most people's professional careers to be ruined, their lives completely upended for seeking nothing more than the truth.

Arvo Ikänen, a retired Finnish scientist was one of these people, someone deeply at unease with what he sensed was happening. The approvals were rushed, shuffled through the country's public health system with reckless abandon. The safety tests were hurried. Placebo groups were manipulated. Participants who developed issues during the trials were pulled, labeled as *Pre-existing Condition Discovered* or simply *Unable to Complete.* Every trick he could imagine was being employed, in plain view of anyone who dared to look.

Ikänen attempted to channel his frustration through his nation's scientific boards but was immediately shutdown. His career had driven his official duties away from the laboratory, but he could not shake the feeling something very wrong was happening.

Eventually, the Finnish man connected with other researchers throughout the world, a network of scientific skeptics cobbled together through veiled articles and forum postings. Whether they'd been infiltrated or their communication was simply being monitored, they could not be sure. Despite their official silence on the issue, they began receiving the same treatment those who had gone public did. Promotions denied. Forced resignations. Unexpected illnesses, in some cases.

With no way to freely communicate, news of a global science conference gave them the perfect opportunity to gather and talk openly. They would still have to meet behind closed doors and knew their anonymity would be at risk—possibly, even their physical safety. Regardless, they realized time was running out to alert the public to what some were beginning to sense may have happened.

* * *

Ikänen knocked five times on the door at the end of the hallway and waited for someone to open it. His cart was full of equipment, the tenth trip he had made over the past few days. Another older gentleman opened the door and pulled the cart through.

"I was about to come looking for you."

"It's getting slim down there," Ikänen said. "Less police. Less equipment."

They walked into the conference side of the two-roomed suite. Two desks were pushed against each other to make for a bigger work surface. The room's mini-fridge was perched on the end beside an assortment of other pieces of equipment connected together with clear piping and gas lines. Insulated cables ran under the door into an electrical closet down the hall, providing the increased amperage they needed to run the specialized equipment."I think that's everything," Ikänen said. "Just a couple of hours left."

"We need to hurry."

"You're sure we have all the samples ready?"

"They're in the fridge."

"And we have enough enzymes?"

"I don't know. It will be close."

Ikänen pulled out his list and looked it over, shaking his head at the incredible scenario they found themselves in.

"I can't believe we're actually trying this," the other scientist said. "If he could see it, Finch would be proud."

"Take some pictures," Ikänen replied. "I'm afraid he may be right."

CHAPTER 40

Connolly fell back against the wall, his eyes staring vacantly at the floor.

"You killed him," one of the protestors screamed, furious over the news Mongchai was dead.

"You should have never brought him here," another shouted.

The promise of the evening—the promise of his entire life mission—evaporated into nothingness as images of the blazing hospital played on television screens and mobile phones throughout the hotel. Without the boy, the gathering at the Cathedral was meaningless. There would be no healing. No miracles. No reconciliation.

Connolly's mind spiraled into darkness. Every rocky relationship he'd ever patched over had been leveraged. Payback for every favor he'd ever done, cashed in. Doubters—on both sides—circled his claims of a miraculous discovery like buzzards looking for carrion to devour. They *wanted* him to fail. They *wanted* to deny what faith was capable of. He envisioned a better world, one where miracles were once again possible. They delighted in a fallen world of suffering, one where God ignored their pleas and prayers.

One protestor broke through and wrestled Connolly to the ground.

"You don't believe this," the protestor shrieked, tearing the *Finch Saves* shirt from his body. "You don't deserve to wear this!"

"None of you care about children!" another shouted in his face.

Chants of "Child Killers!" broke out, the crowd screaming with anger.

With the crowd growing increasingly agitated around him, Connolly could think of only one thing.

Eva.

His only granddaughter, consigned to a lifetime of paralysis—by her own father's actions. Her endless cheer never faltering, despite the horrors forced upon her. She deserved this. If the world's attention would be turned towards one child, if the prayers of the faithful could be directed at once at anyone, it should be her.

Eva.

The thought of her being lifted from the gurney she'd called home for the last three years, set upon the floor, and lifting her knee—a tiny first step towards walking—brought tears to his eyes. There would be months of therapy, of course. Without use, her muscles had atrophied terribly. Without any demands placed upon them, her bones had not grown like they should have.

She would struggle. She would have setbacks. She would have to shoulder the weight of the entire world waiting for the day she could walk in public unassisted. Like being born into royalty, she might receive a lifetime of expectations she had never asked for. But, Connolly felt it was worth it. For her, it was worth it. If anyone could bear those burdens, if anyone could handle being considered the world's first global royalty, it was Eva.

A few of the protestors grabbed Connolly and dragged him from the lounge area into the lobby.

"Take him outside," one of them screamed. "Take him outside so all the cameras can see him."

They lifted Connolly from the ground and carried him outside as the rest of the mob spat, punched, and kicked at his body.

Dear God, save me, Connolly prayed, convinced they were about to kill him.

Outside the hotel, crowds ran to encircle the world's most famous health official. Years of hatred and anger fell directly upon Connolly, his career representing to them nothing but intellectual arrogance and careless disregard for human life. News directors cut their video feeds once they realized what was going on but it was too momentous for the world not to notice. A hundred phones streamed his humiliation live for the rest of the world to watch, a spectacle a decade in the making.

"Let me through!"

A voice boomed through the din of shouts of the protestors, clearly audible above the chaos.

"In God's name, let me through," the voice said.

The crowd parted on one side of Connolly as someone forced their way through the havoc that filled the street, a rotund man dressed in red.

"Cardinal Gordillo," Connolly said. "Thank God you are here. Please help me calm these people."

Gordillo grabbed protestors by the arm, his enormous grip forcing them to release their hostage.

"Let this man go!" he said, daring the protestors to challenge him.

The Cardinal tried to push the crowd away. "Back up. Back up! You will not take an innocent man's life."

The mob roared with mocking laughter.

"Innocent?" one of them screamed. "He's killed probably millions."

"He's killed no one."

"You're just as guilty," another demonstrator screamed at Gordillo. "You supported him every step of the way."

The crowd roared in agreement.

"All of you should hang!" yet another person yelled.

"He'd break the rope," someone from the other side replied, sending howls of laughter into the air, followed by group chants of "Break the rope! Break the rope!"

The crowd began to press in again on Connolly, this time pushing Gordillo over him, sending the Cardinal falling headlong onto the ground. Kicks began to fly as the mob of protestors sensed they'd, once again, gained the upper hand.

Just as Connolly and Gordillo were lost within a mass of furious people, gunshots rang out, echoing between the high-rises that lined the streets. Some of the protestors fell flat onto the ground while others tripped over each other to seek cover within the buildings.

As the sea of humanity began to run away, Connolly noticed a group of men jogging towards them, their sub-machine guns pointed in the air.

"Move back," their leader yelled at the protestors. "Move back."

The men encircled Connolly and Gordillo—both bloodied and dazed on the ground—and formed a protective line around them.

"Get up," the man said. "You're coming with us."

"Who are you?" Connolly asked.

"We're your guardian angels," the man said, his sarcastic tone unmistakable.

Gordillo was unsure of what to do. "I don't believe in angels with guns."

"Neither do I. Now come on, get up. We need to move."

"Who sent you?" Connolly asked. "Who do you work for?"

The leader of the men slung his gun over his shoulder and reached down to help Connolly stand. "You won't believe me if I tell you."

CHAPTER 41

Vickers stared up into the air as the rumble of Yuval's helicopter faded away. At first, he thought they were going airborne to help spot Finch, but as the sound of gunfire rang throughout the hills, he realized something had probably gone wrong. For Yuval to have left without confirmation of Finch's death meant something must have gone *very* wrong. As the helicopter turned and flew away, he realized he and his men were on their own.

Vickers descended past the wrecked ambulance and tactical vehicle with no sign of Brinkley or Garcia.

"They should have been back by now," one of the soldiers walking by his side mentioned. "Where'd they go?"

"Looking for Finch, I'm guessing."

"You don't think he's dead?"

Vickers shook his head and looked at the crumpled body on top of the JLTV. "No. I don't think that's him."

"Why?"

"Just a feeling."

"They're going to want us back at the cathedral soon."

"I realize that. First, we have a mission here."

The sound of a vehicle rounding a corner below them startled Vickers. "Get off the road," he snapped to his men.

"Too late."

A white truck stopped just around the bend plainly visible to all.

"Alive," Vickers whispered. "Remind your team. If this is him, we need him alive."

Vickers cautiously walked toward the truck, motioning for the others to fall behind him.

"Don't let them past," he said. "No matter what."

As he approached, he could clearly see Garcia and Brinkley sitting in the front seat, their faces full of concern.

"You get the picture?" Vickers asked.

"What picture?" Garcia asked.

"The picture of Finch, remember. It's why you came down here."

Vickers moved around the side of the truck, checking the cab more closely.

"Why'd your guy leave?" Brinkley asked. "We saw his helicopter fly away. Or did he decide to stay?"

"It's not your business. I'm asking why you returned to the cabin. You were supposed to get a picture."

"I lost an officer down there this morning. Just like you."

Brinkley pointed to the bed of the truck. "I retrieved his body. Just like you should yours. The animals will get them during the night if you don't."

Vickers walked to the back of the truck and saw the body of a mangled deputy, his torn pants and jacket soaked with blood.

"That's an active crime scene down there, Sergeant. You know better than to do this."

"Sue me."

Circling around to the other side of the truck bed, Vickers tried to turn the body over, but it was too heavy, its arms locked to its sides with rigor mortis. He grabbed one of the man's hands and let go, satisfied his fingers were completely cold to the touch.

Brinkley opened the passenger door of the truck. "I'm going to take the picture of Finch."

"Stay in your truck," Vickers boomed, his soldiers stiffening with tension.

"What the hell?" Brinkley asked. "I'm about done with you. I still have no idea who you are."

Vickers slammed the door shut. "You told me you had a blue Chevrolet up there. Why?"

Garcia shot a puzzled look at Brinkley, his eyebrows wrinkled in confusion.

"This isn't my truck."

Brinkley glanced to see where Garcia's gun was resting. The truck had a magnetic mount under the dash where he sometimes kept it. Unfortunately, it was empty.

Vickers motioned towards the wreckage. "That isn't Finch, is it? You said so at first, before you changed your story. Before you lied to me about your truck."

"Then you go take the fucking picture, champ," he said. "I noticed all your men are real skittish around an unarmed doctor. Especially you. You think I haven't noticed your little oddities?"

Vickers was taken aback at Brinkley's observation, something which further emboldened the sheriff.

"Yeah, you go take that picture. You want my phone? Here—here's my phone. Get real close so we can see everything real clear."

A buzzing sound startled the men from their impasse. It was a phone, not ringing, but vibrating—so loudly it was clear it was pulsating against the metal of the truck bed behind them.

Vickers turned to search for the phone but first motioned to the soldiers standing by. "Don't let them out. Don't let them through or out."

He reached over the side of the bed and felt the empty pants pocket of the fallen officer. Feeling nothing, he hopped up into the bed, reached onto the other side, and removed what he was looking for.

"Who's Natalie?" he asked, holding the phone towards the men so they could see. "That your officer's wife? She's not going to like what I have to tell her."

Suddenly, Vickers felt both of his legs sweep out from under him. His body spun sideways, crashing onto the railing around the bed. Another boot kicked into his chest, knocking the wind from his lungs, sending him sliding into the gate.

"Go!" Brinkley screamed. "Go now."

Garcia popped the clutch, flinging gravel everywhere as the truck's wheels spun in place, the vehicle sliding sideways towards the edge of the drive. The engine roared as he sawed at the steering wheel, trying to keep them pointed uphill.

With no room to stand, two of the soldiers were forced to jump from the road into the trees below. On the other side, a soldier forced his rifle into the cab, directly at Garcia's chest. Brinkley grabbed the barrel and yanked it from his hands, causing the man to slip underneath. Ahead of them, a soldier began firing into the cabin, spider webs of cracked glass exploding across their windshield.

With the rifle facing forwards, Brinkley fired through the windshield, blindly shooting at whoever might be in front of them. The truck finally gained traction and began to accelerate towards the next curve. Again, gunfire rang out as the back windshield disappeared, shattered into thousands of pieces.

Vickers raised himself out of the bed, trying in vain to signal for the men to stop shooting. "It's him! Cease fire," he screamed, his lungs burning with effort. Bullets continued to fly, pinging through the truck's metal body.

Finch slid to the back of the vehicle and wrestled Vickers off the tailgate, slamming his head on the metal bed. The truck bottomed out in a rut in the road as its suspension bounced Finch over the back, his feet dragging behind the truck —his only handhold, a death-grip on Vickers' uniform.

Garcia glanced in the rear-view mirror. "Finch fell out!"

Brinkley turned around and saw Vickers hanging over the tailgate, his shirt stretched and pulled up over his head. With speed that belied his stout frame, Brinkley scrambled through the rear window, grabbed the bloodied jacket Finch was wearing and hauled him back into the bed.

Vickers spun away from them and sat up, his handgun now pointed directly at Brinkley. Without thinking, the sheriff pulled Finch on top of him, using his body as a shield.

"Stop the truck," Vickers yelled at Garcia. "Stop it now!"

Garcia cut across the inside of the next corner, forcing the truck through a perilous dip. The front wheels whirled, looking for traction as the vehicle's rear end dropped into the slope, flinging Vickers out of the bed and into the undergrowth below.

Again, Garcia waggled the steering, waiting for the truck's rear wheels to catch onto something. Finch and Brinkley were pressed against the tailgate, hanging tightly to the railing. The vehicle continued shuddering around inside of the curve, pointed upward towards the sky, hanging precariously by its front wheels.

They slid into a tree, its bark providing the side of the rear wheel just enough traction to lift them up and onto the road. Sporadic gunfire cracked through the air as Garcia accelerated around another curve, putting enough distance behind them they felt they were safe.

"Stop," Brinkley said, trying to catch his breath. "Garcia, stop a minute."

"It's too dangerous. They'll catch up with us."

"No, just stop just a minute. We've got problems."

"Yeah we've got problems."

"What do we say when we get up there? Those troopers are going to have questions."

Garcia stopped the truck, looking in the mirror for soldiers. Finch clutched his chest, his heart racing far above anything he'd likely ever counted. Racked with uncertainty, Finch fumbled around the truck bed, another problem becoming painfully obvious. He looked at Brinkley, alarmed.

"Where's my phone?"

* * *

Vickers rolled away from the truck that had stopped his descent. He pulled his shirt up and could see the entire left side of his torso blossoming red with internal bleeding. Some twenty feet above him, one of his soldiers limped up the road, his rifle held to his shoulders—a chase, for the moment, he was unconcerned with.

He reached into his pocket and pulled out a black phone, it's screen displaying a notification.

4 Missed Calls: Natalie. (981) 420-4950

His body wracked with pain, he pulled out another phone and made a call.

"This is Special Agent Vickers. I have a number I need you to pull a trace on. Identity. Geo. Whatever you can find."

CHAPTER 42

"How much fuel do we have?" Yuval asked the pilot.

"You mean how long can we just sit here? Depends on where we're headed. If we're going back to the mansion, probably another twenty minutes."

They had been hovering, watching scenes of chaos unfold below as the white truck stopped for a moment, then began driving wildly, careening up the gravel drive.

"We've got to get that door closed first. That's a bigger problem."

Yuval crawled toward the side and reached down towards the handle as the door shook violently with the aircraft's vibrations.

"Don't let me fall out."

The pilot tilted the helicopter away towards the other side so that Yuval wasn't staring at the ground five hundred feet below. By wrapping his arm through some cargo netting that lined the interior, he was able to reach out far enough to grasp the handle and raise the door.

The white truck remained stopped on the road.

"You think that's him?" the pilot asked.

"Yes."

"I saw muzzle flashes."

"I told them no lethals."

"Yeah, but looks like he got past Vickers."

"Which means he's still alive. For now."

Still hugging Eva, Martta trembled in fear. Yuval picked up the fire extinguisher and slammed it into the weapons locker, smashing the door in further. He grabbed Martta's hair and pulled her face toward his.

"You will pay for that," he hissed. "Dearly."

Martta turned away and buried her face in the blankets that covered the bed. With an open hand, he slapped her head as hard as he could, sending her reeling onto the floor.

Eva looked at Yuval, her face wet with tears.

"Still not want your daddy?" Yuval asked.

She stiffened her lips and looked at her nurse on the floor. "Don't be afraid,

Martta."

Yuval felt his phone ringing and pulled it from his pocket. It was Vickers.

"We missed him."

"I can see that. Tell me he's still alive."

"He is very much alive," Vickers said.

"Looked like a firefight from up here. I said no lethals."

"Your plan wasn't working."

"So what *is* the plan?"

"Can you see what're they doing?"

"They?"

"It's all three of them. Those two locals. Finch was in the back."

Yuval sighed deeply. He knew there were many sympathetic to the man but didn't expect it to extend so far.

"*They* are sitting still. A couple of turns up the road from you. Can you ambush them?"

"Negative," Vickers said. "I lost a couple more guys. Down to two or three of us. We heard gunfire up towards you. What happened?"

"One of our guests tried to escape. It got messy."

"I'm guessing those troopers are not going to be real friendly with us once we get up there."

"No, you can't go up there. So what's the plan?"

"I got his phone," Vickers said. "Someone named Natalie has been calling him non-stop. Do you know who that is?"

A sliver of hope entered Yuval's bleak assessment of their current situation.

"That would be his wife. Or ex-wife."

"She's been messaging him. Saying, *They took her* and *Please help us.* What's that mean? Took who?"

"She's asking him for help?"

"Over and over."

"Interesting," Yuval said. "What did he say?"

"I can't see. Phone's locked. I can just see the incoming messages."

"Can't your team unlock it?"

"It would take some time."

"How much time?"

"Probably too long."

"How much time?" Yuval asked again, his voice intensifying.

"Three hours once they got the phone. Who knows how long it would take to get it to them."

"Figure out where the nearest airstrip is. Commercial, private, I don't care. Go there. I'll have a plane waiting for you."

"What about Finch?"

"I'll handle it."

Yuval hung up the call and immediately dialed another number—a public relations firm he employed for such emergencies.

"Call every media outlet we know," he said to the woman who answered. "Tell them we have a new guest for the Summit tonight, and we want to introduce her to the world."

"Who is it?" the woman asked. "They'll want to know."

"It's a surprise," Yuval said. "But I'm sure they'll be delighted."

CHAPTER 43

Natalie hung up the call and tried her father again. She hadn't expected an answer from Finch but her father—his inability, or unwillingness, to answer—began to fill her with a sense of dread.

She noticed his demeanor had changed in the last few weeks. With news of the epic discovery, her father's initial response had been jubilant. Publicly, he made every boast possible, assuring anyone who asked they would be dumbfounded at what he and Yuval had been able to accomplish.

Privately, however, Natalie sensed he wasn't completely at ease, a sentiment that had recently become more pronounced. The loss of his decades-long collaborator, Walter Faucett, had been a huge blow. The identity of Faucett's murderer—and his recent escape—an even more somber restraint on what should have been a joyous time. But, something else was off. Something seemingly unrelated to the night of the car crash.

* * *

In the aftermath of his colleague's death, Connolly temporarily picked up the work Faucett had been involved with. With free access to his laptop and emails, he carried the torch Faucett had so famously held aloft for decades as the *de facto* public face of public health. Connolly worked tirelessly to ensure lectures were rescheduled with other speakers, sometimes substituting himself if the subject matter allowed for it. Ambitious programs Faucett had sponsored continued to be funded, a list of initiatives that went on for days, their intent often completely lost on the aging scientist.

One such program concerned Connolly greatly, particularly the scope of those involved. Emails to pharmaceutical company CEOs were common at the higher echelons of public health. Emails to all of them—at the same time—was nearly unheard of outside press releases. One evening, as Connolly scoured through Faucett's emails, looking for a forgotten contact, he saw a strange subject line.

Re: All hands on deck. ██████ green.

The email's author, Dr. Yuval Naftali, struck him as odd. The recipients—

besides Faucett, the CEO of every major pharmaceutical company on the planet —gave him even more pause. The fact the subject line had been redacted—directly within the email itself—set his mind spinning.

Gentlemen and women–

On behalf of Walter and me, I want to thank you for all the incredible work that has gone into the ██████ program. We are all afraid as the pandemic rages around us and the world eagerly awaits our vaccines. You should take great comfort in knowing we are poised for a momentous shift in human health, something our children and grandchildren will undoubtedly read about some day. It should go without mentioning I appreciate the fact nothing has leaked anywhere as far as I can tell, a momentous success in its own right!

Nevertheless, everyone has signed off on their manufacturing processes and I believe we are green and ready to go. Walter speak up if you have any outstanding concerns.

Otherwise, good health to you all (and the rest of the world, of course).

–Y

P.S. I think now would be appropriate to switch our communication channels over to ████. I'm ██████ in case you forgot.

Butterflies darted across his chest as Connolly began to grasp what was going on. During the early days of the pandemic, Faucett was working directly with Yuval on what was clearly a massive project—without Connolly's knowledge or approval. Together, they had involved at least seven of the world's largest drug manufacturers in something so secretive not even he—the head of the nation's public health agency, was aware of.

The black bars weren't something Connolly had ever seen within agency emails. They were commonly used to obfuscate sensitive facts and figures shared with the public through freedom of information requests. But, censored internal emails—their digital form as they sat on the computer's hard drive—that was something entirely new to him.

Clearly, they were expecting trouble. Switching over to a private communication channel. Blacking out sensitive data before it could even be archived for the pubic requests that would inevitably follow. And not involving him. He hadn't even caught a whiff of what had been going on for years behind his back.

Connolly had dialed Yuval's number but immediately hung up, realizing the fact they believed him unaware of the program might offer some value. He couldn't comprehend what they might have been discussing but, given Yuval and Faucett's questionable ethics, he didn't imagine it was anything good. It scared him, in fact. The players involved. The fact they had mentioned the word *manufacturing*.

Natalie learned of her father's concerns soon after. He trusted her more than anyone. Despite her marriage to public health enemy one, he still believed she wouldn't divulge his secrets to anyone—not even to her husband.

"What do you think it is?" she asked after he had relayed portions of the email to her.

"I don't know, but there's one commonality I'm really worried about. Everyone on that email is making malkavirus vaccines."

* * *

Natalie thought of heading to the cathedral to look for her father. He would comfort her, as he always had, with a towering hug from above her. Quiet words of assurance that everything would be okay. His hand on the back of her head, holding her in the same way he had since she was Eva's age.

Eva.

Natalie winced in pain as she snapped from her daydream and thought of her daughter crying in fear on a helicopter. Crying out for her.

Natalie looked at her phone again.

1:37p.m.

Where are you, Tom? she thought to herself. *We need you.*

She picked up the remote to the television and turned it on, hoping the news might offer more information. A reporter stood outside the smoldering embers of a large white building, fire trucks still spraying water in the background. A graphic crawled across the bottom of the screen.

Asian boy hero Mongchai dead in hospital fire. Cathedral Summit for tonight in doubt.

Natalie stood up, the television remote and her phone dropping to the floor.

That's why they took her, she thought. *They're going to put Eva on display for the world to see.*

Immediately, several other dots began to connect, a patchwork of things her father had told her, conversations that began to form a dark picture in her mind.

They want him there. They want Finch to show up.

CHAPTER 44

Connolly and Gordillo were led away from the hotel, around the block to a side street, protestors screaming at them the whole way. As they entered a small alleyway, one of the men guarding them stopped and prevented the demonstrators following them from going any further.

"Where are you taking us?" Connolly asked.

"Somewhere safer than lying in the middle of the street, getting beat up by thugs."

"I had them under control," Gordillo said.

A few of the guards snickered.

"Some of them hate you more than Connolly," their leader said.

"My associate is back there. In the wheelchair. He must come with us."

"We've got eyes on him. He'll be alright."

"Who are you?" Connolly asked the leader of the men.

"We're not called anything."

"No. *Your* name."

"Gabriel."

"Gabriel, the angel, I suppose?" Connolly asked.

"If you say so. Gabe is fine."

They turned down an even smaller alley, just wide enough to fit them in single file. Gabe looked up as a helicopter passed overheard then knocked a strange cadence on the rusted metal door they stood beside.

"You didn't hear that."

The door opened into a dark room, its only source of light the open doorway.

"Grab the railing," Gabe said. "We're going down two flights. There's some light down there."

The group proceeded slowly down the stairs. Gordillo trudged nearly sideways, gripping the railing with both hands as he tapped each step with his toe before he would descend.

A source of light illuminated the last few stairs as they finished going down. They walked through another hallway and into a low-ceilinged room filled with decrepit washing machines, dryers, and an overpowering stench of mildew. A few other armed men stood in the room, two of them looking intently at the screens of their laptops.

"Impressive operation, Gabe," Gordillo said, sarcastically.

"Sorry to disappoint," he replied with a sheepish grin. "We're just angels. Not priests with airliners."

Connolly took off his coat to inspect the beating his body had suffered. "Okay, now what?"

"I call your benefactor and ask. We wait for his answer."

Gordillo shifted uncomfortably, visibly agitated. "Time is wasting, gentlemen. Both Dr. Connolly and I have extremely tight schedules this afternoon."

"As do we."

"Whose side are you on?"

"Whose side are we on again?" Gabe smirked at the other men in the room. "I'll have to ask our benefactor. I seem to have forgotten."

"Well call him, then," Gordillo snapped, tiring of their inside jokes.

Gabe gestured to one of the men with a laptop. "We're working on it right now."

"Can't you just use a phone?" Connolly asked.

"No. We cannot."

The man at the laptop handed Gabe a headset, its long black cable leading back to the side of the computer. He placed the plastic band over his head and pointed his thumb upward, indicating he needed more volume.

After waiting thirty seconds, Gabe began to speak.

"Hey. It's me. We've got him. He's safe. And one other person—a Cardinal."

Gabe looked towards the priest. "What's your name?"

Bruised the man didn't recognize him, Gordillo shot back with his own sarcasm. "I'm Cardinal Gabe."

"It's Gordillo," Connolly said. "Cardinal Gordillo."

"Okay," Gabe said. "We have Connolly and Cardinal Gordillo."

Gabe waited for what seemed like a long response. He held his hand over the mouthpiece and relayed a message to them. "He wants to come talk to you. He says he'll be here in a little while."

Like Gordillo, Connolly began to grow flustered. "Unless you can tell me who you are, who you're talking to, or what you intend to do with us, I'm going to start trying to escape real soon. I don't care about the protestors."

Gabe returned to the call.

"I don't think they're going to want to wait that long."

Outside the room, the sounds of shouting could be heard coming from down the hall. One of the men ran towards the commotion to see what was happening.

"They're coming through!" he yelled. "They found us!"

Gabe ripped the earphones from his head. "We're going to have to use the tunnels."

"It's too hot," one of the other men replied. "They'll never make it."

Gabe yelled a few commands to the other men in the room. "Grab everything. No cables. No chargers. Don't leave anything. Kill the lights when you're done."

Someone threw a large black coat over Gordillo, hiding his bright red robe as the shouting from the stairwell grew more intense.

"Where are we going?" Connolly asked.

"We're going to see the benefactor."

Gabe grabbed Connolly's arm and pulled him into the darkness of the hallway. "But we'll have to go through hell to get there."

CHAPTER 45

"Don't get up yet," Brinkley said as they sped away from the troopers. "They can still see us."

Finch rolled over onto his other side, trying to get comfortable.

Garcia shifted gears as the truck gained speed. "How long before they figure us out?"

"Not long," Brinkley said.

They'd just scrambled up the road onto the highway where a dozen angry state troopers had their rifles trained directly at them. Brinkley flashed his badge and pointed to the truck bed.

"Officer down! Officer down!"

Finch had again taken his place in the back, this time as an injured Monroe, rather than dead.

A trooper flagged them down. "Where's your patrol car?"

"Destroyed," Brinkley said, the quickest explanation he could think of.

Garcia revved the engine. "We need to go."

"What's going on down there?" the trooper asked.

"Shooter is down. Multiple fatalities. Couple of injured. They're probably walking up now. We need to go."

Garcia snaked past the patrol cars that blocked the highway as the diesel engine sprang to life.

"I can't see shit," he said, the windshield pocked with bullet holes.

"I'll tell you if we're going to hit something."

Finch crawled up to the back window. "Where are we going?"

"I don't know, but that was really dumb what you did back there."

"He took my phone," Finch said.

"That was still dumb."

Garcia shook his head. "We're in it deep now."

Finch looked around the bed and realized his canvas bag was gone. Inside, the medical supplies he was counting on to keep his heart from destroying itself. Instinctively, he checked his pulse.

152bpm.

Again, too high. But somehow, still alive. According to his intuition, the fight in the truck should have stopped his heart. Ever since his diagnosis, he had minimized physical strain. Avoided all possible contact with danger. It's what everyone had learned to do to manage the threat of what they called "sudden adult death"—the opposite of what his military training had equipped him for.

It'd been easy in jail. Since his escape, he'd been pushed to the limits. Yet, he survived. In fact, he felt invigorated. Finch had just risked his life several times that morning and, for the first time in years, felt like a human being—not a caged animal.

"Any idea who that was on the ambulance? He must've killed ten of them."

"I don't suppose that was you that called 911 this morning from the cabin?" Brinkley asked.

"No way."

"Well then, *he* did, whoever he was."

"Wonder why?"

"Wanted to kill more people? I don't know."

"He could have shot me," Finch said. "But he didn't."

"Me too," Brinkley said. "He threw me in the basement. Like I weighed nothing. Got right in my face. Talking crazy."

"He tried to kill me alright," Garcia said.

Brinkley flipped through the morning's events, trying to make sense of everything. "Well, he's dead now."

"You're sure?" Finch asked.

"Yes, I'm sure." Brinkley's stomach turned at the thought of the image of the man lying on top of the ambulance, his twisted corpse nearly unrecognizable—the second possible suicide of the day.

"That was seriously Naftali in the helicopter?" Finch asked.

Brinkley shook his head. "It was. I'd recognize him anywhere. Guy strikes me as completely evil."

"You know about him?"

"Oh, yeah. I know all about him."

"How do you know so much?" Garcia asked.

Brinkley pointed his thumb at Finch. "Well, I've been listening to this man for years."

Finch was taken aback and laughed—something he hadn't done in a very long time. "You know me?"

"I watched all your videos. I was a big fan."

"You're both loonies," Garcia said. "That's how you knew his riddle."

Brinkley allowed a smile to creep across his face as well. "Yes. I followed everything. When they started rolling all that crap out, just months after malka-virus hit, I knew something was up."

Finch's mind lit up. He hadn't discussed much of anything of importance since he'd been in jail—the occasional interaction with another sympathetic prisoner, all he was willing to risk. With almost no internet connection, his knowledge of world events lagged months behind.

"You believed what I was saying?" Finch asked.

"Well, not everything. But, I'm a natural-born skeptic, like you."

Garcia rolled his eyes at their interaction. His wife was a nurse and had studied these things in school. He deferred to her advice for any important medical matters.

"Never bullshit a bullshitter," Brinkley laughed.

"That wasn't bullshit," Finch replied. "Nothing I said was false."

"Oh, I know. I'm just pulling your chain. I was obsessed with the whole Bootstrap thing. Went *way* down the rabbit hole on that one."

"What's the Bootstrap thing?" Garcia asked.

Adrenaline flooded Finch's veins as he remembered the night he'd first talked about it. He knew he was a marked man. There were few people who would believe what he said was true. The only thing he felt would keep him safe were his close ties with the Connolly family.

Lies will get you jailed. Truth will get you killed.

Finch closed every show with those same words, a motto his followers used to identify each other with bumper stickers and hats.

TWGYK.

So long as he kept that phrase at the front of everyone's minds, he felt his death might be too costly for those who wished harm upon him.

"What was it?" Garcia asked again. "The Bootstrap thing?"

"You tell him," Finch said. "Brinkley, is that what you're called?"

"Brinkley. Brinks. Whatever, I don't care. But, sure, I'll tell you what the Bootstrap project is."

Garcia tilted his head in an obvious show of doubt. "Good. I'm dying to know."

Brinkley thought back to the first time he'd heard Finch mention it. He took a deep breath and looked at the man he'd originally heard about it from.

"This is a little intimidating."

"No, go ahead," Finch said. "You probably remember more than I do."

"Well, I doubt that, but here's what I recall. You asked for it, Garcia. The Bootstrap program was something that went into all the MALKA shots. It was a new technology that every one of them got."

"M-RNA," Garcia said.

"No, not that shit. Something different. It was secret. No one talked about it. All the companies that made the shots put it in there. Didn't tell anyone."

"What was it for?"

"Well, supposedly it would make it so you'd never have to get another vaccine—that right, Finch?"

Finch nodded his head.

"Yeah, it was like something that would allow them to *program* you. I suck at this. You tell him, Finch—Garcia understands computers better than me."

Garcia shifted in his seat, uncomfortable with Brinkley's description.

Finch thought of how to best explain it. He'd done a few videos, each an attempt at reaching different audiences. Other scientists and doctors. Mothers and fathers. It was a strange concept most people had trouble understanding.

He turned towards Garcia. "You've heard of booting a computer, right?"

"Of course. Rebooting, boot-up, all that."

"Yep. The Bootstrap sequence is the first thing a computer loads when it turns on. It doesn't know anything at that point. Its mind is completely blank. It has to start somewhere. It needs a tiny set of instructions just to get things going. With that tiny set of instructions, it can do anything. It can be a supercomputer. It can be a phone. At first, it doesn't even know what *it* is—until that Bootstrap sequence loads something else in, telling it what to do."

"Okay," Garcia said. "I get it."

"So think of your immune system like a computer. When you're just a clump of cells in your mother's belly, your immune system doesn't know much. It can't do anything. As you grow into a baby, your mother's immune system starts teaching it what's good and what's bad."

"You don't have to talk down to me like that."

"No, it's the best way to explain this. I'd say this to anyone. Your immune system starts off with almost no idea of what's harmful and what's not. You learn over time what's right and wrong—through getting sick and recovering."

"Or a vaccine."

"Sometimes," Finch said. "But actually, vaccines were the problem. Vaccines were why they created the Bootstrap project. They didn't want to have to give people a new vaccine every time a new disease or variant or whatever came out. People felt like there were too many."

"I can agree with that."

"So, they came up with a way to essentially put a Bootstrap sequence directly into your immune system. A way they could *instruct* your immune system what to do—without having to give you another shot every time."

"Sounds amazing to me."

Brinkley shook his head. "Y'all always think everything sounds amazing. You don't see a problem with that?"

"No. I hate shots. Just like everyone else. You're telling me I could get one more shot and never have to worry about anything again."

"You really are that stupid, aren't you?"

"What, Brinks? What's wrong with that?"

"Well, you already got *the one shot* just so you know. You probably got five of them. So it's already in you."

"Okay, so what?"

"So now they can program you to do whatever they want, and you can't stop them."

Finch broke in. "Well, it's not exactly like that. They can't *program* you to do whatever they want—like mind control or something—and it's obviously an extremely complex thing to be able to pull off."

"So they can put out a new program if they're sure it will help."

"Who is *they*, Garcia? Who is *they*? That's the problem with you people. You don't even care who *they* is."

"*They* are the authorities. The scientists. The people who care about public health."

"If you trust *they* will always do the right thing, then you're dumber than a refrigerator."

"I trust they will," Garcia said. "What could they possibly gain by screwing around with something as important as this?"

Finch and Brinkley locked eyes.

"What?" Garcia asked. "What? You seriously believe people would mean to harm us with this?"

Brinkley broke the awkward silence. "It only takes one person, Garcia. That's the problem. You've got nearly the entire world all bootstrapped up and now anyone who has their heart set on it can come along and do very bad things. To everyone."

"You don't even know if this is real," Garcia said. "You just make these things up to freak everyone out and sell your books."

Finch sighed.

"Let's hope so," Brinkley said.

"Look, even if this were real—let's say this were totally real and everyone who got a shot has the Bootstrap thing—you'd have to do another global rollout to *program* them as you call it, right? Nobody's going to do that again. If some freak decided they wanted to kill everyone on the planet, it'd only affect a few people before they caught on to it."

Again, both Finch and Brinkley were unsure what to say.

"I'm right, aren't I?" Garcia asked. "Admit it—I'm right."

Brinkley flinched. "How do you think they program the Bootstrap, Garcia?"

"How should I know?"

"You think they ask your permission and say *Pretty please* and have you sign a form?"

"I have no idea. Tell me."

Finch stared out onto the road ahead, his mind still reeling from the reminder this entire scheme was even possible.

"Tell him, Finch," Brinkley said.

"Yeah, Finch. How do they program it?"

"Viruses," Finch said. "They program it with viruses."

CHAPTER 46

Some thirty miles north of Washington, D.C., Yuval's helicopter touched down on the grass of the Prince George State Hospital campus. A few firetrucks remained, dousing the last of the flames that consumed one of the buildings.

With media already on the scene for the fire, it was an ideal location. Reporters and their camera crews were directed by their producers to encircle the designated landing zone and roll their cameras as he arrived. From high above, Yuval could see the smoldering carcass of the structure as they descended, most likely still containing the boy's body—a bit of reality he was completely unaffected by.

Death was an abstract concept for Yuval. Besides his parents, he had never lost anyone dear to him—not because such people were fortunate to have good health, but because he was unfortunate enough not to have anyone dear to him. He grew up with no pets. Few friends. And a struggle to understand the joy or sadness of everyone around him.

In a similar way, his religious upbringing was similarly devoid of meaning. Rituals. Prayers. Songs. All of it, absurd incantations to an invisible deity who would never answer a single request. He was made to attend a religious school for years but outpaced the curriculum its teachers could sustain. And so, with two years left to complete his high school education, he left for the university, where his intellect might be more properly channeled.

What was God? he asked in an early college paper. *An improbable mathematical equation that cannot be solved? An artificial bridge of faith and belief meant to conjure happiness from sorrow?* He posed sophisticated questions with answers that escaped the understanding of his most astute professors, unsure if he was that much smarter than they, or simply had such an incredible command of the language he could baffle even himself into believing what he said was true.

One teacher—an old rabbi who wasn't so easily impressed—graded one of Yuval's papers candidly.

Your word count is too high. Your ability to clearly explain your thesis is too low. I suggest you cut half of this and try again. This time, pretend children will be reading it. Try and explain yourself so that children can understand.

Yuval—seventeen-years-old and a sophomore in college at this point—stormed into the rabbi's office, demanding an apology.

"Absolutely not," the rabbi said. "I will do no such thing."

"What possible good can come from trying to relate these concepts to children?"

"They are your most important audience. Sell them on it, and you can convince anyone."

"There is not a single word in that entire paper that is unnecessary. Everything is perfectly ordered. Not a sentence goes to waste. I demand a written apology—in the university paper."

The rabbi couldn't believe the brash demands of his young student, the first of many troubling conversations Yuval held with his professors while at university. Graduate school proved no less awkward, despite the faculty who insisted he would eventually mellow with a bit of age. He couldn't keep lab partners, his advisors would not meet with him, and eventually, many of his professors graded his papers with perfect scores just to avoid confrontation.

His Ph.D. focused in esoteric studies on the nature of religious belief. What was faith? What was prayer? What drove otherwise intelligent humans to close their eyes and whisper requests to a phantom being no one had ever seen? Why did they continue to think their petitions would be granted, when hundreds of others had not?

The solitary nature of his study was a relief to those around him. There was little need for interaction, even from his core advisers. He took these questions into the lab, trying to quantify and qualify what humans had always regarded as mysterious. Unmeasurable. Unquantifiable.

* * *

"I won't be long," Yuval said to the pilot.

"Want me to leave things running this time?"

"It'll be too loud. Just be ready to go as soon as I'm done."

"Okay."

Yuval grabbed Martta and pushed her into the empty pilot's seat, wrapping the seat belt around her tightly and snapping it in place. He grabbed her chin and pointed her face directly at him.

"Don't move. Do you understand me? Don't move from here."

She stared back and said nothing.

"Kill her if she tries to move," he said to the pilot.

Toward the back of the helicopter, Eva's gurney was strapped to the floor with cargo hooks. Through the back window, he could see cameras pointing directly at them, their reporters waiting with microphones in hand.

Brushing the wrinkles from his coat, Yuval forced a smile from his lips and leaned into Eva's ear so that only she could hear him.

"We're going to talk to a few people about something exciting that's happening tonight. You are going to be the star."

"I don't want to die," she said.

Yuval grabbed her hand, a slip of emotion he found embarrassing. "No, you're not going to die. This is a good thing. Tonight, many people will be praying for you. They will be so happy to see you."

"What are you going to do to Martta?"

"Listen. We are going to go out there and talk about some things. There are news people out there with cameras, and they love you. They want to hear that you're happy. They may ask you a question or two. They're going to say something like *Are you excited about tonight?* or *Are you ready for all of this attention?* Just say yes. To any of those questions, say yes. You *are* excited. You *are* happy."

"What if they ask me where my parents are?"

Yuval slammed his fist down on the gurney. "Just say you can't wait to see them tonight. And that you are so happy."

"My daddy won't be there."

A spark of light formed in Yuval's mind.

"That's it. Eva, that's it! Tell them you wished he would come. Tell them you miss your daddy so much and that's the only thing that would make you happy is if he comes tonight."

"But that's not true."

Yuval grabbed Eva by the throat, a sensation she could only partially feel.

"Say it," he hissed. "I will throw your nurse from this helicopter if you don't say that. We will go way up in the air, and I will throw her down to the ground so that she dies—if you don't say you miss your daddy and you want him to come."

Eva tried to speak, but nothing would come out. Unable to turn from his gaze, she squeezed her eyes shut.

"You better say it," he said, flinging her head away from him.

Yuval stood up and, again, straightened his clothing. He opened his eyes as wide as he could, blinking them repeatedly as if to mentally reset.

"Okay," he told the pilot. "I'm going out there."

With cameras rolling, the back cargo door slowly lowered to the ground, the interior of the aircraft shrouded in darkness. Yuval Naftali slowly walked down the ramp towards a small podium already set in place. All over the world, news programs switched to the live video feed, everyone anxious as to whether the evening's event would still take place.

Yuval paused at the microphone and made eye contact with every reporter before he started speaking, a purposeful trick he had learned to increase people's expectations.

"Ladies and gentlemen. Thank you for allowing me to speak to you on this historic day. You will, no doubt, have learned by now that Mongchai was tragically killed in a fire here at the hospital. As some of his biggest supporters, Dr. Connolly and I were shocked to hear of his death. When we first discussed who might help us unveil our recent discovery to the world, Mongchai was the first and last person that came up. His bravery, courage, and desire to help others is a model for children everywhere. Even for us adults."

A few of the reporters nodded their heads in agreement.

"I realize that many people have traveled from across the globe in hopes of seeing improvement in Mongchai's condition tonight. I assume that many are asking will the event go on? How is it possible to hold such an event with the loss of its heroic star? I've asked myself that many times since I heard about Mongchai's death. But, I'm here to tell you the event will go on, and with someone else—another star I know many of you have already prayed for."

Yuval returned up the ramp and unstrapped Eva's gurney from the hooks that ran along the floor. With the regal air of a king presenting his successor, he rolled her bed down the ramp and across the grass to the podium. To their great delight, Yuval turned her bed around to face the cameras, inclined the backrest, and tenderly brushed the girl's hair from her face.

Audible gasps could be heard from the reporters when they realized who she was.

Yuval beamed with pride. "Ladies and gentlemen. I present to you tonight's *new* guest: Eva Connolly. Granddaughter of our very own Albert Connolly."

Several of the reporters lowered their mics and applauded the incredible reveal. Another burst out with a question she could not contain.

"Do you expect she might be healed tonight, Dr. Naftali?"

Yuval held his hand in the air. "I'll answer a few questions in a moment. Maybe Eva, too, if you're lucky. I doubt that anyone is unfamiliar with her story, but in case you haven't heard, Eva was tragically paralyzed in the same car accident that killed our beloved Walter Faucett. Her mother was also severely injured, but little Eva—just three-years-old at the time—little Eva was the true victim."

Some of the police and firefighters began to gather around as a hush fell over the growing crowd.

"Now some of you may think I'm going to not mention the man who perpetrated this horrendous act out of reverence—if we can call it that—for tonight's historic event. But, I am. I am going to mention it, or *him* I suppose I should say, because of a very specific reason. Little Eva here was paralyzed by her own father, a man by the name of Thomas Finch. Murdered Walter Faucett. Nearly killed his wife. Paralyzed his own daughter. Thomas Finch. You have probably heard of Thomas Finch because of how viciously he attacked those of us who work in public health. Those of us who've pledged our lives to better humanity. He constantly attacked his father-in-law, Dr. Connolly. He's said all kinds of horrible things about me over the years, made up all kinds of rumors about things that weren't true—all in hopes of terrorizing you into buying more of his books and T-shirts."

Yuval shook his head and pursed his lips in contrition. "What kind of man would do that?"

He gestured towards Eva's bed. "What kind of man would do this? To his own three-year-old daughter?"

Yuval straightened his glasses. "I'm mentioning Thomas Finch because I—on behalf of the entire scientific community...on behalf of the entire public health community...on behalf of everyone in the world who wants to move on from the terrible last few years of pandemics and fighting—I want to bury the hatchet. I want to make amends. We all want to make amends, do we not? Tonight, as the world lifts Eva up in their prayers and asks for healing, you know who I want standing behind her? You know who I want standing amidst me and Dr. Connolly and all the scientists and priests and everyone else he's disparaged over the years? I want Thomas Finch there, right in the middle, praying alongside every one else that God would heal the very child he destroyed."

CHAPTER 47

Unable to sit, Natalie stood trembling at the sight of her daughter on the television. Every major news station had a camera at the hospital as Yuval rolled her gurney out of the helicopter. The words that came out of his mouth—the deceit; the betrayal; the smile covering it all—it was only the second time she'd ever felt rage like that in her life.

The thought of calling the police passed through her mind, but she knew it would go nowhere. Natalie was aware how these things worked. As head of the World Health Alliance, Yuval had nearly every immunity possible. A call would be placed. A chief would be alerted. A few phone calls would be made. And they'd call her back to tell her they'd passed it up the chain to higher authorities.

As word began to spread Eva would be taking the dead boy's place, news programs began to air archival footage of anything related to her father and the wreck that almost killed her. Flashing blue and red lights of police and fire trucks cut through the dark night at the top of a bridge. With long ropes, emergency crews hoisted something from the car that lay destroyed beneath it—a tiny body lashed to an orange rescue board.

Natalie was extracted next, the hydraulic cutters shearing the crumpled metal away from her. Her leg fractured in three places, missing several pints of blood, she was unable to comprehend what was happening. As they strapped her to another board and slowly raised her away from the wreckage, Natalie said nothing.

The front-seat passenger was completely entangled within the crushed car and there would be no extraction. It was every first responder's nightmare, a horrific death that so mangled the victim, they could no longer be recognized as human. A rescuer was able to spot the license plate and called it in.

Vehicle Owner:
Walter Raymond Faucett
4814 Fairlawn Avenue
Falls Church, Virginia

DNA confirmation would take a few days, but for those reporting on the story, it was just a formality. Shocks of silver hair. The black tuxedo. A mangled dress shoe. Once the vehicle owner's identity became known to the rescuers, it was clear who the victim was.

"No pictures," the cry came down from above. "No pictures."

A gray nylon tarp was lowered to the team and tied around the wrecked car before it was dragged from the ravine by a crane, shielding the man inside from any further indignity given the media that had arrived on the scene.

Natalie was about to turn off the television when the video feed switched to a disheveled Thomas Finch being led out of an unmarked car, his arms bound behind him in handcuffs. It was footage she'd never seen before—early morning, just hours after the wreck.

Finch had been found near the wreckage, ushered away by emergency crews that soon arrived. A witness had called in a description of his car followed by details of the crash. Finch had run them off the road, they suggested, an accusation he reluctantly admitted to police.

The show cut to footage of him handcuffed in prison scrubs, walking from the courthouse into a van.

Thomas Finch, Disgraced Doctor, Sentenced for Life in Fatal Wreck.

The conviction had taken over a year, but for much of the public, it couldn't have come soon enough. For them, Faucett represented the calm voice of reason during a turbulent time of pandemic-related hysteria. The fact others hated him for his efforts only served to elevate his near-angelic status. When Finch—his greatest detractor— was convicted for murder—Faucett's martyrdom was complete. He would be forever revered as one of public health's greatest heroes, his name taught in history books, his likeness depicted in paintings and sculptures throughout the country.

Another segment began on the television.

Convicted Doctor Missing After Improbable Escape.

Aerial footage showed police cars surrounding a small-town grocery store, intercut with interviews of local townspeople—witnesses who claimed to have spotted the recently escaped convict.

"I think it was him," the cashier said. "I knew I recognized him when I saw him. He wouldn't look at me, so I knew something was off."

A reporter appeared on camera in front of the grocery store, summarizing a stunning event that had just happened over the previous week.

"Finch has been missing for days now after an apparent mix-up at the Lee Penitentiary. Prison authorities are still unclear as to what exactly happened, but it sounds like—as unlikely as it may sound—they left the transport vehicle's door unlocked."

The television ran pictures of Natalie's father holding his granddaughter—paparazzi-style photos taken from afar with powerful zoom-lensed cameras. One of them included Natalie, laughing at Eva as she ran in front of her, a long-forgotten smile she hadn't felt the urge to use in years.

Eva Connolly To Replace Mongchai At Health Summit Tonight.

Natalie flipped the television off, unwilling to endure any more. Unable to call the police—and unable to reach her father or Finch—she felt powerless to stop whatever was about to happen.

They can heal her. Images of the men praying around the empty wheelchair flooded her mind.

They can heal her.

Natalie tried to envision her frightened six-year-old daughter being able to simply walk into her room in the middle of the night and climb into bed with her. Children got scared, but Eva could do nothing beside call out to her through the intercom, hoping her mother would wake up and comfort her.

There was little Natalie wouldn't do to grant her daughter even a tiny bit of recovery. Perhaps Yuval meant well. Perhaps his intellect prevented him from conveying things as he should. But, why would he have taken her? Why did he kidnap her without bringing Natalie? Perhaps he thought she would say no.

It's tonight or never!

A threat from Yuval. An unexplainable threat. For all the promise of their discovery, why did it have to be tonight? Eva could wait another day. She'd probably insist others go before her—*everyone* else—such was her endless charity. But, Mongchai was dead. Maybe there was no one else they could get in time. Yuval was under tremendous pressure, of course. Maybe his anger stemmed from that.

Natalie tried to reason her way through a constellation of confusing memories, piecing together why Yuval had taken her daughter. A constant source of anxiety stemmed from one of the last things she could remember Faucett telling her before the accident.

Your husband may be planning an attack. Something big. Something sophisticated.

Why did Faucett tell her what felt like an obvious lie? Discernment was more difficult with Yuval, but for Faucett, it might as well have come with a bright red warning light. Something was off. His insistence she drive him home. The big story about millions of dead. It felt so completely implausible, particularly for such an esteemed man of science.

The fact it was the last thing he ever spoke—coupled with the reality that the man he warned her about was the very person who killed him—did not sit well with her. Finch was full of hate and anger—sometimes for those he loved most. But for random people? To wish death upon millions of people who he didn't even know? That didn't sound like her husband. It sounded like fantasy. Like a laughable Hollywood script with comically evil villains.

Natalie wanted Eva to walk again more than anything else, but couldn't shake the uneasy feeling she began to develop. A sense that Finch had been right about some of the things he had told her. A sense that something was about to go very wrong.

CHAPTER 48

"That was Finch," Vickers screamed at one of the highway troopers blocking the road. "You let him get away."

"Finch who?"

"Thomas Finch. Fed's number one most wanted? Heard of him?"

"That truck had three officers. One of them appeared badly injured."

Vickers pointed to the blood running down his head. "This look like the work of an injured officer? That was Finch in the back. He tried to kill me."

"And whoever was in that helicopter may have kidnapped someone and killed one of my troopers. Word is you know who he was."

"I need you to get on your radio and call in help to track down that truck and get him."

The trooper was unimpressed. "I need *you* to get on your radio and tell your guy he's about to see fighter jets in his rearview mirror. We've already called the F.A.A. who I'm guessing have already called the Air Force. I advise he land and surrender peacefully."

"That man is wanted for murder. And he just slipped right through your fingers."

"Sir, we are not here on a federal manhunt. We have a rogue military aircraft with a homicide and possible kidnapping suspect on it. What agency are you?"

"NIH."

The trooper laughed. "NIH? You're a *health* agency."

Vickers showed his badge, bristling at the lack of respect. "You may not have dealt with us before, but I can assure you, we are *much* higher up the chain than you."

"Maybe in D.C. This is West Virginia, and I have no idea what health officers with guns and helicopters are doing in my county. Until you get a better explanation, you're not going to get any help from me other than an escort to the hospital for that little boo-boo on your head."

Vickers felt his pants leg vibrating. He pulled his phone out but realized it was the other device—Finch's phone—that was buzzing. Its screen displayed a notification, another message from Natalie.

Don't come Finch. They want you here. It's a trap.

Vickers considered the implications of the text. Two other notifications appeared as he read the first.

Yuval wants to humiliate you. Or worse.

DON'T COME!

"Is there a problem?" the trooper asked.

Vickers stumbled for a moment. "Uh...let me...I'm going to have to talk to my commanding officer and get some more direction."

"Okay, you do that."

As he walked away from the troopers, Vickers called Yuval on the other phone.

"You missed him again, I presume?" Yuval asked.

"Correct."

"Where is he?"

"In a white pickup with two local deputies. Headed towards the hospital, I'm guessing."

"I don't think he'll go to the hospital," Yuval said. "He can take care of himself."

"I got another text from his wife, Natalie."

"What is it?"

"Now she's telling him *not* to come. She's saying it's a trap and that we want him there."

"How is she still messaging right now? I thought you sent people over there to prevent this from happening."

"They're on their way. Everything's jammed up. No one can get out of the cathedral. The highways are crawling. There's protestors everywhere."

"Did she say anything else? What does she suspect?"

"I don't know. She's just messaging like crazy telling him not to show up tonight."

"Do you know where she is?"

"Still at the mansion, according to what I'm told."

"How long would it take you to get there?"

"I don't know—an hour maybe?"

"Take whatever men you have left, and go shut her down."

Vickers looked at the two agents that stood by him. "I've got wounded down here. Several more are dead."

"Leave them!" Yuval shouted.

"What about Finch?"

"I'm handling Finch. Go shut her down now."

CHAPTER 49

Gabe was the last person to enter the tunnel, making sure Connolly, Gordillo, and all his men were inside before he closed the door and slid a pair of locks closed.

"This is going to be challenging," Gabe told them. "It's going to be tight in some spots. You may have to crawl in others. But, the heat will be the worst part. Make sure you let us know if you start to feel like you're going to pass out."

Steam powered many of the heating systems of the buildings above them. Physical plants with huge boilers connected buildings together underneath the streets of Washington, their service tunnels filled with scalding pipes that ferried steam to the radiators and convectors warming each structure.

In a single-file procession, they continued down a low-ceiling tunnel until another set of metal stairs took them down another level. The ambient temperature began to rise as Connolly felt sweat beading on his forehead.

"I don't want this extra layer," Gordillo said as he removed the black cloak they had wrapped around him.

"You will," Gabe said. "It's going to be a tight squeeze up ahead. You don't want to be touching these pipes anymore than you have to."

Metallic banging on the door behind them echoed throughout the passageway as angry protestors discovered they had escaped.

"You think they'll get through?" Connolly asked.

"Eventually. Hopefully we'll be long gone by then."

"They sure are ticked. You think they would have killed me?"

"Oh, for sure. Maybe not right away. They wanted to make a spectacle out of you first. But, someone would have cracked. Someone would have wanted to be the one at the end of your Wikipedia page—in the death or assassination section."

"You sure are a great comfort, Gabe."

"It's a pleasure," he said.

They entered a new section of tunnel where the ceiling got lower. Gordillo's height presented no problem, but Connolly had to stoop in order to fit.

"Watch your head," Gabe told them as they turned a corner and sensed the floor sloping downwards beneath them.

The corridor's height continued to grow shorter, forcing Connolly to shuffle his feet as they walked. Extreme heat wafted down the passage from an opening in front of them. Once they reached the doorway, the source of warmth stood directly before them. Nearly filling a room two stories tall, an enormous iron vessel glowed red, its gas-powered flames boiling water, sending pressurized steam into the hundreds of pipes that forked away from it.

A metal walkway led around the opening, its flimsy railing scalding hot.

"Yeah, I meant to tell you don't touch that," Gabe said as a struggling Gordillo recoiled in pain after grabbing hold of it.

"Holy hell," Gordillo said as he inched his way around the boiler, his red robes beginning to show discoloration as sweat poured off his body, soaking through the thick garments. "Does it get any hotter than this?"

Gabe gestured into another passage on the other side of the walkway. "Ladies first. Watch the pipes."

Reluctantly, Gordillo followed Connolly into the passageway, wiping sweat from his head with the sleeve of his robe. Slowly, he began to crawl forward, his immense form undulating as it vibrated along the ground.

"Dear God, how much farther?" he asked, his voice weakened with effort.

"Almost there," Gabe answered.

A draft of cooler air passed over their face as they neared the end. Gordillo reached through the opening as several men picked him up by his robes and lowered him to the floor, his chest expanding and contracting violently.

"Thank God," Gordillo said, struggling to speak. "I could have died in there."

Gabe opened his mouth wide, trying to get more air into his lungs. "Where's Dr. Connolly?"

"I'm here," Connolly said, his face—like everyone else—covered in sweat, his suit nearly ruined.

"We need to get moving. He's waiting on us."

"I'm ready."

Gabe motioned for one of his men. "Take Dr. Connolly up to the room. Stairs might be faster."

"What are you going to do?"

"I'm going to take the Cardinal up the elevator."

"Elevators are out."

"Not the freight elevator," Gabe said, as Gordillo still gasped for breath. "There's no way we'll make it up the stairs. You all go on. We'll be there in a moment."

"Thank you for saving us," Connolly said. "I realize you were trying to help."

"Go on. we'll be there in a minute. They know where to go."

Connolly and the other men left the room towards a large set of stairs that ran upward into the ceiling.

"How far's the elevator?" Gordillo asked.

"Not far."

"Just give me a second, and I'll be alright."

Gordillo straightened his body, resting his hands on his knees for balance as what little fluid remained in his body drained from his head. "Let's get on with it," Gordillo said. "Where is the elevator?"

Gabe scrambled up a flight of stairs and opened a metal door into a large carpeted hallway.

"The hotel?" Gordillo asked as he stepped out of the stairwell. "How did we get here?"

"Secret," Gabe said, holding his finger to his lips. "Elevator's that way."

They continued down the hallway past a few double doors, then turned left down another corridor and walked through a large commercial kitchen. At the rear, a wide sliding door marked the presence of a freight elevator.

"Up, I'm guessing?" Gordillo asked as he pressed the only button available.

"Nowhere but up from here."

After a few moments, the elevator car arrived and the door slid open. Gordillo grabbed a towel from a rolling cart that sat nearby and began to wipe his head.

"What floor?" he asked.

"Thirteenth."

Gordillo pressed the button, and the door closed shut.

"Where I come from," he said, "buildings don't have thirteenth floors."

"Used to be the same here. I think everyone got tired of the superstition."

Gordillo held his towel by the corner and spun it around in a circle. "You're not taking me to the same floor as the others, are you?"

Gabe shifted uncomfortably. "Why do you ask?"

Gordillo grasped both ends of the towel in each hand. "I don't know. Superstition can be a good thing, sometimes."

CHAPTER 50

"Where are we going?" Garcia asked.

"Hospital," Brinkley said.

"Thanks, but I can patch myself up," Finch said.

"Not for you—for me. I think I cracked a rib."

"We can't go there. They'll have that place staked out for us by now."

"For *us*?" Garcia asked. "We're not criminals like you, Finch."

"You are now."

Brinkley realized he was right. It had happened so fast. Finch attacking Vickers in the back of the truck. Garcia speeding off around the mountain drive. Something about Yuval and the men working with him turned his stomach. He couldn't explain why, but decades of working in law enforcement—in *obeying* the law—were thrown out the window in the split second he decided to help the world's most wanted man.

"This was *your* idea," Garcia said. "I'm not a part of this."

The sheriff raised his hand in apology. "I know—this *was* my idea. Why don't you drop us off at my house."

Despite his fears, Garcia seemed reluctant to abandon their captive.

"And then what?" he asked.

"Still working on it."

Again, Brinkley tried to parse the morning's events. A typical day might include a few traffic stops or assisting fire and rescue after a car crash. This particular day included the grisly scene in the young girl's bedroom and a mass shooter in the woods with multiple fatalities. Now he was essentially running from some paramilitary government force he couldn't even identify.

"Hey Finch—before those guys got here, they were asking me if I'd gotten the shot or not. Any idea why?"

"No clue," he said.

"We're probably the only two people within fifty miles of here that didn't get it."

Finch sighed deeply. "*You're* probably the only one."

Brinkley snapped his head around. "What?"

"I said you're probably the only one."

"What are you saying? Surely you didn't get it."

"Not willingly."

"But how?" Brinkley asked.

"In prison."

"They strapped you down and injected you against your will?"

Finch sensed his lips beginning to curl. "Something like that."

Garcia started to say something but thought silence the better option.

"Those sons of bitches," Brinkley said. "I would kill them if they did that to me."

"Well, I got *one* of them."

"Yeah, you did. Faucett was the worst of them all."

"But they got you back, I suppose."

"Yeah, they did."

"Is that why you keep checking your pulse and all that?"

"Yeah."

"Did it 'f' up your heart?"

"Yeah."

"What'd they do? I can't imagine the fight you must have put up."

Finch knew his heart was accelerating into a dangerous place. "Actually, I didn't fight at all. They drugged me somehow. Food, I'm guessing. I woke up on a gurney with them pulling a needle from my arm."

"I would have exploded on them."

"I wanted to. I could barely think straight I was so out of it."

"They give you just the one?"

"I don't think so. They did it again. It was either starve to death or...."

"They would have just done it anyway I suppose."

"Probably."

"And now you've got what? Myocarditis or something?"

"Yep," Finch said, his jaw clenched tight with rage. "Ticking time bomb."

"You got the clots, too?"

"I'm guessing. Couldn't bring myself to look."

"Jesus, Finch. I'm sorry, man. I had no idea."

"Yeah, it's not been fun."

"Why in the world would they have done it?"

"I don't know. The symbolism was probably important."

"World's number one anti-vaxxer triple-vaccinated?"

"Exactly."

Brinkley rubbed his eyes with his hands, trying to ease the stress building in his body. "Look, Finch. I know you've been through a lot. I think the world owes you a debt of gratitude. I really do. I wouldn't trust Naftali or his men with anything. They're bad news in my book. But, they're dangerous. They can probably get away with anything. For some reason, they're being careful with you. But me? They'd knock me off and have my case closed without a single suspect."

"Brinkley—you can just walk away. Both of you can just walk away. Tell them I escaped. Tell them I had you at gunpoint and made you do all those things back there."

"I'm not opposed," Garcia said.

Brinkley sat up. "I'm surprised you're not headed down to D.C. for the big event."

"You said that was tonight?"

"Yeah—my wife and her girlfriends drove down this morning to try and go."

They took her.

Natalie's last message to Finch flooded through his mind. He'd completely forgotten about it in their fight to escape.

They can heal her.

Suddenly, his heart filled with darkness—dread at what they might be set to do to his daughter.

Finch reached toward Brinkley. "Can your phone get the news up here?"

"Sometimes. Depends on where we are."

"Can I hold it?"

"Yeah. What do you want?"

"I want to check the news."

Brinkley tapped on his phone a few times. "Here, I'll pull it up for you. What are you looking for?"

"Just hand it to me."

Brinkley tapped the screen again. "Oh no," he said.

"What is it?"

"Um..."

"Just hand me the phone!"

"I...I think you should probably check your pulse first."

CHAPTER 51

Yuval was beaming. The crowd of firemen and police standing behind the row of media continued to grow. He had set the stage in such a way he felt Finch would have to show up. A reporter asked a question Yuval had already prepared an answer for.

"Thomas Finch has been on the run for days. He could be in another country by now. What makes you think he'll show up tonight?"

Yuval paused to give the impression he was carefully considering his response.

"I mentioned burying the hatchet. This is something I hope we can all take very seriously. The world is so divided right now. Those who are fans of Mr. Finch hate me with every fiber of their being. Those who believe in science and technology hate Mr. Finch and his followers with every fiber of *their* being. I wasn't going to mention this until the event tonight, but given the fact we've been unable to reach him, I feel I must make this announcement now.

"Dr. Connolly and I have worked out an arrangement with the appropriate authorities. If Finch will show up tonight, if he will participate in the event as I've suggested, he will be granted a full pardon. All charges against him will be dropped. He can return to his family and walk away a free man."

"How is that even legal? He's the most wanted man in the country."

"I want to thank Dr. Connolly for working tirelessly with the governor and the D.O.J. on executive clemency."

"Do you know where Dr. Connolly is? He's evidently been reported missing."

"I wasn't aware of that. I'm sure he's practicing for tonight—he has a very important role to play."

Another reporter stepped closer and spoke.

"Dr. Naftali? Rumors are circulating that someone was healed this morning. Has the technology already been demonstrated? And if so, what can you tell us about who it was?"

"Dr. Connolly and I had hoped that would remain a secret but given the miraculous nature of what we've been able to accomplish, you might expect that people would want to talk about it. Jesus had similar problems, if you could call them that."

"What was their condition?"

"ALS. Unable to walk or even speak."

Several of the reporters shook their heads in disbelief.

"And you were able to cure him this morning?"

"Well, let's just say he didn't leave in the wheelchair he arrived on. And I must interject here—actually, *I* wasn't able to heal him. It was the faith of those who prayed for him and the God they prayed to. I simply facilitated the exchange."

"How does it work? Can you say *anything* about that?"

"I'll explain it fully tonight."

Another reporter piped in. "Can't you just give us a little something? A tease?"

Yuval stroked the corners of his mouth while he contemplated what he might reveal at such an informal gathering.

"Faith is an interesting thing," he said. "Hundreds, maybe thousands of years ago, most everyone believed in miracles. According to the old accounts, miracles actually occurred. We read about their accounts in the Bible and other places. The focus of my research has been—what happened? If God is still interested in the plight of humanity, why do we no longer see miracles anymore? We still pray for our loved ones, do we not? Do we love them any less than our ancestors?

"Through years of study, I came to the realization that most people have lost their *belief.* They may *say* they have faith, but if you were somehow able to measure it, you would see it is nearly non-existent."

"Why is that?" a reporter asked.

"The jury is still out on that. Either the old stories were lies, or something has changed. People no longer believe. Their faith is weak. They may *feel* it is strong, but again, if you were able to measure it, they would see it is very weak. This is a big part of what we've been able to develop."

"A way to *measure* faith?"

Yuval felt he was beginning to reveal too much but couldn't stop himself.

"Yes," he said. "That's exactly what we have been perfecting. A way to measure your faith."

"How could measuring your faith increase it?"

"That is where I'm going to stop and save something interesting for this evening. You need to see it to believe it."

CHAPTER 52

Arvo Ikänen dreaded what they were about to do—not the process itself, but what the results might reveal. It was just a cobbled together lab in a two-room suite at the hotel, but regardless, properly-conducted science was often this way. A hypothesis was proposed. A set of experiments designed and conducted to prove—or disprove—whether the hypothesis appeared to be correct. Over time, a given hypothesis might gain credibility as additional research confirmed what it suggested might be true. Or, as it sometimes happened, the hypothesis would lose standing, relegated to the dustbin of history as experiments provided new data to disprove it.

For old school scientists, *truth* was always in short supply. A hypothesis might appear *more* true based on recent data, but there was always the chance new information would come along that made it *less* plausible. For someone like Arvo Ikänen, to call something *absolutely* true—beyond question or scrutiny—wasn't in his nature, a maddening trait for those who interviewed him, their modern obsession with binary answers never satisfied in the muddled responses he often provided. But, his insistence on interpreting the plausibility of a hypothesis in light of the corpus of data available—regardless of media pressure or the risk of losing funding—was something he felt necessary to the rigorous pursuit of truth.

As Ikänen and his partner began a complex set of experiments, there was a foreboding sense of what they might find. Typically, the confirmation of a hypothesis might bring great joy. What they were working on promised something much different—a very personal sense of terror and fear.

Each scientist had a particular job to do, their roles clearly defined weeks before the conference. They set about their work in near silence, readying the equipment and prepping the samples as if they'd done it a thousand times before.

Ikänen stepped out onto the balcony and returned holding a cage filled with several birds, their chirping, the unmistakable song of red cardinals.

"Good luck, Stobnicki," he said, holding the cage for the other scientist to see. For many, the sighting of the bright red plumage of the Northern cardinal was considered a sign that good fortune was imminent. For the scientists in the room, the irony of the morbid joke was not lost on them. Both of them had received multiple doses of the malkavirus shots, and the gravity of the experiment weighed heavily upon them all. They knew if they were proven right, they—and hundreds of millions of others—would need more than just luck.

In the months leading up to their meeting, some of the scientists confirmed the presence of something odd in the vaccines. Each tested a different manufacturer's product. Each found the same tell-tale markers. Despite the various manufacturing techniques each company employed, they all contained a sequence that appeared to have nothing to do with malkavirus at all.

Initially, they were loathe to accept the possibility Thomas Finch was right. He'd proposed the concept in a few of his shows, discussing the *Bootstrap* project as if its reality were beyond question, a nonchalance many of them found off-putting. Out of curiosity, Dr. Arvo Ikänen pursued the idea. After discovering the existence of something that fit Finch's description, he passed word along to his colleagues within the secret group—a request that they might attempt to substantiate his claims.

All of them were successful. No matter the maker, no matter the date on their manufacture, they all contained the markers of what Finch had described. It was confirmation of the grandest conspiracy theory ever attempted—nearly the entire world, injected with a technology that might allow others to manipulate their immune systems in ways that defied belief.

"*This* was the reason for malkavirus," Finch repeated over and over in the last video he ever made. "*This* was why they pushed so hard. They had to get everyone afraid enough to take the vaccine, sight unseen. Because it contained *this*—the last injection they'll ever need to give you."

That last line—*the last injection they'll ever need to give you*—caused many of Finch's most devoted followers to abandon him. For them, pharmaceutical companies didn't want cures, they wanted lifetime customers. To suggest that they would willingly create something that would lessen their profit margins was ludicrous. Pharmaceutical companies wanted *more* vaccines, not *less* of them.

Finch tried to preempt the pushback he knew would come from his fans. "You think they're about nothing but money. Money is important, but it's not the only thing. The most powerful people in the world don't need more money—they have enough of it. They want prestige. They want immortality. They want to live beyond the seventy or eighty-years they get on earth by influencing humanity in a way God apparently can not."

In an uncharacteristic move, Finch brought his infant daughter on camera, holding the baby in his arms for the world to see before he signed off. "If you value anything in this world, the future of humanity is at stake here. You are giving control of your body to an unnamed, unelected, unaccountable group of people who will not hesitate to destroy you in the name of *health* or *progress*. If you haven't gotten the shot yet, I *beg* you—don't get it. We need as many as we can if we, as a species, are going to survive this."

It was an over-the-top, melodramatic call to action nearly everyone ignored, the last time Finch was seen on camera. In the time that had elapsed, the existence of *something* all the vaccines contained had been proven. *What* it actually was, had not.

Like many of the other men in the room, Ikänen was initially a skeptic. He didn't doubt the ethical and regulatory lapses required to pull such a thing off but, instead, was more dubious about how such a thing could be guided or controlled after the fact—an uncertainty someone posing as Finch tried to address.

Despite being held in maximum-security prison, several short messages were smuggled out, communications supposedly authored by Finch himself.

It's the viruses. That's how they're going to do it, one such message read.

You know I think masks are dumb, another note read. *If you got the shot, you might think about wearing something to protect you from infection. Sorry I don't have better news.*

The immune system controls everything, his final note read. *It's the key to everything else in your body. If they take over that, they own you.*

It was these few messages from Finch that most troubled the scientists gathered on the twelfth floor of the hotel. The realization that everyone who took the vaccine might now be controlled in some way was devastating—something they hadn't fully come to terms with yet. The possibility this thing could be manipulated remotely through specially-made viruses was something they could barely comprehend.

Ikänen placed the cage on the table in the middle of the room. After putting on latex gloves, he pulled each bird out, placed it in its own glass container, and addressed the man standing beside him.

"Stobnicki, for a bit of decorum, I want to quickly summarize what is about to happen. As you already know, four of these animals have been given one of the malkavirus shots—we've confirmed it through blood analysis. Two of them have not. They will serve as our placebo. None of us know which ones they are—unless you've somehow identified some unique markings on them I cannot see. In which case, more power to you."

Stobnicki laughed uncomfortably, happy to break the dark moment.

"We've developed two viruses to see if we can engage the Bootstrap sequence in these animals. If it works, one of them may suppress the dopamine receptors in these birds. The other virus may activate adrenaline production. I want to emphasize *may* here. We're obviously not exactly sure how this works and are flying blind."

Again, Stobnicki broke out into muted laughs.

"Based on the efficacy of the vaccine itself—the amount of self-amplification that has taken place—the effects may take longer. Given the less-than-ideal conditions we're working within, the results of this experiment should not be considered valid. Not *too* valid, at least."

Stobnicki spoke. "What do you think will happen?"

"If it works, we don't know. If it doesn't work, we think nothing will happen. If it *does* work, we might expect to see signs of suppressed dopamine production or heightened agitation or anxiety. That's probably the best guess we have for now."

"Are these all the birds?"

"These are all of them."

"Shouldn't we save some for another test?"

"We *should*... but we don't have enough time. We need to know if this is real. We may need to warn people accordingly if it is."

"There's only a few hours left. How long might we do observations for?"

"As long as we can," Ikänen said. "Until five if necessary."

Stobnicki connected tubes to the top of each container and tightened the lids they were attached to. Another scientist placed a video camera along the row of glasses and started recording.

Ikänen took a deep breath and shook his head. "Okay, go ahead and flood the containers."

Stobnicki twisted a valve on each of the six containers and pulled a large mask over his face.

"Now we wait," Ikänen said, half-smiling.

"Don't you want to put on a mask?" Stobnicki asked.

"If we need the masks, we're as good as dead anyway."

Two of the birds continued to chirp, their song barely audible through the glass containers.

"How long before we might see anything?" Stobnicki asked.

The fourth bird began fluttering around the glass, unsettled by something.

"Who knows?" Ikänen replied. "Their metabolism is accelerated compared to ours. No idea how that might affect their immune response. I'm guessing twenty minutes minimum. Probably more like an hour."

Stobnicki adjusted the camera and stepped back as the fourth bird continued to flutter around within his container. "You think that's anything of note?"

Ikänen bent down to take a closer look. "Possibly, though this one is more concerning."

He pointed to the third bird who appeared to be leaning against the glass.

"I'm not familiar with bird behavior, but I don't think that's normal."

"Me neither," Stobnicki replied.

"I suppose if I shake the glass it will invalidate our results?"

"Yeah, don't do that. We'd have to shake them all equally. And I don't want those hoses coming off."

"Shouldn't we close the valves now, just in case?" Ikänen asked.

"Probably."

The first bird began to flutter around his container, just like the fourth. The scientists began to step back.

"Okay," Ikänen said. "I'm guessing one and four got the same thing. Possibly the adrenaline virus by the looks of it. Agreed?"

Stobnicki took a closer look. "Too early to say, but they are exhibiting the same distressed behavior."

Ikänen breathed in deeply. "Let's close the valves."

"Why don't you put on a mask?"

"I will. But, just in case, let's close the valves."

Stobnicki reached on top of the containers and closed the valves in the same order he opened them. A rhythmic clinking filled the room as the fourth bird began flying directly into the glass container.

"He's trying to get out," Stobnicki said.

Ikänen walked to a nearby counter and pulled a respirator mask over his face. Another series of pings overlapped the first as the first bird began crashing into the glass.

"He's doing it, too," Stobnicki said.

Ikänen returned to the table and held his face directly beside the glass. "It's definitely odd. Seems too soon to be related, but they're both doing it. Maybe they're both distressed?"

Like one of the other cardinals, the bird in the sixth jar was completely inactive.

"Asleep?" Ikänen asked as he pointed at the sixth. "Are these our dopamine birds?"

The fourth bird began to fly wildly inside his container, hitting the sides so violently it began to move.

"Okay," Stobnicki said. "This is not good. We're going to have to stabilize these containers somehow."

"No. Leave them alone."

"They might fall over."

"Leave them alone," Ikänen repeated.

The first jar began to move as well as the bird inside began ramming its beak into the sides.

"If they fall off, the tubes will come undone."

"You closed the valves. We have on respirators."

"But the jars contain the virus as well."

"Leave them alone," Ikänen shouted.

Stobnicki backed up from the table. The bird in the third container was now lying sideways, its curled feet locked in the air beside it. The two birds in the second and fifth containers remained apparently unaffected by the proceedings.

Ikänen pointed towards the balcony. "Close that door. We don't want anything getting out."

Someone knocked hard on the door to their room.

"Who is that?" Ikänen asked. "See who it is."

The fourth jar inched closer to the counter as the bird continued pinging around inside.

"This is not good," Stobnicki said. "End this now, Ikänen. We can all see what's going on."

"No. We finish the observations."

Ikänen bent closer to the sixth container to inspect the red cardinal inside. Like the other, it was lying on its side with clenched feet held in the air.

The person at the door pounded again, this time five separate knocks.

"It's one of ours," Ikänen said. "Who could it be?"

The fourth container rolled off the table, hanging from the edge by its tube. The bird smashed into the side, rocking the glass just hard enough it detached from the tube and smashed onto the floor. Shocks of red streaked around the room as the bird escaped from its container and collided into mirrors and windows.

Stobnicki grabbed the first jar to prevent it from also falling over. The escaped bird continued to dart throughout the room as they covered their heads to prevent more attacks. The cardinal plowed into Stobnicki's hand, sending waves of pain as its beak pierced his skin to the bone. Flinching in self-defense, Stobnicki sent the container flying across the table, shattering it into pieces against the refrigerator.

Now two red cardinals bolted throughout the room, looking for an escape.

"Open the balcony door!" Stobnicki shouted.

"We can't let this out. We have to kill them."

"They're going to kill us first!"

One of the birds smashed into another jar, sending it crashing to the floor. Crawling along the ground, Stobnicki moved toward the balcony. Ikänen leapt onto his body in an attempt to stop him.

"We can't do this," Ikänen told the younger scientist.

"It's too late," Stobnicki said. "The birds aren't the problem. It's the viruses."

Stobnicki flung the sliding glass door open and crawled out onto the balcony. Seconds later, Ikänen threw the curtain across the opening as both cardinals streaked towards the outside, trapping the birds within the folds of fabric. He ripped the top of the curtain off its rod and began stomping his feet until the fluttering movement beneath the cloth stopped.

Ikänen leaned against the balcony wall and breathed deeply, trying to catch his breath. Chants from the protests taking place on the streets below floated up around them.

"What the hell are you thinking, Stobnicki? You know we can't let those escape."

"They were going to kill us," Stobnicki said.

"So what if they kill us? You know what could happen if they got out."

Someone thumped the door again—five separate strikes.

Two birds, likely the unvaccinated ones, remained in their jars, apparently unaffected. The other four were dead. The realization of what they had just witnessed began to fill Ikänen with dread. Months earlier, they had confirmed all the malkavirus shots contained something unusual—a shocking enough discovery, by itself. They had just discovered something much worse—the Bootstrap sequence could be activated through a virus. It didn't take standing in lines or million-dollar advertising campaigns. One of them could smear it on a New York subway handle and eventually the entire world could be affected.

Finch was right. The malkavirus shots were the last injection they would ever need to give.

"For God's sake, who is that at the door?" Ikänen asked.

Stobnicki tiptoed around the broken glass and looked through the peephole. Standing in the hallway was a filthy-looking group of men. In their midst stood the disheveled, sweating, unmistakable six-and-a-half-foot frame of Dr. Albert Connolly.

CHAPTER 53

Natalie again tried to reach her father on his phone. There was no answer but, instead, a message that his voicemail was full—a clear indication others had also been trying to reach him.

Something's wrong, she thought.

Her father was reliable, a trait he'd taken great care in passing on to her. It had been a couple of hours now, and she'd neither seen or heard from him, despite her many attempts to get in touch. Again, she considered calling 911, but stopped herself short. The local police would shut down the moment she mentioned Naftali or the World Health Alliance. They knew the rules. They knew when they were overstepping the unspoken boundaries that governed international politics.

Natalie's head ached with indecision. There were few options—none of which offered her any meaningful chance of getting help. Wracked with anxiety, she walked to the library, the sole source of comfort she could think of, and collapsed into the leather chair within one of the reading nooks.

Lying on the table was the *Metamorphosis* book she had discussed with Yuval.

His research is here, she thought.

Yuval had always disturbed her. For most of her life, he was *Dr. Naftali*, the temperamental research partner her father nearly worshiped. More recently, he had insisted she call him by his first name—his awkward attempt at flirting. Finch was an easy sell. In many ways, he was everything her father hated. Daring. Reckless. Unable to compromise on anything. A loner who was faithful to no one but a select few. His ability to forge and maintain alliances, non-existent.

Yuval did not even register as a potential mate. Any thought of a relationship with him instantly repulsed her. Months after the wreck, she could begin to sense her father's desire.

"Dr. Naftali is in town this week," he mentioned to her one morning at the breakfast table. "I don't believe he has anything going on Thursday if you two wanted to get some dinner."

For Connolly, her marriage to Finch was inconvenient. Embarrassing. A public relations disaster since the beginning. A constant strain on the relationships he had so carefully manicured. With Finch in jail for the rest of his life, Natalie's father sensed a possible opening—a political alliance through an entirely different marriage—that might amend a thousand wrongs.

"No," she told her father.

"It would make things so much easier—for all of us."

"Not a chance. Never."

"Natalie, you'll never see Tom again. Eva will never see him again. He will die in prison."

Like so many other times, Natalie's temper exploded whenever she felt someone trying to steal the anger towards Finch she—and she alone—deserved.

"Don't try to manage my personal affairs," she snapped at her father as she stormed out of the kitchen.

It wasn't the last time he would try. Over the next few months, Connolly was relentless as he attempted to discuss divorce and custodial matters with her—always followed with hints that Yuval was interested in spending time with her.

"Dad, I appreciate the respect you have for Dr. Naftali."

"Yuval," he said, a correction Connolly had attempted before.

"Dr. Naftali nauseates me. There is nothing there. There will never be anything there. I don't care if Tom dies in prison a thousand times over—I will die alone and miserable before I eat a single meal alone with that man."

With her daughter taken from her, Natalie felt her intuition about Yuval to have been proven correct. She stood up and looked at the books that lined the shelves behind her—groupings of works organized by subject rather than author.

Somewhere in here are his thoughts.

Natalie moved from the historical section and into a grouping of books that appeared to be related to biology and nature. Within each category, the works were alphabetized by author. She ran her thumb down row after row until she came to the *N*s. To her surprise, there was a folder with Yuval listed as the author. Inside was a short scientific paper documenting some research he had done many years earlier.

Memory of the Soul: Do Butterflies Remember Their Lives As Caterpillars?

Natalie pulled the pages from the folder and read through the abstract summarizing his research and its findings.

Caterpillars undergo a remarkable transformation during their metamorphosis into moths and butterflies. Within the cocoon that protects them, they digest themselves with enzymes into a primordial soup—a nearly primitive state as they begin their journey into a new life as a butterfly. In this experiment, we seek to understand whether the butterfly stage of their life retain any memory of their lives as caterpillars.

The metamorphosis of caterpillars had always been one of Natalie's favorite miracles of nature, an incredible example of evolution occurring in real-time, something she had eagerly explained to Eva during the nature walks they frequently took. The question of their consciousness—before and after that metamorphosis—was something she'd never considered. With such a dramatic transformation, were they the same creature as before, albeit with a new body?

Like seemingly everything related to Yuval, the research had a disturbing quality to it. The thought of dissolving one's self with enzymes into a biological soup was odd. The notion that what emerged after might somehow be a different creature altogether upset Natalie in a way she couldn't quite explain. Science was driven by a natural curiosity, but there were, perhaps, some questions best left unanswered. Best left unasked, even.

A strange sound echoed down the hallway outside the library, something far enough away Natalie couldn't identify it. She peeked through the window at the lengthening shadows growing behind each tree outside but saw nothing else. Old houses always made sounds with changes in wind or humidity. A conversation almost, a protest against growing old.

Despite her aversion, she continued to read through the paper, curious if caterpillars did, indeed, retain any recollections of their previous lives.

To make this determination, we will teach the caterpillars aversion to a particular odor. We will expose them to the target smell and administer electrical shocks to their bodies. Eventually, they will associate such smells with pain.

Pain, Natalie thought to herself. *Of course he would use pain.*

She wasn't opposed to using animals in scientific experiments—she knew that progress was nearly impossible without sacrifice somewhere along the way. Why caterpillars, of all things, would bother her—insects with minimal sensitivities or emotions—she wasn't sure. The thought of purposefully shocking those tiny creatures every time they were exposed to a certain smell bothered her. After some consideration, she realized it was the man conducting the experiment. If it had been anyone else, she may have felt differently. But, with Yuval at the controls, with him pressing the button—that made her nauseous.

Another noise startled Natalie. This time it was closer—and definitely not outside. She tried to calm herself but, given the events of the day, found her heart racing uncontrollably. Her knees trembled with fear as she stumbled to the back of the library within a reading nook not visible from the door.

Did they remember? Natalie asked herself as she poured through the paper, trying to find the results. It seemed impossible given the way in which a caterpillar's entire being dissolved so completely.

Upon completion of their metamorphoses, we exposed the butterflies to the odor to measure their reaction. The control group (those not trained with electrical shock) did not respond to the smell in any perceivable way. Amongst the eight butterflies trained with the electrical shock, seven of them (.875%) attempted to escape their restraints when exposed to the particular odor. This leads us to conclude that despite their miraculous transformation, moths appear to retain at least some portion of their memories.

Further study is needed to understand how these memories are retained and why one of them (.125%) apparently did not. The results do raise interesting metaphysical questions. Is there a store of memory that exists outside the physical space of this world? Might this be evidence of the soul, long assumed to be a spiritual dimension of humans alone?

Again, the questions bothered Natalie. They were something akin to a scientific version of the *Ouija* board game she'd been forbidden from playing as a child. At a sleepover late one night, a group of her girlfriends lightly rested their fingers on a glass monocle that would slide around a board of letters and numbers, highlighting a character one by one and, in so doing, spell out answers to questions the group had asked. What had started out as playful interrogations regarding boys and crushes turned serious.

"Is there a spirit here with us in this room?" a friend had asked.

The monocle drifted over the numbers and towards the end of the alphabet.

Y.E.S.

A chill filled the room as Natalie and her friends looked at each other, regretting the eeriness of the dim candlelight they had staged for maximum effect.

"Are you an evil spirit?" Natalie asked, a question she immediately regretted.

Still resting on the *S*, they were relived to watch the monocle float toward the beginning of the alphabet. It circled around, past the numbers towards the middle of the board. Chills ran down their spines as the monocle passed directly over the *N* and didn't stop until it again rested on the *Y*, an event which sent them all screaming to her parents' bedroom.

Despite the parlor-trick of the game, it was still a question she'd regretted asking. Over twenty years later and she continued to be haunted by seeing the monocle hover past the *N* and land on the *Y*. In the time since, her faith in the good had constantly wavered. Unfortunately, her faith in what might be evil had not.

* * *

From reading the paper, her revulsion for Yuval blossomed beyond what she thought possible. The fact he had taken her daughter in order to offer her up before the world in what amounted to some bizarre ritual made her feel even more sick.

I have to get to the cathedral, she thought. *Finch might not be able to stop him.*

Natalie put the papers down on a small table and stood up, testing the strength of her legs. Still shaking, she resolved to walk to the kitchen where her purse and car keys were. Every step through the library seemed to resonate in a way she'd never noticed before, cutting through what had become an unbearable silence.

Beyond the library was a long hallway that turned halfway into the center of the house where the kitchen was. Despite its cavernous dimensions, the library's numerous nooks and crannies offered her a sense of safety. The rest of the house would not.

Natalie stepped from the library into the hall and felt her resolve waver.

I can't do this alone.

She cursed the terror that kept her frozen. A shadow passed over the bend in the hallway, and Natalie crumpled to the ground in fear.

Someone was in the house with her.

CHAPTER 54

Finch felt like he could explode as he read the headline again.

NIH HEAD CONNOLLY'S GRANDDAUGHTER TO REPLACE MONGCHAI AS STAR OF HEALTH SUMMIT.

"Give me that," Brinkley said as he snatched his phone from Finch.

"What's this mean?" Finch asked. "Who's Mongchai?"

"That Asian kid who saved all the other kids."

"Never heard of him."

"A bunch of them were trapped in an underground cave. He tried to swim his way out and nearly drowned. He's alive, but barely. All the other kids are fine."

"Why are they replacing him?"

"That, I don't know."

Garcia interjected. "Read the article—it'll probably say."

Brinkley scanned through article, mumbling the words as he skimmed over the text.

"Oh. He died this morning. In a fire or something. He was supposed to be the star of the show tonight."

Finch shook his head in confusion. "What did you say was going on tonight?"

"They're calling it a Health Summit or something like that. They've had stuff going on all week. Everyone who's anyone is in D.C. I think tonight is supposed to be the grand finale."

Something about his implausible escape triggered a thought in Finch's mind. "You said something about healing?"

"Yeah, supposedly they have some new technology that can heal people."

"Sounds bogus to me," Garcia said.

"*Now* you're a skeptic?" Brinkley asked. "You believe anything else they say *except* this?"

"Sounds impossible. Call me crazy."

Finch cut back in. "And they were going to have this boy there to try and heal him?"

"Well that's what everybody was thinking. They wouldn't quite say exactly what was going to happen. Trying to build up some mystery or suspense I guess.

But, yes, supposedly they were going to heal him in some way from his injuries."

"And what were they?"

"I don't know. He basically drowned. He was kind of in a coma. Couldn't move. Couldn't talk. Just a vegetable, really."

"No way they can fix that," Garcia said. "At that point, he's a goner."

Garcia's assessment struck a nerve with Finch.

"You never know," Finch said. "Kids are resilient. They can come back from all kinds of stuff."

"Not something like that."

"Don't say that. You don't know what it's like to have a kid in such bad shape."

"I've never tried to kill my kids, either."

Finch leapt towards Garcia and wrapped his arms around his throat, crushing his windpipe. With surprising agility, the deputy spun around and sent his elbow flying into the side of Finch's face. Brinkley grabbed for the steering wheel, but the truck swerved off the road, skidding into the grass bank that lined its side.

"Let him go!" Brinkley screamed as he grabbed Finch's throat with his powerful hand and squeezed hard.

Finch pulled Brinkley's hand away and spat up blood as Garcia stepped out of the truck, doubled over in pain.

"Stop it!" Brinkley said. "Both of you. We got enough problems as it is."

Garcia and Finch breathed deeply as they tried to catch their breath.

"What the hell's gotten into you, Garcia? I expect as much from Finch. But not you."

Brinkley rubbed his head and looked behind them to see if they'd stopped any traffic from passing. "Both of you, just relax for a minute. I need to figure out what we do next."

* * *

With the headlights off, Finch pulled out of the parking garage, the distinctive silhouette of Faucett's Bentley rolling in front of him. Living in a hotel had its advantages, but even for Finch, the loneliness could be overwhelming. And so, he would sometimes follow Natalie and Eva, watching them from afar, imagining what life might have been like had he been able to accept the lies most others held to be true.

An invitation to Faucett's retirement party had never been offered, unsurprising given the fact he and Natalie had separated, their relationship fractured. Weeks earlier, Finch had followed her home from a clinic, the tell-tale sticker on her arm, the puffy eyes and colorful band-aid on Eva's thigh, clear indicators as to what had happened.

The MALKA shots, still in clinical trials, were an unspoken red line, a threshold from which both Finch and Natalie knew—once crossed—they wouldn't return. With their marriage already struggling, the sight of his wife and daughter getting out of their car with band-aids on their limbs sent Finch over the edge. His public-facing antagonism towards Connolly and Faucett became unchecked, his unsurpassed rage clearly visible in his videos.

As he followed Faucett's car out of the downtown area and onto the interstate, Finch grew concerned with the way in which it would occasionally cross the lane markers, the driver clearly distracted. He pulled beside them, just behind their eye line and could make out the soft curve of the driver's arms.

Natalie, he thought. *Why's she driving?*

Faucett's car began to speed up and crossed into the rumble strips that lined the right shoulder before overcorrecting hard to the left, scraping against Finch's vehicle.

She's drunk, he thought as he slammed the brakes to put more distance between them.

Natalie continued to accelerate forward, unable to stay within her lane. Finch smashed the gas pedal, intent upon getting in front of her and slowing her down. After flying safely beyond her car, his eyes locked on the rear-view mirror. In horror, he saw Natalie veer from the road far behind him as her headlights bounced wildly up and down before disappearing into the darkness of the night.

Finch slammed on the brakes, skidding to a stop in the middle of a bridge he'd just crossed. He raced out of his vehicle and peered over the side, fearing the worst. A hundred feet beneath him, tangled within trees just before the water's edge, sat the crumpled wreckage of Faucett's car, one headlight still shining diagonally up into the sky.

CHAPTER 55

Arvo Ikänen opened the door and stepped out of the room towards a stunned Albert Connolly, waiting in the hallway.

"Dr. Connolly," Ikänen said, staring at the director's rumpled appearance. "I wasn't expecting you here."

"I wasn't expecting you either," Connolly said, his voice a cracked whisper.

"I was going to come meet you. Why are you here?"

"We were being chased. I didn't know you had your own mercenaries."

"Desperate times.

"Do you have water?" Connolly asked.

Ikänen looked over the men that surrounded him. "Where is Gabriel?"

"With the Cardinal," one of them replied. "They're coming up the service elevator."

"Could we please have some water?" Connolly asked again.

Ikänen opened the door and asked someone inside to bring them something. After a few moments, Stobnicki handed him a large beaker, brimming with clear liquid.

"I'll assume this is water?" Connolly asked.

"Yes, of course. I'm not here to poison anyone."

Connolly downed half of the beaker's contents. He offered the remainder to the men beside him, but they refused.

"Can we go inside and sit down?" Connolly asked.

Ikänen moved in front of the door. "No, we cannot at the moment. People are changing clothes and what not."

"Who's in there?"

"Just a few others. Getting ready for tonight. Very excited of course."

"Dr. Ikänen..." Connolly started to ask.

"Arvo is fine."

"I'll stick with Dr. Ikänen. I appreciate you rescuing me and Cardinal Gordillo from the protestors, but I must ask, what's going on? Why do you have armed men working for you? What are you hiding in this room?"

"I'm not at liberty to discuss these things."

"Not at liberty to discuss them with *me*? Or anyone?"

Ikänen continued to look concerned. "Could someone go find Gabriel and the Cardinal?"

One of the men left the group and jogged down the hallway.

"The rest of you—could you give the doctor and me some privacy?"

Ikänen pointed towards the center of the building where the main elevators sat locked in place. "Just around the corner there will be fine."

He waited for the men to be well clear of them before he continued to speak. "Dr. Connolly, you know that you and I have had some differences over the years."

"Yes, I know."

"You're probably aware I'm part of a consortium of scientists and doctors that have been labeled terrorists and other vile things."

"I'm aware."

"Do you agree with those labels?"

Connolly tried to ferret out where he was going. "Keep talking. I'll let you know once you're finished."

Ikänen attempted to force a smile. "You're familiar with the Bootstrap project?"

Connolly sighed with annoyance. "I am. I'm led to believe you and your group have been obsessed with it."

Ikänen laughed, this time accompanied by a genuine smile. "Obsessed? I suppose you might call it that, although *extremely concerned about the future of our species* is probably a better way of putting it."

"Finch really got you guys spooked, didn't he?"

"Why are you so cavalier about this? We've proven every mRNA vaccine has it. That's billions of people that could be manipulated by a rogue actor."

Connolly continued to give the man speaking to him a glassy stare.

"Why does this not concern you?" Ikänen asked again, this time with anger. "This was on your watch. Billions of lives are at stake."

"No one knows how to activate it, Dr. Ikänen. It died with Faucett. Not even Yuval's figured it out."

"Who told you that? Yuval?"

Connolly thought back to years ago when conversations regarding the technology first surfaced.

"How do we keep it secure?" Connolly had asked the task force that had met to discuss its possibilities.

"It will be triple-key protected," Faucett assured him. "The sequence would be impossible to activate without all three parties participating."

"And who might they be?"

"Well, we would be one of them."

"The National Institutes of Health?" Connolly asked. "Or *we*, meaning members of the task force here in this room?"

"Probably just us here in the room."

"And what's the chain of command here? How do *we* guard the secret? How do *we* decide when to authorize its use? How do we pass it on to those who come after us?"

Faucett flapped his hand in the air as if he were shooing away an annoying fly. "We can figure those things out later. This is a high-level discussion right now."

It wasn't the first time Connolly's concerns were brushed aside by Faucett.

"And who are the other two parties?"

"The World Health Alliance would be the second."

Connolly's anxiety continued to rise. "Our goals are nearly always in alignment. That seems dangerous to me."

"That's why the Church would get the third."

"The Church? Who represents the Church? The Catholic Church? The Pope?"

"No," Faucett replied. "Don't be silly. They have too much power already. We don't need to give them more."

"Then who?"

"That would be a secret. Several high-ranking members of different church organizations would be given a key—most of them fake, one of them genuine. No one would know who else had one. And no one would know if they had the real key or not."

"Like the executioner's fake bullet?" Connolly asked.

Executions were often staged with multiple shooters, one of whom received a dummy round that sounded and felt like the real thing. As all shooters fired simultaneously, every one of them could at least imagine they may have been the one with the fake bullet, free from the guilt of having contributed to the condemned person's death.

"Yes," Faucett replied. "Something like that. They would be instructed that no one give up their key unless they could all agree to do it. That way, no one would ever know whether they had the actual key or not."

Connolly was unconvinced. "And no one would be riddled with guilt if something went very wrong."

"That's not the point here."

"It's the reality, though."

"Albert—it would take the cooperation of all three parties to be able to activate the Bootstrap sequence. And within one of those parties—the Church—it would take additional layers of cooperation for them to produce their key."

Discussion of the Bootstrap project had fallen off his radar as health officials grew concerned with a novel malkavirus charging across the globe. After Faucett's death, as Connolly realized the Bootstrap project had been activated without his knowledge, he assumed the keys were distributed safely.

* * *

"Faucett had the NIH key," Connolly said to Ikänen. "No one has been able to find it."

"You're sure of that?"

"I've asked everyone. I have his personal laptop and had someone from the NSA scan it. The key is nowhere. All of us may have the Bootstrap sequence inside us, but without that key, it's useless."

"I'm afraid you're far too optimistic, Dr. Connolly."

"The Bootstrap project died with Faucett, Dr. Ikänen. Finch killed it, and he doesn't even know it. He's more of a hero than they even realize."

Ikänen considered what Connolly had told him, trying to decide whether to reveal the experiment he had just witnessed.

"You know that Faucett and Yuval were working closely together, correct?"

"I do now. I didn't realize it at the time."

"And you don't think it's possible that Faucett shared his key with Yuval?"

"I can't imagine he would have been that reckless. Even if he was, they'd still need the third key."

A fire door opened from the end of the hallway as one of Ikänen's men ran towards them.

"Where are they?" Ikänen asked. "Did you find them?"

"The Cardinal is gone. Gabriel was in the elevator. He's dead."

CHAPTER 56

Covered in dust, Cardinal Gordillo descended the stairs and tapped a message into his phone.

On my way. Package ready?

He stopped at the second floor and exited the stairwell onto the enormous mezzanine that adjoined the convention center halls. On the opposite end, a large glass-covered walkway spanning the streets below connected the hotel to another building filled with shops and restaurants.

With no signs of security, hooligans ran through the wide-open space, in search of anything they might destroy. Gordillo adjusted the black robe, covering his vestments to minimize the distraction their bright red colors might create.

The Cardinal glanced at a response that appeared on his phone.

Ready.

He reached the other end of the mezzanine and crossed the walkway to the other building. An expanding metal gate was stretched across to block access but lay in ruins on the ground. Gordillo stepped over the debris and rounded a corner onto the upper balcony of shops that lined the retail center.

Some of the stores' security gates still stood closed, but most had been ripped from their anchors. After passing by a demolished shoe outlet, Gordillo stopped at a large bookstore, its security gate apparently untouched.

I'm here, he typed into his phone.

Someone walked from the back and raised the barrier that extended from floor to ceiling across the doorway.

"Where is it?" Gordillo asked.

"It's in the back. It's heavy."

"How am I going to carry it?"

"It's in a rolling suitcase."

"Will it fit under the wheelchair?"

"No idea. That's your problem."

The man walked Gordillo to the back of the store, behind the retail area, where shelves of unopened boxes lined the unfinished space.

"You missed quite a show back there," the man said.

"What are you talking about?"

"Back at the hotel. You know they've got a lab set up and everything."

"Who? Ikänen and his gang?"

"Yes. Stobnicki messaged me and said they'd activated the Bootstrap sequence in some birds."

Gordillo's face flushed white with fear. "That's impossible."

"The birds part?"

"No. They shouldn't be able to activate it. They don't have all the keys."

"Well, Ikänen figured something out."

* * *

The Cardinal thought back to a cryptic phone call he'd received years earlier. A familiar voice with a face he could not recall.

"Write this down. Don't use your computer or phone. Write it on paper."

The voice listed a random sequence of letters and numbers, over one hundred in all.

"Now read it back to me."

The Cardinal slowly relayed the string.

"What is this?" Gordillo asked.

"Memorize it."

"I can't memorize this—it's too long."

"Memorize it, then destroy the paper you just wrote on."

"What's it for?"

"It's your life insurance. Don't tell anyone else about this call or the code. If people find out you have this and can take it from you, you're as good as dead."

"What if I don't memorize it?"

"They'll kill you anyway, just to be sure."

"What's it for?"

"You'll find out soon."

Gordillo spent days storing the sequence in his head. Terrified for his life, he broke the pattern onto different index cards and hid them around his apartment, their order carefully preserved through a color-coded system he created.

He didn't hear of anything regarding the sequence again until months later. While attending a papal conference, someone slipped a note under his hotel door during the night.

The code will be needed soon. Only give it to the right person.

The right person? Gordillo asked himself. *How will I know who that is?*

Eventually, Gordillo burned the index cards he had employed to memorize the sequence, confident it was forever locked in his brain. Soon after, he returned home one Sunday afternoon from the morning services to find his apartment completely ransacked. Every book or magazine was taken. Every piece of clothing or shoes he owned was gone. Any couch or seat cushion had been ripped apart. Pictures were torn from the walls. Each container of food in the pantry, refrigerator, and freezer was opened and left on the counter.

He regretted his call to the police once they arrived, their curiosity piqued by the oddity of what had been done to his apartment. Upon their suggestion, they raced to his office at the church to find it had also been rummaged through.

"I have no idea what they might want," he told the police searching for clues throughout the Columbian cathedral, an answer they were clearly unsatisfied with.

Again, months passed without anything of significance related to the 100-digit code Gordillo had stored in his brain. He moved to another apartment registered in someone else's name. Increased the level of security that surrounded him. While attending a charity event in Europe, he was surprised to find Yuval Naftali approach his table and ask to speak.

"Cardinal Gordillo," Yuval said with an air of humility. "I don't believe we've ever met."

"I don't think we have either."

Yuval pulled out a chair and sat down. "You have something that I want. Something very important."

Gordillo stopped. "What is that?"

"A healthy appetite. No matter what I eat, I'm stuck in this wraith-like body of mine. How do you maintain your figure?"

Gordillo smirked at his taunt. "Some of us are blessed in ways others are not."

"I suppose there's no hope for me, then."

"We will pray for you."

"I would appreciate that very much."

"What can I do for you, Dr. Naftali? Surely you're not here to discuss epicurean fantasies?"

Yuval leaned back in his chair and looked to see who was near them.

"Should we go someplace more private to chat?" Gordillo asked.

"No, no. This will be better here. Don't want anyone asking questions."

"Very well. How may I help you?"

"*The code will be needed soon*. Does that mean anything to you?"

Again, Gordillo hardened. This wasn't the voice of the man who'd relayed the sequence to him. For over a year he'd agonized over what the code might mean, with no one to discuss it with. Clearly, Yuval had knowledge of what was going on.

Fearing his life might be in danger, Gordillo proceeded carefully. "I may have heard something like that before."

"Or read it, perhaps? On a card, slipped under your hotel room door last

April?"

The details of the way in which Gordillo received the message were unmistakable.

Yuval continued. "Room 548, if memory serves me correctly?"

"That was you?"

"No, it wasn't me. Someone who works for me."

"Was that you that broke in to my apartment and tore the whole place upside-down?"

"When did that happen?" Yuval asked as he bolted upright. "Did they find anything significant?"

"It was a few months ago. Suppose that wasn't you?"

"No, that wasn't me. Bad people looking to do bad things, most likely."

"What's this all about? The code? The secrecy."

Yuval struggled with how to proceed.

"Is this some cryptocurrency thing?" Gordillo asked. "Billions of dollars stored somewhere and I'm the only one who can access it?"

"No, it's not crypto. Something else."

"What?"

"Did you know Walter Faucett?"

"I met him a few times. Shame what happened."

Yuval shifted in his chair. "I'm going to tell you something in confidence that must not be repeated—to anyone."

"Okay."

"Can you handle that burden?"

"I guarantee I know more secrets than you."

"Very well. Faucett's team discovered something extremely important."

"A cure for cancer?" Gordillo joked.

"How did you know?" Yuval asked. "That's actually what it was."

"I wasn't being serious."

"That's evidently what his team found."

Gordillo tilted his head. "And they hid it because all the drug companies would go out of business if it was discovered?"

Yuval narrowed his eyes and studied Gordillo closely.

"Dr. Naftali, you're going to have to come up with a better story than that if you want my help. This one is awful."

Yuval flushed with anger. He'd never experienced someone pick him apart like that.

"I've heard confessions my whole life," the Cardinal said. "Try telling me the truth—it'll go much faster that way."

"Okay. I need the code. How's that?"

"The message under the door at the hotel—why were you so certain I had the code?"

"I wasn't. I assumed you might. I gave everyone at the conference the same message."

"But now you *are* certain I have it?"

"If your apartment got raided in the way you mentioned, yes."

"Other people's residences could have gotten raided."

"You're the only one I've heard of. And I've asked a lot of people."

"And I can assume you were trusting I would think you are the *right* person to share it with?"

"Perhaps."

"I need the code, Cardinal Gordillo."

Gordillo sensed he had more leverage than he originally assumed.

"I can tell."

"I will pay for it."

"I'm sure you will. What's it for?"

"I will tell you once you give it to me."

"You don't even know that I have it."

"You'd be dead by now if you didn't. What's it going to take? Name your price."

Butterflies filled the Cardinal's stomach as he suppressed a wry smile. "I'd like the papacy."

"You know I can't do that."

"I think you can. You have tremendous influence."

"The Vatican is nearly completely closed off to me. My network is not positioned to being able to sway something like that."

"Well you should start working on it then."

"Gordillo, I will have $50 million wired into whatever accounts you like by tomorrow."

"I'll take $25 million—and the papacy. That's half off your asking price."

"You are asking for too much."

"Then tell me what it's for."

"I can't."

Gordillo stood up and brushed some crumbs from the folds of his clothing. "Well, that's my price. $25 million now. $25 million later—once you've made me the Pope."

They figured something out.

The Cardinal struggled to understand how anyone could have activated the Bootstrap sequence. He hadn't revealed his key to anyone. Days after their heated conversation, Yuval called Gordillo and promised he would get him what he had asked for. Once the initial funds were wired, the Cardinal knew Yuval was serious.

As months passed, rumor began to spread suggesting the vaccines contained something serious—something others might leverage as a biological weapon of some kind. Knowing Yuval was heavily involved with their global rollout, Gordillo assumed the code was related to this discovery and considered upping his price. After unanswered messages to Yuval, he relented to accepting the terms of their original deal.

* * *

"Stobnicki was sure they figured it out?" Gordillo asked the man rolling a small suitcase towards him.

The man offered his phone to Gordillo. "Call him yourself."

The Cardinal could feel himself beginning to struggle breathing.

"Gordillo? Are you okay?"

"I just need to sit down for a minute."

"There aren't any chairs back here."

Gordillo leaned onto the counter where the man had placed the suitcase.

"How's this work?"

"Give me your phone. I'm going to store a contact in there. All you have to do is call it."

Gordillo unlocked his phone and handed it to the man.

"Is there a code or something I have to enter?"

"No. Just call the number. Let it ring a while. Probably ten times."

"What's the name of the contact?"

The man saved a number, locked the phone, and handed it back to the Cardinal.

"You can't miss it: The name is Boom."

CHAPTER 57

Garcia pulled out his phone.

"What are you doing?" Brinkley asked. "Who are you calling?"

"Relax. I'm not calling anyone. I just want to check the news myself."

Garcia scrolled through an article on his phone. "Did you read the whole thing, Brinks?"

"No."

"The part at the end from that guy in the helicopter?"

Finch reached for Brinkley's phone. "Give it to me."

Brinkley pulled it away from his grasp. "I'll read it to you. Hang on."

He flipped through his phone, glancing at a few quotes from Yuval.

"Oh, this is real interesting," Brinkley said. "He *wants* you there."

"I'll bet he does," Finch replied. "And every federal agent in all of D.C., too."

"No, he wants you there because he wants to forgive you."

Finch rolled his eyes. "Yeah, right."

"He says they are going to have Eva front and center—in front of the world. And the world might see a miracle happen. They are going to all be praying for her recovery. And he wants you there, right in the middle of it all."

Finch couldn't even begin to stomach the thought of groveling before Yuval, praying that he might use his demonic technology to heal her.

Brinkley continued to read. "You're going to love this, Finch. He's saying if you show up and play along with whatever he has planned, he'll get your charges dropped. Said he's already got it lined up. All you have to do is show up."

"And apologize, probably."

"*Apologizing's* a deal breaker?" Brinkley asked. "You've been in jail for almost three years because of something *you* did. This guy's offering a deal for you to walk, and you're concerned he might make you *apologize*—for something you admit you did?"

Finch ignored the sting of the accusation, his commitment to shield Natalie from the horrible truth about the wreck, unfaltering. "He's lying."

"Looks like he's on all the media outlets saying the same thing. Why would he lie about something like that—all your supporters would crucify him if he didn't follow through on that."

"They'd crucify him already if they could catch him."

"I know. You know what I mean."

Brinkley made partial sense, but Finch still perceived something was off. Why did his participation matter so much? Faucett had been Yuval's most valuable research partner, even more important than Connolly. Why would Yuval go to the extent of getting Finch's murder charge cleared just to share the stage with him—and his daughter?

Garcia spoke up. "Look, Finch. From what I can tell, seems like he wants to bury the hatchet. This looks like the perfect opportunity for both sides to move on from all the bickering of the last few years."

"You trust this guy, Brinkley?"

"Naftali? Hell no. But, he's in a bind—you can tell. He lost the Mongchai kid. For some reason, you have leverage right now. I'm not sure why, but some reason you have leverage. Maybe he's changed. Maybe he really does want to bury the hatchet."

"A lot of people hate him," Garcia added. "A lot of people like you. If he could negotiate a peace between the two of you, it might solve a lot of problems."

The entire situation was difficult for Finch to believe. The night of the wreck, he knew his life was over. He knew he'd likely never sleep at home with his wife or daughter ever again. Now, things had changed. The person he considered the most evil character on the planet was offering him not only his own freedom, but healing for his daughter as well—the only apparent cost, apologizing for crimes he'd never committed in front of the entire world. A few seconds of humility is all it would take. Just two or three sentences of contrition and he could have everything he thought lost forever—back in an instant.

"Is there video of him talking?" Finch asked. "I want to hear what he said."

Brinkley held his phone up in the air, trying to get better reception. "There is video, but it'll probably never play up here. Not enough signal."

"Can I see it?"

Brinkley handed his phone to Finch, a thumbnail of the scene as it played out on the hospital lawn—Yuval standing in front of a podium of microphones, Eva in her hospital gurney beside him.

Eva.

Finch swelled with anxiety as he saw his daughter for the first time in years. She was bigger, but a bit skinnier than he remembered. Her hair had grown longer, her eyes swollen—likely from tears.

"When was this video taken?" Finch asked.

"Looks like today," Brinkley answered.

"Like since he left here?"

"Yeah, I think so."

"So he was here, in front of you. With my daughter in the helicopter?"

Brinkley sank at the thought. "I didn't know, Finch. I'm sorry."

"I was that close to her?" Finch asked, his thoughts clouding with anger at failing his daughter again.

"*We* were that close to her," Brinkley said. "*You* were still down by the cabin."

"How far away is that place that burned down? Where he was doing that interview?"

"No idea. By car, probably forty-five minutes. Maybe more with traffic."

Finch climbed through the window from the bed into the driver's seat of the truck and re-fired the engine.

"We're going there. Now."

"You're not taking my truck," Garcia said.

"I am. And you're coming with us."

"Us?" Brinkley asked. "I'm not going down there on some witch-hunt with the head of the World Health Alliance."

"Both of you are going."

Finch put the truck into reverse and backed away from the embankment it was stuck within.

"If they're offering me a deal, I can get both of you one, too. Get in the back, Garcia. Brinkley, you're coming, too—unless you want to go back to jail with me."

Garcia rolled into the bed as Finch threw the shifter into first gear and accelerated the truck onto the highway towards Washington, D.C.

CHAPTER 58

"Could we ask Eva a few questions?" a reporter asked.

Yuval backed way from the microphones and spoke to the young girl.

"Just one," he said as he returned to the podium. "Make it good."

"Eva—what do you think is going to happen tonight?"

Yuval grabbed a few microphones from the podium and brought them to her bed, holding them for her to speak.

Eva remained silent. The world hadn't heard her speak a word since the accident. Yuval attempted to encourage her.

"What do you think is going to happen tonight, Eva?"

Finally, she spoke, her voice quivering with fright.

"I miss my daddy. I will be happy if he can come."

Yuval exploded with pride as she did what he asked.

"Isn't that amazing?" he asked into the microphones. "Little Eva here wants to see her daddy."

Yuval placed the microphones back onto the podium and offered one final word.

"Let's hope she's not disappointed this time."

With the solemnity of a religious procession, Yuval rolled Eva's gurney back up the ramp and onto the helicopter. Cameras continued to track him as he locked the wheels and attached the cargo straps that held it in place.

"Should I close the ramp?" the pilot asked.

"Not yet. The world is watching. I want them to see everything."

Yuval swung to the side of Eva's bed. After caressing her head, he bent down to give her a tender kiss.

"Start the motors," he shouted to the pilot, his face still buried within the bed sheets.

"Ramp?"

"No! Leave it down to the very last second."

The pilot initiated the startup sequence and slowly the rotors began to turn. A female reporter ran up to the side of the ramp and yelled inside.

"Dr. Naftali? Let me and my crew go with you. Someone needs to document what's happening today."

The momentous occasion deserved to be recorded—Yuval was certain of that. He glanced towards the cockpit and saw the back of Martta, still bound by the seatbelt wrapped around her.

"I'm afraid that's not possible," he said. "Come to the show tonight. That's what needs to be documented."

"Are you sure?" she asked, her eyes locked onto his. "I will make it worth your while."

Yuval struggled to decline her offer. Despite the tremendous power he wielded, women rarely showed any interest. Money could buy many things. But attraction? That was an emotional rush he'd almost never experienced.

After a moment of weakness, the gravity of the evening returned to the fore and he found the strength to refuse. Yuval had suffered a lifetime of rejection—not just potential suitors, but from professors, colleagues, even friends and family. He was not going to let anything derail his gift to everyone who'd doubted him his entire life.

"I'm sorry, but it's just not possible."

The reporter dropped her shoulders as the helicopter blades began to pick up speed.

"Watch your head," he said, as he smiled and motioned for her to leave.

Crestfallen, she ducked and backed away from the helicopter.

"Are we ready?" Yuval asked the pilot.

"Just about. Want the ramp up yet?"

"Raise it as we lift off. I want them to see me leave."

Yuval grabbed onto one of the hydraulic struts which powered the ramp's movement as the rotors reached full speed. He crouched down low for balance and began waving.

The helicopter lifted from the ground as the long grass swirled underneath it. Yuval smiled broadly for the cameras and waved his hand in a wide figure-eight pattern. The ramp began to close. Just as he turned away from the rear of the helicopter, a figure dashed toward the opening and leapt onto the ground below.

Yuval raced down the ramp but it was nearly closed, making it impossible for him to see what had happened. He ran to the cockpit and instantly realized one of the seats was empty.

"What happened to the girl?" Yuval screamed at the pilot. "How'd you let her escape?"

"Hang on a minute. We've got power lines everywhere."

The pilot looked from left to right, judging the narrow clearances as they ascended.

Yuval looked out of the side window, trying to get a view.

"What happened?" the pilot asked.

"She jumped out. The nurse jumped out as we took off."

Directly below them, Yuval could see the female reporter rushing towards someone on the ground.

"You want me to go back?"

"Leave her," Yuval hissed. "She's nothing to me."

"Not too late to try and grab her."

Yuval looked towards Eva's gurney. "We've got what we need."

"She's going to be talking to that reporter. Lots of awkward questions are going to start getting asked."

"Just a few more hours. I can deal with questions later."

The helicopter continued to lift into the air and began to turn.

"Where to now?" the pilot asked.

Yuval walked to the gurney and noticed that Eva was buried deep within the sheets. Concerned they might obstruct her breathing, he pulled them away.

"Stop!" he yelled to the pilot. "Don't go anywhere!"

"What's happening?"

Yuval quivered with rage as he realized the bed was completely empty.

"They're both gone."

CHAPTER 59

With one arm wrapped tightly around Eva's tiny frame, Martta rolled to the ground, the wind from the helicopter blades whipping her clothing painfully against her skin.

"We're okay," she shouted to Eva. "We're okay. Just hang on. We'll be okay."

The roar of the helicopter faded as it ascended above them.

"Why's it stopping?" Eva asked.

"I don't know. We need to get help."

A woman appeared above Martta and kneeled beside her.

"You fell," she said. "Are you okay?"

"You're the reporter?"

"I am a reporter."

"You tried to get on the helicopter as we were leaving."

"Yes, that was me."

"We didn't fall. We jumped."

The reporter gasped as she realized Eva lay underneath Martta's body.

"There's two of you."

"I'm Eva's nurse. We were kidnapped by that man. Can you help us? He's coming back to get us."

The helicopter remained hovering just fifty feet above their heads. The reporter looked behind her at the remnants of people leftover from Yuval's appearance.

"I'll get the police."

Martta grabbed her arm. "No, please don't."

"They'll help him," Eva said.

"What's your name?"

"Martta."

"Martta, I'm Iga. Are you Polish?"

"My parents are. So yes, I guess."

"Me too."

"Why are they not coming over here? How did they not see us fall?"

Iga looked at the few police and fire as they returned to their vehicles. "I don't know. The grass is too high I guess."

"You say this man kidnapped you?"

"He took us from our home. Or the place we were staying."

"Doesn't he need Eva for the thing tonight?"

"Nobody told us. We were just in our bedroom when they barged in and took us. It happened so fast I couldn't do much of anything."

"Where was Eva's mom?"

"I don't know."

"Was she home?"

"Yes."

"Could she have given him permission to take Eva without you knowing about it?"

"I don't think so. They were so violent with us. I can't believe they'd do that if they weren't scared of something."

"I see."

The grass around them began to swirl as the helicopter descended closer.

"Please," Martta said, "we have to go. He'll kill us if he catches us."

Iga sensed an opportunity as she stood up and motioned to her cameraman.

"He won't hurt anyone. I'm going to make sure nothing happens to you."

"How?"

"We're going to come with you."

CHAPTER 60

"Hello?" the voice asked. "Natalie? Are you here?"

It was a female—a friendly voice Natalie recognized. She tried to respond but couldn't force enough air from her lungs.

A figure rounded the corner and ran towards her, bending down to wrap her arms around her.

"Brooke," Natalie whimpered as tears ran down her face. "I'm so glad it's you."

"You're shaking," she said.

"I was terrified. I thought you were someone else."

Brooke had only been Dr. Connolly's assistant for a year, but Natalie had already developed a deep affection for her. About eight years apart in age, their natural inquisitiveness and endless optimism proved them to be kindred spirits.

"What's going on?" she asked.

"Yuval came here in a helicopter and took Eva."

Natalie began sobbing as voicing the reality of what had just happened brought the grim reality of the situation in focus.

"It's going to be okay," Brooke said.

"I can't reach my father either. He won't answer my calls."

"That's another Yuval situation. He's gone crazy. I don't know what's going on."

"Where's my father? Have you seen him?"

"We were headed here in the limo. Then a police man or security guard or somebody that works for Yuval took over and was taking us somewhere near the hotel. It felt like he was going to try and kill us."

"How'd you escape?"

"We ran into a crowd of protestors, and once they recognized him, it was just chaos after that. We got separated, and I don't know where he is now."

Natalie could feel the room begin to close around her.

"Do you think he's alive?"

"I think so," Brooke said as she began to tear up uncontrollably. "They were beating him pretty bad. I'm sorry. I tried to stop them, but there were too many of them."

"You don't know where he is?"

"I don't. I'm sorry. I didn't know you were here. I just came because it felt safe."

Natalie couldn't stop herself from shaking.

"What do we do?" Brooke asked. "He took Eva?"

"Yes, he took her. And Martta. They're going to use her tonight in the show."

"Why?"

"Have you not seen the news?"

"No."

"Mongchai died in a fire at the hospital this morning."

"Oh my."

"Exactly. Oh my."

As Connolly's assistant, Brooke was the one who initially contacted the boy's parents. Several phone calls later, they had agreed to bring him over, a journey she felt directly responsible for.

"He's dead?"

Natalie nodded her head in sorrow. "According to the news, he is."

Brooke buried her face in her hands. "It's my fault."

"No, it's not. It was an accident. He was at a hospital and it caught on fire. A terrible accident. Don't blame yourself. It wasn't your fault."

"And now Yuval wants to use Eva in his place?"

"Yes. He asked at first. But, I refused."

Brooke hugged Natalie tightly again. "I'm so sorry. Eva must be terrified."

"She's got Martta with her."

"Thank God for that."

"Why is this happening?" Brooke asked. "Why is he acting like this?"

"I don't know. Something strange is going on."

"Your father trusted Dr. Naftali completely."

"Mostly. Not completely."

"Can we call the police?"

Natalie shook her head. "I don't think that will help. He's too powerful."

"What should we do?"

"I don't know."

Natalie's pocket buzzed with an alert from her phone.

"Is there anyone we can we trust?" Brooke asked.

Natalie removed her phone and checked the screen.

I'm coming, the text read. *Stay put.*

It was a message.

From a contact she'd created hours before: Thomas Finch.

CHAPTER 61

"How far away are we?" Finch asked.

"Driving like this?" Brinkley replied. "We'll never get there. You need to slow down. We can't afford to get pulled over."

Finch checked the speedometer. It had been pegged at 85mph for the last fifteen minutes.

"What's the speed limit here?"

"Seventy."

"Won't they give us a little bit of wiggle room?"

"Not in this truck. Bullet holes? Blown out windshield? It's basically screaming *Pull me over, we're criminals*."

Finch eased off on the accelerator pedal. The needle barely moved.

"We're going slower now. You just can't see it."

Garcia spoke from the bed of the truck. "We're going to need to get gas at some point."

Finch pointed at the dash. "We're still full."

"It's broken."

"When did you fill up last?"

"I can't remember. The other tank works." Garcia pointed towards a control on the dashboard. "Flip that to the other one."

Finch toggled the switch from *Front* to *Rear*. The needle dropped to just over one-quarter full.

"Okay we drive the other one till we run out, then we switch to this and we can get a little farther."

"Perfect," Brinkley said, sarcastically.

"We'll never get there on that," Garcia responded.

"I better speed up then." Finch floored the accelerator again.

Brinkley unlocked his phone and dialed a number.

"Who you calling?" Garcia asked.

"Tamara. She needs to know about Monroe."

Brinkley waited for the emergency dispatcher to pick up. "Tamara, it's Brinks."

Tamara immediately interrupted him with something urgent.

"I know. You did the right thing. They all showed up. Look, I don't know how to say this gently so I'll just put it to you straight. Monroe is dead. His body is still at the cabin."

Brinkley paused to listen to her response.

"Yes, I know, but I can't talk to them right now. Garcia and I are going to be offline for a bit. Don't send anyone after us. I'll explain later, but if you could just make sure someone goes to the cabin to get Monroe, that's the best we can do right now."

Again, Brinkley listened to what Tamara had to say.

"Okay. I understand. You did the right thing. I've got your back. I will talk to you later. Probably tomorrow."

Brinkley hung up the call and turned to Finch.

"We've got a world of problems. She's got another agency there now looking for you. Not sure who, but she said they acted pretty pissed."

"They'll be tracking us, then. Both of you should turn off your phones. Meaning totally off—not just in standby mode."

Brinkley held the power button on his cell until the screen went black.

Garcia hesitated. "What if someone needs to reach us?"

"Oh," Brinkley said, "they're going to try and reach us alright."

"What if we need to look something up?"

"We'll just have to use Wi-Fi for now."

Garcia sighed and pressed the power button on his phone.

"What's the plan, Finch?" Brinkley asked.

"I'm going to find my daughter."

"Yeah, and then what? Something-something *guns*? Something-something *explosions*?"

"Probably."

"We've got one 9mm Smith & Wesson between the three of us. We're going to need to get real good at sharing."

"And we get about two shots each," Garcia added.

"Don't worry. I'll figure it out."

"And what about Mr. Naftali?" Brinkley asked.

"I will figure that out, too."

"Okay, you do that."

"Shit," Finch said, tapping the brake pedal as they passed a state trooper going the other way. Brinkley tracked the officer to see if he turned around.

"He's not stopping."

Finch ramped the truck back up to its previous speed.

"What was your beef with Faucett?" Brinkley asked. "If you're comfortable talking about it."

"Well I hated him, if that's not obvious."

"That's obvious."

"And not just for the reasons you might expect."

"What reasons might we expect?" Garcia asked.

"Well, for starters, the reason everyone hated him—he made sure all the malkavirus gain of function research had plenty of funding. That goes way back. A decade or more."

"Gain of function? What does that even mean?"

Brinkley interjected. "It means they were trying to weaponize it."

"Not necessarily," Finch said. "It *could* mean weaponizing it. Viruses can be hard to study. They can be expensive to work with. If you're going to test something on a monkey, you want to make sure the virus infects or does whatever it is you hope it does. Otherwise, you're out a couple of thousand dollars each time, with nothing but an angry monkey to show for it."

"So they wanted to make it more reliable," Garcia suggested.

"That's an optimistic way of putting it. *Reliably dangerous* is probably a better way of stating what they were doing. This started way back when they were first studying the poliovirus. They could inject it directly into the spinal tissue of monkeys, but it wouldn't *always* paralyze them. So they did things to make it more *reliable*, as you put it. They wanted it to paralyze them every time so they weren't wasting so many monkeys. That was really the first gain of function work."

Brinkley shook his head in disgust. "Gain of function? That's weaponizing an already harmful virus."

"I don't think they meant to harm anyone—at least not at first. They were doing this research in New York City—trying to make the poliovirus stronger—when something strange happened. Just a few miles from the lab where they were doing the testing, a strange outbreak of polio happened—something bigger than the world had ever seen before.

"Most people hadn't even heard of polio back then. But, something happened and thousands of people were struck. It was the worst summer ever recorded in the United States. All the black and white pictures you might have seen as a kid are from the 40s and 50s. Those never came close to that 1916 outbreak—right around the corner from the Rockefeller Institute where, like I was saying, they were purposefully trying to make the poliovirus more dangerous."

"You think they released it on purpose—like Wuhan?" Brinkley asked.

"I don't think so. And I'm not sure they were related at all, though the proximity in time and space is really difficult to ignore."

"Bastards," Brinkley said. "How many people died?"

"In New York City, it was over two thousand—just that one summer. Something that never happened again."

"Shut the whole thing down, probably. Too much attention. Too many people asking questions."

"Maybe. But, that was really the first big gain of function research. They weren't trying to hurt anyone. They were really trying to help."

"Yeah, right," Brinkley said, rolling his eyes.

"No, I think they were legitimately trying to understand what was going on. Whether it was an accident or even related to their research—again, I don't know. Seems like it was probably connected."

Garcia spoke up. "Okay, so fast forward to today—or yesterday or whenever it was—what were they doing with the malkavirus? It doesn't paralyze anyone, as far as I can tell."

"Well, that gets into kind of a weird area. There were all kinds of things going on with malkavirus research. Mixing it with other pieces and parts of this and that microbe. Trying to make it more infectious. Trying to make it infect humans more easily."

"That sounds like weaponizing it."

"Yeah, it does. You could make the argument it was just scientists being scientists—little kids in lab coats trying to see how big they could blow things up."

"But why?" Garcia asked.

"It's part of the curiosity all scientists have. They want to understand things better. You have to do weird things to be able to isolate certain behaviors or attributes of microbes to study them. They're extremely difficult to study. You really can't even see most of them—they're so small a regular microscope won't work. You have to use an electron microscope or other tricks."

"So, you don't think they were purposefully trying to weaponize the malkavirus?"

"I didn't say that. I don't think *everyone* was. And I think some people were doing weaponization work but were told it was for something else. Each person or lab or university was working on a tiny piece of a bigger puzzle. Not all of them really knew what role they were playing."

"And that's where Faucett comes in?"

"Correct. He was definitely aware of what was going on. He had the 50,000-foot view no one else did. He asked for particular research. He approved the grants. He wrote the checks. He knew exactly what he was doing."

"I thought you people believed the virus was released from a lab in China or something."

"The nation of China doesn't have complete control of its laboratories. The *government* of China doesn't have complete control of its laboratories. At the end of the day, we're all humans just trying to pay the bills."

"You think Faucett was working with someone on the inside, so to speak?"

"I think it's likely. They were doing research there, just like we and a hundred other places were. But that's where it originated. I don't think the Chinese government—as an organization—had anything to do with it."

Brinkley sat up. "But what about all those videos of people falling over in the street at the beginning of the whole pandemic? They were obviously trying to freak people out."

"Oh, they were. The videos worked perfectly—everybody *did* freak out. But who are *they*? I don't think *they* is the Chinese government. There were people making those videos in China. They were probably Chinese for all we know. But who were they working for? Who wrote their checks? That's the real question."

"And you think it was Faucett?" Brinkley asked.

"I think so, yes."

"But why?" Garcia asked. "Why the whole thing? Just to kill a bunch of people? Why would anyone go to the trouble of all this—if it was on purpose like you believe?"

"To make a trillion dollars, that's why," Brinkley said.

"No, actually I don't think it was about money at all. Lots of people made a *lot* of money, that's for sure. But, for Faucett and the other higher ups, I think it was something else."

"Depopulation."

"Possibly a bit of that. But, you've got to see these things through their eyes. In their mind, they're doing *good*. They're not twisting their mustaches, hoping to commit acts of evil. They're patting themselves on the back, convinced they are doing the world a great service. We may see things differently, but if you want to understand them, you've got to realize they genuinely believe they are doing good, not evil."

"They think depopulation is good."

"They would describe it as lowering infant mortality. Fewer childhood deaths means families need to have fewer children in order to seed the next generation."

"What's the difference?" Brinkley asked. "If they have more children and more children die, you still end up with the same number of people at the end of the day."

"Forget the depopulation crap," Garcia interrupted. "If Faucett was managing this whole program to weaponize the malkavirus, what *good* did he think would come of it?"

Finch inhaled deeply and breathed out through his nose. For him, this was where the trail had gone dark. He had a source within the NIH who'd been feeding him bits of information—news of grant applications or travel plans of top officials. With their help, Finch was able to piece together some of what was happening. The gain of function research. The Bootstrap project. The way in which it could be programmed.

One day, his contact stopped responding. Finch didn't know their actual name. He didn't know how old they were. Gender. Ethnicity. He knew nothing about this person other than they were a ghost who felt something very bad was happening. Someone had either gotten cold feet, fired, or possibly something worse—a price they told Finch they were willing to pay if he could stop whatever was going on.

"This is what I *think* Faucett was doing. I'm not sure of it, but my best guess? They had the Bootstrap technology in place. They wanted every person on the planet to get it. But, to do that, they needed the one thing people have always used to get what they want."

"What's that?" Garcia asked.

"Fear. They needed something serious that would drive nearly the entire world into a hysterical panic to get a vaccine."

"A vaccine with the Bootstrap thing in it," Brinkley said.

"That's right."

Garcia scowled. "This is so completely batshit crazy I can't even believe I'm listening to you guys."

"Well it happened, as far as we can tell. Crazy? Sure. And bats were involved at some point."

"You're trying to tell me they spent years—and who knows how many billions of dollars—developing a weaponized virus just to scare people into taking a special vaccine?"

"Well, half the research was for the Bootstrap technology itself. For the scientists doing the work, they had no idea."

"I'll ask it again—why? Why would Faucett go to all this trouble? Just for a special vaccine?"

"Garcia, the Bootstrap technology—if it works like we think it does—will allow them to do all sorts of things to you. Without you even knowing or asking for it. It will allow the single biggest shift in DNA any species has ever experienced since the dawn of creation—just by catching a cold from someone else. Do you have any idea what kind of threat this poses to our very existence?"

"Maybe they'll be able to cure cancer? How about Alzheimer's? AIDS? Isn't that kind of the point of science like this? To end sickness? Disease? Suffering? Wouldn't that be *good*? Isn't that probably the *good* Faucett was hoping for?"

"Then why all the secrecy?" Finch asked. "Why use fear to compel people to inject this technology into themselves? Into their children? A technology that is completely untested—possibly harmful?"

"You have such little faith."

"You are absolutely correct. I have zero faith—in humanity. If we can screw something up badly, it won't be long before we figure out a way to use technology to screw things up even worse."

"Don't we have to take some chances here and there to risk doing something serious like curing cancer or AIDS?"

"Not like this," Finch said. "This is a bridge *way* too far in my book."

"Mine, too," Brinkley added. "I have a question. If Faucett is hoping to do good—curing cancer or something—then what do you make of Yuval? What's he trying to do?"

Finch swallowed hard. "Whatever it is, I don't think it's good."

"You don't?"

"No. Absolutely not. I think he means nothing but evil."

CHAPTER 62

"What happened?" Ikänen asked.

"He was slumped on the floor of the elevator. No blood. No shell casings."

"Any sign of the Cardinal?"

"None."

"Someone kidnapped him," Connolly suggested. "They killed Gabriel, then kidnapped him. He traveled with heavy security for a reason."

Ikänen raised an eyebrow. "Cardinal Gordillo is not the person you think he is."

"I don't think much of him, to be honest with you. But, I don't think he's a murderer, if that's what you're suggesting."

"Dr. Connolly, I had someone following Gordillo this week. Would you believe me if I told you he was at the hospital where Mongchai was killed?"

"That's ridiculous. No, of course I wouldn't believe you if you told me that."

"What if I told you Gordillo had gone to visit Mongchai just minutes before the fire started? Would you believe me, or is that too much of a leap for you to consider right now?"

"Why were you following him? He's a Cardinal. He's being considered as the next Pope. So far, you're not impressing me, Dr. Ikänen."

"We followed him for the same reason we followed you—to keep tabs on things."

"You've been following me?"

"Yes."

"How long?"

"Months. Maybe years."

"To keep tabs on things? That's a lot of effort just *to keep tabs on things*."

Again, Ikänen felt the need to hold back even though he knew time was running out.

"Albert—we were there in case things went off the rails."

"In what way?"

"We believed that if someone got hold of all three of the Bootstrap keys, it could have led to some very bad things."

"So you followed everyone you thought might have a key?"

"Precisely."

"To protect someone else from getting them?"

"Correct."

"I'm surprised you didn't just kill us. Wouldn't that have been easier."

"Yes, it would have been much easier. We considered it, but ultimately decided against it."

Connolly was shocked. "So I guess I'm supposed to say thank you for saving my life?"

"Don't thank me. I lost the vote."

"So you voted to kill me?"

"Not just you. All the others we felt might have had a key."

"You think Gordillo had one of the other keys?"

"We're fairly certain."

"Well, make sure to tell your friends thank you for saving my life. I don't have a key, for what it's worth. My death would have been for nothing."

"I wouldn't say that, Dr. Connolly. You've played an important role in this whole thing in other ways. Your death would still certainly have been deserved."

Flushed with anger, Connolly stepped directly in front of Ikänen. "You have no idea the things I've had to do to keep everyone in your group from going to jail."

"For what? An insatiable desire to know the truth?"

"For ruining people's trust in science! For ruining people's trust in medicine! People like you and Finch set us back two hundred years."

"I'd gladly take two hundred years of jail if it could undo what's happened under your watch."

"Dr. Ikänen, I know the shots have problems. We all know that now. What's done is done. But, the Bootstrap project is dead. Gordillo may have one of the keys, but Faucett had one as well. He's dead, and his key—and the Bootstrap project—died along with him."

Ikänen pressed his lips together and decided it was time that Connolly learned of their discovery. He knocked on the door five times and waited for Stobnicki to unlock it.

"I wish you were right," he said, as the door opened and they stepped inside.

CHAPTER 63

"Don't be scared," the reporter told Martta and Eva. "It will be me and my camera guy with you. He's big and strong. We won't let anything happen."

Yuval's helicopter touched down on the ground about thirty feet away from them.

"We need to go somewhere else," Martta said. "Please take us to your house. He'll kill us."

Iga stroked Martta's head. "Don't be scared."

"Why are you doing this?"

"I'm a reporter," Iga said. "You're part of the biggest story in the world right now. And it's all mine."

The door on the side of the helicopter opened. The pilot stepped out onto the grassy field and paused.

"Are you streaming this?" Iga asked her cameraman.

The burly assistant switched on his camera and stepped back to recompose the shot with Iga in the foreground, the massive helicopter behind her.

"I am now."

Iga strode towards the helicopter, her heels cutting into the deep blades of grass. She turned around and held her hand out towards Martta.

"Stay there. Don't come until I call you."

With an air of complete confidence, she bent underneath the spinning rotors and spoke to pilot.

"I need to speak to Dr. Naftali."

"He's busy."

"I have something he wants."

The pilot shot her a stern look. "And I'm here to get it. If you would fetch those two girls, we need to be leaving."

"Sorry," Iga said. "No deal."

"I will get them if I have to. I'm not afraid to make this ugly."

Iga shot him a curt smile. "We're streaming right now, just so you know. Seven hundred thousand followers. I'm sure they'd love to see you make this ugly."

"What do you want?"

"Me and my cameraman will ride with you to Washington, D.C. A few questions with Dr. Naftali in the helicopter along the way."

The pilot laughed. "That will be a firm *No Deal* as well."

Iga turned from him and began to walk away.

"Wait," the pilot said.

Iga stopped and spoke. "Yuval needs her *way* more than I do."

"I don't know about that."

"I have *all* the leverage here, Mr. helicopter pilot. Go let Dr. Naftali know we'd like to come along with our special guests. We will leave you alone as soon as you land in D.C."

Raging with anger, the pilot spun on his boots and ascended the stairs back into the helicopter.

Iga returned towards the camera and straightened her hair as she lifted a microphone to her mouth.

"Dr. Yuval Naftali has agreed to let us ride aboard his executive aircraft with young Eva Connolly and her nurse on their ride to Washington, D.C. We will have an exclusive interview with Dr. Naftali along the way that I'm sure will leave you stunned."

The camera zoomed in on the open door of the helicopter, looking for signs of movement inside the darkened interior.

"We're just waiting for his signal to board," Iga said into the microphone.

After a full minute, the pilot leaned from the side of the opening and beckoned them towards him.

Iga's eyes glowed as she moved to gather Martta and Eva from the grass.

"Come with me, girls. We're going back on the helicopter."

Iga reached for Eva, still wrapped within Martta's arms.

"Give her to me," she whispered. "I'm going to carry her onto the helicopter.

Martta tightened her grip.

Iga grabbed the nurse's arm and sunk her thumb deep into the muscle. Martta winced in pain and let go.

"Let's go, Eva," she said as she laid the little girl's head over her shoulder. "You, too, Martta. Time to go."

Iga walked toward the helicopter slowly, waiting for her cameraman to catch up with her.

"How much battery do you have?"

"Tons."

"Good. Don't stop streaming. No matter what."

CHAPTER 64

Gordillo stepped outside and left in search of Maduro, wincing every time the black suitcase rolled over a crack in the sidewalk. The streets were teeming with people readying themselves for a march from the hotel all the way to the Cathedral, a grand parade of a hundred different groups and protests that had descended on the Capitol.

"Where in the hell is he?" Gordillo asked, scanning the crowd for signs of Maduro or his wheelchair.

Someone bumped into the suitcase, wrenching the handle from his grasp.

"Watch it," the Cardinal screamed, gingerly tilting the container back onto its wheels.

A marching band had spontaneously formed, filled with drums and a few other instruments. Half of them rehearsed some of the chants and patterns they would employ during the march, the other half content to carry on with improvised beats in a circle to the side.

An assortment of four-wheeled trucks were staged along the street with trailers behind them—improvised floats covered with thousands of plastic grocery bags, a purposeful affront to the environmental groups they so frequently sparred with. A nearby formal shop had been completely pillaged, its most gaudy dresses and gowns now worn by men and women standing on the trailers—self-appointed kings and queens of the parade—mockingly waving at their friends.

Gordillo noticed a man readying a drone to capture footage of the spectacular event.

"Could you help me find someone?" he asked.

The drone operator looked up from his equipment and noticed the Cardinal's red robe underneath the grungy black cloak that nearly covered him.

"Are you with them?" he asked, pointing to the protestors nearby.

"Not really," Gordillo said.

"I'm not either. What can I do for you?"

"I'm looking for a friend. He's a young male in a motorized wheelchair. Shouldn't be too hard to spot."

The man put on a pair of goggles and launched the drone up into the air.

"What do you see?" Gordillo asked.

"A crap ton of people. Jesus, it goes on forever."

The drone took off down the street towards the front of the parade, its camera spinning in circles as it flew.

"I'm not seeing him."

"It's a black, motorized wheelchair."

"I'm not seeing *any* wheelchairs at all."

"How about behind us? Can you look behind us?"

"Sure."

After a few moments, the drone buzzed over their heads towards the rear of the parade. The operator shifted the joystick in his hand, continuing to turn knobs that controlled the camera angle.

"Sorry. Still not seeing anything at all. Just thousands of people."

"May I look?" Gordillo asked.

"Sure."

The man removed his goggles and placed them over the Cardinal's head. Gordillo instinctively held out his hand for balance as the camera spun.

"Don't fall," the man said, as he grabbed Gordillo's arm to steady him.

"I can't get my bearings. Where are we? Can we see ourselves in this?"

The man spun the camera towards them.

"I think that's pointed at us now."

He held his arm up in the air and swung it from side to side.

"Can you see me? I'm waving."

"I think so."

Gordillo scanned up and down the sidewalks for Maduro's wheelchair but saw nothing other than a throng of people. At the bottom of the frame, he could barely make out the man beside him waving his arm. At the top, he noticed some commotion as a group of men ran through the crowd.

"Can I zoom in on something?" he asked.

"Sure," the operator replied as he placed the controller in Gordillo's hand. "Just turn this knob."

The Cardinal adjusted the zoom but now the advancing men were out of frame.

"I missed. How can I control the camera?"

"Just use your thumb to pan with that little joystick."

The man placed Gordillo's thumb on the control and wiggled it for him.

"Oh, I see."

Gordillo widened the angle and spotted the men again. After centering the camera on their progress, he tried to zoom in on them again.

"Oh, okay. That's interesting. I think they're coming for me."

Gordillo recognized they were some of the men from the tunnels.

"Who's coming for you?"

"I need to go."

Gordillo threw the goggles to the ground. Completely disoriented, he was unable to figure out which direction the men were coming from. Beside him, protestors continued to revel on the trailers and trucks that awaited the parade before it got underway.

Through a sea of humanity, the Cardinal finally saw the group of men moving towards him. With only fifty feet between them, he realized he was trapped. He beat on the side of the truck nearest him, trying to get the protestors attention.

"Help me up," he said. "I'm coming with you."

A protestor, wearing a sequined blue gown pulled over his clothes, reached down and helped raise him and his suitcase up and over the side of the bed. The group of men surrounded the truck, their rifles bulging underneath their coats.

"Cardinal," the dress-wearing protestor said, slapping him on the shoulder. "Good to see you!"

Gordillo looked up and couldn't believe what he saw. Trimmed in pearls, sequins, and a long blue gown, stood Mr. Maduro.

CHAPTER 65

"We're getting closer," Brinkley said.

"How far?" Finch asked.

"Depending on traffic, maybe thirty minutes."

"How's your pulse?"

"Bad, I'm sure. About to get worse probably."

"You really think that's going to do you in?"

"Maybe I'll get lucky and get shot first."

Garcia spoke up. "You said you thought Naftali was evil. Is that how you describe people you hate?"

"Oh no, I actually think he's evil. Like legitimately, spiritually evil. Not an ounce of good intentions in his blood. I've never met anyone like him."

"Oh, you met him?" Brinkley asked. "That had to have been good."

"Yeah, it was before I went public with my opinions. He didn't know where I stood on things."

"What was he like?"

"It was a big meeting with the NIH and the World Health Alliance and all the people trying to save the world. Connolly—my wife's father—brought me along. I think he sensed I was rebellious and was hoping to win me over to their side. Thought I'd be a good spokesperson or something."

"Little did he know...."

"Yeah, little did he know I wanted to strangle nearly everyone there—including himself."

"What'd they talk about?"

"Oh, all the usual stuff. Economic disparity. Environmental concerns. Gender this. Racial that."

Brinkley laughed. "Sounds like a nuclear bomb of good intentions."

"They meant well. *Real* well. Had all kinds of plans for fixing everything, of course."

"Why the NIH and World Health Alliance? Isn't that kind of talk the realm of other players—World Economic Conference and those guys?"

"In the past, yes. But, they just don't have the Pharma relationships in place like the NIH and WHA. Fear of economic disparity is not a very powerful tool for control. The fear of death is."

Garcia shook his head. "Thousands have died because of people like you. Because you taught them not to fear death."

Brinkley contorted his face in contempt. "No they haven't—that's bullshit."

"What are you afraid of?" Finch asked. "What are you afraid of dying of? Polio? Measles? Chicken pox?"

"Yes. To all those."

"There's thousands of other infections that can also kill you. Yet, you're only afraid of the ones they have shots for. Why do you think that is?"

"Because they're the worst ones. That's the ones they made vaccines for."

"Tuberculosis kills millions of people every year. Are you afraid of it?"

"Never heard of it."

"Exactly. They've got a piece of crap vaccine for it, but you've never heard of it. That's why you're not afraid of it."

"You are so full of shit I can't tell your mouth from your ass."

"You do whatever your wife tells you, don't you?" Brinkley asked.

Garcia leaped towards Brinkley and wrapped his arm around his throat. Scrambling to crawl through the window, he began punching the sheriff in the head with his free hand. Brinkley crunched his body forward, dragging Garcia's head across the broken glass that edged the missing window.

Pushing through the pain, Garcia latched onto Brinkley's shoulder with his teeth, biting through layers of fabric.

"What in the hell?" Brinkley asked as he wrenched Garcia's entire body into the cabin, the deputy's feet smashing into the side of Finch's head. The sheriff rammed Garcia's head onto the floor and directed all his body weight onto the deputy's neck.

"What are you doing?" Brinkley asked again. "Get a fucking grip on yourself, Garcia."

The deputy writhed around in anger, but couldn't break free. Finch pulled the truck to the side of the road and jumped out of the cabin. Brinkley opened his door and readied himself to leap clear.

"I'm okay," Garcia said. "I'm good. Let me go."

"What's your problem?"

"I'm okay. I'm okay."

Finch looked at Garcia in shock. "Maybe we should just leave him here."

"No, I'm good," Garcia said. "I just lost my temper. Brinks knows I'm sensitive about my wife. I'm sorry, Brinks."

Brinkley moved one of his legs from the back of Garcia's neck and replaced it with his iron grip.

"I'm going to let go of you and step out of the truck. You better not try anything or else I will hurt you this time."

"I'm totally good, Brinks. I'll get in the back. Just let me go."

Carefully, Brinkley released the pressure he had applied to the deputy and leapt from the truck. Garcia sat up in the cabin, blood dripping down his face.

"I swear. I'm good now. I don't know what happened."

"Jesus, Garcia. Your head is shredded. You got a rag or towel or something in here we can use?"

"I don't think so. I'll just use my sleeve."

"Don't do that—it's too much. You'll ruin your coat."

Garcia ignored him and wiped the blood from his face onto his sleeves. "That any better?"

Red stains were smeared all over his face.

"Close enough, I guess."

Garcia reached into his hair and pulled out a piece of glass.

"What'd I cut it on?"

"The window."

"Strange," Garcia said. "Don't remember that part."

"You good now?" Brinkley asked.

"Yes. Totally fine."

"Sure?"

"I'm sure."

Garcia crawled out of the floor of the truck and onto the ground. He stood up and hopped into the bed.

"See, totally fine. Let's go."

"Why don't you sit at the back of the bed?" Brinkley suggested.

"It'll be freezing back there."

Brinkley met Finch's eyes for a moment as he stepped into the truck.

"I think you'll be fine."

CHAPTER 66

Natalie's mouth fell open as she read the message from Finch.

I'm coming. Stay put.

It had been over a year since she had heard a single word from him.

He's alive, she thought to herself. From week to week, from month to month, her feelings toward him changed. At times, she wished he were dead. At others, she longed to close her eyes and bury her head in his chest, confident his embrace could protect her from anything.

He'll fix this.

If anything, Finch was a problem solver. An eternal optimist. Often delusional, but at least confident things would end well even when others had lost all hope. Perhaps, specifically *because* others had lost all hope.

"What is it?" Brooke asked, sensing Natalie's shock.

As it was with everyone else, Brooke sensed nothing from Natalie but disdain for her missing husband. Despite many intimate conversations, Dr. Connolly's assistant knew only one side of the story—Finch was a scoundrel who deserved to die. Natalie's actual feelings—the struggle between intense loathing and a passionate desire to fall in love with him all over again—that was something kept carefully hidden from everyone.

"Just an old friend," Natalie said. "They saw the news about Eva. Wanted to check in on me."

"Everyone's concerned. They love you and Eva so much."

"Why is he doing this?"

"Yuval?" Brooke asked.

"Yeah."

"I'm not sure."

"He was always a little odd—I'm not talking about that. He took Eva—*kidnapped* her. Then you and my father, too? Something is seriously wrong."

Brooke nibbled on a fingernail as her eyes darted from side to side.

"What is it?" Natalie asked.

"It's nothing."

"No, seriously—what is it? There's something you want to tell me."

"Your father wouldn't want me talking to anyone about it."

"My father is missing, Brooke. If this has any possible connection to why, I don't think he would care."

Brooke rocked her head in indecision.

"Brooke, tell me. I know nearly everything he does already anyway."

After a series of deep breaths, Brooke spoke.

"Your father had me tracking something very strange. It wasn't covered by the news—I'm not sure why. Either they were told to stand down or they just didn't notice it, but Dr. Connolly noticed it and had me tracking it. Gave me access to everything I needed."

"And...what was it you were tracking?"

"Yeah. You're not super religious like your father, right?"

"We're different in some ways."

"Well, I don't know if you believe in ghosts and evil spirits and things like that, but over the past week or so, there've been a string of deaths that seemed to have some—I don't know what to call it really—some supernatural element to them."

"Supernatural?" Natalie asked. "But not in a good way, I'm assuming?"

"Definitely not in a good way. *Paranormal* might be a better word."

"Why in the world would you and my father have ever gotten involved in that?"

"I can't say for sure, but I think there were two reasons. The first is it had a vector to it. Meaning we could kind of track its progress."

"Like an infectious disease or something?"

"Yes, something like that."

"So it was like demon possession, but also contagious?"

Brooke still couldn't believe what she was suggesting. "As crazy as it might sound, yes. That's what I think he was afraid of."

"Sounds like MPI to me."

"I'm not familiar with that term."

"Mass psychogenic illness. *Mass hysteria*, basically."

"Oh, yeah—like when Tourette syndrome becomes contagious?"

"Yes. Maybe it's something like that."

"It might be, but I don't think so. These cases were unrelated. No one knew each other. They weren't interacting with each other as far as we can tell. And all of them ended up committing suicide."

"That's horrible," Natalie said.

"Yeah. It is."

Brooke was about to relay news of the young girl who had apparently killed herself that morning but thought of Eva and decided it was better left unsaid.

"So that's the first reason you and my father got involved. What was the second?"

"This one's way out there, but Dr. Connolly had a feeling—an intuition, really—he wanted me to follow up on."

"What was it?"

"Some line of research Yuval had done at some point in his career."

"Please don't tell me he was studying demons?"

Brooke cocked her head sideways, unsure of how to describe what she knew. "Well, not exactly. Some people might say it's related."

"What?" Natalie asked. "What was he studying?"

Brooke looked into the enormous room behind them, its two stories of shelves filled with books and papers.

"I'm guessing we can read all about it in there."

Natalie clutched her hands together. "Please don't tell me this has something to do with Eva or tonight's event."

Brooke grabbed Natalie's hand and pulled her out of the hall and into the library.

"Can you turn on more lights, Natalie?" she asked. "It feels dark in here."

CHAPTER 67

"What in the hell?" Connolly asked as they stepped into the hotel room.

Lab equipment was strewn everywhere, sitting on every horizontal surface amidst cabling and hoses that connected them together. Shards of glass and mirror littered the floor as a scientist attempted to clean it up.

Stobnicki looked stood up, his face turned in confusion as he recognized who Ikänen had brought with him.

"Stobnicki—Dr. Connolly of the NIH has decided to join us for a moment."

"I've said no such thing! You brought me here against my will."

Ikänen ignored him and continued speaking. "I am sorry to have to tell you that Gabriel has died."

"What happened?" Stobnicki asked.

"He was bringing Cardinal Gordillo up the service elevator. They found Gabriel's body slumped onto the ground."

"Gordillo killed him."

"Probably so."

Connolly was furious. "This is ridiculous. Is this how easily you and your kind are swayed? No evidence at all and you're pronouncing this man guilty of two murders?"

Ikänen was unshaken. "You are ignorant of many things, Dr. Connolly—chief of all, the extent of your knowledge."

"Well then, tell me. Tell me all the things I don't know so that I can share in your infinite wisdom."

"Do you know what an Overton window is, Dr. Connolly?"

"No."

"Well, in the context of this particular conversation, you can think of it as the range of things you may find at least plausible. The edges of what you're able to consider possible."

"I have an open mind."

"Of course you do. Everyone does. Unfortunately, your Overton window is much too small to handle all the things you don't currently know."

"Try me."

"I just did. I gave you a tiny slice of reality and you are already about to lose your mind."

"What reality?"

"That Cardinal Gordillo, a man you hold at least in some high esteem, is capable of murdering someone. Or is the murder of *one* person plausible—but *two* that you find impossible?"

"Okay. I'll consider it. Cardinal Gordillo, a man being considered as the next Pope of the Catholic Church murdered two people today. An invalid boy who posed no threat to anyone and a man who just risked his life to save him. Sounds totally plausible to me."

Ikänen made eye contact with Stobnicki. "Your sarcasm is a clear indication of how far off you are."

"Then enlighten me. Explain to me why it *is* plausible. What am I missing? Why would Gordillo kill the boy this morning? Let's start there. What possible reason would a Cardinal have in going out of his way to kill one of the world's most beloved children?"

Ikänen blinked deliberately as he searched for patience. "Mongchai was an important part of your event tonight, was he not?"

"Of course."

"Maybe Gordillo had an extremely pressing reason he didn't want the event to happen."

Connolly started to speak, but Ikänen held up a finger and stopped him.

"Hang on just a minute. Hear me out. Maybe there is something—something you don't know about right now—but something extremely important to him or other people—that made him act in a way he felt might get the event cancelled."

"But murder? Really?" Connolly asked.

"See—this is where your Overton window cuts off too narrowly. You can't think of anything important enough to *you* that you would purposefully kill someone for, so you can't imagine *others* would have something so important to them *they* might kill."

Connolly tried to respond but couldn't think of what to say.

Ikänen continued. "Other people have a different moral compass than you. They have a different ethical framework than you. They have more ambitions than you. They're willing to risk more than you to achieve those ambitions."

"So what do *you* think it is, then?" Connolly asked. "What was so important to him he was willing to kill someone to get the event canceled?"

"I don't think that was it at all, actually."

Connolly through his hands up and rolled his eyes in frustration. "Well, now we're getting somewhere."

"I think he did it for *another* reason—something that will be even harder for you to accept than getting the event cancelled. I just wanted to take a few baby steps so you can see how far off you are from being able to consider a reality beyond what you currently accept as true."

"So he found an interplanetary portal of space and time that would only open with the sacrifice of a small boy. How's that? My Overton window getting bigger yet?"

"It hasn't changed a bit. Your sarcasm is just an expression of your frustration."

Ikänen returned to the door and opened it. "I think we're done here. This is pointless. I'll have some of the men escort you to wherever you feel you are safe."

Connolly put his hand on the door and attempted to close it. "No, I'm not leaving. I want to hear the truth. Ignore my sarcasm. Just push through it. Let's go all the way to the end."

Ikänen got directly in Connolly's face. "Gordillo killed Mongchai because they want your granddaughter at the event tonight."

Connolly fought the urge to speak. His mouth moved but stopped himself before a sound emerged.

"And why do they want your granddaughter at the event tonight?" Ikänen asked. "Because they want *Finch* at the event tonight. Eva is the lure."

Connolly's head began to shake in confusion, an involuntary gesture he was unable to control.

"And why do they want Finch at the event tonight?" Ikänen asked, holding a finger in the air.

"Because..." he paused and walked to the other side of the table in the middle of the room and held his arms out around the jars and debris that littered it.

"Because the Bootstrap sequence is alive and working. We just tested it, minutes before you showed up, and it is very alive and well."

Ikänen looked at the other scientist. "Isn't that right, Stobnicki?"

He nodded his head in agreement.

"I don't understand," Connolly muttered.

"That's right, Dr. Connolly. The Bootstrap sequence, that modification that nearly every one in the world has sitting in their bodies—right now—is not dead. It did not die with Faucett. It is alive and well and open for business. And we just made the first transaction."

Connolly's hands trembled. "How is this possible? How'd you figure out the key?"

"We didn't figure it out. We stole it."

Connolly was visibly shaking now. "From who? Who figured out?"

"Your dear friend, Dr. Connolly. Your partner in crime."

"Yuval?" Connolly asked, his voice barely audible.

"I think you know the answer to that question."

CHAPTER 68

Yuval cut a wry smile towards Iga and her cameraman as they boarded the helicopter.

"Welcome aboard," he said, gesturing to the spartan seating that lined the sides of the aircraft.

The reporter took a seat. Just behind them strode Martta, who held Eva in her arms, an entrance Iga's cameraman took great pains to film.

"We're streaming live," Iga told him. "Just so you know."

"I should have closed the ramp before we left," Yuval said.

The cameraman spun around and pointed his gear directly at Yuval.

"I should have closed the ramp before we left," Yuval said again, this time with a saddened look on his face. "That was so foolish of me."

The helicopter lifted off the ground and rose high into the air before moving forward. Iga tapped on her cameraman's shoulder to indicate she wanted to speak. He kneeled on the floor to get the perfect angle before she began talking.

"I am delighted to report we are onboard Dr. Yuval Naftali's helicopter and are in the air, presumably headed to the National Cathedral in Washington, D.C., where the world awaits his arrival. Dr. Naftali has agreed to this exclusive interview as we make our way there."

She gestured to Yuval and motioned for him to sit down beside her. Cords showed in his neck as he fought the rage boiling inside him.

"Please, Dr. Naftali. Have a seat."

Again, Yuval tried to smile as he sat in the chair beside her.

"Dr. Naftali—before we begin, the world is mourning the loss of our beloved Mongchai. What do you know about his death?"

Yuval's eyes thinned as he bristled at being humiliated in this way.

"I'm sorry, I didn't catch your name."

"My name is Iga Witecki. I'm an independent reporter. Over seven hundred thousand followers."

"Thank you, Iga. I'm happy to have you with us."

The reporter continued her question. "Mongchai—what do you know about his death?"

"Mongchai was everything to me. And to Dr. Connolly. We had fallen in love with his story just like everyone else. When we confirmed our technology worked, it was obvious Mongchai was the perfect patient on which to demonstrate things."

"And now he's dead."

Yuval waited for Iga to feed him a question.

"And now he's dead. Do you in any way feel responsible for that?"

"Yes. Of course, I do. We asked him over here. He and his family, of course. It was a long trip. A difficult trip. I suppose that might have had something to do with it. But, with the promise he might be healed, they were more than eager to take that chance."

"Dr. Connolly was in agreement with you on this choice?"

"He was. We knew Mongchai was the right person."

"Do you know the whereabouts of Dr. Connolly? Some media outlets are reporting that he is missing."

"I hadn't heard that. That's terrible, if true. He's obviously an important part of the show tonight."

"Some outlets are suggesting Dr. Connolly wasn't happy with the choice to use Mongchai and that he wanted his granddaughter to receive the first treatment instead. Do you have any comment on that?"

"I don't. We all love Eva very much. No one more than Dr. Connolly, of course. Like all of us, I'm sure he'd love to see her walk again."

"Any possibility Dr. Connolly would have had something to do with Mongchai's death? Some people are suggesting it's possible he's responsible."

Yuval was intrigued with this particular question. "I hadn't thought of that. Though his disappearance does seem strange. He's always been a reliable partner in my work."

"It looks like you've chosen Eva to replace the boy tonight. Was that done with Dr. Connolly's blessing?"

"Yes—he was happy to consent to my suggestion that Eva take Mongchai's place."

Iga's questioning was relentless. "Was that something you and he discussed before today—as a contingency plan or something?"

Yuval considered how to answer her question.

Iga continued to pepper him. "Given that he's missing, it would seem you would have had to have discussed this before today. As a contingency plan, perhaps?"

Yuval assented to her line of thought. "That is correct. It was a contingency plan we had in case something happened to the boy."

"How powerful is your technology, Dr. Naftali? If something less traumatic happened to the boy, could you have saved him?"

"You mean something other than his body being burned to a crisp?"

Yuval's attempt at humor was remarkably odd considering the tone of the conversation. The reporter tried to steer it back on course.

"You haven't spoken much about what's possible with this technology. Is it safe to assume bringing the dead back to life is impossible?"

"That is correct. It's important for people to know this is a healing technology, not a *resurrection* technology."

"Just how close might someone be to death before their restoration is still considered healing, rather than resurrection?"

Yuval couldn't stand to play along with her game any longer. He stood up and put his arm behind Martta, still holding Eva in a tight embrace.

"Here is the hero of the hour—Eva's nurse, who kept her from being hurt as they fell out of the helicopter. Why don't you ask her a few questions?"

Yuval reached for Eva as Martta turned him away from her.

"Don't do this," he whispered to the nurse, just out of earshot of the video stream. "Let me have her. I will put her on the bed and tuck her in. That is all."

Yuval turned to the camera and showed the palm of his hand.

"One moment, Miss Iga. We just need to get little Eva secured into her gurney."

Again, Yuval turned his back to the camera and bent down to Martta's eye level.

"Look, you little bitch. Give me Eva right now or I will kill all of you. I promise you I'm not kidding."

"I know you're not kidding," Martta said. "Go ahead and kill me first."

Yuval backed away and smiled at Iga, unsure how to respond.

"Go on," Martta said. "Do your thing."

Yuval stepped towards Iga and whispered in her ear. "One moment. Martta has a special request."

Using the handrails above him for balance, Yuval walked to the front of the helicopter and spoke into the pilot's ear. After a few moments, the pilot put on an oxygen mask and lifted the aircraft straight up into the air.

CHAPTER 69

"Maduro, what are you doing here?"

"I'm having fun."

"Why are you wearing that dress?"

"They said I'm King of the Handicaps."

"My God, you're drunk, aren't you?"

"I'm not junk. I'm a king!"

Maduro reached into a bag and tossed candy to the revelers beneath them.

"Gold and silver for everyone!" he shouted. "It's free!"

One of Ikänen's men surrounding the truck stepped onto the rear bumper and was about to swing his leg over the rear gate when the protestors grabbed him and pulled him back to the ground.

"Kings and Queens only!" they shouted.

Another man stepped onto the rear wheel but was quickly wrestled away by several demonstrators guarding the truck.

"Infiltrators!" a protestor screamed, pointing at the fallen men.

"Infiltrators!" the crowd continued, taking up the chant in unison as they pushed the men away from the truck.

One of the men brandished his gun, sending the activists scurrying away. Another guard came up beside him and pushed his barrel back towards the ground.

"Not here," he said.

"He killed Gabriel."

"We can't do this. It's too crowded."

"He'll get away."

"No, we can just follow him. He can't stay up there forever."

The men sulked away from the truck and disappeared into the crowd, content to track the Cardinal's progress from a distance.

Ahead of them, a band of musicians and percussionists began to assemble. Drummers lined up beside each other in rows that stretched across the entire street. A bevy of young women holding ferns in their hands served as cheerleaders. Three trumpet players wearing Mariachi outfits took to the front, just behind a wide banner that read "Walter Faucett Memorial Band."

Beyond the musicians were more trucks and improvised floats. Hundreds of protestors were sprinkled throughout with random signs and banners: "American by Birth. Pureblood by Choice." "Miracles > Science." "Finch Is My Homeboy." Two people dressed as enormous syringes staged mock injections for anyone willing to get jabbed by their foam needles.

Gordillo surveyed the chaos around them, looking intently for the two Cardinals he was told would be present.

"Please tell me you know where the wheelchair is," he said to Maduro, giddy with joy as he continued throwing candy.

"Someone's watching it for me."

"Where are they?"

"I don't know. In the parade somewhere."

The procession extended ahead of them farther than Gordillo could see, but it was clear it had begun to move. Black exhaust from the diesel trucks in front of them belched into the air as they rolled forward, the dignitaries standing in the back waving excitedly.

"Did you see the other Cardinals?" Gordillo asked.

"I think so. I think I saw them up towards the front."

Gordillo ducked underneath the top-mounted exhaust as their truck started to roll forward, a blast from its air-powered train horn startling everyone around them.

"That's loud!" Maduro laughed.

"Do you know what's happening?" Gordillo asked. "Where are we going?"

"We're going to the Cathedral," Maduro said, thrusting his arm forward into the air like a sword. "We're going to shut the whole thing down!"

CHAPTER 70

"How close now?" Finch asked as they slowed to a crawl on the outskirts of Washington, D.C.

"Real close," Brinkley answered. "Phone says traffic's going to be a bitch the whole way though. Everything's red."

"What's going on? Is this all because of tonight?"

"Probably. They've had stuff going on all week though."

Finch grew uncomfortable driving by so many people in close proximity. For years he'd lived in near isolation in prison, a way of life he'd grown comfortable with. Just hours earlier, he'd awoke in a cabin thought to be occupied by only himself. Now, here he was, in the nation's capital, surrounded by millions of people—most of whom probably hated him.

"You never finished that story about you and Yuval," Brinkley said. "At that conference."

* * *

Finch thought back to the days of awkwardness he'd endured—painful discussions and presentations from enlightened globalists confident the world would soon end without their intervention of choice. For Finch, it was a diplomatic mission, an attempt to convince Natalie's father her marriage would not ruin his career.

At the time, Thomas Finch was a respected doctor and had made a name for himself as a distinguished military veteran. He checked nearly all the boxes anyone with political aspirations might seek to fill except one: his inability to speak comforting lies. It was a trait anyone in power had to excel at, almost above anything else. Voters were swayed, elections were won, and diplomacy was secured by speaking what the listener wanted to hear, something Finch was squarely unable to do—unless it happened to coincide with the truth.

As he sat through hours of presentations on "Environmental Justice" and "Health Equity," his blood began to boil as speaker after speaker recited buzzwords and mantras they knew would resonate within their echo chamber most freely.

A thousand solutions in search of a single problem, Finch thought to himself. Africans didn't *want* the hassle of digital identification. With electricity never a given, they relied on more primitive means to ensure commerce could always be conducted, a reality the presenters were clearly unfamiliar with. South Americans didn't *want* Zika vaccines. Hundreds of millions of dollars were spent on their development, but with the public's fear of birth defects long since passed, they would have to be mandated by the government if they were to be able to sell them—a suggestion everyone in attendance seemed to have no problem with.

After three days of suffering, the conference wrapped up with a closing keynote from Dr. Yuval Naftali, the organizer of the event.

"Why are you here?" Yuval began. "Why are you here today?"

Finch laughed and rolled his eyes at the thought of answering the question honestly.

"We have had three days of engaging speakers. Difficult questions. Poignant answers. Disagreement. Resolution."

Again, Finch couldn't believe the sanctimonious dribble he was hearing. There had been no disagreement. Almost no one had said anything remotely controversial. The only resolution was that they needed more power, more control, and more money to achieve their goals.

"We represent over forty different nationalities here. Many languages. Many ethnicities. Many genders. But, my guess is that we are all here for the same reason—we want to leave the world a better place than how we found it."

Everyone nodded their heads in agreement.

"Many of you have suffered for your commitment to this cause, have you not? You have declined higher-paying jobs. You have turned down lucrative book deals. You have faced constant ridicule by those who hate us."

Finch looked around at the opulent conference room in which they sat. Five-star meals were served at every opportunity. Their accommodations had them staying in a private castle the public had no access to. A hundred private jets sat waiting at a nearby airport to whisk everyone home. It was a lifestyle Finch felt would be impossible to describe as "suffering."

Yuval continued. "And yet, here we are. Pushing through adversity. Determined that, despite the nay-sayers, despite those who hate us so, we will all leave this world one day with more justice, rather than less."

A few in the crowd murmured their approval.

"We will leave this world with less inequality, not more."

Scattered applause emerged through the giant room.

"Better health—for everyone, not just the rich and famous. More diversity. More economic opportunity. More acceptance."

People began to stand up and cheer. Yuval's voice began to rise in pitch and volume, distorting the microphone.

"More everything and anything those who hate us want less of!"

As the only one who remained sitting, Finch stood up and held his hands together in a frozen moment of silent applause.

"Friends—no matter why you've come here today, we can all at least hold this in agreement: There is darkness in the world that would rather us remain silent. It would rather us stop what we're doing because it's too hard. Or it's too complicated. Or it seems impossible."

The crowd, now completely lathered into a frenzy, screamed wildly after every sentence.

"Do not let them win!" Yuval yelled, shaking his fist in the air.

The volume that filled the room was deafening, their unbounded passion for Yuval's declarations frightening.

"Don't let them win," he chanted with an infectious cadence. "Don't let them win."

Yuval stepped away from the microphone and continued to shout, holding both fists in the air as if some miraculous victory had just been accomplished. Finch was deeply unsettled at what he witnessed. Intelligent, respectable scholars, officials, and reporters had all been stirred into near emotional hysteria through a melodramatic invocation of triumph against an imagined enemy, a profoundly disturbing experience that would change the course of Finch's life.

After the event was over, Dr. Connolly surprised a clearly-rattled Finch when he introduced him to Dr. Naftali.

"Dr. Naftali, this is my son-in-law, Dr. Thomas Finch."

"I know who this man is," Yuval said as a smile wound across his face. "Albert may have not told you this, but I wouldn't let Natalie marry just anyone. I had to approve it first."

Dr. Connolly laughed at an apparent joke Finch couldn't parse.

"Look at him," Yuval said. "He doesn't know I'm her real father."

Connolly squeezed Yuval's shoulder as he bent over laughing but, again, Finch could not follow the humor.

"Is he always this serious?" Yuval asked.

"Only when he meets his new in-laws," Connolly quipped.

"What's been the highlight of your week, Dr. Finch? So many good presentations, no?"

Finch considered how to respond. In actuality, there was just one talk he could honestly say he enjoyed, a speech he was sure was the only possible point of dissent throughout the week.

"I enjoyed Arvo Ikänen's talk, actually."

Yuval lowered his jaw and scratched the hint of a beard on the side of his face. "Interesting. Why is that?"

"I don't know. Less bullshit than everything else?"

Connolly began laughing nervously. "That's Dr. Finch for you, Yuval. I told you—he's direct."

Ikänen was researching ways to address the mysterious clots that were forming in people's blood vessels, clumps of protein so massive they couldn't be removed without surgery.

Yuval's eyes narrowed. "I thought you might like Dr. Ikänen."

"I did," Finch responded. "Highlight of the week."

"Well, it was a pleasure to meet you," Yuval said as he offered Finch a limp handshake. "Take care of Natalie, for me, will you?"

Finch offered a half-smile and walked away before more damage was done.

* * *

Finch checked the gas gauge. Like his pulse, it was still locked in place.

"Yuval and I did not hit it off."

"I could have told you that," Brinkley said.

"I think my father-in-law's the only person who's been able to do that. To crack the code, so to speak, of Yuval."

"I'm sure the conference was a globalist's delight?"

"Of course. Except for one guy they let in. Can't figure out why he was there. Talking about the clots and how to clear them."

"Oh, I'm sure you were interested in that."

"Well, sort of. I hadn't had any shots at the time, so I was just kind of curious about the fact they'd even talk about it. Most people couldn't even admit it's going on so, at this place—of all places—I had to see who was brave enough to do it."

"A kindred spirit, I suppose?"

"Definitely."

"Who was it?"

"Some guy from Norway or Finland. Something Ikänen. Dr. Ikänen. Wished I could have met him and shaken his hand."

Brinkley's mind registered something significant. "Hang on. How do you spell that?"

"I don't know. *I–K–A–N–E–N* I think. One of the letters has the little dots above it."

Brinkley unlocked his phone and started scrolling through the speakers listed for the conference being held in Washington.

"Look," he said, holding his phone up to Finch. "This your guy?"

It was a headshot of a slightly younger Dr. Ikänen with a short biography below.

"It was a few years ago, but yeah, I believe that's him."

"He's here. He's in D.C. Spoke at the conference this week. He'll be at the event tonight, I'm sure."

A surge of curiosity ran through Finch.

"Wonder why he's here. I thought they would have shut him up by now."

"No, he's here. Spoke on Thursday."

"What about?"

Brinkley clicked through a few pages on his phone. "Says *Healing the Heart: New Strategies in Cardiovascular Care.*"

Finch's pulse surged involuntarily. Ever since the global conference years ago, something about the scientist had intrigued him. The confidence in which he spoke. His matter of fact presentation style. His apparent lack of concern with winning the adoration of his peers.

It was too late to hear Ikänen's talk but, clearly, he'd been researching two of Finch's main concerns.

He can help me.

The thought crossed Finch's mind like lightning. Ever since being injected against his will in prison, the cloud of death hung over his every thought. Even as Natalie texted him with news that healing was possible, he never once considered himself a possible candidate, deprived of any hope of life beyond a few years.

"What time is it?" Finch asked.

"Three-thirty."

"Where's that thing at? The conference?"

"Looks like the Capitol Suites Hotel."

"How far is that away?"

"Not far. Closer than the Cathedral. Less than half a mile."

Finch put the truck into neutral and opened the door.

"Brinkley, I need you go to the Cathedral and watch for Eva. I will be there as soon as I can."

Finch stepped out of the truck as the vehicles behind them began honking their horns in anger.

"Hey, wait a minute," Brinkley said. "You're our prisoner. Where are you going?"

"To get some help."

"We don't need help," Brinkley responded sarcastically. "We've got at least six bullets."

"This isn't for Eva," Finch said. "This is for me."

CHAPTER 71

"Where do you think it might be?" Natalie asked Brooke.

"I don't know. Something about faith? Or religion, maybe?"

Brooke heard only bits and pieces from Connolly to even guess what Yuval might have been studying. Regardless, it was enough to know it wasn't going to be located anywhere near the natural sciences.

"Before you got here, I was reading about some study he did with moths and caterpillars. Something to try and see if they could remember things after they'd turned into butterflies."

"Huh," Brooke said, speaking plainly. "Did they?"

"I'm not sure. It's just a weird question to me."

"Yeah, it *is* kind of weird."

"And he had to use pain to figure it out."

"Yuval's a strange bird, no doubt about it."

"You don't know the half of it," Natalie said.

"What do you mean?"

"I'll tell you some other time. Let's find this research you're talking about."

The two ladies climbed a spiral staircase onto the balcony that ran around the perimeter of the room, a set of bookshelves and reading nooks at each window, mirroring the ones below.

"This looks like biographies," Brooke said as they passed another section with titles containing famous painters and musicians.

"This must be the Arts," Natalie said.

"Definitely not here."

They came to the corner of the room where the window didn't look outside the home but, instead, was completely dark, covered up by an addition or renovation at some point.

"Of course it will be here," Brooke laughed nervously. "I can barely see a thing."

Natalie ran her finger along the spines of some of the books and read out the authors. "Philo of Alexandria. Justin Martyr. Origen."

"Those are religious guys, right?"

"Yeah, I think so."

"We should be close then. His stuff won't be books. It'll be papers, unless they're in a folder or something."

"You think it will be more than one?" Natalie asked.

"Might be."

"Seems strange for his work to be stored here, doesn't it?"

"At the house?" Brooke asked.

"No, in this part of the library. He just doesn't seem like he'd be interested in spirituality."

"He's fascinated with it, for some reason."

"A perverse fascination, probably."

"For sure."

Natalie spotted a blue binder just before a book on Numenius and pulled it from the shelf.

"Anything?" Brooke asked.

The binder contained a collection of papers—some joined by staples, others held together by paper clips. One had obviously been torn from a journal, its glossy pages filled with flash charts and graphics. Natalie flipped through each of them, looking for each author.

"These must be them. Naftali's listed as the author or co-author on each one."

Brooke headed back toward the staircase.

"Let's go back down where there's more light. I don't like it up here."

"Me neither," Natalie said.

They settled into a reading nook that contained a coffee table between two plush leather chairs.

Natalie opened the binder and laid all the papers out in order. "I want to be able to put them back just like we found them."

"I don't think anyone's going to be interested in these," Brooke replied.

"Let's hope you're right. What do you see?"

Brooke picked up one of the papers and read the title out loud. "Author of Life. Author of Death: God and the Problem of Good."

"How's that even a science paper?" Natalie asked.

Brooke flipped through the pages and scanned for anything meaningful.

"Isn't there something about *The Problem of Evil*? Isn't that a thing people talk about?"

"Yeah."

Brooke shook her head in confusion. "Why's he asking about the problem of good?"

"So weird."

"Yeah. So weird. Anything interesting in there?"

"I don't see anything. How about you?"

Natalie held an older set of papers closer to her face. It was a photocopy of something composed on a typewriter, an age that seemed thousands of years before the laser printers she was accustomed to using.

"That looks old," Brooke said.

"Yeah, it's real old. Like something he wrote when he was a kid."

"Let me see."

Brooke reached out and grabbed the paper from Natalie's hand.

In the center of the first page, the author had typed his name in all capital letters.

YUVAL S. NAFTALI.

TWELVE YEARS OLD.

The title above, however, is what caught Brooke's attention.

DEMONS IN THE BEAKERS: THE SCIENCE OF EVIL.

CHAPTER 72

Yuval walked to the back of the helicopter and grabbed several ratchet straps as the helicopter continued to ascend.

"Where are we going?" the reporter asked, nervously peering out the window.

"Somewhere very special. I want you to see things from my perspective."

With his back turned to the camera, Yuval grabbed a mask from a mount on the interior wall and slipped it over his face. He traced his hand up the hose it was connected to and turned on the oxygen supply.

Iga's cameraman tapped her on the shoulder and pointed towards the screen on his device.

No Service. Streaming Stopped.

Iga fought the urge to scream.

"How's your battery?"

"It's fine. I think we're too high up."

"Don't lower your camera," she said. "Don't let him know it stopped. No matter what."

He squinted his eyes as his arm began to shake. "I'll try not to, but I'm starting to feel dizzy. Are you?"

"Yes."

Leaning against the gurney, Martta fell over, spilling Eva onto the floor beside them. Iga tried to force her muscles to move toward the little girl, but they would not cooperate.

The reporter squinted her eyes and fought hard just to think. "We're going to die," she said.

Beside her, the cameraman dropped his device onto the floor as his head collapsed into his chest. Iga rolled her body over and tried to raise his chin but felt no sensation of muscle strength at all.

Yuval spun around and picked Eva up from the ground. After placing her on the gurney, he ran a few cargo straps around the bedding and cinched them down tight around her body.

"What are you doing?" Iga somehow managed to ask, her weak voice inaudible over the roar of the helicopter's engines.

After pulling back the sheets from around Eva's head, Yuval took a deep breath, removed his mask, then placed it over the young girl's face. After a few seconds, Iga could see her eyes blink as she regained consciousness.

"Pick up Martta," Yuval said to Iga.

"Why?" she mouthed.

Yuval opened the weapons locker and removed a small handgun.

"Just do it!" he screamed, holding the barrel of the gun directly in her face.

Iga tried to move to the floor but was unable to even tip her body over enough to fall. Yuval took another deep breath of oxygen from the mask, then held it over the Eva's face again.

"I can't," Iga said. "I can't breathe."

Yuval moved closer to the pilot. After speaking something in his ear, the cargo ramp at the back of the aircraft began to open. Freezing air rushed inside, numbing any motility Iga had remaining.

With another gulp of air, Yuval moved the mask to Martta's face and held it tight until she showed some sign of recovering.

"What's happening?" she whispered, unable to stand.

"Please," Iga said. "I can't breathe."

Yuval grabbed Iga by the hair and threw her to the ground. Martta reached out to grab her hand as she slid past her reach.

"Move to the back," Yuval screamed at Martta, showing her the way with his gun.

Her body trembling with weakness, Martta pulled herself up by the gurney rails and slammed the mask over Eva's face.

"Now," Yuval said.

He grabbed the cameraman by his jacket and pulled him onto the floor. His own strength now failing, Yuval stumbled to the gurney, and after tugging on the straps over Eva's body, grabbed the mask and pulled it back over his face.

"What're you doing?" Martta asked, the world turning black around her again.

Yuval returned to the cockpit and wrapped his arm through a handrail.

"I'm doing what you asked."

After wedging his foot behind a metal bulkhead, he tapped the pilot on the shoulder. Without a moment of hesitation, the helicopter nosed straight into the air. Iga fell over and grabbed one of the straps that held Eva's gurney in place. The cameraman spun down the length of the helicopter and disappeared out of the back.

Iga snaked her arm around the strap to save herself. Burning pain seared through her body as she hung by one hand, completely constricted with blood.

"I don't want to die," she said as the strap cut into her bone, her tendons tearing in half.

The helicopter continued to angle upwards and, finally, Iga's grip failed her. She reached for the side of the helicopter but fell through the opening as a blood curdling scream filled the aircraft.

"Don't hurt her," Martta cried, clinging to the gurney as her feet lifted off the floor of the helicopter. "Don't hurt her."

Yuval smiled. "Haven't you heard? I'm a miracle worker, Martta."

With his free hand, Yuval raised his gun and fired, unleashing a bullet that tore through the length of Martta's body—a blast that sent her tumbling out of the helicopter into the clouds below.

CHAPTER 73

Connolly sat down on the couch.

"I'm going to need some more water, I think."

Ikänen had just suggested something to him so disturbing he felt as though he was floating outside of his body, looking at the pitiful shell that remained. Just minutes earlier, Connolly was under the impression only a few people in the world knew of the Bootstrap project. If Ikänen was speaking truthfully, not only did his team know about it, they'd been able to activate it—something supposed to have been impossible.

"But how?" Connolly asked. "Without the keys, they said it was unbreakable."

"Millions of years to crack it, right? That's what they told you?"

"They said *hundreds* of millions of years, if I remember."

"Well, Yuval did it. We're not quite sure how, but he did."

"And how did *you* get it? Surely Yuval kept it protected from anyone. He has more money than God. How could you have possibly gotten it from him?"

"You're asking about what they call *sources and methods*—something I'm not prepared to talk about right now. I'll just say we preyed upon a particular weakness of Dr. Naftali."

"A honey trap, then."

"Perhaps."

"Amazing how a woman could gain access to something so dangerous just by nature of her gender."

Ikänen raised his eyebrows but kept silent.

"It was a woman, I'm assuming?" Connolly asked.

"As I was saying, we were able to retrieve the unencrypted Bootstrap code. We've spent the last few months trying to understand if it would even work. Was the code legitimate? Could it be encoded in a virus to activate it? Basic questions like that. Today—just thirty minutes ago, really—we confirmed it was real. It does work."

Connolly still struggled to believe what he was hearing. "So, you can activate it through a viral infection?"

"You didn't know that already?"

"Yuval and Faucett began working privately somewhere along the way. I'm not sure when, but there are parts where I'm afraid you may know more than me."

"So then I'll tell you a viral infection appears to be the *only* way to activate the Bootstrap. I don't think there's any other technique that will work."

Connolly looked up at the ceiling and sighed deeply. "Dear God. What have we done?"

"You've created a few billion human video games that can be dramatically changed just by sticking a new cartridge in them."

"And the cartridge is just a virus, I suppose?"

"Not just any virus, of course. But yes."

"And there's nothing they can do to stop it if they don't want it?"

"They could wear a mask."

Grimacing, Connolly squinted his eyes and massaged his forehead with his hands. "They could wear 99 masks, and it wouldn't stop anything."

"*Now* you tell us."

"What did you see here just now with your experiment? What did you do?"

"Nothing too dangerous—I hope. We manipulated the dopamine receptors in a few birds."

"*Dopamine*?"

"Not just dopamine. Dopamine *receptors*—the things which bind to dopamine. The things which make dopamine even work in the first place."

"How is that even possible?"

"I think you already know this, Dr. Connolly, but this is child's play compared to what someone could do with this technology."

"What happened to the birds?"

"They died."

"From just increasing the dopamine receptors?"

"It would appear one can be *too* relaxed. Too early to say. We ran another virus that manipulated some other adrenergic receptors. Epinephrine, specifically."

"Adrenaline?"

"Yes."

"And?"

"They broke out of their jars, and did this, essentially."

Connolly looked at the cracked mirrors and glass that filled the room around them.

"They didn't die?"

"They escaped."

"You let them out?"

"They were going to kill us."

"Ikänen, you are playing with fire here. There's no telling what you've done. Those birds could infect others and create a real problem."

"Dr. Connolly, there's an event in just a few hours where nearly everyone who's anyone in the entire world is going to be. A few presidents of countries. Celebrities. Clergy. Hundreds of others. An event that Yuval Naftali orchestrated, no doubt."

"We did it together," Connolly interjected.

"I'm sure you did. Did *you* draw up the guest list?"

"We did it together."

"Have you looked it over recently? Notice anything strange?"

"Like what?"

"Anyone close to Yuval on there?"

"Me."

"You and he are close?"

Connolly thought back to this morning, the smug look on Naftali's face as he was berated for revealing their discovery.

"We've had some roughness here and there."

"Anyone else."

"Yuval doesn't have many friends."

"Notice anyone on there he *might* be friends with. He might care about?"

"He and Cardinal Gordillo are close."

"Does Gordillo have a role in the proceedings? Speaking? Presenting? VIP seating? Anything like that?"

"I haven't looked at a seating chart. I have no idea. What are you suggesting?"

"Think it through, Dr. Connolly. This entire production tonight is for a reason. And I doubt it has anything to do with your miracle discovery—if that's even a thing at all."

CHAPTER 74

With Gordillo and Maduro standing in the bed of the enormous truck, the mass of demonstrators and media continued to roll forward. It was a strange parade, with more participants than onlookers—their route a straight line from the Capitol Suites hotel to the National Cathedral, where they hoped their massive numbers might overwhelm the security team tasked with ensuring the evening's show could go on as planned.

While Mr. Maduro thoroughly enjoyed the spectacle, parroting any cheer he could grasp the words to, Cardinal Gordillo's mind wandered to a more concerning matter.

They figured out the code, he thought to himself.

The one-hundred digit sequence he had carefully memorized had—through his deal with Yuval—granted him not only enormous wealth, but a path to secure the highest seat in all of Christendom. Secret meetings were held, deals were made, and Gordillo was nearing his life's ambition—the Holy Father of the Christian church.

All had not gone smoothly. Some would not agree to what was clear disregard for the safeguards put in place to guard against such manipulation. Two Cardinals stood in his way—two men whose presence Yuval convinced was necessary in Washington. Additional promises were made, and they reluctantly agreed to march in the protest, their appearance cast under the theme of reconciliation Yuval preached.

Confident their normally rigorous security might be at a minimum, Gordillo knew the parade offered him an opportunity to end the threat the two Cardinals posed. And so, with an untraceable exchange of cryptocurrency, Gordillo paid a scientist in town for the event to make him something special.

They figured out the code, he thought again.

If it had been hacked, Yuval no longer needed him. In fact, Gordillo realized he might know too much. With the code a secret, he was guaranteed no one would lay a finger on him. If they didn't need the code anymore, they didn't need *him* anymore, a reality he knew might mean death.

* * *

Gordillo studied the protestors walking beside the truck, looking for any sign of Ikänen's men. Far ahead, the silhouette of the National Cathedral came into view. It was still a quarter of a mile away, but seeing the parade's end doubled his sense of urgency. Somewhere within the horde in front were two men he desperately needed to find.

To his right, the Cardinal spotted the drone operator, stumbling along with the march, his vision consumed by the goggles he wore over his face.

"Hey!" Gordillo yelled. "Hey!"

The man was completely absorbed in the video feed his drone provided. Gordillo grabbed Maduro and pointed at the pilot.

"Mr. Maduro, go get that man's attention. I need to speak with him."

"Too dangerous," Maduro said. "A King can't leave his chariot."

"What are you even talking about? These people love you."

Gordillo looked up and saw the man's drone flying over his head, towards the back of the parade. He waved his arms at the camera, trying to get the operator's attention. As the drone circled around and approached them from the rear, Gordillo took off his black cloak and threw it in the air, entangling the drone with the folds of fabric.

The pilot lifted the goggles from his face as Gordillo caught his cloak and removed the drone. Unable to locate what had happened to his aircraft, the operator put his goggles back on. The Cardinal held the drone's camera up to his face and smiled.

"I need to see you. Right away."

The pilot removed his goggles again and saw Gordillo waving at him from the back of the truck.

"What do you want?" he asked as he ran towards him. "I'm streaming this live for a gazillion people."

"Are you still?" Gordillo asked.

"What do you mean?"

"Is it still going? Is there a mic on this thing?"

The pilot saw a small red light on his remote.

"Yes, it's still streaming. There's no audio, though."

Gordillo held the drone above the truck and pointed the camera towards the front of the parade.

"You sure there's no audio?"

"Yes, I'm sure. Doesn't transmit audio. Just picture. No mic on the camera even if it did."

"Listen, I need your help again. I'm looking for two friends. They're dressed just like me. They're somewhere in the parade. I really need to find them."

"I've got literally tens of thousands of people watching this stream right now. It's the biggest thing I've ever done."

"I'll pay you."

"How much?"

"Name your price."

"A thousand dollars."

"Done."

"Two thousand dollars, then."

"Can your drone reach to the front of this parade?"

The operator glanced up the road.

"Clear line of sight? I think it should. Though it'll be sketchy."

"If you can tell me where my two friends are, I'll give you two thousand dollars."

The pilot reached up towards the truck bed.

"Deal," he said, offering to shake in confirmation of their agreement.

Gordillo reached with both hands for the operator's and pulled him up into the bed.

"Find me those guys," he said. "We're running out of time."

CHAPTER 75

Finch walked up the asphalt, weaving his way through the cars that crowded the interstate exit. From an elevated vantage point the overpass afforded, an endless stream of traffic extended as far as he could see.

"Do you know where the Capitol Suites Hotel is?" he asked a stopped motorist.

"Across the bridge. Down a ways. Look for the parade."

Finch listened to the sounds of drums in the distance, their rhythmic cadence matched by the intonations of people chanting.

"That what I'm hearing?" he asked.

"Yeah. They're everywhere."

With his finger pressed to his neck, Finch counted his pulse as he crossed the bridge.

148bpm.

"What the hell?" he asked himself out loud. "I'm barely jogging."

He realized the press of people surrounding him had him spooked. He'd come to prefer the solitude of the last year and hadn't been near more than one or two people at a time. The streets of the nation's capital were ordinarily crowded, but the madness around him was something far beyond.

Is this claustrophobia?

With years of special operations training, Finch had come to despise *phobias*. They were enemies, their danger just as clear and present as flesh-and-blood enemies and their weapons. Many a fine soldier hadn't made it past "water week," such was their fear of drowning. Training for parachute drops normally went off without a hitch—until they were standing at an open door ten thousand feet above the ground.

As an elite soldier, he was taught how to conquer fear—a much different attribute than courage or bravery. There were some things for which anyone might find their legs give way, things for which all the courage in the world might not help them push through. In those cases—and with practice—Finch had learned how to temporarily disable the physiological responses to fear that might otherwise leave one incapacitated.

With a thousand unfamiliar faces surrounding him—staring at him as he crossed traffic on foot—Finch still couldn't find the handle to settle himself.

Ikänen has to be close.

Brinkley and Garcia could deal with Yuval. For the time being, he had questions he needed answered and, for that, he just needed scouts. Was his daughter with Yuval in the helicopter? Was Natalie with her? What were their conditions? Finch had a more pressing matter to deal with—keeping his heart from exploding inside his chest.

Following the sound of drums just blocks away, Finch walked across an intersection clogged with traffic. The odor of a street vendor selling pretzels and hotdogs wafted through the air as he realized he hadn't eaten in almost a day.

Keep walking, he thought to himself. *You can eat later.*

Two blocks ahead, Finch clearly saw people and trucks rolling through a street running perpendicular to the one he was on. Chancing a light jog, he lifted his feet and scampered towards them.

Hundreds of people filled each block, singing songs and shaking their fists at an imaginary enemy before them.

"Finch saves! Finch saves!" one group chanted, echoing a phrase written across their signs—a tune that caused him more fright than embarrassment.

Finch lowered his head and raised an arm in front of him as if to ward off evil spirits as he continued past them onto the route of the main procession. The parade extended far beyond his left toward the cathedral. As he looked, something hit him in the head and fell to the ground—a piece of candy thrown from a truck that rolled by.

Finch picked up the candy and noticed a man in a blue dress staring at him from the truck bed high above him.

"Hey, you're Thomas Finch!" the man said, pointing directly at him.

"Sorry, bro," Finch replied. "I get that all the time."

Finch ducked his head and jogged away from the truck, crossing the street to the other side. Yards behind him, a man emerged from the crowd and crossed the street, grabbing a sign from the ground to hold above his head.

A group of people stood around a fire, warming their hands from the cold. Finch approached one of the protestors and took a chance at being recognized to ask them a question.

"Where is the Capitol Suites Hotel?" Finch asked, pointing behind them towards the back of the parade. "Is it that way?"

"Yeah, it's back there. We're all going to the Cathedral though. That's where the action is going to be."

"What action?" Finch asked.

"We're going to shut the whole thing down."

"I'll be there," he said as he took off running towards the hotel. The parade began to thin as it became clear he'd reached the back of the procession. Trucks drove side by side, bringing up the rear in style with a single banner that stretched across all their grilles. It read: *THIS IS NOT THE END.* A miniature electric-powered truck followed close behind, a child at the wheel holding his own tiny sign that read: *THIS IS THE BEGINNING.*

Despite the darkness he knew he must soon confront, Finch couldn't help but to laugh at the spectacle of it all. Thousands of protestors, gathered in the nation's capital to prevent what they felt might be the final injustice against the dignity of humanity—a scientist and his minions taking things a final step too far.

They were hopelessly outnumbered. Perhaps not on the streets of Washington, but throughout the world, their steadfast refusal to believe science and technology could solve the world's problems—to believe they were, in fact, *responsible* for many of them—made them hated by many. And yet, here they were—outnumbered, outcasts, and outlaws—and having fun. Full of joy, despite the horrors they felt awaited humanity.

These are my people, Finch thought, wanting to embrace their indomitable spirit openly.

The hotel and convention center began to loom large as he continued farther away from the parade. As the crowd grew less dense, the man following behind Finch allowed more space between them, hopeful his sign would serve to disguise his identity.

Finch crossed the street and entered the hotel lobby, its furnishings destroyed. An attendant at the front desk picked up her computer monitor from the ground and set it back in place on the counter.

"I'm looking for a Dr. Arvo Ikänen," Finch told her. "Do you have any idea if he's staying here?"

The attendant held her hands in the air, her face full of exasperation.

"No internet. No computer. No nothing right now. Sorry."

"What happened here? Where are the police?"

"They're all at the Cathedral," she said. "Trying to stop them."

Without knowing where he was going, Finch took off jogging through the lobby towards the convention center floor.

"Elevators don't work," the attendant called to him as he disappeared from the lobby.

Debris littered the floor of the mezzanine. On one side, a few large rooms were employed for the scientists' presentations. The other opened into the massive hall where vendors displayed their equipment. Finch scanned the placards attached beside each entrance listing the speakers and their presentation times. At the third door, he found what he was looking for.

Dr. Arvo Ikänen.

Healing the Heart: New Strategies in Cardiovascular Care.

1:00pm

Finch rolled his eyes. *Lunch slot, of course.* It was the last place anyone wanted to speak. Stragglers often showed up late, if at all, often exhibiting *postprandial somnolence*. Otherwise known as *food coma*.

He was too late for the presentation, but it was confirmation Ikänen had spoken just hours earlier. Finch opened the door and walked in, hoping to find the handouts some scientists were kind enough to reward their attendees with. He walked down the center aisle of the darkened room but saw nothing. An empty lectern lay on its side atop a small stage. What had once been a projector screen was destroyed, ripped to shreds by someone with a knife and a lot of anger.

A figure flashed across the doorway outside, drawing Finch's attention back towards the light. Two red exit signs sat above doors at the front of the room, fire escapes he knew he could use if needed. He crept to the door and listened for movement. Hearing nothing, he thrust his head outside and quickly brought it back within the darkness of the room. Across the mezzanine, Finch detected the tiniest bit of movement as one of the doors to the vendor hallway closed shut.

Confident someone had just entered, Finch stole across the tile floor of the mezzanine, painfully aware of the tap each step of his hard boots sent echoing through hall. The double doors were set just far enough apart they afforded him a sliver of visibility beyond. Peering into the dim light beyond, Finch could see nothing but the remnants and wreckage of displays and equipment scattered across the cavernous conference hall.

Without the slightest warning, the door opened outward, slamming into his face. Finch reeled backward, clutching his nose and bracing for another attack.

A cart was pushed against the door, full of odds and ends from the ruin beyond. Behind it stood a scientist, scrounging for equipment.

"I'm so sorry," he said. "I didn't see you there."

"Dr. Ikänen?" Finch said in complete shock.

"Not hardly. He's slightly better looking. And shorter."

"Do you know him?"

"Possibly."

"Do you know where he is?"

"Possibly."

"Can you take me to him?"

"Who are you?"

Finch's heart raced as he considered how to answer.

"Have you heard of Thomas Finch?" he asked.

The scientist paused and raised his eyebrows before looking to the side.

"Possibly," he said.

CHAPTER 76

"What the hell?" Brooke asked. "Did you see the title?"

Natalie grabbed the paper back.

"Careful," Brooke said. "This might be the only copy."

Natalie read the title out loud in shock. "Demons in the Beakers: The Science of Evil? What the hell is right."

"Eleven years old?" Brooke asked.

"Twelve."

"Twelve years old? What kid thinks about stuff like that?"

"What adult?"

"Not me."

"Me neither."

Natalie read the introductory paragraph out loud for Brooke to hear.

Where does evil come from? The book of Genesis tells the story of the fall of man and woman as they disobeyed God and ate from the Tree of Knowledge. It never explained where the serpent came from. Two thousand years ago, there were Jews and Christians who believed the serpent was actually good. They believed he was trying to right the wrongs of God, a deity who wasn't the supreme being of the universe at all, but a lesser god who mistakenly made a fallen world.

"What is he even talking about?" Brooke asked. "Is this real?"

"If I had to guess, yes—I would guess this is real."

Natalie continued reading twelve-year-old Yuval Naftali's paper, skipping to the next page.

As science has progressed to understand the inner workings of the human mind, the question must be asked: Where does evil come from? Are animals evil? They might slaughter innocent creatures, but it is almost always for food. Occasionally an animal may appear to purposefully torture another—such as when whales toss seals or penguins into the air—but scientists are beginning to sense even this behavior is simply exercise. Possibly practice for a future meal.

"What is it with this guy?" Brooke asked. "Even at that age?"

Humans are uniquely suited for cruelty in a way animals aren't. They can use their creativity to harm others. They have the ability to purposefully prolong the suffering of a particular animal. Where animals may seek to kill for no apparent reason, humans may seek to inflict agony in such a way their victim cannot escape, not even through death.

"I can't take this," Brooke said. "Stop it."

Natalie quit speaking but gazed at Yuval's paper, reading its contents silently to herself.

Brooke swatted it away from her.

"Stop it, Natalie. Seriously. This stuff is demented."

Natalie stopped reading, but her mind was locked away in thought.

"You can't read this stuff," Brooke said. "Not until you get Eva back."

Brooke waved her hand in front of Natalie's face, trying to get her attention.

"Hello? Come back, Natalie. Come back to earth. Where are you?"

Natalie shook herself loose from the daze she'd fallen into. "I'm sorry. Just some old demons still haunting me, I guess."

"You've spent time alone with him, haven't you?"

"I have."

"Is this the way he talks all the time?"

"No. He can be pleasant sometimes."

Brooke raised her eyebrows. "I've never seen it."

"Most people haven't."

"Your father said Yuval had a thing for you."

"Had?"

"Still does?"

"I think so. It's hard to tell. If loathing is a sign of infatuation...."

"Which it sometimes is," Brooke interrupted.

"Yes, which it sometimes is. If loathing and contempt are a sign of infatuation, then perhaps he still has a thing for me."

"Has he ever been married?"

"No way. He doesn't even have any friends. Not at least as far as I know."

Brooke began to connect some dots Natalie was avoiding speaking about.

"You spurned him."

"No, I didn't."

"You spurned him, didn't you?"

"No."

"He's a jilted lover. That's what this is all about, isn't it?"

"Not really."

"Not really? Okay, now you have to tell me. What happened?"

"Eva nearly died. I was in constant rehab. Finch was in jail."

"You were lonely."

"Of course, I was."

"And Yuval reached out to you, knowing you were vulnerable."

"No. Actually, my father set us up."

"A royal marriage?"

"Hoping to rid us of any ties to Finch."

"A royal marriage," Brooke repeated with emphasis.

"I suppose that's what he was thinking."

"Were you..." Brooke started. "Did you...Were you fond of him?"

"I was fond of not being lonely."

Brooke flinched and drew her head back.

"We attended a few galas and other events together."

"I *know* that. I saw the pictures."

"That was all. Just a few dinners and the stuff you saw in the press."

Brooke looked unconvinced that was the extent of their relationship.

"Was he ever normal?"

"Sometimes."

"Was he ever happy?"

Natalie wracked her brain, trying to conjure a memory of him caught in laughter.

"He smiles occasionally."

"Certain smiles are signs of pathological killers. Do you know how to recognize them?"

Natalie dropped her shoulders. "Brooke."

"You don't think he would kill Eva, do you? Serious question. Seems like you'd be more worried if you did."

"I don't know. I *didn't* think so. But, sitting here reading his paper, thinking back on a few things—now I wonder."

"How does the paper finish? What's the conclusion? Maybe that will make us feel better?"

Natalie flipped the report to the last page, her stomach churning in anticipation of what they might find.

CHAPTER 77

Brinkley tried to switch lanes to make the exit, but the interstate had turned into a parking lot. Tempers flared as drivers, eager to get home, watched the afternoon sun draw closer to setting.

"I'm sorry but y'all are not going to like this one bit," Brinkley said as he turned off the truck and got out in the middle of the interstate.

"Come on, Garcia."

Brinkley looked in the bed of the truck, but it was clear.

"What in the hell?" Brinkley asked out loud as horns began blaring behind him.

He walked around to the other side of the truck but saw nothing. After bending to the ground, Brinkley could see it was clear underneath. Cars behind him forced their way into the lanes that ran on either side, causing even more rage to build.

"Where in the hell did he go?"

In desperation, Brinkley checked the cabin one more time. It was vacant, the blood-stained upholstery the only sign of Garcia. The magnetic gun mount under the dash once held the deputy's firearm, but it was also clear.

"Well shit," Brinkley said, ignoring the blasts of horns and epithets being hurled at him.

He left the truck behind him and walked across three lanes of traffic to the shoulder, jammed with vehicles trying to make an early exit lane. Brinkley pulled himself up onto the railing and looked for any sign of Garcia but saw nothing. Completely confused, the sheriff unlocked his phone and called the missing deputy.

Call failed.

Brinkley tried again but got the same message. He flipped to his GPS, hoping to plot a route to the cathedral, but a search wouldn't even pull it up on the map, a spinning wheel the only sign of activity on his phone.

Networks totally jammed, he thought to himself.

Thousands of trapped motorists sat immobilized all around him, no doubt engrossed in whatever entertainment their mobile devices could provide.

Brinkley walked toward a car to ask them directions, but they rolled their window up as he approached. Other cars locked their doors the moment they spotted his disheveled appearance.

Brinkley turned toward the exit and began walking, his boots more suited to the rough-and-tumble mountain terrain of West Virginia than miles of Washington asphalt. Ignoring his cracked rib, he tried to jog, but the stabbing pain was too intense.

Hope I don't need to run anytime soon.

Minutes later, Brinkley crested the exit ramp, a throng of cars continuing as far as he could see. Each block was a perfect clone of the previous, lined by multistory buildings looming above, a concrete jungle he wished he could escape.

How in the world did I end up here?

Again, Brinkley thought back to the early morning call that woke him from his sleep—the dispatcher relaying details of hysterical parents who'd just discovered their child. He replayed the scene in the cabin as he was thrown into the basement, surrounded by the bodies of dead mercenaries.

He moved every one of those bodies in there.

An image of the man's remains was seared into his mind, a giant billboard of carnage splattered across the side of the overturned ambulance. How Brinkley was still alive, he couldn't fathom. The man had killed a dozen people that morning, sparing only Finch and himself.

Though far away, Brinkley detected the sound of a helicopter, a rumble that cut across the hum of thousands of idling vehicles. He glanced upward and saw nothing but the blue-gray fog of winter sky.

Garcia.

He attacked me.

Brinkley and his deputy had plenty of differences between them but enjoyed a professional relationship. Each knew the other's boundaries—what could be discussed and what was better left unsaid.

He bit my shoulder.

It was a blur of violence, an outburst of anger triggered by Brinkley. He knew not to suggest Garcia's wife wore the pants in their relationship. He knew that was off-limits, but he did it anyway.

Brinkley had wrestled him to the floor of the truck with ease. Yet still, Garcia's reaction seemed remarkably strange for the normally even-keeled deputy. He had latched onto the sheriff's shoulder with his teeth. His blood-stained face seemed to have caused him the least bit of discomfort, shards of glass stuck in his hair nothing but an annoyance.

And now he was gone. He had disappeared.

Additional connections formed in Brinkley's mind, the detective machine his brain had become churning through seemingly irrelevant points of data. Over decades of gruesome puzzles, he had a sense of when things were related and when they were not.

Unfortunately, Garcia had, for him, just become related.

* * *

Brinkley tried his phone again, hoping to pull up anything that might point him towards the cathedral, but nothing was working. The rumble from above grew louder, but the source was obscured by the buildings that encompassed him.

"Do you know where the cathedral is?" he yelled at a frightened motorist, unable to decipher his question through their closed windows. With his hands, he tried to form a steeple, a gesture they interpreted as an impassioned plea for money from a crazed lunatic.

Suddenly, a huge aircraft cleared the buildings and passed directly overhead, the concussion from its rotors battering Brinkley as if he were being punched.

Yuval, Brinkley thought.

He's going to the cathedral.

Bracing himself for agony, Brinkley pressed his arm against his ribs and began to run.

CHAPTER 78

A storm of confusion brewed within Connolly's mind. "I don't understand."

"Your Overton window is still constraining you to things that make sense. Free yourself. Stop making sense for just a moment, if you can. This technology Yuval and you are unveiling tonight. Has anyone else been able to replicate it?"

"We haven't... not yet. It's too early for that."

"Have you ever seen it demonstrated?"

"Yes."

"In person?"

"In videos he sent to me."

"Videos?"

"They just did it this morning. Someone with ALS was healed."

"You saw it?"

"I wasn't there. But others were and...."

Ikänen interrupted him. "Do you understand how it works?"

"Basically."

"And you're confident this discovery is even real? You don't understand how it works. You haven't seen it work firsthand. And no one has been able to replicate it?"

"Yet."

"Dr. Connolly, these are the basic building blocks of science, and you've failed every single step."

Connolly was stunned, nearly unable to speak.

"Is it possible your discernment on this was clouded?"

"By what? I'm not as old as I look."

"The fact your life's mission has been a marriage of science and religion. The fact someone you care deeply about, your own granddaughter, might get her life back in some meaningful way—if it works."

"This is not true. What you're suggesting is not true. It's real. It works."

"You *want* it to be true. That much is not in doubt. And it may be. I cannot say. But, the fact is *you* cannot say for certain at this point. What we can say is—*if it is not*, your dear colleague Dr. Naftali may have something extremely nefarious planned for this evening."

"I'm sorry. I just can't understand what you're suggesting."

"Think about what we've just admitted. Talk it out. The event. The guest list. All of it."

Connolly spoke slowly and deliberately, trying to ferret out what Ikänen suggested as he spoke. "Dr. Naftali is hosting the event tonight with a certain group of people..."

"I just told you something Dr. Naftali discovered. What was it?"

"He's figured out how to trigger the Bootstrap sequence."

"Yes. With a virus...."

The NIH director froze.

"Big event..." Ikänen suggested. "Hundreds of important people. Including you. Your daughter. Your granddaughter."

"Oh my God," Connolly said.

CHAPTER 79

Gordillo watched the drone hurtle into the air towards the front of the parade. Next to him, its pilot rested against the side of the truck bed, his face covered by goggles.

"What's he doing?" Maduro asked.

"He is going to find my friends—the other two Cardinals."

"Okay."

"You still have a mission, remember."

"I don't."

"You don't know where the wheelchair is?"

Maduro pointed at the drone operator. "Maybe he can find it."

"No, he's looking for something else. Look, we can just skip the wheelchair, okay? I've got this suitcase here, and it has a gift for the Cardinals. I need you to take it to them."

"What is it?"

"It's a surprise."

"You can tell me."

"No, it'll be a surprise for you, too."

Maduro smiled and hugged the Cardinal. "I like surprises."

"Me too," Gordillo replied, pulling away.

"Do you want me to bring the suitcase back when I'm done?"

"No. It's part of the gift. You can let them keep it."

"Okay."

Gordillo looked at the drone operator, his fingers busy flexing the joysticks on his controller.

"Anything?" Gordillo asked.

"Not yet."

"How far are you?"

"About halfway down."

"You sure you haven't skipped them?"

"They'd be wearing red robes, like you, right?"

"They should."

"I haven't seen them yet. Still a ways to go, so sit tight a minute."

Gordillo took some of the candy from Maduro's bag and opened it.

"Hey," Maduro said, "that's for the peasants."

"Kings have to eat, too."

"You're not a king."

Gordillo smiled and swallowed a piece of caramel whole. "I will be soon."

The operator sat up as something caught his attention. "I think I see them."

"Two of them? Dressed like me?"

"Well. Sort of."

"What do you mean?"

"They're sort of dressed like you. But, there's not just two. There's probably a hundred of them."

CHAPTER 80

Yuval winced as the helicopter passed between two buildings.

"You said you wanted to be close," the pilot said.

Dr. Naftali knew Washington had sophisticated anti-aircraft batteries stationed throughout, hidden on rooftops in the unlikely event the capital was ever attacked. Sensing his time running out, Yuval instructed the pilot to return directly to the Cathedral, a dramatic breach of controlled airspace that would, no doubt, trigger all kinds of alarms.

"There's people everywhere," the pilot said as he peered down street after street of vehicles and protestors—one of the few things Yuval was currently pleased with.

"They're here for the show."

"They're here because they want to kill us."

"Oh no," Yuval said. "They love us. They love us, and they love Thomas Finch, and they want to see everyone come together tonight and hug and make up. It's going to be marvelous."

The distinctive silhouette of the National Cathedral began to loom in front of them.

"I don't know where I'm going to land this thing."

"Don't worry. They'll get out of the way."

In the rear of the helicopter, Eva Connolly lay motionless as the aircraft streaked across the D.C. rooftops. Yuval walked towards her and loosened the cargo straps that held her firmly in place.

"You've been very brave, Miss Eva."

He waited for her to respond, but she would not open her eyes. With the tenderness of a father, he wiped a tear and its trail of moisture from her face.

"Don't worry, Miss Eva," he said. "It's almost over."

CHAPTER 81

Albert Connolly reeled from the possibility his colleague had lied about their discovery as images of his granddaughter walking towards him melted away. The notion Yuval would go far beyond and do something harmful—to everyone attending the evening's event—was impossible for him to consider.

"But what would it be?" Connolly asked. "Why would Yuval want to harm anyone? We have the same goals and aspirations."

"The marriage of science and faith?" Ikänen asked.

"Yes."

"You're in complete alignment on that?"

"Complete."

"There's nothing about him that's ever struck you as odd?"

"He's got a darkness about him. Most everyone is aware of it. I've told him that, directly."

"Dr. Connolly, you work within a bubble. I'm not sure if you realize that. You work within a protected sphere of influence and feedback that protects you from knowing how others outside that bubble feel."

"I do outreach all the time. Events with schools and churches. I have my finger squarely on the pulse of things."

Ikänen laughed painfully. "No, you do not. Even those events are staged. They're coordinated by your allies, populated with people—even children—who are either known to agree with you or are instructed to agree with everything you say. You don't realize this because they don't tell you."

"And I suppose you're able to somehow see everything clearly then?"

"No. I do not. I *know* I don't see things clearly. That's the difference. I *know* this and try to account for it whenever something new or strange or unsettling is presented to me. I *assume* people are lying to me rather than assume they are telling me the truth. You assume the opposite."

"Forget truth and lies," Connolly said. "*Why* would Yuval do something sneaky like what you're suggesting? What does he have to gain from it? He has all the money in the world. All the prestige. All the power. Why would he sacrifice all of that to do something harmful? Everyone will find out eventually."

"Were you going to the event tonight?" Ikänen asked bluntly.

"Yes."

"And so was I. And so was everyone else working on this research with me. We were all invited and have assigned seats at the Cathedral."

Connolly was speechless.

Ikänen continued. "Everyone on that guest list has this Bootstrap sequence just waiting inside us because everyone on that guest list got the shot. I can guarantee you that."

"What about Yuval?"

"Almost everyone."

"You don't seriously think Yuval...."

"No. Way," Ikänen interrupted. "You are out of your mind if you think he got any of those shots. He knew what was in them."

Ikänen stepped closer to Connolly and put a hand on his shoulder.

"Your daughter. Your granddaughter. I'm assuming they got them?"

Connolly paused for what seemed like minutes, his eyes glazed over in thought. "They were in the trials. The very first ones. Both of them."

"I'm truly sorry," Ikänen said.

"What about you?" Connolly asked. "You and your team. I thought you were opposed to the vaccines."

"We are now. We weren't when it mattered, unfortunately."

"Am I safe to assume you aren't going tonight?"

"I am not going, and I wouldn't let anyone you love anywhere near that event."

The aging NIH director felt the weight of the world upon his shoulders. "I take it you haven't watched the news today?"

"No, why?"

"My granddaughter is now supposed to be the featured guest. The boy died in a fire this morning."

"Oh," Ikänen said. "That's troubling. I'm guessing it's too late to cancel the event?"

"Me? Me cancel the event? What little influence I have is fading by the moment. Only Yuval could stop it now."

The silence of the room was broken by five sharp knocks. Ikänen moved to the door and looked through the peephole.

"It's Stobnicki," he said. "He's got someone scary looking with him."

CHAPTER 82

"Before you read the conclusion, keep in mind he was twelve years old."

"Got it," Natalie said.

"Kids are weird. They can think and say and dream all kinds of crazy stuff."

"Yeah. I agree. I guess."

Natalie looked for the final remarks of Naftali, a summary of what his research found. Despite its grown-up themes and vocabulary, the paper was still obviously the work of a child, its malformed hypotheses supported by rambling denunciations and grievances Yuval appeared obsessed with. Regardless, the passion with which he argued his position was fierce, an unmistakable intensity that continued to define him.

"Here it is," Natalie said. "I guess this is it."

If humans represent the pinnacle of evolution, then perhaps the fact evil appears to be uniquely human suggests it, too, is the pinnacle of spiritual evolution. If survival of the fittest is the determining factor in human progress, if brutal self-preservation is the difference between greatness and failure, then perhaps we should reconsider whether evil is really...evil after all.

Brooke's eyes opened wide in shock. "I can't believe he said this."

"I can," Natalie said.

Just as we watch in mistaken horror at baby seals being tossed into the air by playful whales, perhaps our disgust at human cruelty is similarly mistaken. Perhaps we should celebrate such things as the summit of the human experience—an evolutionary expression of progress. Advancement. Escape from the primordial soup from which we first arose.

"I've never heard something so disturbing in my life," Brooke said. "From anyone—forget the fact it's a kid."

"He talked about this kind of stuff all the time in private."

"He told you evil was good? That humans at their worst was actually a sign of progress?

"Not exactly. But, something along those lines, I suppose."

"Nat, this guy is seriously fucked up. I'm sorry, but I just don't know how else to say it."

"I know."

"I'm not a religious person—you know that. But, this is just so mentally deranged it feels like it couldn't just come from an atheist or somebody who doesn't believe in spiritual stuff. Feels like it has to be from somewhere very dark.

The opposite of light. The opposite of good."

"I know."

"How can you even stand to be around him? I'm surprised."

Natalie wrinkled her forehead and looked down. "I'm scared of him."

"I can see why."

"I'm scared he'll do something."

"You're not leading him on, are you?"

Natalie stuttered. "Not really. But, I did do something I'm sure he's extremely angry about."

"What?"

"I took something from him. Something precious to him."

"Does he know?"

"I'm not sure, but something about tonight makes me think so."

"Why?" Brooke asked.

"I think he wants Tom there for a specific reason. He wants to make a final example of him."

"Kill him?"

"Possibly. But more than that, he wants to humiliate him in front of the world so that, perhaps, I'll choose him."

"Him, meaning Yuval—not Finch."

"Yes."

"Whether he knows what it was, I think he senses I betrayed him."

"What did you take?"

"I can't say."

"You can trust me. You know that."

Natalie sniffed as her eyes welled up with tears.

"Seriously. I really can't talk about it. Maybe one day. Not today."

"Alright," Brooke said. "That's okay. Maybe one day is fine."

"I just want Eva back. That's all. I want her back and okay."

Brooke walked around the table and hugged Natalie tight as her tears turned into sobbing.

"We'll get her soon. I promise."

Natalie wiped her face and tried to regain control of her emotions.

Brooke sat down on the table and grabbed Natalie's hands in hers. "I understand if he might have something against your ex-husband. But Eva? Surely you don't think he'd hurt her."

"This paper we've been reading—does it mean anything to you? The stuff my father and you have been tracking... Does it seem like this might be related?"

"It's hard to say. Did you ever get to the end? Was there anything after the 'calling evil good' part?"

Natalie picked up the paper again. "Actually, yes. Looks like he proposed some kind of solution. A solution for *the problem of good,* I suppose."

"What is it?"

This leaves one thing standing in the way of human progress. One thing preventing humankind from reaching our penultimate destination. One last remaining fetter upon humanity blocking our species from reaching our evolutionary destiny. And what is that? Goodness. Some may call it righteousness. Some may call it virtue. Whatever the label, it is the constant tug of morality our religious faith enshrouds us within.

"Oh my God," Brooke said.

From afar, the arc of human evolution might seem to be a perfect crescent from nothing to the living, breathing creatures we are today. From amino acids to artificial intelligence, from one-cell organisms to quantum computing—no matter how you view the start and end points, most would consider the human species to be a remarkable success.

The evolutionary tree, however, is not perfect. Errors are made along the way, mistakes which are often naturally pruned by natural selection and the struggle for survival. Occasionally, however, such errors persist, despite the valiant efforts of nature to correct them.

"Oh my God," Brooke said again. "I know where he's going with this."

"Hang on, let me finish."

Occasionally, such errors survive, frustrating the cause of progress. The source of goodness—of morality and virtue—may be one such error, one giant blot on the arc of humanity that will forever hold us back. What is their source? Religious faith. Belief in the unknown. Trust in a deity that exists outside the bounds of physical space or time, a spiritual being that may one day hold you to account for what you do when no one's looking.

Brooke stood up. "I think I know what's going on."

With things like artificial intelligence and quantum computing, we may see ourselves as perfectly evolved. In the absence of religious faith...

"The cases your father had me following. The demon stuff and all that."

Natalie held up her finger, asking for time to finish.

In the absence of religious faith, the arc of human evolution might extend far beyond their current station to a domain we cannot even imagine.

"What is it?" a flustered Natalie Connolly asked.

Brooke stared vacantly into space, the color completely drained from her face.

"What?" Natalie asked again. "What's going on?"

"He's going to try and end it."

"End what?"

Brooke's body began to wobble.

"Faith," she said.

CHAPTER 83

"Let me see that," Gordillo demanded as he grabbed the goggles from the drone operator's head and placed them on his own.

"Come forward a bit, they're moving."

The drone glided along the street. Beneath it were dozens of spectators, dressed in white and red bathrobes looted from a nearby shop. Some of them had soap-on-a-rope hanging from their neck, carved into crude crucifixes.

"What are they doing?" Gordillo asked out loud.

"If I had to guess, I'd say they're mocking you."

The Cardinal looked more intently and realized the protestors had stuffed rolls of towels under their robes and were waddling down the street, a purposeful caricature of the way in which his elephantine figure required him to walk.

Gordillo felt a spasm of fury beginning to twirl inside him.

"Move forward some more," he said to the operator, who flicked the controls in response.

"A little more. And down a bit."

Flying blind, the pilot trusted his instincts and pushed forward on the joystick that controlled the drone's movements. He twisted another, lowering the aircraft by a few feet.

Gordillo could now comprehend the scene clearly. In the middle of the scarlet mob walked two proper Cardinals, their faces beaming with apparent delight at the charade.

Gordillo ripped off the goggles and peered into the distance ahead of them, trying to gauge their actual location.

"Mr. Maduro, are you ready?" he said, setting the suitcase up onto its wheels.

"No."

"How far away is your aircraft?"

The operator lifted his drone into the air, high above where it had been resting.

"Do you see that?" the pilot asked, pointing in the air at his machine.

Gordillo squinted his eyes, trying to spot the drone.

"I see it," Maduro said. "Is that where I'm going?"

"Yes, Mr. Maduro. Fantastic idea."

He turned to the drone pilot. "Could you help lead Mr. Maduro to that fine group of people?"

"Of course."

"Like a pillar of fire," Gordillo said as he pushed Maduro to the back of the truck and helped him step over the tailgate onto the bumper. He searched the crowd around them for signs of Ikänen's men but saw nothing.

"Mr. Maduro, this man's drone will lead you to the Cardinals. Got it?"

"I think so."

"Here," he said as he lowered the black suitcase to the ground. "Make sure they get this gift."

Maduro extended the handle and tilted it onto its wheels.

"Are you ready, Mr. Maduro?"

"No."

"One final mission."

"Okay."

Gordillo leaned over and tapped Maduro on the head.

"Follow that drone."

"Okay."

"No more miracles."

"No more miracles," Maduro said as he staggered away, the black suitcase rolling behind.

CHAPTER 84

Ikänen turned from the door and looked at Connolly. "You should go in the other room. Lock the door. I don't know who Stobnicki has with him."

Connolly had tired of being shuffled around but, with law and order completely broken down, decided not to take any chances. He walked through the opening into the adjoining hotel room and locked the door behind.

After latching the security bolt, Ikänen cracked the exterior door open for a better look into the hallway.

"Stobnicki," he said. "Come closer."

The scientist outside leaned against the opening.

"Are you under duress?" Ikänen asked.

Stobnicki glanced toward the disheveled man beside him.

"A bit."

"Is it safe to let both of you in?"

"Yes. It's me. And a Mr. Thomas Finch."

Ikänen launched the door open, confident Stobnicki and the man were playing some joke on him. Stobnicki walked in and made an introduction.

"Arvo Ikänen, this man calls himself Mr. Thomas Finch. He says he is looking for you."

The scientist looked the man over. Streaks of grey ran through his black mop of hair. A similarly colored beard, full enough to have made a viking jealous, covered his face.

"You don't look like Thomas Finch," Ikänen said.

"You don't look like Dr. Ikänen."

"How would you know?"

"I saw you," Finch said. "In Oslo. Years ago. Talking about clots."

"The most poorly attended presentation I've probably ever given."

"I was there. There were seven or eight of us."

"Yes."

"You were talking about Nattokinase."

"Got in a lot of trouble for that one."

"Me too," Finch said.

Ikänen's face beamed as he wrapped his arms around Finch and hugged him tightly.

"Dr. Thomas Finch, I can't believe I finally get to meet you. You were such a source of inspiration to us those last few years."

"I'm sorry for the smell. It's been a long few days. Or weeks, probably. I don't really know anymore."

"You were happy to find your van door unlocked, I take it?"

"That was you?" Finch asked, still perplexed at his improbable escape.

"No handcuffs during transport, either? Guard distracted? What an amazing set of coincidences, no?"

Finch couldn't believe what Ikänen had been able to arrange.

"I don't understand. Why did you do all of that?"

"We got word Yuval was taking you into his custody. At the time we didn't know what for."

The other scientist piped in. "Couldn't be good. We knew at least that much."

"So we intervened," Ikänen continued. "I'm glad you took advantage of the opportunity."

"I did. They nearly caught me this morning, but somehow I'm still a free man. I don't suppose that was your doing, as well?"

"Nope. Just the escape."

"And the messages," Stobnicki said. "We got all of them."

"That was you?" Finch asked.

"Neither of us were physically there," Ikänen said, "but we did have someone sympathetic to our cause."

"I assumed those notes went nowhere special."

"No, we read them. Saved them. Framed them."

"You didn't."

"No, we did."

"I said things in those letters," Finch said. "Personal things—about me and Natalie. I hoped she might read them one day."

Ikänen waved his hand. "Don't be embarrassed. We didn't frame those, though the Elmer Fudd jokes did give us a good laugh. Stobnicki, get this man some coffee or water or something."

"Coffee would be amazing."

Stobnicki walked into the kitchen and moved aside some of their equipment to make room for the coffee maker. Finch looked around at the impressive collection of equipment that filled the room.

"What's going on here? You guys up to no good, I'm sure?"

Ikänen took a deep breath. "No good, is correct. Though it's others we are worried about. Deeply worried."

"Yuval?" Finch asked.

"Yes, of course. I'm afraid it's much worse than we thought."

"Anything to do with tonight?"

Ikänen and Stobnicki looked at each other.

"Yes," Ikänen said. "I'm afraid so."

Finch sensed a familiar pressure building in his chest and remembered why he was there.

"Dr. Ikänen, I'm here because I need your help. I'm worried about my heart and wanted to see if you could advise me."

"What's the problem?"

"Oh, the usual. Myocarditis. Inflammation. Clots. Etc."

"Why?" Ikänen asked, his face warping in confusion.

Finch went silent for a moment.

"Not you?" Ikänen asked. "Surely not you? Why? Or how? If you don't mind me asking."

"When I was imprisoned. They forced it on me."

Ikänen spat on the floor. "Consider us at your service. We will do whatever we can, though we're poorly equipped here for that kind of thing."

"Could have fooled me," Finch said, holding up a bundle of tubing that ran onto the table beside him.

"I'll tell you about all of this," Ikänen said, gesturing to the gear that surrounded them. "You must know. It's urgent. But, let us talk about *you* for the moment. We need you healthy. We have very difficult things to deal with."

"Okay. Where do we start?"

"Well, let's see. Tell me about your diagnosis."

Stobnicki brought a steaming mug and placed it in Finch's hands. He took a sip and winced.

"Any sugar, by any chance?" he asked.

"Incredibly, no." Stobnicki said. "We have nearly everything else."

"Creamer?"

"Well, we have *anything* for lab work. Coffee is kind of on the primitive side right now."

Finch forced another sip. "May we sit, Dr. Ikänen?"

"Yes, of course. Let's sit and chat quickly. Tell me about your diagnosis again."

Both men cleared a spot on the cushions and sat down on the couch.

"Self-diagnosed," Finch said. "Elevated pulse. Shortness of breath. Heart skips every now and then."

"Do you ever get dizzy? Fatigued?"

"Yes. All of that. Really bad sometimes."

"Swelling in your feet?"

"I wouldn't know. Never take off my boots."

"That's not good."

"Yeah, that and a million other things."

Finch pointed to the stapled wound on his leg, the extent of it impossible to see underneath the dried blood that covered it.

"Can we take your boots off and have a look?"

"I'll never get them back on if we do."

"Okay, fair enough. Stobnicki, can you get a blood sample and run it under the microscope? Let us know what you see?"

Stobnicki retrieved an empty slide and brought it to Finch.

"That totally dried off?" he asked, pointing at Finch's wound.

"Yeah, I think so. You have any lancets or anything?"

"We don't. Sorry."

"Then I'll need something sharp. What do you have? Scalpels?"

"This is basically a laboratory, unfortunately. Best I can do is a butter knife or a stiff piece of paper."

Finch recoiled at the thought of dragging a piece of paper across his fingertip. "I'll take the butter knife."

"That wound closed up yet?" Ikänen asked. "I know it's stapled, but is it scabbed over?"

Finch looked down and squeezed the staples. "Actually, it's not. That might be easier."

Ikänen and Stobnicki looked away as Finch pressed the glass rectangle into his wound.

"Does it have to be in the middle?" he asked. "Or can it be towards one side?"

"Whatever you can do will be fine."

Finch held the slide up for them to see. "I can smear it in the middle if that helps."

"No," Ikänen said, still recoiling at Finch's blunt technique. "That will be fine as is. Just hand it to Dr. Stobnicki."

The scientist took the slide from Finch and placed it on the kitchen counter beside a large microscope. After flipping a few switches, a light came on underneath and Stobnicki clipped the sample into place.

"What's he looking for?" Finch asked.

"Well," Ikänen began, "protein clusters for one thing."

"Protein clusters? What are they?"

"Clots, basically."

Finch felt a pit form in his stomach. "I see. I'd almost rather not know."

"We just want to determine how bad they are. Some people respond more aggressively and have thousands. Others form the really giant ones I'm sure you've seen pictures of."

"Anything else?"

"What's your blood like in general? Abnormalities. Malformed red blood cells. I think we can get some enzyme tests to check for troponin, can't we, Stobnicki?"

The scientist continued peering into the microscope. "I'm sure there's some down there."

"Do you think you've had any heart attacks? Even minor ones?"

"Every day, it seems like. I just can't keep my heart rate under control. It feels like I'm going to keel over the minute I wake up to the minute I go to sleep."

"How are you feeling right now?"

"Awful."

"Coffee helping any?"

"Sugar or cream would."

"What's your pulse?"

Finch held his finger to his neck and counted. "One thirty."

"Yeah, that seems abnormal. It's not going to go down when you hear what we just discovered."

"Can we just deal with my heart for now?"

"You're going to need to hear about it. It concerns your daughter. And your wife. All of you, actually."

"And everyone else in the world," Stobnicki added.

"I don't know if I can take that right now." Finch said.

"The Bootstrap sequence," Ikänen began. "You know about it, of course."

"I do. Real?"

"Yes. You were right. It's real."

"Has anyone been able to activate it yet?" Finch asked.

"Not that we know of. Besides us."

Finch sagged into the couch. "That's what this is for? This is your lab?"

"Yes."

"And what happened? What about the keys and all that? I thought it was protected. Did you crack it somehow?"

"We didn't. Yuval did."

"How did you get it from him?"

"We stole it."

"Why?"

"To confirm the Bootstrap was real. To confirm activating it was even possible."

"And it is possible?"

"I'm afraid so."

Finch nearly broke into tears. "I knew it," he said. "I knew it. I tried to warn people, but they wouldn't listen."

"You've reached millions."

"I was too late."

"Well, perhaps it's not too late. You may be able to help."

"How?"

"Like I said, as far as I know, we're the only people that have been able to figure out how to activate the sequence."

"How does it work?"

"You're not going to like this."

"Just tell me."

"It's a virus."

Finch clenched his jaw and felt like he was going to pass out. "I said that's how they'd do it. No one believed me."

"I know. We didn't believe you either. Not until an hour ago."

"What happened?"

Ikänen exhaled. "Oh, we played around with some dopamine receptors. Some adrenaline. Killed some things. Nearly got killed."

"Shit," Finch said. "With a virus?"

"That's right. Without another needle. Without another visit to your local pharmacy. Without anyone knowing it, no matter how many times they wash their hands or how many masks they wear. We can activate the bootstrap with a virus. And it will spread."

"Which means," Finch said, "Yuval can probably do this as well."

Ikänen's head dropped to his chest. "We think so."

"Which means he's planning on something tonight."

"We think so."

"Hundreds of the most important people in the world there."

"Yes."

Finch stared at the floor. "A super spreader event."

"We think so."

"We have to stop him. Stop the event."

"Yes, ideally. Stop the entire thing from happening."

"My daughter will be there. My wife as well."

Finch stood up, his breathing labored.

"What time is it?" he asked. "We have to go. How far away is it?"

"We can't," Ikänen said. "It's a suicide mission."

"We have to stop him."

Stobnicki looked up from his microscope and adjusted the magnification.

"Dr. Ikänen?" he asked, trying to get his attention.

"Dr. Finch, I don't know what Yuval may have planned, but if any of us who've had the shots get anywhere near there...."

"What?" Finch interrupted. "What do you think he's going to do? What's the worst thing he could do?"

"Dr. Ikänen?" Stobnicki repeated, this time more forcefully.

"What is it?" Ikänen said.

"Can you come take a look at this?"

"What is it? What do you see?"

"Just come look and tell me."

Ikänen got up from the couch and raised his glasses as he approached the microscope. He wrapped both hands around the controls on either side, panning and focusing the cells that floated on the slide beneath him.

"Do you see anything?" Stobnicki asked.

"I don't," Ikänen replied.

"Me neither."

"Anywhere."

"Me neither."

"What is it?" Finch asked. "What's wrong?"

"Your myocarditis," Ikänen asked. "You said that was self-diagnosed?"

"Yes."

"I've got some news for you. I'm guessing your heart is fine."

"Why? Why do you say that?"

"Because your blood is completely clean. You never got the shot."

CHAPTER 85

"End faith?" Natalie asked as they left the library for another side of the great mansion. "What does that mean?"

"He's going to kill it. Make it so people can't believe."

"How is that even possible?" Natalie asked.

"I know it's possible because I've read the research."

"Yuval's research?"

"No, this was something else. It was a famous thing in the agnostic circles a while back. A team isolated a gene that had something to do with religious belief. With faith, actually. The *Teoma* gene, they called it."

"Hard to see how a gene could have anything to do with that."

"Yeah, well I thought that, too. Most everyone did. But, they thought differently and seemed to be able to prove it."

The two women walked through the kitchen and stopped just beyond in the living room.

"If I remember correctly," Brooke continued, "there's a gene that everyone carries that directly affects that tissue that connects the two sides of your brain together. What's it called?"

"The *corpus callosum*," Natalie offered.

"Yeah, the *corpus callosum*. That's it. That's what connects your left and right brains together, so they can work properly."

"No idea where you're going with this, just so you know."

Brooke exhaled and tried to order her thoughts.

"Right. The left side of your brain is for rational, linear thought. And the right side of your brain is more for creative, abstract thought."

"Correct."

"If someone has a deficit in the left side of their brain, the right tends to take over. This is where we get savants. Artists. Mozart. Michelangelo. That kind of thing. If someone has a deficit on the right side of their brain, the left takes over, and they can become extremely good at math. Language. Science."

"Sounds like Yuval."

"Yeah, it does. Abstract thought—this is what the research actually discovered,

I think—abstract thought is necessary for religious belief. God or gods or whatever deity you believe in isn't really *rational* at the end of the day. You can't see it. You can't touch it. You can't speak with it—at least most people can't. It takes something more to accept there is something that may be true that you can't verify with your own experience."

"Faith."

"Exactly," Brooke said. "Faith. But, you can't *just* have abstract thought. The creative side—the right-side brain—by itself doesn't automatically become Mother Theresa. You have to have that rational belief in what you *can* see anchoring you to reality for religious faith to happen at all. If you don't have that, it's not faith. It's just myth. Fairy tales."

"I think I see where you're going."

"It takes both sides of the brain, working in tandem like this for religious faith to be possible. Or at least, for it to excel."

"This is what the research suggested."

"Yes. And I believe it. Or I believed it at the time, at least. I haven't really thought about it much until now."

"So back to the research itself. You said there was a gene that affected the *corpus callosum*?"

"Yeah, exactly. Suppress that gene and the tissue that connects the left and right withers away."

"And then they stop talking to each other."

"Yes. And when they stop talking to each other...," Natalie suggested.

"Religious belief becomes difficult."

"Faith dies."

"Yes," Brooke said. "Or maybe something worse."

"What do you mean? The supernatural stuff? Demons, and what not?"

"Yes. Like the two incidents from this morning. The stuff your father had me tracking."

Natalie waited for a moment to consider the implications. "You think Yuval is behind those somehow?"

"I'm not sure, but it concerned your father enough he gave me access to anything I needed to track it."

"Did he know about this stuff?"

"Not that I'm aware of."

"You think it has anything to do with tonight?" Natalie asked. "Why are you seeing these cases all of a sudden?"

"I don't know, but we should tell him. Your father needs to know."

"I've tried calling and texting him all day, but I can't reach him. The lines are jammed or something."

"You have a car, right?

"I do."

"Then we need to leave. Now."

Natalie's phone buzzed with an alert. "At least someone's phone is working," she said as she glanced at the screen.

"Who is it?" Brooke asked.

Natalie's hand went to cover her open mouth. It was a message from Finch.

I'm here.

CHAPTER 86

For nearly the first time in decades, Finch's voice cracked.

"I'm sorry. What?"

Ikänen made some adjustments on the microscope and continued to pan the slide.

"Yeah, I'm not sure what to tell you. Either you are some sort of human-like species I've never see before—highly unlikely, I think—or... you never got a single shot."

"How do you know? How can you tell?"

"It's obvious, once you know what to look for."

"How obvious?"

"Completely obvious. A child could be trained in five minutes to tell the difference."

"Can you show me?"

"I can show you *your* blood. I'm not cutting myself with a butter knife, though."

"It will look completely normal," Stobnicki interjected. "You wouldn't notice anything."

"What's the other kind look like?" Finch asked.

"Oh, it's all kinds of fun," Ikänen said. "Clusters, clusters, everywhere. Red blood cells that look like they're a hundred years old."

"We're walking miracles," Stobnicki added sarcastically.

"Let me see it," Finch said. "I want to see it with my own eyes."

"Step right up," Ikänen replied as Finch pressed his face against the eyepiece.

Finch racked the focus, trying to gain clarity on the red and white blood cells floating through the frame.

"I can't believe it," he said. "All this time."

"You're a *pureblood*," Ikänen said. "Isn't that what they call themselves? Wish I would have known."

"Me too," Stobnicki replied.

Finch felt a deep sting of guilt. "I'm sorry, Dr. Ikänen. Stobnicki. I truly am."

"Oh, it's okay. We've come to terms with our lot in life. We've outlived our warranty by—what do you say, Dr. Stobnicki—a couple of years?"

"At least," Stobnicki said.

"But my heart?" Finch asked. "What's wrong with it?"

"What's wrong with it?" Ikänen replied. "You're a doctor who, like every doctor who ever lived, has misdiagnosed themselves with something horrible. Something they don't actually have."

"My heart rate is constantly through the roof."

"My God, Finch—you've been on the run for what? A week or two now? Poor sleep. Poor nutrition. Terrified of being caught."

"A family who hates me."

"All that," Ikänen said. "All that adds up. Plus the fact you were convinced you had the shots."

"So, you don't think I have myocarditis?"

"Heavens, no. We could go get some enzyme tests but I can almost promise they'll be completely normal."

For nearly a year and a half, Finch lived under a dark cloud—a constant source of anguish he could die at any moment. With no future to look forward to, he'd squandered every human relationship he ever had, including those with his family.

Eva.

A wave of anger he'd suppressed since the night of the tragedy flooded through his body as he collapsed to the floor.

"My daughter," his shoulders shaking as he covered his face with his hands. "My own daughter."

"It was an accident," Ikänen said, trying to console him. "It was a terrible accident."

"I abandoned them. When they needed me most."

"They'll forgive you."

"I cut them out," Finch said as he wept. "I completely cut them out. I couldn't even let myself think about them. It was too painful. It was either end it all or block it out like it never happened."

"You did what you had to do to survive."

"She texted me this morning," Finch said. "I hadn't heard from her in forever. She said, 'They can heal her.' And I wouldn't let her have a moment of joy or hope—even then."

"Well, you're a real son of a bitch, aren't you?" Stobnicki asked, an attempt to stanch Finch's heartache with some much-needed levity.

Through his tears, Finch laughed. "Yes, I am. I'm a real son of a bitch alright. I want nothing more than for her to be healed. I'd give up anything. My life. My whatever—if only they could undo her suffering."

"I'm sure you would," Ikänen said. "We'd do it for you, if we could. That's how much we owe you. So, all is not lost. You've been a net positive in the whole scheme of things."

Finch wiped the tears from his face with the back of his hand. "Do you think they can heal her? Do you think it's true?"

Ikänen looked at Stobnicki. "I'm not sure. There's always hope."

"Wouldn't that be amazing?" Finch asked, trying to sit up straight. "I want to believe. I really do."

Ikänen's face drew into a strained smile. "I don't know if you know this, but I think your wife and daughter got the vaccine."

"I know they did. They were some of the first."

"Finch, if Yuval's planning something tonight—which I think he is, *you* can go. You just got a get-out-of-jail pass, right here on this microscope."

"Okay."

"They can't. You can't let them go there. I'm not sure what Yuval has planned, but if what I'm sensing is true, I think we can guess it's not good. Healing will be the last thing on his mind. You can't let that event happen, Finch. You have to stop it. We can't help you."

Deep in thought, Finch rubbed his hand over his heart. He was still in unbelief at the possibility he might live a long, healthy life. He remembered a picture he once kept on his desk at work—a photograph of a visibly pregnant Natalie, radiant with the joyful expectation of motherhood. She wasn't posing for the camera at all, but had been caught unaware while she slept, her hand resting atop her head, fingers delicately curved as if she were a ballerina.

It was the most beautiful thing he had ever seen in his life—not just Natalie herself, and not just the wonder growing inside her, but the complete trust and abandon required to sleep in someone else's presence. She had done that. She had completely given herself to him in a way no one else ever had. He was not an easy man to deal with—that much he'd learned in the half-dozen failed relationships sprinkled through his adulthood. And yet, Natalie trusted him completely, despite his flaws.

"Finch," Ikänen said, grabbing the man's arm. "They need you."

Lost in thought, Finch's gaze returned to the man standing beside him. "I don't think they'll ever forgive me. I just don't see how they can. And I wouldn't blame them."

Ikänen walked to the door that joined the two rooms together and knocked. "There's someone you need to speak with. Forgiveness will take time, but he may help it get started."

The door opened and Finch stumbled backwards, amazed at who he saw.

CHAPTER 87

"*Who's* here?" Brooke asked in shock.

"Tom. My husband."

Natalie turned on the television and flipped the input to the security system. Outside the mansion's gate sat a lone vehicle, its driver obscured behind the window.

"That's Finch?" Brooke asked, pointing at the screen. "Right outside?"

Natalie couldn't believe it. "Yes."

"I thought he was your *ex*-husband?"

"Ex-husband. Whatever."

"How'd he find us?"

"I don't know."

Natalie grabbed a remote for the security system from the coffee table. "I'm going to let him in."

"Stop," Brooke said, pulling the control from Natalie's hand. "Won't he kill us?"

"No. He won't kill us. He probably thinks Eva's here."

"You're sure about that?"

"I am."

Reluctantly, Brooke handed the remote back to Natalie. "I've never met your... Tom before. You know that, right?"

"He's much different than they make him out to be."

"Sounds like all is forgiven between you two," Brooke said.

"It's not. If he can get Eva, it will be."

Natalie pressed the button on the remote and watched the screen as the ivy-covered gate slowly rolled open.

"What's happening?" she asked.

The car pulled forward but stopped in the opening, pausing to the side to let two other cars go by. Once they passed, the first car followed.

"There's three cars," Brooke said as they watched the entourage wheel into the courtyard just outside the living room. "I thought Finch didn't have any friends."

"He doesn't!" Natalie cried as she dropped the remote. "Hurry! We need to hide!"

With lightning speed, Natalie bolted toward the bedroom wing of the house, bouncing against the furniture that lined the hallways as she ran. Brooke had trouble keeping up but stayed hard on her heels. In the living room behind them, an explosion of wood and glass showered across the tile floor of the foyer.

"Follow me," Natalie whispered as they entered one of the bedrooms and locked the door behind them. It was a room she was well familiar with—a child's room, decorated like a dungeon.

"Where can we hide?" Brooke asked. "They'll find us."

Natalie pointed to an off-colored tile of carpet in the middle of the floor. "Stand there. It's a trap door. You can hide underneath."

Brooke stood on the square and braced herself for the fall as Natalie grabbed the lever that would trigger it.

"Stop!" Brooke whispered as she stepped off the tile.

"What are you doing?" Natalie asked. "Get back on there. I'm going to pull it."

"No," Brooke said. "They want you, not me. They don't know what you look like."

"No."

"You go. You hide. Let them take me. They don't know there's two of us here. Maybe I can hide somewhere else."

"No," Natalie said. "I'm not doing it."

"Natalie, Eva needs you. This is not Finch coming to your rescue, if you can't tell. No one is going to save her. You have to do it yourself. Hide for now. They will take me. Then go find her."

Brooke grabbed Natalie from the wall and pushed her into the center of the room.

"We can both do this," Natalie said.

"They know at least one of us is here. They won't leave until they find one of us. It might as well be me."

Brooke pulled the lever and Natalie gasped as she dropped into the darkness below.

CHAPTER 88

Gordillo watched Maduro until he disappeared into the mob of people ahead of them. The parade continued to move slowly, inching towards the National Cathedral where thousands of other protestors waited for their arrival. Devoid of its king, Gordillo was pressed into service waving to the crowd that cheered his truck's passing.

"Do you see him?" Gordillo asked the drone operator tracking Maduro's progress.

"Not yet."

"Can you move back closer?"

"I don't want to lose track of them."

The drone continued gliding along the parade route, hovering thirty feet above the group of Cardinals—two actual clergy and a hundred other imaginary ones. Its camera panned back and forth between the red mass below and the stream of people and vehicles behind, sweeping the road for signs of Maduro.

"Let me see," Gordillo said, reaching for the goggles.

"I can't fly this thing with you watching. You're going to have to let me handle it."

The Cardinal leaned over the top of the cabin, looking for flashes of light from the sequin dress Maduro wore over his clothing.

"What's in that suitcase, anyway?" the pilot asked.

"Just a gift."

"Why don't *you* deliver it?"

Gordillo grew increasingly frustrated with the man's interrogation. "Just shut up and let me know when you see him."

As the band in front of them passed through a crowded intersection, they paused their marching and spread out, eager to perform a poorly rehearsed song and dance.

"What are they doing?" Gordillo called out loud. "Why are they stopping?"

The drums began a rhythmic cadence as others in the band circled around, cheering them on. Gordillo beat on the roof of the truck, trying to get the driver's attention.

"Go around them!" he yelled. "We can't stop!"

The truck turned towards the edge of the intersection, inching forward in the tiny space between the curb and dancing protestors.

"Just push through! They'll get out of the way."

Onlookers began booing the truck as it tried to bully its way past, prompting the driver to completely halt the vehicle.

The drone operator stood up, trying to get the Cardinal's attention. "You're gonna want to see this."

"What is it?"

"I see your guy. He's running, if you can call it that."

"Good."

"No, he's being chased."

Gordillo snatched the goggles and slammed them onto his head. The drone floated above the street, its camera pointed backwards to the rear of the parade. Despite the commotion of the procession, a man in blue could be clearly seen, dragging the suitcase. Behind him, Ikänen's men were giving full chase, trying to minimize the disturbance mercenaries with assault rifles running through a crowd might cause.

"Oh no," Gordillo said. "They're going to catch him."

He lifted his goggles and looked beyond the intersection as the front of the march grew further away.

"Move!" he screamed as he beat down on the roof of the truck. The driver threw his door open and spun out of the side of the cabin.

"Beat my truck one more time and I will bust your skull open."

The Cardinal ignored the threat and handed the goggles back to the operator. "Where is he? I lost him."

The pilot twitched his controller until he had caught up with Maduro's progress.

"They haven't reached him yet, but it looks like he's getting close to the red guys."

"How close?" Gordillo asked as he unlocked his phone.

"He's at the edge of the main group. He hasn't reached the main two guys yet."

Gordillo pulled up his contacts and pressed the one labeled *Boom*.

"How close?" Gordillo asked again, staring at his phone.

"Oh, this is interesting," the operator said, ignoring the Cardinal's question. "There's a few dogs up there. They've got vests on—like bomb dogs or something. They're really freaking out."

"What?" Gordillo asked, staring at the readout on his phone.

Call failed.

CHAPTER 89

Natalie tried to slow her breathing, confident the invaders would be able to hear her heart beating through the trap door. As soon as she fell, muffled steps and bumps made it clear Brooke was trying to hide somewhere else within the room.

The sound of wood crunching filled the tiny compartment as someone kicked the bedroom door in, ripping its latch through the door frame. Natalie held her breath as hard boots struck across the floor above. They walked across the room towards the bathroom, opening the closet within.

Brooke, Natalie thought to herself. *Why did you do this?*

The steps returned across the middle of the room and swung open the main closet door. Again, they returned to the center, a sliver of light appearing around the edge of the trap door as they stopped directly on top of her.

Suddenly, Natalie's phone begun buzzing. Frantically, she reached for her pocket, trying to silence the noise. The person standing above shifted their weight, pressing the trap door even harder against its spring-loaded lock.

Where are you? the message read.

Her phone started buzzing, this time from a call. Natalie held the phone away from her body, pressing it into the foam blocks beside her. The person moved from the trap door, no doubt searching for the source of sound. In horror, Natalie watched as the mechanical latch above her moved slowly open. She braced her hand up against the panel, hoping it wouldn't move and give away her location.

Confident she was about to be discovered, Natalie unlocked her phone and sent a short message to Brooke.

Where are you?

Instantly, the person above her moved towards another section of the room and toppled something onto the floor. Brooke screamed as her hiding place was discovered.

"Don't hurt me!" she cried as they dragged her across the room.

"Who are you?" the man asked.

"I'm Natalie Finch," Brooke said, defiantly. "What have you done with my husband?"

"Give me your phone. You're coming with us."

"Where is he?" Brooke screamed.

Natalie wept silently—not only over Brooke's quick wit, but her acting ability as well. Brooke struggled with the invaders, but other men came running into the room and took her away.

Just as she was about to move, Natalie went rigid as the latch above the trapdoor slid open once more, someone apparently still trying to discover its location. After waiting what seemed like minutes, the person's curiosity evidently exhausted, they walked across the floor and left.

Convinced she was alone, Natalie crawled from the hidden compartment and up the ladder into the tower above the bedrooms. In the courtyard below, men filed back into their cars, hauling Brooke along with them.

Again, Natalie started to dial the police but was sure they'd be unable to help. Something big was happening. Brooke had explained it clearly—Yuval was set to do something diabolical. Realizing her husband was unreachable, Natalie called the only other person she felt she could still trust, even if only partially.

She dialed the number and pressed the phone to her ear, hoping that, somehow this time, the call would go through.

After several rings, a familiar voice picked up on the other end, a comfort she had badly needed all day.

"Natalie?" the voice asked.

"Dad?" she said, her voice cracking with emotion. "Something horrible is about to happen."

CHAPTER 90

"Who are you?" Albert Connolly asked the bedraggled man staring at him.

"Dr. Connolly," Finch said, a voice whose timbre triggered a flood of memories. "It's me. Tom."

Connolly looked at Ikänen for an explanation but received nearly nothing.

"I'm sorry?" Connolly asked.

Finch pulled his hair back to reveal more of his face. "It's me. Tom. Thomas Finch."

Connolly stepped back, his skin white with panic.

"What are you doing here?" Connolly asked, his face instantly transformed with rage. "I should call the police right now."

Ikänen placed himself between the two. "Dr. Connolly—we should probably put aside our differences for just a few hours. Time is of the essence."

"Why are you here?" Connolly asked again. "You here for *me*? Are you going to take me out, too? Like you did Walter?"

The two hadn't spoken since before the night of the accident.

"Yuval has Eva," Finch said. "I'm afraid he means to harm her."

"*Harm* her?" Connolly asked. "*Harm* her? You're afraid he's going to *harm* her?"

Finch lunged forward directly in Connolly's face. "I didn't know she was in the car. You know I didn't know that."

"You knew Natalie was."

Finch backed off.

"You knew Natalie was in the car, didn't you? You *knew* she was in the car, and you tried to kill them anyway."

Finch vowed he would always protect Natalie—no matter the cost. "I wanted to hurt Faucett. That was the only thing on my mind. There was no planning. No forethought. Just unbridled rage at the man who ruined so many lives."

"You have ruined *their* lives—your daughter. And your wife. Do you know that? Have you ever stopped to feel an ounce of remorse for what you did?"

"Not for Faucett. I'm glad I did it. I'd do it a thousand times over if I could."

"Why? Why did you do it? He was a dear friend. A hero to public health."

"He was a scoundrel whose pride and arrogance may end up costing millions of lives. And you know that. Don't tell me you don't."

Ikänen pressured Finch into the other room with Connolly and grabbed the doorknob. "I'm going to close this and let you work things out privately. Quickly please. Time is wasting."

Silently, Ikänen closed the door, leaving them alone in the room.

Connolly started to speak but was interrupted by Finch.

"Where's Natalie?"

Finch thought he was invincible. He thought nothing could hurt him. The way in which Connolly took shallow breaths through his open mouth made him feel vulnerable, something he hadn't felt in a very long time.

"Is it Eva?" Finch asked. "Tell me they didn't hurt her."

"I just got off the phone with Natalie."

"Where is she?"

"She's on her way."

"No!" Finch screamed. "She can't come."

"I know. I tried to tell her not to."

"Yuval's going to...."

"I know," Connolly interrupted. "He's got something planned."

"We have to stop him."

"I don't think it's possible."

"What are you talking about?" Finch asked. "We can stop him. There's thousands of people out there that want the same thing. We can shut the event down. They'll listen to me."

"Oh, they're big fans, that's for sure. But, it's too late, I'm afraid. Yuval is in complete control now. I think he'd prefer me dead. Him, and you, and many others."

"Look, Dr. Connolly. We're not going to get over our differences in the next five minutes—if ever. But, I need your help *right now* if we're going to stop this thing. If we're going to get Eva back."

"But they can heal her," Connolly said with a half-smirk.

"You believe they can? You believe it's real?"

"I don't know anymore. Nothing makes sense right now."

Connolly walked toward the sliding glass window leading onto the balcony and looked outside. "You were called a conspiracy theorist for all your Bootstrap talk, weren't you? For suggesting it was the main reason for the malkavirus vaccines?"

Finch laughed with anger. "Called a conspiracy theorist? Is that the worst thing you people can think of? Losing the respect of your peers? I lost my medical license. I lost my family. Caged like an animal. Not because I lied, but because I told the truth. You think being called conspiracy theorist means anything to me?"

"The Bootstrap project is real. It is a *real* thing. I suppose you know that by now."

"I do. Dr. Ikänen told me. Why'd you allow it?"

"I didn't. I didn't know about it until after Faucett died."

"You're telling me you'd never heard of it at all?"

"Not exactly. I'd heard of the concept for years. We had a few meetings to discuss it. Ultimately, we decided it was too dangerous and shelved it. At least, that's what I thought had happened."

"How could you have not seen it during the trials? During the approvals?"

"We caught one of the manufacturers adding something—didn't know exactly what it was at the time. I pulled their license. People were real unhappy with me about that. The others paid who needed to be paid, and everything looked clean on paper."

"Those trials are fabricated—you know that. How could have not looked more closely at what was going?"

"There was a lot of confusion during that time. A lot of things slid under the radar."

"It's always been that way," Finch said. "You were responsible for protecting millions, *billions* of people's lives, and you just throw your hands up in the air and say, 'Too much confusion?' 'Can't stop what they're trying to do?' Is that really your excuse?"

"What would you have done differently, Thomas?" Connolly asked, sensing time was beginning to run short.

"I would have shut the whole program down. I would have told the world what was going on. I would have done a hundred things, any single one of which might have saved thousands of lives."

In a way, Connolly pitied Finch. His ignorance. His indifference to the continuity and stability Connolly was tasked with maintaining, despite the most difficult trials they'd ever faced. He opened the sliding glass door and stepped onto the balcony, the cold air sending a chill through his body.

"Do you have any idea how thin the razor's edge we have to dance on every day is? Do you have any idea how much work it takes for us to maintain people's faith in medicine? In science?"

"Why is that?" Finch asked, furious. "Ask yourself. Why is that? Why do people have so little faith?"

"Because of people like you."

"People like me? People who tell the truth?"

"Yes. People who tell the truth."

Finch couldn't believe the admission he was hearing.

"You think everyone's like you, don't you, Finch? You think everyone's just walking around every day thinking how much better their life would be if they just knew the truth about every damn thing."

"Sounds reasonable to me."

"No," Connolly screamed back him. "It's not reasonable. It's foolish. The world is full of horrors beyond most people's imaginations, things they don't want to know about. Some people protect the innocence of children. There are those of us who protect the innocence of adults. It may be a different kind of innocence, but the job description is the exact same. People may live within a sea of lies, but they're happier for it. You may not like it, but the world is better for it. You think the truth is a miracle salve, a cure for all the world's ills. It's not. It's a curse. It harms more than you can possibly imagine."

Finch had never heard things explained like that but pressed on with his commitment. "I will always want the truth. I do not need to be protected. This is admirable. This is what we should teach our children. This is what you should have taught Natalie."

Connolly lit up like a torch. "Natalie has suffered more than you will ever know—because of you. Because of your truth obsession. You're not the knight you make yourself out to be."

"You think you're noble because you've hidden the truth from millions?"

"What's more difficult?" Connolly asked. "Telling the truth, or telling a lie?"

"Both can be impossible," Finch replied.

"Wrong. Tell the truth, and you can sleep like a baby. Tell lies, and demons will haunt you every waking minute. You may have been caged like an animal for the past three years, but I guarantee you've slept better than I have."

"The truth can be just as bad," Finch said, longing to share the secret of the Natalie's car accident with someone.

"So, what do should I do?"

"Tell the truth!" Finch said. "While you still have a platform. Tell them what's happened. They need to know."

"It's too late for me, I'm afraid."

"What are you talking about?"

"I wouldn't be given a microphone now if I begged for one. Yuval's taken everything from me. I'm an old man, ready to be put out to pasture."

"What are you doing?" Finch asked, concerned at how Connolly was peering over the balcony. "Move away from there!"

"My life has been full of faith, Thomas Finch. More than you can imagine. I will not die without it."

With a spryness that surprised Finch, Connolly jumped onto the railing and stood straight up, grasping the bottom of the balcony on the floor above.

"What are you doing?" Finch asked again. "Don't do this. Please don't do this. We can make things right. One video. One sixty-second video and we can make things right."

Connolly looked down, the wind swirling his hair in knots.

"Come with me," Finch said. "To the cathedral, before the event starts. We'll tell everyone what happened."

Connolly stood motionless, no longer paying attention to the conversation.

"Why are you doing this?" Finch asked.

"Do you want the truth?"

"Of course."

Connolly looked down the other side of his body, checking for pedestrians fifteen stories below. He let go of the balcony above and lowered his hands to his side.

"Stay away from Natalie," he said. "Eva, too."

Finch sensed an opening. "There's something you're not telling me Connolly. I asked for the truth."

Connolly wouldn't look him in the eye. "You'd come with me if I told you."

Finch's heart squeezed hard as a surge of adrenaline shot through his bloodstream.

"Don't ever talk to them again, Thomas. Do that, and they may live in peace. That's the truth."

Connolly leaned back but reached for the railing as he began to fall. Finch grabbed for his hand, but it was too late. Connolly's lanky frame tumbled end over end until he slammed into the sidewalk below.

CHAPTER 91

Gordillo tapped on the contact labeled *Boom* and redialed the number again.

"What's going on?" he asked the drone pilot. "Where's Maduro?"

"He's fighting some of the guys in red. They're trying to wrestle the suitcase from him."

"Where are the dogs?"

"They're all around."

The air above them split in two as an enormous military helicopter slipped in between the buildings and traced the parade route towards the Cathedral.

"What in the hell is that?" the operator asked.

Gordillo looked at his phone again.

Call failed.

He redialed the number and began beating on the roof of the truck, slamming his fists down hard. The driver slammed on the brakes and jumped out onto the pavement.

"I'm going to split your fucking skull open."

"I'm waiting for you," Gordillo said, egging him on.

The man grabbed the side of the truck, put his foot on the hub of the wheel and hoisted himself up. Just as he twisted into the bed, the Cardinal kicked him squarely in the jaw, sending him tumbling headfirst into the pavement.

"Get in the cab with me," he said to the pilot.

With surprising agility, Gordillo lowered himself onto the street and jumped back into the cab. He slammed the truck into gear and pressed forward, spectators jumping left and right out of his way. As they rolled forward, the drone pilot climbed headfirst into the open passenger window.

"What is that thing?" the pilot asked again, stunned at the aircraft streaking in front of them.

"That's our ticket out of here if things go wrong."

"If?" the operator asked. "Aren't things going wrong?"

The Cardinal checked his phone and dialed the number again. "What are they doing now?" he asked.

"I can't see him. It's chaos. Everyone's running from the helicopter, I think."

"Find him."

Maduro pressed on the accelerator, slamming through members of the band in front of them. He checked his phone.

Call connected.

0:03.

0:04.

0:05.

The drone operator flicked the joysticks, trying to spot Maduro. "Oh, I seem him. He got away! He's running past them, towards the cathedral."

Slate tiles dislodged from the Cathedral's roof as the helicopter circled, unable to find a place to land.

"Has he got the suitcase with him?"

Gordillo held his finger over the *End Call* button.

"Has he got it?"

0:07.

0:08.

"No."

Gordillo took his finger off the button.

"Wait, yes—he's got it. I can see it."

0:09.

"You're sure?"

"Yes."

Gordillo pressed the *End Call* button, but it was too late. A blinding flash of light exploded from ahead of them followed by a concussive boom—a shock-wave that shattered every window within a quarter of a mile.

The helicopter spun counterclockwise as the pilot tried to keep it aloft, its tail nearly severed from the blast. After several rotations, it crashed into the ground, its rotors shearing off and slicing through the protestors that stood nearby.

Behind it, a cauldron of smoke rose into the air.

The cathedral was on fire, a gaping hole in its side.

CHAPTER 92

Finch stumbled in a daze away from the balcony, his ears buzzing in pain.

"What was that?" Ikänen asked as he burst into the room. "Sounded like a bomb went off."

Finch bent over onto the bed. "What?" he asked, unable to hear his own voice. "Can you hear me?"

Ikänen nodded his head. "I can hear you," he said, loudly. "Sounded like a bomb went off."

"Yes," Finch said as he walked back outside see what was happening. "Must have been a bomb."

"Where's Dr. Connolly?"

"Huh?"

"Where's Dr. Connolly? You were in here talking to him?"

Finch tried to replay the previous few minutes of his life—the Bootstrap sequence was real. They had just confirmed it. He'd never received a MALKA shot at all. His blood was completely clean, meaning he might live a full life. He'd walked in and was as shocked to see Dr. Connolly staring him in the face. Finch was furious Connolly knew about the Bootstrap project but did nothing to warn people. Then he had stepped onto the balcony....

"Oh God," Finch said. "He jumped."

"What do you mean he jumped?"

Finch reeled in anguish at the likely repercussions of what had just happened. They would say he had killed Connolly. Pushed him to his death. Natalie would never forgive him now. Finch's face creased with worry.

"He jumped off the balcony."

Ikänen peered over the railing and felt sick as he saw a crowd gathered around a body on the street.

"No," he said. "It can't be."

Ikänen couldn't believe the man he had just been speaking with, the titan of public health for nearly half of his life, was dead.

"What's happening?" Ikänen asked, looking at the chaotic scene playing out below them. Hundreds of protestors were pouring out of the hotel, running up the street towards the cathedral. In the distance, a dark column of smoke coiled up into the air.

"Maybe someone tried to blow it up?"

"Did you hear that helicopter fly over?"

"I didn't notice."

"It was huge. Flew right over us."

Eva.

Finch raced back inside and rifled through the closet, looking for anything he might be able to wear.

"What are you doing?"

"I'm going to get my daughter."

"Try and stop Yuval while you're at it."

Finch caught a glance of himself in the mirror on the closet door. "Anything in here I can cut my hair with?"

"No one will recognize you. Leave the hair."

"They'll never let me in like this."

"We've got bigger problems than a shower and shave can fix." Ikänen opened the front door of the hotel room. "Go."

Finch started towards the hallway, but Ikänen blocked the doorway.

"Connolly," Ikänen said. "What happened in there?"

"I didn't kill him, if that's where you're going."

Ikänen dropped his chin. "I didn't mean that. Did he *say* anything? What was wrong?"

Finch tried to recall the conversation with Connolly, but there was nearly nothing there, his immediate memory erased by the concussion of the blast.

"I can't think of anything. It's blank."

"He liked you, Finch. I believe in his heart of hearts he had faith you and your family would sort things out."

Ikänen's comment triggered a fragment of a memory, an odd phrase that stood out in his mind.

"I remember something he said. Before he jumped."

"What?"

"He said his life had been full of faith. He said he wouldn't die without it."

Ikänen stared intently into nothingness, searching for Connolly's intent.

"What'd he mean?" Finch asked.

The scientist's gaze began to bounce from place to place as a horrible possibility formed in his mind.

"Do you know?" Finch asked again.

Ikänen broke from his trance and stepped away. "Be careful. Your daughter needs you."

"He told me never to talk to them again."

"The world needs you," Ikänen said, ignoring his question.

"Why would he have said that?

Ikänen put his hand on the door and began to close it. "Don't let them down."

CHAPTER 93

Gordillo steered the truck through the confusion on the streets, but found any movement nearly impossible. Glass from blown-out windows littered the sidewalks as the walking wounded began to file past, their bloodied shirts and missing shoes evidence they had just narrowly escaped a brush with death.

"I don't suppose you can see anything?" he asked the drone operator crouched beside him, still dazed from the blast.

"No way," he said. "I can't see shit. Drone is destroyed I'm sure."

The Cardinal got out of the truck and began walking towards the Cathedral.

"Hey—I need my money," the operator yelled to him.

"Don't go anywhere," Gordillo said as he waved him off in annoyance. "I'll be right back."

While those who were injured instinctively ran away from the blast, those who were not, a far great number, were drawn to the scene. Gordillo trudged alongside the protestors, eager to see what had happened.

Occasionally, a flash of scarlet would catch his eye, but they were all impostors in ruby bath robes, the real Cardinals still nowhere to be found. Dark smoke filled the air as he approached the Cathedral, an impressive chunk of its side completely missing, giving outsiders a full view into the sanctuary.

Movement grew difficult as the density of onlookers increased. The siren of fire trucks wailed in the distance as they coaxed their vehicles safely through the crowd. Some of the trees outside the cathedral were blown over, their root balls resting up in the air. Others had broken limbs and bark stripped from their trunks.

Gordillo worked his way around the side of the building, away from the main entrance. Despite being in the middle of the city, the cathedral was situated amongst a small wooded campus—an oasis of green surrounded by the stone and concrete buildings of Washington. Leaning against a clump of trees, partially hidden, lay the hulking ruins of a helicopter, its tail section folded in half against the fuselage. Two rotor blades were still attached, though broken in half. The others were missing, the thirty-foot blades sheared off during the crash and embedded within trees or earth, a trail of dismembered corpses laying behind them.

With a blazing inferno now engulfing a portion of the cathedral behind it, the helicopter wreckage attracted much less attention. Gordillo crawled underneath a detached rotor blade and approached the aircraft, laying on its side, the cargo ramp ripped wide open. Laying on her side, still strapped into her gurney, lay Eva, her gaze focused directly at him.

"Help me," she said, her voice barely a whisper.

Gordillo glanced around to see if anyone was looking. Content he was not being watched, he scooted closer to the debris and peered into the cabin. The helicopter's frame had crumpled when it hit the ground, the metal bulkheads sheared apart and thrust like knives in every direction. By craning his head, Gordillo was able to imagine the original orientation of the aircraft. He traced his way to the front and saw the upper body of someone familiar.

It was Yuval.

The Cardinal climbed into the helicopter, expecting to see Yuval's legs laying separately somewhere else but realized they were pinned behind a bend in the metal airframe. With his finger resting on Yuval's neck, he checked for the thump of a pulse.

"Anyone in there?" someone shouted into the helicopter from outside.

Gordillo scurried out of the wreckage and turned the onlooker away.

"Everyone's dead," he called out, looking Eva directly in the eyes. "I smell fuel. We better get away."

CHAPTER 94

Once the last car had cleared the gate, Natalie burst out of the tower and into the bedroom below, its door hanging in pieces from its hinges. She leapt down the stairs and through the kitchen, pausing to grab the keys to her car. Before she turned toward the front door, she saw the stack of Yuval's research papers on the living room coffee table.

One more question, she thought to herself. *One more question I need answered.*

Natalie stuffed the papers into the binder and left the house through the front door. Across the courtyard, her Range Rover sat just as she had left it earlier that morning when she rushed home, ecstatic they might be able to heal Eva. Now, the thought of Yuval with her daughter made her nearly vomit.

I'm coming, Eva. I don't know where your father is, but I'm coming to get you.

Trembling with anxiety, Natalie fumbled through the keys, trying to get the door open. The car's computerized dashboard lit up once she started the engine.

"Shit," Natalie said when she saw the clock appear.

6:12pm.

The event was supposed to start at 7:00pm and Natalie was at least 40 minutes away—with no traffic.

No way I can make it, she said.

The car's engine roared to life and Natalie threw the gearshift into reverse.

Maybe they're running late, too.

Before the gate had opened wide enough, Natalie pressed through the crack, clipping her passenger mirror against the barrier as it snapped off and spun onto the street. She turned the wheel hard, pressed the accelerator, and streaked away from the mansion.

Her mind a blur as she passed car after car, Natalie set the National Cathedral on her GPS to help her navigate congestion.

ETA: 1 hour 35 minutes.

I'm going against traffic, she thought, confused as to why the trip would take so long. With one hand, Natalie scrolled to an overhead map of her destination, a sea of red roads covered with "Do Not Enter" icons.

Eva is somewhere in there.

Natalie's heart filled with dread at the thought of Eva being shuffled around in Yuval's helicopter.

Thank God Martta is with her.

Natalie pressed the wrinkles from her jeans, embarrassed at her appearance. The dress she was going to wear sat hanging in the bedroom closet beside the matching outfit she had found for Eva, even down to the shoes—an accessory her daughter seldom wore.

Shoes, she thought. *What if Eva needed shoes again?*

Natalie tried to imagine a grown-up Eva. Sixteen years old. Training to get her driver's license, her feet working the accelerator and brake pedals. Her feet wearing shoes. It was a fleeting vision she could not hold on to.

Let me see it.

Completely stunned, Natalie was shocked to find herself praying.

Let me see it, God. Let me just see her healed. Even if it's just in my mind. Let me see it.

As it was, Natalie hadn't prayed in years. *I refuse to beg*, she had told herself. The hope that often accompanied such humility was, for her, not worth it. Now, as she raced down the highway, her daughter taken from her, it was a sacrifice she was more than willing to make.

I should have asked Dad to pray for her.

Natalie regretted not talking more candidly with her father when they had just spoken over the phone. He was someone for whom it had come naturally, someone who was always happy to pray for others, a trait completely missing from her genetic lineage. She was private. Never needed help—not publicly at least. Finch was the only person who'd ever broken through those defenses.

* * *

Just twenty minutes earlier, as she spoke with her father, Natalie struggled to control her emotions as she relayed what she and Brooke had discovered.

"Yuval has something terrible planned for tonight," she told him.

"I think so too," Connolly replied. "But what?"

"Do you know what the *Teoma* gene is?"

The phone went silent.

"Dad? Are you there?"

"I'm here."

"Brooke mentioned something about the *Teoma* gene. Have you heard of it?"

Connolly breathed out a long stroke of air. "I do. *Teoma* is Aramaic for twins."

"What's it have to do with twins?"

"They first confirmed it in a set of identical twins. One they left untouched. The other, they manipulated."

"And I'm guessing it ruined the second one's *corpus callosum*?"

"How do you know about this?"

"Brooke told me. What happened to them, dad?"

"We don't know."

"We don't *want* to know, probably."

"Probably not."

"It ruins people's faith, Dad. That's what it does, right?"

"I'm afraid so."

"I don't want her to *not* believe in God."

"Me neither."

"I don't want her *not* to pray," Natalie said, weeping. "I don't want her to be like me."

"She's going to be fine."

"I want her to hope and not feel like everything depends on her."

"She will."

"I want her to feel someone or something else is out there that will take care of her. That's how you feel, isn't it?"

"I do."

"I don't want Yuval to take that away from her."

Again, the phone went silent.

"Dad? What's the matter?"

"Nothing," he said.

"Just tell me."

"*Teoma* is Aramaic."

"You told me that."

"You know what other languages call it?"

"No."

"Thomas."

CHAPTER 95

Ikänen's hand shook as he closed the door, his mind racing towards a rational conclusion that filled him with dread. Outside the balcony, sirens continued to fill the air as first responders arrived to deal with the carnage outside the cathedral.

"Where's Connolly?" Stobnicki asked as he walked into the bedroom.

"He's dead."

"Please don't tell me Finch killed him."

Ikänen gazed at the wall, lost in thought. "He jumped."

Stobnicki turned toward the balcony. "Why?"

"I'm afraid to say. But, I have a hunch."

"The world won't mourn his passing."

"Many will," Ikänen said. "He was a man of great faith, despite our disagreements. I don't wish death upon him. Not like that, especially."

"His faith failed him in the end."

"I think it was beginning to."

"You think that's why he jumped? Guilt or something?"

Ikänen looked around at the cluttered mess of equipment that littered the other room. "Something? Perhaps. Guilt? I don't think so. Guilt would have served us a world of good years ago. Now? I'm afraid it's too late."

"His hubris will serve as a lesson to others."

"Let's hope so," Ikänen said as he stood up and walked into the kitchen. Seized with curiosity, he grabbed the slide with Finch's blood, opened a laptop, and placed the slide on an electronic tray that connected to it.

"What are you doing?" Stobnicki asked.

"Like I said, I have a hunch."

"You think maybe we missed something? Maybe he got the shot after all?"

"No. I want to know why Connolly jumped."

"He's dead. We've got bigger problems."

"I know," Ikänen said as he closed the tray, pressed a key on his laptop, and looked over his glasses directly at Stobnicki.

"*We* may be next."

CHAPTER 96

Covered in debris, Brinkley staggered to his feet, coughing up dust that coated his lungs. Scenes of chaos played out in nearly every direction. Fire trucks continued to rush in. Ambulances left in the other direction. Lifeless corpses were scattered throughout the street, half their clothing blown off in the blast. One sad figure hung draped over a second-story window, its body precariously balanced on the sill. Another lay motionless, wrapped around a utility pole.

Someone handed Brinkley a water bottle. After a few swigs, he closed his eyes, looked up, and poured the rest over his face.

"What happened?" he asked the Samaritan.

"Nobody knows. Some kind of bomb."

Well, that's obvious, I guess, Brinkley thought to himself.

Just minutes earlier, he'd been following the rumble of a helicopter, racing towards the cathedral. Just as he rounded a corner, he saw the aircraft circling near some trees, trying to find a place to land. The next thing Brinkley remembered was lying on his side, his ears ringing in pain as people screamed in shock around him.

"Did you see a helicopter?" Brinkley asked.

"Yeah. It was really low. Maybe it blew up."

"Where'd it go?"

"No idea."

Brinkley stumbled across the street and onto the wooded campus that surrounded the cathedral. Firemen had concentrated their efforts on the side of the building, where the explosion had caused the thick stone wall to cave inwards, sending one of the giant stained-glass windows above it shattering onto the stone floor. Although their wooden frames were still in place, most of the colorful works of art that once decorated the cathedral's other windows were completely obliterated.

Through toppled trees, Brinkley caught sight of a small fire burning beyond. After walking closer, he recognized the wreckage of the helicopter, now starting to burn.

"Hang on," he said to Eva as he realized she was alive, still strapped into her bed. “I’ll get you out.”

Cradling her body with his arm, Brinkley unlatched each strap until he was able to gently pull the girl from her gurney. Flames began to appear underneath the debris.

“That man killed Martta,” Eva said, whimpering.

“What man?”

“The man in the helicopter.”

Brinkley craned his neck and realized someone was still pinned inside.

“Is that Dr. Naftali? The bald guy with the glasses?”

Eva began to cry. “Yes. He shot her, and she fell out.”

“I’m sorry,” Brinkley said, trying to comfort her. “Maybe she’s okay.”

“We were way up in the sky. She’s not okay. She’s dead.”

“I’m sorry.”

The intensity of the heat began to rise and Brinkley backed away. Inside the helicopter, he could see Yuval stirring.

“He’s alive,” Brinkley said, as he laid Eva down on the ground. “I’ll be right back.”

“He’ll kill you, too.”

Brinkley crawled up into the interior of the helicopter, grasping onto bent pieces of metal for grip. Inside, Yuval was pinned at his waist by an aluminum spar that ran from floor to ceiling.

“Help me,” Yuval’s raspy voice said. “I don’t want to burn.”

Brinkley braced his leg against the metal and pulled, but it wouldn’t move. The metal was getting too hot to touch so he pulled his sleeves over his hands and wrapped both of them around the bent pole, pulling hard. Grunting with intense effort, it still wouldn’t budge.

“I can’t move it,” Brinkley said. “I’m not strong enough.”

“Use the straps,” Yuval replied.

Brinkley ran outside and grabbed the ratchet straps from beside Eva’s bed. After looping them around the hooks on the cargo door, he connected them together behind the pole and began swiveling the handles back and forth. With each click the slack began to lessen and, eventually, the metal began to groan in complaint.

“Hurry,” Yuval said. “Please.”

The nylon webbing stretched near its breaking point as Brinkley swung both handles with his hands. With a chilling scream, the aluminum spar bent in an entirely new direction, freeing Yuval’s lower body. He dropped to the ground and, with his legs completely disabled, tried to crawl out using just his hands.

“Pull me out,” Yuval said. “We’ve got to get away.”

Flames licked along the entire length of the helicopter, the smell of spilled fuel now clearly noticeable. Brinkley grabbed Yuval’s hands and, after wrestling him free of the ruined machine, collapsed onto his side in exhaustion.

"Her bed," Yuval said, pointing back inside the aircraft. "Undo the straps and grab her bed."

"No way," Brinkley replied, trying to catch his breath.

"It's got her oxygen on it," Yuval lied. "She'll die without it."

Brinkley raged with anger. Bracing his face against the heat, he stood up and walked back within the aircraft, undoing the straps that locked Eva's gurney in place onto the cargo ramp. Yuval crawled around the front of the aircraft, reached through broken glass inside the cockpit, and flicked a hydraulic switch. With the weight of the aircraft resting completely on the ramp, it began to close quickly.

Unaware of what was happening, Brinkley screamed for help.

"Hey!" he said. "I'm stuck."

Yuval crawled back to the side of the helicopter and gathered Eva in his arms as flames continued to engulf the wreckage. From the outside, Yuval could clearly see Brinkley's arms stretching through the narrow opening, pleading for someone to give him aid.

"I can't get out! Please, someone help me! I'm going to die!"

CHAPTER 97

Miles ahead of Natalie, Brooke sat anxiously in the passenger seat of a black sedan, its driver weaving through traffic.

"You're going to get us killed," she said.

"Be quiet."

"That's the whole point, I suppose, right? You want us killed? Me and my husband."

"You talk an awful lot about your husband."

"Do you work for Yuval?"

"You know, I saw him this morning," the man said, lifting his shirt to reveal his dark purple torso. "Your husband, that is. Gave me a nice gift."

"Lovely," Brooke said, turning away in disgust. "You work for Yuval, don't you?"

"Of course I do. Everyone works for him, in one way or the other."

"Not everyone," Brooke replied.

The driver raised an eyebrow and looked over his shoulder as he made a quick lane change.

"Do you even know what's going on?" Brooke asked. "Or are you just some grunt being told what to do to get your paycheck?"

"Probably somewhere in between. A grunt who knows what's going on."

"With a paycheck."

"Man's gotta eat."

"What's your name?" Brooke asked.

"Not your concern."

"I don't think you actually have any idea what's going on."

"I do."

"No, you don't."

"And I suppose you do?"

"I have the plans," she said, pointing to her temple. "Locked in here."

"Yuval's plans?"

"Yep."

"Your father give them to you?"

"My father?" Brooke asked, forgetting for a moment who she was pretending to be. "He's dead."

"Really? Not last I heard."

"Dead to me," Brooke said, stumbling to recover. "We fight constantly."

"You're not Finch's wife, are you?"

Brooke locked up but was able to recover quickly. "You don't really work for Yuval, do you?"

She reached her hand towards the driver to attempt an awkward handshake. "I'm Natalie Connolly. Or Natalie Finch—depending on who's asking."

The driver looked unconvinced. "*I'm* asking."

"Well, then it's Natalie Connolly. What's your name?"

The driver looked in the rear-view mirror before changing lanes again. "My name is Vickers. And I want to know why you haven't asked a single question about your daughter."

CHAPTER 98

Cardinal Gordillo ignored the maelstrom around him and traced his way back down the parade route, searching each cross street or alleyway for red. He'd already passed several protestors still wearing their red bathrobes and soap crosses, but to his dismay, none of them appeared to have been close enough to the blast to show serious injuries.

Maduro got too far away, he thought to himself.

From what he could tell, bomb-sniffing dogs sounded the alarm once Maduro got close to the two Cardinals they were trained to protect. In his blue dress, pulling a black suitcase behind him, he wasn't hard to miss. Once the dogs caught the scent, security guards disguised as protestors moved into place. Unaware of Gordillo's plan, and with guns pointed directly at him, Maduro panicked and ran away as fast as he could—a challenge for anyone with cerebral palsy.

The wheelchair probably wouldn't have mattered.

After a few rings, Gordillo ended the call, hoping to make another attempt on the two Cardinal's lives. But, it had come too late—a red LED on the flip phone taped inside the suitcase lit up, sending voltage down a wire that started a ten-second countdown sequence. If the call had ended a moment earlier, the light would have turned off, the voltage would have dropped, and the countdown sequence would have reset.

As things happened, it did not, and so, primers were fired deep within the compound the suitcase was filled with. Normally, *octanitrocubane* would have been impossible to obtain. With hundreds of the world's most brilliant scientists in town—and cash to spare—Gordillo had little trouble finding someone willing to help. And so, a violent chemical reaction occurred, unleashing a blast of energy twice as powerful as C4, the explosive of choice for military operations.

Most smaller bombs relied on a blast propelling shrapnel—hundreds of tiny shards of metal—in every direction, each one a potential deadly knife slicing into flesh. The suitcase Maduro pulled behind him contained nothing that would serve in that way. The shockwave from the blast itself was powerful enough to lift two-hundred-pound humans up into the air and fling them against buildings as if they'd been hit by freight trains. Anything within twenty feet of the explosion would likely have been pulverized.

Unfortunately, Maduro had evidently made it far enough away to spare the two Cardinals Gordillo so badly wanted dead. The exterior Cathedral wall, its mortar weakened by nearly a hundred years of expansion and contraction, could not hold. A single stone broke loose in the blast, loosening others around it. Like dominoes, the stones above cascaded into the initial opening, a fissure which eventually reached from the ground to hundreds of feet above, stopping just short of the roof.

The road to the papacy was never going to be easy—the Cardinal knew that from the start. His alliance with Yuval was supposed to have ensured his ascendancy within the church but, as it stood, he was out over two million dollars with nothing to show for it but a pile of bodies cluttering the street.

At least Yuval is dead.

With the recent revelation his Bootstrap key was no longer needed, Gordillo knew he was a marked man, his attendance at the summit likely requested by Yuval simply as a way to more easily dispose of him. There were too many secrets between them. Too much money exchanged. Too much at stake for both of them. It was either him or Yuval. One of them would have to die. It was simply a matter of who would act first. And by good fortune, the suitcase explosion had knocked Yuval's helicopter to the ground, crushing him within the wreckage.

After passing a series of newer retail stores, their shatter-proof windows splintered in place, Gordillo peered within an old coffee shop, the plate glass that once lined its facade completely destroyed. A group of people surrounded a body lying atop a couple of tables pushed together. Underneath, a large red robe lay crumpled across the floor, discarded in apparent haste.

Someone fanned a laminated menu above the body in an attempt to recycle the air. Gordillo stepped through the door and realized an EMT was working on the man, a bag of saline already held above him. Beside the table, another man knelt in prayer, a sub-machine gun slung from his shoulder, his shirt covered in blood.

Cardinal Olevnik.

Gordillo couldn't believe his luck. He'd found Cardinal Olevnik lying in the coffee shop. A security guard bowed beside him, also wounded from the blast, no doubt begging God to save Olevnik's life.

"How's he doing?" Gordillo asked the EMT tightening a tourniquet.

"I'm not sure. Vitals seem okay. Bled a lot. Not sure how much. It's stopped, for now."

"Has he spoken any?"

"Just a little. Asking where he is—that kind of thing. Fluids should help."

Gordillo knelt beside the security guard and clasped his hands in prayer.

"What happened? Bomb?" he asked.

The guard looked up. "Must have been."

"Any idea who would have done it?"

"I don't know. Both Cardinal Olevnik and Vallcorba seem well-liked. By everyone—both sides, I mean."

"Indeed," Gordillo said. "You think they were the targets?"

"Definitely. Someone came up and tried to detonate something. A container, I think. It had wheels. I didn't see much of what happened. Just heard the dogs and it was chaos after that."

"Do you know where Cardinal Vallcorba is?"

"No idea."

"Have you seen him at all since the explosion?"

"No. I wandered for a few minutes. Just happened to see Cardinal Olevnik in here and started praying."

"You've done good. You may have saved his life somehow."

Gordillo patted the security guard on his shoulder and surveyed the room. He walked behind the counter and noticed an espresso cup, still warm to the touch. With both hands, he raised the glass to his lips and drew off a tiny sip.

"Whew," he said to the EMT, smacking his lips. "Don't need a triple-shot right now, do we?"

Glancing out towards the street, Gordillo dumped a silver cup of ground beans into his pocket and returned to the table.

"Men, I need just a moment with Cardinal Olevnik."

"He's not stable yet," the technician replied.

The security guard shook his head. "I'm not leaving."

Gordillo tried again. "It's a rite. A secret rite we use for situations like this."

"I'll leave once he's stable."

"I'll leave when he leaves," the guard added.

The Cardinal smiled, trying to suppress the anger bristling up and down his spine. "Very well. I'll wait."

He grabbed the saline bag from the EMT and raised it up high. "At least let me help."

"Thank you."

With a pair of shears, the technician cut more of Cardinal Olevnik's sleeve away and prepared to dress a wound. Gordillo turned away from the table and reached behind him to grab the shears.

"How many dead, you think?" he asked as he sliced the corner of the saline bag open.

"I don't know. At least fifty. Maybe a hundred."

Gordillo reached into his pocket and began transferring the ground beans into the saline bag. After a few handfuls, he took an enormous swig from the glass of espresso, held the bag to his mouth, and spit into it. Pinching off the corner, he rotated the bag, mixing its contents thoroughly.

"You got to hold that up high," the EMT said, noticing Gordillo's odd positioning. "Let gravity do the work."

Gordillo swept his arm over the table, toppling the technician's bag onto the floor. The instant the EMT looked away, he took the saline bag in both hands and squeezed it as hard as he could.

On the table, Cardinal Olevnik twisted in pain as ounces of caffeinated fluid were forced into his bloodstream. Gordillo yanked the line from his arm and dropped it on the floor.

"It came out," he said as the technician tried to gather the contents of his bag.

"What came out?"

"The tube. It came out of his arm."

"That's never happened before."

"I better clean it," Gordillo said, crumpling the tube into a ball.

"You can't do that. We'll have to use a new one."

"I can clean it good. It's no problem."

"Stop," the EMT said. "Just stop. You're not helping. Just back up until I'm done. I can hold the bag."

The table began to vibrate as Cardinal Olevnik's legs quivered.

"What's going on?" Gordillo asked.

"I don't know."

The shaking overtook his whole body as he began to convulse violently.

"What's happening? Is he okay?"

"I don't know. He's having a seizure or something."

"Can you stop it?"

The security guard braced the tables from toppling over as the Cardinal began to flinch wildly.

"I don't have the right medicine."

"What do you need?" Gordillo asked, headed for the door. "I'll go find it."

"We need an ambulance. He needs to go to the hospital."

"Okay. Just keep him alive. I'll be right back."

Gordillo stepped through the doorway and wiped the grounds from his hands, scanning the mayhem for one more red robe.

CHAPTER 99

Keeping to the back streets, Finch followed the smoke until he reached the rear of the campus surrounding the Cathedral. People sat with their backs against trees, sipping water, inspecting each other's wounds. Others sat slouched over and didn't move, a haunting reminder of what had just happened.

Again, the instinct to hide nearly overcame him. Finch put his finger to his neck and had begun to count his pulse when he recalled what Dr. Ikänen had told him.

Your blood is completely clean, Ikänen had said. *You never got the shot.*

For Finch, it had become a death sentence, a future guarantee of an early exit from the mortal coils of earth. With access to medical care, he may have been okay. Without the stressors and travails of living in hiding, perhaps then, he might have also been okay. But, as he'd been forced to live, he'd woken up each day believing his time was short, his entire body turned into a spike-protein-making factory that would one day kill him.

You don't need to do this anymore, he thought.

Having grown accustomed to the frequent pulse checks, he kept his finger in place and finished the count anyway.

114bpm.

In defiance of the fear that still remained, Finch had run nearly a quarter of a mile from the hotel and felt nothing. No dizziness. No shortness of breath. He wasn't yet ready to push himself to the limit, but still, the desire to set things right with Natalie—with Eva—exploded within him.

Out of habit, Finch grabbed his upper arm and rubbed it, a custom he developed when released back into his jail cell after being drugged, taken to the infirmary, and injected.

Injected? he asked himself. *With what?*

Lee Penitentiary was a federal prison—a serious place for serious offenders. Finch assumed combat had hardened him enough that incarceration wouldn't challenge him. He was wrong. With an hour a day of exercise and a library of books he had no interest in reading, Finch struggled to maintain his sanity.

Life in prison. With no release.

He remembered the shock of hearing the sentence come down from the judge. The unbridled applause that broke out in the courtroom and spread into the hallway outside. It was all part of the end of a chilling turn his life had taken when he followed Natalie to Faucett's retirement party and waited for hours in the parking deck for her to leave.

Injected with what? he asked again.

Visits to the infirmary at the prison were typically on a routine schedule—a basic check-up every four months. A more thorough, yearly check-up took place in the presence of an armed guard, despite any indignities it might cause. Requests for medical care were often ignored, the risks of dangerous felons engineering a miraculous escape simply too great.

At first, interactions with the doctor were a welcome chance for Finch to break the monotony of prison life with something different—an interaction with one of his peers. Although his opinions were clearly unwelcome, he made the most of every opportunity to spread *the gospel of truth* as he called it.

One day, his lunch sat especially heavy on his stomach. His eyes grew heavy, and he was more than happy to waste the afternoon with sleep. Sometime during his nap, he realized he'd been transported to the infirmary. Barely conscious, completely unable to move his body, he realized there were other people in the room, doctors he'd never seen before.

When he finally awoke, it was 9pm at night. His arm was throbbing with pain, but he had no other recollection as to what had happened. A few days later, a note arrived, tucked within the folds of his laundry.

I tried to stop them. Next time, I'll warn you.

Weeks passed without another medical visit. Finch had nearly forgotten about the message when another piece of paper fell out of his clothing.

Something's brewing. Nothing specific yet. Leave me a note in your clothes and I'll get it to the right people.

"The right people?" Finch asked out loud. Killing Faucett and nearly his wife and daughter, there seemed to be no one that might defend him. Who would care about what he had to say?

With nothing to lose, Finch traded his autograph for some paper and a pen from a guard desperate to turn a buck from his notoriety. Afraid he might completely forget the research he'd done, he set out to document everything he knew in the most concise wording he could think of.

A month passed and a third note appeared in his laundry.

Message received with many thanks. Trouble brewing. Probably tomorrow morning or the next. Skip your breakfast.

Finch ripped the note into tiny pieces and flushed them down his toilet. After a sleepless night, he received his breakfast through a slot in his door and set about inspecting it. He smelled the coffee, confident they could hide something within such a distinctive tasting liquid. Full of apprehension, Finch took two sips of coffee and poured it down the sink. He chopped the eggs and sausage into little bits, smelling each morsel for something foul. Again, there seemed to be nothing wrong. Regardless, Finch took the contents and dumped them in the toilet.

Just thirty minutes later, someone opened the flap in his door. Sitting upright in his bed, Finch realized someone was peeking in to check to see if he was awake or not. With the expectation they would come around and check again, Finch laid down in his bed and pretended to sleep.

Another half hour later, Finch heard the flap open again. Seconds later, it closed gently. Electric solenoids buzzed as the spring-loaded locks that secured the door were temporarily retracted. Three men came in, secured Finch to a stretcher, then rolled him away towards the infirmary.

Unwilling to take any chances, Finch kept his eyes closed until he felt sure no one was looking. When he opened them, two physicians stood with their backs to him by a laptop, one of them pointing at the screen. They spoke in hushed tones, quiet enough they could barely be heard.

Despite the precautions he had taken with his breakfast, the room began to rotate slowly, causing Finch to spin his head to counteract its effect. It became clear the coffee had been spiked, his two sips enough to send him reeling.

Let's have a look, shall we?

One of them had spoken, though distorted—as if it had come through a broken speaker.

He closed his eyes as they approached his arm and rolled up his sleeve. Fearing the worst, Finch readied himself to tip his gurney over should he sense them bringing a needle nearby. Unable to keep his eyelids closed, Finch relaxed and let them part just enough to see what was going on.

Hovering beside him, one of the doctors wrapped an elastic band tightly around his elbow. The other had a syringe in his hand, the silver needle glistening under the fluorescent light. Without a thought, Finch twisted hard beneath his straps, trying to rock the gurney over.

He's awake, one of them said, their digitized voice emanating from a speaker in the front of a full-faced helmet they both wore.

Shoot him, the other said, as he dropped the needle on the table and grabbed a jet injector. Half-conscious, Finch continued to struggle to break free of his restraints until a doctor pressed the injector into his shoulder and fired twice. Within seconds, Finch felt a wave of dizziness pass through his body until everything went black.

* * *

The memory of the event came in bits and pieces every time Finch tried to remember it. The conversation the doctors had with each other. The strange attire they wore. The elastic band above his elbow.

They weren't there to inject me, Finch realized as he pictured the doctor holding a needle at the bend in his arm.

They were taking my blood.

They were checking something.

Assuming Ikänen was right, Finch couldn't imagine why they hadn't taken the opportunity—one of apparently several—to give him the vaccine. It would have been so easy. He was completely immobilized. Unconscious. They could have done it with ease.

But they hadn't. They hadn't done what any other scientist or doctor in the world—the thousands upon thousands of those who hated him deeply—would have gladly done.

Why? Finch asked himself. *Why didn't they do it?*

* * *

Still wrestling with the mystery, Finch resolved to press onwards to the cathedral in hopes of finding Eva or Brinkley. The last of evening light was nearly gone, the ruined trees and broken bodies outside the cathedral casting an eerie gloom over the entire scene.

The terrain rose steeply towards the ground level of the giant building. Though the majority of smoke appeared to come from the cathedral itself, Finch noticed another source of fire to his right within a large clump of trees.

Gripping his chest out of habit, he clambered up the slope toward the blaze. Finch froze in terror as he realized the raging flames encircled the ruined helicopter, broken in half and toppled onto its side.

"Eva," he screamed, suffering the scalding heat to get close enough for her to hear.

Finch scurried to another side of the aircraft, trying to find some way in.

"Eva!" he cried out again. "Eva, are you in there?"

Nearly overcome with burning pain, Finch backed off until he could gather himself for another approach. He scoured the surroundings for anything that might put out the fire but saw nothing.

"Help!" he wailed, cupping his hands to his mouth for amplification. "Someone help me."

Through the flames, Finch saw a hand emerge from within the debris. It reached out and, unable to withstand the heat, pulled back in. Just feet away, Finch saw a large tree branch, severed from its trunk, jutting from underneath the flaming hulk of aluminum.

He interlocked his fingers underneath it and pulled up, trying to roll the wreckage down the hill. Unable to see any movement, Finch crawled under the branch and pushed his back into it, using both his arms and legs to lift.

Someone staggered up the hill behind him, stopping just feet short.

"Help me!" Finch said. "There's someone trapped inside."

"Who is it?" the voice said, full of anger.

Finch turned around. Lit by flaming ruins stood a man holding a gun, pointed directly at him, his eyes white and full of rage.

"Who is it?" he screamed, spit flying from his mouth. "Is it Brinkley?"

Fire leapt from the hulk of metal as something exploded, a source of light that made it clear who Finch was looking at.

It was Garcia.

And something about him had changed.

CHAPTER 100

With Eva in his arms, Yuval lurched up the rising ground toward the main elevation of the National Cathedral. Unaware of the damage it had suffered, Yuval felt his throat tighten when he saw the yawning opening into the building. Inside, firefighters had nearly contained the blaze that followed the explosion. Burnt rows of pews sat still smoldering. Priceless artwork was ruined. An entire chapel was destroyed when the stone wall collapsed.

Dressed in black gowns and tuxedos, a hundred musicians and singers waited outside for shuttles to pick them up. Media technicians trudged through the water-soaked floors of the sanctuary, wrapping up cables and putting away light stands.

"No," Yuval said as he realized what was happening. "What's going on? What's happening?"

He approached one of the musicians shivering in the cold. "What's happening? Why aren't you inside?"

"It's over. They've canceled it."

"Who's canceled it? I haven't canceled it."

"It's destroyed in there. We can't perform like that."

Yuval raced inside and stopped someone breaking down their camera equipment. "What are you doing? We're about to start."

"The fire marshal came in here and told us all to leave. Said the building was unsafe."

Yuval stared openly at the destruction in front of him. Nearly half of the right side of the sanctuary stood in total disarray. A mound of stone and mortar had fallen inside, crushing wooden structures and toppling rows of seating. The acrid smell of smoke filled the air. At the front of the giant room, the stage built for the event was still intact. Toward the rear, the media risers sat unmanned.

"Where is he?" Yuval asked. "The fire marshal?"

"Probably outside. He's doing some interviews out there."

Yuval climbed over the mound of rubble to the exterior of the building and saw a group of lights and cameras pointed at a small podium. As he approached the press conference carrying Eva in his arms, every reporter and camera operator turned their attention squarely toward him. The fire marshal stopped talking mid-sentence, curious as to what everyone was looking at.

"It's Dr. Naftali," one of the reporters whispered in shock.

"With Eva Connolly," another said.

"Dr. Naftali, what happened?" the reporter asked.

Yuval attempted an answer. "I was arriving in my helicopter...."

"Speak up!" someone yelled.

"Can you step up to the microphones?" another reporter asked.

Stunned, the fire marshal stepped aside as Yuval approached, stroking the back of the girl he was carrying.

"We were arriving in my helicopter for the event. Trying to land. Something happened, and we crashed onto the ground. There was fire everywhere. We barely escaped."

"How is Eva?"

"She is okay."

"Can we see her face? Can you show us her face?"

Yuval craned his neck to gauge her reaction but thought better of trying to parade her. "She's fine where she is."

"What do you make of tonight being canceled? Do you plan to reschedule?"

"Actually, that's why I came up here. To talk to the fire marshal."

The marshal stepped up to the microphone. "It will take months to repair this. Maybe years...."

Yuval interrupted. "I am hoping we can find a way to salvage the evening."

"Not happening," the marshal said. "Not tonight, at least."

A reporter jumped in with another question. "Have you heard about any other bomb threats?"

"I haven't," the marshal replied.

"Dr. Naftali, what do you make of rumors Thomas Finch was behind the bombing?"

Yuval was stunned. "I hadn't heard. Why are people saying that?"

"Have you not seen the footage?"

"What footage? We just nearly died. I haven't seen anything."

A reporter handed Yuval their phone and hit play. "People are saying this is Finch. Not in the blue dress—the one on the ground speaking to him."

Security camera footage showed the parade at a standstill. In the back of one of the trucks stood two men. One was dressed in red robes, the other, a sparkling blue dress atop his clothing. A shaggy-bearded man walked by the truck, looked up, and spoke.

"The man in blue is the one who had the bomb. People are saying that's Finch, giving him instructions. Just minutes later, the guy leaves with something and a bomb explodes."

He's here, Yuval thought to himself as a wave of emotion nearly overtook him.

It can still happen.

Yuval fought the urge to smile as he straightened his posture and moved Eva to his other arm. "The fire marshal has a confession to make."

The man standing beside him looked confused.

"I do?" he asked.

Yuval stepped away from the microphone and pulled the marshal with him.

"Do you know who I am?" he whispered.

"Of course."

"How many children do you have?" Yuval asked.

"Two. Why do you ask?"

"Do they have any children of their own?"

"Both of them do."

"Are they important to you? Your grandchildren?"

"Why are you asking these things?" the fire marshal fired back.

"Because, if you know who I am, you will know that I am capable of doing very bad things to your entire family—your children and your grandchildren—and nothing you can do, no police force you can call, no federal agency, can stop me. All I need is for you to allow this event to happen."

"What are you talking about?"

"Make an announcement right now and tell them Thomas Finch paid you to shut this event down. Tell them you want to set the record straight. Tell them you refuse to take bribes and that the building is safe, and that the event will go on tonight as planned."

"Are you threatening me?"

"Most definitely. I am threatening extreme suffering for your family. Not you —I will make sure you're around to see it all happen—but for your extended family. Make the announcement and this conversation never happened."

"But the building isn't safe."

"Make the announcement," Yuval hissed.

Yuval turned around and smiled at the cameras. "As I said, the fire marshal has a confession to make."

The man standing behind him swallowed hard.

"What is it?" a reporter asked.

The fire marshal stepped up to the microphone, his face pulled taut with anguish. "I...I spoke dishonestly about the building closure."

The reporters struggled to understand what was happening.

"I was paid a large sum of money by Thomas Finch to shut this event down. It was wrong, and I want to set the record straight. The building is safe. The event can go on."

A hundred questions exploded from the reporters' mouths, shocked at the official's strange turn.

"What about Finch?" a reporter asked. "He's nearly killed his daughter twice now. Does he still have an invitation for tonight?"

Yuval pushed the marshal from the microphone. "Does Finch still have an invitation for tonight?"

He looked at each camera, the reporters hanging in suspense for his answer.

"Yes," he said. "Most definitely yes. In fact, the event couldn't go on without him."

CHAPTER 101

Dr. Arvo Ikänen pulled the slide from the tray and held it to his face as his laptop churned through millions of calculations.

"How long?" Stobnicki asked.

"I don't know. A few minutes. Maybe more."

"You realize what this might mean."

"I guess I don't."

Ikänen swept his arms around the room. "All of this. It has to end here. With us."

"What are you talking about?"

"We have the key for the Bootstrap. No one else does."

"Yeah. So?"

"We can't let it leave this room. The code. The knowledge. It has to end here."

"It could be worth billions to the right people."

"Billions?" Ikänen asked. "Billions? There isn't a number for what this is worth. There's no word for it. Trillions? Quadrillions? No one in the history of the world has ever dreamed of having this kind of power over nearly the entire species."

"In the right hands, that power...."

Ikänen cut him off. "In the right hands? Don't tell me you're turning, Stobnicki. You, of all people."

"Surely, there is some possible good that could come out of this. Something like this will probably never happen again."

"And it *shouldn't*," Ikänen said, nearly beside himself with anger. "Remember Frodo and the Ring? Remember what happened?"

"He couldn't bring himself to destroy it in the end."

"And why?"

"Because he failed the temptation. It was too much power for him to give up."

"Exactly."

"This isn't a fairy tale, Ikänen. This is different. This is possible cures for every known malady humanity has ever suffered from. Without anyone lifting a single finger. They could keep eating whatever they want. They could smoke whatever they want. They could never leave the couch again. They could ignore every single thing a doctor will tell them for the rest of their lives and still—still, we could help them."

Ikänen's pulse began to quicken to an uncomfortable pace. "It's *not* different than the fairy tale. It's worse. It's *much* worse. It's real life. And it's far more power than the Ring ever offered anyone."

Stobnicki sat in silence, staring at the floor.

"I'm losing you, Stobnicki. We knew this was the way. From the very beginning. You were the main one who argued this with the others. You helped me weed them out."

Stobnicki remained silent.

"I'm losing you, aren't I?"

Ikänen glanced around the room, trying to take inventory of what would need to be done. He stood up and began gathering all the respirators and masks lying on the floor and put them in a pile.

"What are you doing?" Stobnicki asked.

"*We* are doing what we promised *we* would do. We are throwing the Ring in the fire. Now help me get everything together."

Ikänen shoved notebooks from the kitchen counter onto the floor and kicked them onto the stack.

"We didn't agree to this."

"We did. You and I agreed to this."

"There's another way," Stobnicki said.

"There isn't. You know that."

"This is against your faith, isn't it?"

"Desperate times."

"You swore an oath at some point. You must have."

A putrid smell filled the room as Ikänen emptied plastic jugs onto the floor and furniture. He checked his laptop and saw that its calculation was nearly complete. Stobnicki walked quietly out onto the balcony and looked down towards the ambulance surrounding Connolly's body.

With the calculations finished, Ikänen adjusted the angle of his screen and put on his glasses.

"Oh God," he said.

"What is it?" Stobnicki asked.

"We have to stop him. We have to go stop him."

"Finch?"

"Yes."

"Why?"

"Because we're dead. That's why."

CHAPTER 102

ETA: 1 hour 13 minutes.

Traffic had begun to slow Natalie's progress considerably. It was nearing seven o'clock, and the interstate was a parking lot, an ocean of red taillights as far as she could see.

On a whim, Natalie toggled her GPS routing icon from a car to a shoe. A spinner appeared on the screen above the words *Recalculating Route.*

ETA: 25 minutes.

With little concern for her own safety, Natalie pulled her vehicle onto the center median, got out, and ran across five lanes of stopped traffic.

Faster to walk, she thought to herself. *That's technology for you.*

Natalie couldn't help but to laugh at her snark, a remnant her husband had gifted her with. Before their marriage, she was studious. Prudish. Almost Puritanical. His biting sarcasm had rubbed off on her. At one point in her life, she'd nearly worshipped technology, confident many of the world's ills could be solved through the advancement of scientific knowledge. Now she rolled her eyes at such things, particularly the irony by which her one-hundred-dollar shoes could get her three miles away faster than a fifty-thousand dollar Range Rover. Such was the legacy of her time with Finch, a bond she found difficult to sever completely, even after it was clear Eva would never walk again.

* * *

Months after the accident, her hatred for Finch seemingly at its peak, someone had gotten in touch with her—a text message from a number she didn't recognize.

I have a favor to ask. Only you can do it. No one else can.

"Who are you?" Natalie texted back.

A friend. You don't know me. Your husband does.

"That's a NO from me, then," she responded immediately.

Pwetty pwease?

The message hit like electricity. It was the literal spelling of a cartoonish tremolo Finch's voice assumed whenever she was firmly set against something he wanted.

"Who is this?" she asked.

It's dain-juh-wus.

"The favor? Or knowing who you are?"

Boaf.

Natalie was nearly positive she was texting directly with her husband, a man supposedly locked away for life in a maximum-security prison.

"Finch," she typed into her phone. "Is this you?"

Maybe.

"What do you want? What's the favor?"

You have a special date tonight.

Natalie hardened instantly. Yuval had asked her to a celebration with his research team—the first such event without her father's presence. Flush with a sense of foreboding, she realized she could hear air whistling in and out of her nose.

Interpreting her delay in answering as unease, another text appeared.

It's okay.

Another message came in—a link to a video. Natalie tapped the thumbnail and the theme song to *The Jeffersons* began playing: *Moving on up.*

At one point, her champagne tastes would have scared off nearly any suitor. Finch's low-brow lifestyle had radically changed that. Yuval, with billions of dollars floating around him at any given time, was, in many ways, a clear upgrade. Natalie clenched her jaw in anger, laughing all the while. His knack for self-deprecating humor was unmistakable. His ability to piss her off while simultaneously having her in stitches, matchless. She was convinced Finch was on the other end.

"I get it," she typed. "What's the favor?"

We believe Yuval has something dangerous. A code of some kind.

"Who's *we*?" Natalie asked. "How many are there of you?"

Several.

"Okay. Just wondering."

The code is long. About 300 characters. 309 to be exact. You'll know it when you see it.

"Will it be on a computer or something?"

Not likely. Too easy to hack.

"What do you want me to do? Take a picture of it?"

Not unless you can't take it with you. If it's something you can remove, take it. If it's something else, take a picture of the code, then destroy his copy.

The messenger no longer sounded like Finch. It was as if a different person was typing.

Natalie quickly decided she would have nothing to do with Yuval's code and their request. It *was* dangerous. Yuval was a dangerous man—she knew that. But dangerous in a much different way than Finch. While she was terrified of what Finch might do to others, she was terrified of what Yuval might do to herself.

Natalie continued to play along. "What's in it for me?"

Kombucha.

"I hate kombucha."

Kombucha is the essence of life.

Finch was clearly back in the driver's seat.

"I will not do this for kombucha. I need something else."

How about a promise.

"Yes?"

A promise your husband will one day earn your forgiveness.

Natalie groaned again, amazed at the way in which Finch could make her love and hate him at the same time.

And kombucha.

"I'll take the promise."

Okay.

"No kombucha or the deal's off."

No kombucha.

CHAPTER 103

Flames continued to engulf the helicopter as Finch raised his hand in front of him, nothing more than a speck of protection from the pistol pointed at his chest. Just hours earlier, he had left Brinkley for the hotel as Garcia sat in the back of the truck. An entirely different man now stared him down—his face drawn tight in distress, eyes bulging from their sockets.

"Garcia," Finch said, ignoring the man's maniacal appearance. "Someone's stuck in here. Help me get them out."

"It's Brinkley."

"How do you know?"

"I can smell him," Garcia said, his lips twitching with hate.

"Are you okay?"

"No."

Finch turned his body sideways to minimize the visual threat he might pose. "What's wrong, Garcia? Can you help me? They're going to burn to death if we can't get them out."

"We're all going to die," Garcia said, his mouth turned upside-down as he lowered the gun to his side.

"Not today. No one is going to die today—if you can help me."

Garcia slouched his shoulders and nearly began sobbing. "No one can help me."

Finch inched closer to the crazed man, crouching in submission as he held out his hand. "I can help you. But, I need your help first. I need you to help me move this helicopter."

Garcia dropped his head. "I'm not strong enough."

"Together we are," Finch said, touching Garcia's shoulder. "Come back here. There's a branch we can lift."

Finch nudged Garcia around the back of the ruined aircraft, where it had fallen on top of a downed tree. The flames had grown more intense, forcing Finch to turn his head as they approached it. Crouching beside the fallen limb, Garcia got on his knees and curved both arms underneath.

Shuddering with effort, he lifted the branch a few inches, enough to swing one foot in front of him. Garcia arched his back, screaming in pain as the crumpled aircraft began to turn over. With an explosion of strength, he brought his other foot underneath him and stood, hoisting the lever above his chest.

The helicopter teetered upside-down as the broken rotor shaft stuck into the ground. Garcia maneuvered his hands underneath the branch and pushed it over his head as the clump of twisted wreckage flipped all the way over, rolling several times down the slope until a standing tree stopped its descent.

Garcia fell away from the flames and collapsed on the ground as Finch looked on, completely bewildered by what he had just witnessed.

"How did you do that?" Finch asked.

Garcia continued lying still. "Now you can help me," he said, his unblinking eyes visible from the fire that continued to burn around them.

Finch stood and walked down the slope. "We need to get him out. He's probably injured."

"No!" Garcia screamed, standing up. "Now *you* help *me.*"

Finch backed up, trying to put some distance between them. "How can I help you?"

"We're all going to die," Garcia said, his mangled lips barely able to move.

"One day. One day far away."

"It's today!" Garcia screamed, holding his gun to his head.

"Stop! Garcia, stop! It's *not* today."

Garcia began weeping. "How do you know? How do you *know* it's not today?"

"It's our choice to make."

"It's *not* our choice," Garcia said. "It's theirs."

"Who?" Finch asked.

Garcia turned his head and looked into the emptiness behind his right shoulder. "Them," he said, pretending to fire his gun in the air at invisible objects. "You can't see them. But I can."

Inexplicably, Garcia's face cycled through an assortment of emotions within the course of a few seconds before landing on a pained look of concern. "And they're telling me something you can't hear. But, I can."

Finch walked slowly towards him, hoping for a chance to wrestle the gun from his hand. "What are they telling you?"

"They're saying—today's my special day."

A troubled smile crossed his face. "My new birthday."

Finch lunged for Garcia's arm, but the deputy was too quick. Garcia sprinted away, held the gun to the back of his neck, and fired it as he ran.

CHAPTER 104

With an exhilarating sense his destiny for greatness might yet be fulfilled, Yuval stormed through the cathedral, rounding up his staff to receive instructions. Water either needed to be mopped up or pushed to the rear of the sanctuary. Pews that weren't salvageable were stacked outside, trundled over the mound of rubble lining the bottom of the break in the cathedral's wall. Musicians set aside their instruments and went to work, assisting anywhere help was needed.

The seating arrangements were reconfigured, a task Yuval took great interest in. With fewer pews taking up space, the media risers at the back were brought forward, their sight lines vastly improved.

Outside the cathedral, National Guardsmen began to arrive and form a perimeter around the building, their belated presence ordered by Washington authorities to quell the protests.

"We found a gurney for Eva," one of his assistants, their forehead drizzled in sweat, told him.

"Good. Does it tilt?"

"It does, but it's not motorized. We have to manually do it."

"Okay. Make sure she's comfortable. Don't say any more about her father. Maybe it will be a surprise."

"You're that sure he's coming?" the assistant asked, her face full of skepticism.

"Yes. Quite sure."

A stiff draft blew through the building, the cold evening air sending a chill through many inside.

"Any progress on getting that hole covered?" Yuval asked.

"We've found a few tarps. Nothing big enough. And the firemen said it was too high for their ladders."

"We have to cover it somehow. This draft will be the end of me."

"We'll keep working on it."

Despite his best efforts to keep them out, VIPs began to wander in, anxious not to miss the start of the event.

"Hello," Yuval said, greeting them in the vestibule. "We are running late, obviously, but I am so glad you are here. Please tell everyone you know everything is still on for tonight. A bit late, but nothing has changed otherwise."

"Tell your soldiers they need to let people through," one of them responded. "We had to sneak around them to get in here."

"Those are National Guardsmen. They were told to allow anyone who had tickets to pass."

"They're under the impression no one is supposed to come through. Said another bomb threat was called in."

Yuval was troubled. Without guests, the entire event was meaningless.

"How many others did you see?"

"A lot. They're all still coming. They just can't get in."

Yuval checked his watch and rubbed his forehead as he approached a group of people working.

"Where is Cardinal Gordillo? Has anyone seen him?"

"I haven't," one of the workers said.

"Not since this morning," another said.

"See if you can find him."

"Have you tried calling him?"

"Phones are useless right now."

Despite the lack of any personal protection, Yuval left the cathedral and began walking along the line Guardsmen had formed. Protestors had begun to file back towards the building, their screams of hatred replaced with a more somber tone, given the events that had just transpired.

"Do you know what the tickets look like?" he asked the soldiers. "Let anyone through who has a ticket."

Unaware his voice carried any authority—and with communication channels completely down—most of them ignored his request. Yuval continued to negotiate the perimeter, trying to give the soldiers clear instructions on who was to be allowed through. With not even half the boundary covered, he gave up and turned back toward the sanctuary.

"Dr. Naftali," someone called out from the crowd, their booming voice cutting through easily.

Yuval spun around and saw a bright red robe cutting through the drab winter tones of everyone else. He approached the line and ignored the obscenities being thrown his way. Three rows back stood the shocked face of Cardinal Gordillo.

"Dr. Naftali," Gordillo said. "I thought you were dead."

"What makes you say that?" Yuval asked him. "I'm alive as I've ever been."

CHAPTER 105

Ikänen opened the bedroom closet and removed the outfit he had brought specifically for the event.

"You're really going to wear that?" Stobnicki asked.

"Yes. Let's go. One final check."

With a tiny notebook in hand, Ikänen rummaged through the pile on the floor, checking things off a list as he went.

"Where's your laptop?" he asked Stobnicki.

"That *is* my laptop," Stobnicki replied, pointing to a black computer in the pile. "Where's yours?"

"No, that's mine. Mine has the dent on the corner."

"It's mine."

Ikänen stood up. "Where'd you put it? Stobnicki. Don't do this. It all has to be destroyed. You and I can't help what's already been done."

"I don't know what you're talking about."

"Stobnicki, I will lock you in the room in here, and you will burn with it."

Without meaning to, Stobnicki's eyes shot outside toward the balcony.

"Oh, is it out there?" Ikänen asked as he marched in the same direction.

With no warning, Stobnicki jumped onto Ikänen's back, tackling him to the floor.

"Stop," Ikänen said, trying to wrestle his attacker away. "Don't do this."

Ikänen was able to spin over onto his side and caught the shine of a pair of scissors in Stobnicki's hand. Over and over, his attacker plunged the blades into Ikänen's back, but the folds of his clothing were able to stop it.

Using his feet to kick off the wall, Ikänen rolled over the top of Stobnicki, onto his other side, trapping the weapon underneath them.

"Don't do this," Ikänen screamed. "We have to stop Finch."

Stobnicki loosened his grip to shift the scissors into his other hand. Ikänen felt the pressure relax and rolled away, crashing into the chairs around the dining room table. Holding the scissors like a dagger, Stobnicki stood over Ikänen, trying to stab downward. Unable to pierce his thick clothing, Stobnicki jumped over the old scientist and grabbed the microscope in his hand.

Ikänen seized the opportunity and scrambled toward the balcony, looking for the laptop. As Stobnicki approached, he slammed the sliding glass door shut, using his foot to keep it from opening. Stobnicki slammed the microscope against the glass, trying to shatter it. Expecting the door to explode at any moment, Ikänen continued scanning the balcony and finally saw what he was looking for—leaned up against the wall, behind a planter, rested a black laptop.

Stobnicki stood back and hurled the microscope with both arms, cracking the glass all the way to the edges. Before Stobnicki could attack again, Ikänen leapt for the computer and hurled it over the balcony.

"No!" Stobnicki screamed, slamming the microscope into the glass until it completely shattered.

Ikänen jumped past Stobnicki towards the hallway door but, again, was tackled to the ground.

"It's too late," Ikänen cried as they flailed along the floor. "Help me stop him."

Stobnicki was able to get on top and, with all his weight, began pressing a plastic tube across the scientist's throat. Ikänen flapped his arms around, trying to break free as he began to lose consciousness. Without knowing what they were, his left hand caught hold of long Q-tips they'd used for testing. He slammed them into the face of Stobnicki, several of which went through his nose, piercing the back of his sinus cavity and into his brain.

Stobnicki tried to pull them out, but his cerebral function was so impaired he was unable to direct his arms where he wanted them to go. After five seconds of struggle, he collapsed onto the ground beside Ikänen, red bubbles forming at his lips.

Struggling to breathe, Ikänen stood up and found the flint lighter he had stored in a kitchen drawer. He held it over the pile of equipment and squeezed it until the sparks caught fire. Flames raced around the room, engulfing nearly everything.

Ikänen reached into the mound of equipment and pulled out his laptop. He started for the door, then paused, coughing from smoke inhalation. Ikänen looked around the room, his mind exploding with temptation.

No Gollum to save this hobbit, he realized.

With smoke completely obscuring his vision, Ikänen bent down, tossed the laptop back into the fire, then opened the door and left.

CHAPTER 106

Finch watched in horror as Garcia's lifeless body crumpled and slid down the hill. Just twenty feet away, the tangled remains of the helicopter rested against a tree, a trail of flaming debris leading away from the original crash site.

Widening his stance, Finch skimmed down the bed of fallen leaves to the wreckage, recoiling in pain when he touched the metal, still blistering hot from the fire. The damage was severe enough determining what was up, and what was down was nearly impossible. Eventually, Finch figured out only the front half the aircraft was laying on its side. The back half—minus the tail rotor—was folded backwards along the main fuselage.

With shards of glass jutting from its frame, Finch lowered himself into the cockpit and stepped into the area directly behind. Through a window, he peered into the back half of the aircraft and was terrified by what he saw—his daughter's gurney lying sideways, tightly secured to what had been the floor of the helicopter.

"Eva!" he screamed, beating on the glass.

Something moved within the sheets of the gurney—a large figure, bound in place with ratchet straps. They turned their head, revealing an oxygen mask they had pulled over their face.

"Brinkley!" Finch cried as he recognized the man's clothing. "Brinkley, hang on! Just a minute! I'm going to get you out!"

Finch ransacked the aircraft interior, looking for a pry bar. A hammer. Anything useful besides a roll of black duct tape. Unable to find a single tool, he re-entered the cockpit when several flashlight beams converged upon the aircraft.

Thank God for first responders, Finch thought to himself.

"Help," he said, stepping into their light.

Temporarily blinded by their xenon beams, Finch struggled to see.

"There's a man trapped in the back. He's badly wounded."

"Who are you?" one of the voices called out.

"I'm nobody," Finch said. "I'm just trying to rescue this guy. He's trapped."

The man stepped forward into the light, revealing himself to be a casually dressed soldier, a sub-machine gun held at the ready. Others around him were similarly dressed—and armed.

"Whoa," Finch said. "I'm guessing you're not EMTs?"

"We're looking for someone. We were told he was seen near here."

"Who are you looking for?"

"Who's in there? Besides yourself?"

"I'll tell you if you tell me."

"You first," the man said, raising his firearm. "Unless you have a bigger gun."

Finch looked down for a moment before answering. "His name's Brinkley. He's a sheriff. From West Virginia."

"How'd he end up in there?"

"No idea."

"How do you know who he is?"

"Long story. What's your name?"

"Cam."

"Look Cam—can you and your friends help me get him out? He's probably bleeding to death back there."

The soldier spoke to someone behind him then turned back towards Finch. "There should be a hydraulic pump in there. A hand pump. If the lines aren't cut, it might open that cargo ramp."

Within seconds, Finch spotted the yellow handle labeled *RAMP OVERRIDE* and started swinging it back and forth. Hydraulic fluid shot everywhere.

"It's leaking," Finch said. "Not going to work."

"Looks like you're out of luck," Cam said as they cut their lights and began to walk away.

"Wait. I need your help."

"You got our help. Now figure it out."

Finch scrounged around and found a small piece of bent metal. He pulled on the lever and located where the leak was coming from.

"Guess this might be useful after all," he said, grabbing the black duct tape. After placing the metal piece over the leak, he began wrapping the roll tightly along the hydraulic line.

After a few revolutions around the small metal pipe, Finch tore off the tape and pumped the handle again, holding his free hand in the air to feel for leaking fluid. Sensing nothing, Finch put both hands on the hydraulic pump and began working it back and forth, the twisted metal hulk screaming in protest as the ramp slowly pressed into the ground, lifting the tail into the air.

* * *

Cam and his men could still hear the helicopter unfolding behind them as they neared the top of the hill, still intent on finding their target. Just beyond the trees they sat enshrouded within, the cathedral was teeming with life as frantic work continued, surrounded by hundreds of armed soldiers.

"If he's inside, we'll never get to him," a soldier suggested.

"I know," Cam said.

"Who do you think that was back there?" one of the soldiers asked.

"No idea."

"You don't think he was hiding him?"

"No."

"We should've looked. Just to make sure."

"We can turn around if you want," Cam said, checking the notification that lit up his phone screen.

It was a text. From a Dr. Arvo Ikänen.

Cam—We have to stop Finch from getting inside the cathedral! IMPORTANT!!!

Forget about Gordillo. Avenge Gabriel later.

Cam searched for answers as to why Dr. Ikänen was calling them off Gordillo when a final text came in.

Do whatever it takes. I will cover for you.

Cam locked his phone and stopped, deep in thought.

"Who is it?" a soldier asked.

"Ikänen."

"What's he want?"

"Finch," he said as he took off running down the hill, back towards the helicopter.

CHAPTER 107

Natalie continued jogging along the streets that led to the Cathedral, glancing at her phone to check her progress.

ETA: 13 minutes

It had just turned seven o'clock, the western sky nearly devoid of any trace of sunlight. Her hope was Yuval's event would start late—late enough, perhaps, she could find Eva first. Unlikely, she admitted, given his obsession with punctuality.

* * *

Hours after the strange texts regarding codes and kombucha, Natalie found herself waiting for the elevator to take her up to the research team's celebration Yuval had invited her to. Another female party-goer entered the lobby and acknowledged her presence.

"Natalie," she said, bowing her head awkwardly. "We've never met, but hello."

"Hello," Natalie responded.

"I'm sorry about your daughter."

"Thank you. That's very kind."

"Finch was very...."

Natalie cut a thin smile. "Yes. He was."

"Yuval's probably a better match, anyway."

The phrase struck her as incredibly odd but, for the moment, she held her tongue.

"He's been talking you up quite a bit. Super excited to have you here tonight."

"That's nice," Natalie said.

"Guest of honor and all that."

"Yikes," Natalie said, her comment betraying an attempt to not look embarrassed.

A bell rang, and they both stepped onto the elevator. The woman pressed the button to the 9th floor.

"Moving on up," she said, laughing clumsily.

As Natalie expected, the research lab was spotless, a piece of architectural wonder notable for its lack of humanity more than anything else. Within the lobby and beyond, she couldn't spot a single naturally occurring material. Even the amber glow of an incandescent bulb would have been a compassionate addition, given the artificial veneer that covered every surface.

The party, if one could call it that, was similarly anodyne. Yuval welcomed Natalie into the center of the crowd that had gathered around him, introducing her one-by-one to every single person, names and faces for which she hadn't the slightest inkling to remember or banter amongst.

The humiliation Finch sometimes caused at her father's events now seemed so innocent. A stodgy group of benefactors, a celebration of yes-men and -women, begging to be jostled from their corpulent stupor. And Finch could deliver—without delay, every time. He could humiliate them five times over before they even realized it was themselves they were laughing at.

Yuval's party would offer no such diversions. Natalie spoke of her life since Finch had gone to jail with all the vividness of a toll-booth operator. Others congratulated her for the nothingness of which she spoke. It was a mirage, the illusion of a life well-lived for those who'd never risked a thing in their life.

"Natalie," Yuval said to her in a whisper. "Come with me. I want to show you something."

He took Natalie's hand and pulled her away from the group. They walked down a long hallway which opened into another two-story lobby. A giant window looked down upon the interstate that passed by beneath them.

"Beautiful, isn't it?" Yuval asked, gesturing out the window.

"Yes," Natalie said, confused as to what he was referring.

"This is my office," he said, looking around the room. "Actually, the lobby to my office."

"It's amazing."

He pointed towards the balcony that ran around the room. "Up there is my personal office, where I work."

"That's where all the magic happens," Natalie suggested, growing increasingly uncomfortable.

"Not all of it," Yuval said, sitting down on the couch, crossing his legs tightly.

"What did you want to show me?"

Yuval patted the couch cushion beside him. "Come here, Natalie. Sit."

Natalie forced a slight grin and wobbled in place.

"Come over here, Mrs. Connolly," he said, tapping the couch again. "I won't bite."

The noxious way in which Yuval smiled at her sent waves of nausea running through her entire gastrointestinal tract.

"Do you have a bathroom in here?" she asked.

"Do I have a bathroom? I have a full kitchen, bathroom, and bedroom—

anything you might need to be comfortable."

Steeling herself, Natalie walked behind the couch where Yuval sat and whispered in his ear. "Give me a few minutes and I will be ready for you."

Yuval sat motionless, unsure of how to respond.

Natalie got closer, the warmth of her breath flowing along his neck. "Go back to the party. I will let you know when I am ready."

Yuval straightened his gawky frame and, without looking directly at her, walked back towards the hallway.

"Leave your phone," she said.

Yuval stopped, took his mobile from his pocket, and laid it on a counter.

"Which way is the bathroom?" she asked.

Without turning, Yuval pointed to his left, at the top of the stairs.

"Okay. I will come get you," Natalie sang, a feminine lilt to her voice. "Don't go too far."

Natalie watched him leave and closed the door behind him. The instant he'd rejoined the party, she bounded up the stairs and began rifling through his office, confident that, without his phone, he couldn't see her through hidden security cameras. Her heart thumped hard as she searched from drawer to drawer, cabinet to cabinet, looking for anything that might resemble a code. One wall was covered from floor to ceiling with a custom bookcase, its contents illuminated by LED lamps. Natalie took a picture of the bookshelf to mark where the rolling ladder was before removing a few books, leafing through their pages to see if anything fell out.

This seems too obvious, she thought to herself—hiding something so important within a book. There were so many. No one would have enough time to check them all, but still, it just seemed too careless for Yuval's manner. After replacing the books, Natalie checked her phone and rolled the ladder back in place.

The kitchen yielded nothing as well. The pantry was nearly empty. Besides several bottles of kombucha, the refrigerator was almost bare. Natalie picked up the bottles and looked inside them, curious if something might have been hidden within.

Not even a sauce pack drawer, she thought, remarking at yet another oddity of Yuval's.

Satisfied the kitchen held no other secrets, Natalie moved to the bathroom, a luxurious mirrored expanse whose infinite reflections unsettled her. At home, her attire seemed tame. Conservative almost. Here, within the thousands of reflections, she saw her figure-hugging dress from every angle, disconcerted at how much it revealed.

Where is it? she asked, knowing Yuval's patience would soon run out. The cabinets under the sink were barren. A linen closet yielded nothing besides a few towels with tags still on them. She opened the door to an enormous walk-in closet and flicked on the light. The center contained a concrete-covered island with something very strange sitting on top—an elaborate house, built with playing cards.

Natalie approached the counter, making sure she exhaled away from the fragile structure. Through the nooks and gaps of the assembled cards, it was clear a folded piece of paper rested beneath them. As it was, there was no way for her to get the note without collapsing the house. Natalie had seen card houses glued together in such a way the entire structure could be lifted in one piece. There was nothing indicating what she could see might have been constructed in that way.

This must be it, she thought. *Not hidden. Just protected.*

With no way to retrieve the paper, Natalie resigned herself to leaving the party without the precious cipher. She left the walk-in closet and turned out the light. Just as she shut the door, she heard an alarming clatter beyond. Throwing the door back open, a jolt of epinephrine rushed through her as she realized the card house had collapsed.

Shit, she thought as she floundered with what to do.

With the realization it was too late to turn back, Natalie raced back into the closet to find a jumbled mess on the counter, every one of them an identical card —the Queen of Hearts. With no time for caution, she removed the piece of paper and unlocked her phone, ready to take a picture of the code within. The message, however, was much different than she expected.

You have my heart, Queen Natalie. I love you. Yuval.

"Shit," she said out loud, shaking her head in dread. "Shit. Shit. Shit."

She folded the piece of paper in half again and returned it under the mess of fallen cards where the house once stood. Natalie turned off the light, closed the door quietly, then raced down the stairs.

"Shit," she kept repeating to herself. "Now I've done it."

She grabbed Yuval's phone and straightened her dress before opening the door and returning to the party. Yuval sat by himself, his hands splayed together on his lap. At once, he stood up and smiled when he saw her.

Natalie handed the phone to him and placed her hand over her stomach, her face twisted in simulated discomfort.

"I'm sorry, Yuval. I have to leave. I'm not feeling well. I'm sure you understand."

Before he could speak, Natalie dashed across the lobby, waving silently to those who wished her good-bye. The door closed behind her, leaving Yuval standing alone, his face warped in excruciating pain.

CHAPTER 108

"Don't get any ideas," Vickers said to Brooke, holding her hand as they dashed through stopped cars toward the cathedral. With roads completely jammed, he guessed they could make better time on foot.

"Sorry. I'm taken."

"I'm talking about you trying to escape."

"Why would I try and escape? If we're headed closer to my daughter, then we're on the same path. The same team, even."

"Don't."

"What?"

"Try to be endearing."

Brooke feigned surprise. "Oh, I'm sorry. Was I?"

"No. You weren't."

Brooke looked behind them. "Where'd all your men go? Your helpers?"

"Couldn't keep up."

"Shouldn't we wait for them?"

"No."

As they got closer, more people began to abandon their cars and walk alongside them.

"Is everyone going to this thing?" Brooke asked.

Vickers ignored her question. "So now you talk about your daughter."

"She's everything to me."

"Now that I mentioned her, she is."

"What is it you want?" Brooke asked. "What do you think is going on?"

"Something," Vickers said. "I'm not sure what. But something."

As Vickers had searched through the mansion for Natalie, something felt off. Her lack of resistance when he discovered her hiding. Her apparent youth for a married woman, mother to a six-year-old child. Another oddity bothered him—he was confident he heard her phone vibrating beneath the bedroom floor after he sent her a message, trying to smoke her out. Impossible, given where he had discovered her hiding, but somehow, his hearing must have completely deceived him. Perhaps it was the two cars in the driveway, but regardless, Vickers sensed somehow he was being played.

Phone.

Vickers realized he had her phone in his pocket, essentially an extensive identification device. He pulled it out and tapped the power button.

Natalie

Where are you?

Befuddled, Vickers pocketed the phone and shook his head, convinced it was the same message he'd sent as he tried to find her.

"Everything okay?" Brooke asked as they slowed their pace to weave through a particularly scrambled intersection.

"I suppose."

Vickers pulled his phone and tried to make a call.

Call failed.

He redialed the number but was met with the same result.

"Stop just a minute," he said. "I need to message someone."

He unlocked his phone and typed with both hands.

I've got Natalie. We're running behind. I'm assuming you want her after the event?

Vickers held his phone up in the air, trying to get better reception. Eventually, the message went through.

"Service is shit," he said to Brooke, embarrassed at the awkwardness of holding his phone above his head.

Two cars trying to force their way through the same spot collided into each other, firing off both of their air bags. Horns blared in anger as one driver got out and screamed at the other.

Feeling his phone vibrate, Vickers lowered it and silently read the response.

Bring her here. I want her now.

"Who are you texting?" Brooke asked.

Vickers grabbed her hand and began to run. "Your new boyfriend."

CHAPTER 109

Yuval and Cardinal Gordillo left a growing number of people pressed up against the National Guard perimeter and walked up a small incline toward the side of the cathedral.

"Why did you think I was dead?" Yuval asked.

"I saw the helicopter go down. Assumed it was you."

"If I didn't know any better, Cardinal Gordillo, I'd assume it was *you* who set off that bomb—specifically in *hopes* of my helicopter going down."

"Well, you know better, don't you?"

"You saw me go down?" Yuval asked, pressing the accusation a bit deeper. "Just happened to be looking in the right direction?"

"Lucky me," Gordillo said. "I prayed you'd land safely."

Yuval clicked his tongue. "Always thinking of others, aren't you?"

"Always."

Yuval stared up at a media helicopter circling above them. "Mongchai is..." he started to ask but stopped.

"He is taken care of."

"Good. His parents, too, I assume?"

"They are not—as far as I know. Unless we got lucky with the fire."

"I suppose we'll need to have someone clean that up?" Yuval asked.

"We will. And quick—before they start talking."

"Who do you think did this? The bomb?"

Gordillo sneered as he waved his hand towards the crowds. "Them. They hate us. They don't want to see us succeed."

"Sounds like a lot of *them* died. The media's saying Finch did it."

"Maybe he did. That'll teach them who the good guys really are."

"Us?" Yuval asked, a small grin creeping across his face.

"Of course," Gordillo said, his harsh laughter transforming into a fit of coughing. "Who else?"

They turned up the sidewalk through a group of evergreen trees that still remained, the emergency lighting being cast onto the building barely visible.

Gordillo slowed to catch his breath and turned toward Yuval. "Cardinal

Olevnik died. In the blast."

"I'm sorry to hear that. One of your rivals, if I remember correctly?"

"A dear colleague," Gordillo said, bowing his head in reverence. "You haven't seen Cardinal Vallcorba, I presume?"

"I haven't, though I will pray he didn't make it either."

"You wouldn't pray for your mother's life."

"Priorities, Cardinal. Priorities."

Gordillo stopped completely, just beyond the emergency lights projected onto the side of the building. He felt his cordial relationship with Yuval would soon end, something he needed to address.

"Someone has the Bootstrap code, Yuval. I assume you know that?"

"I do. It was stolen from me."

"*You* had it?"

"Yes."

"The whole thing?"

"Yes."

"How? I never gave my part to anyone. I kept my end of the bargain."

"You never had the code, Gordillo. No one did. I'm sorry to have misled you. I had it the whole time."

"But why?" Gordillo asked. "Why all the subterfuge?"

"Plausible deniability."

"You didn't want anyone to think you had it?"

"Correct."

The Cardinal was shocked. "But the money. You paid me all that money."

"I paid lots of people who thought they had pieces of the code."

"But why?"

"Keep your friends close? You ever heard that phrase?"

"And your enemies closer?" Gordillo asked, confused. "But, I'm not your enemy."

"You may be one day—depending on your quest."

"For the papacy?"

"Correct."

Gordillo knew Yuval had access to significant funding but couldn't imagine how much money he'd spent just to give the appearance he wasn't completely in control of things.

A brawl broke out among nearby protestors as one of them tried to scale the fence. Others pulled the man back into their midst as he shouted a cryptic phrase impossible to discern.

"You believe Finch is going to show?" Gordillo asked.

Yuval looked around them. "He's already here, somewhere—doing the Lord's work, I hope. It's just a matter of us making sure he feels welcome inside."

"I assume the girl is in good health?"

"She's fine. A little scratched up, perhaps. Not that she would even know."

"A lot of people are going to be disappointed when they wake up tomorrow and she isn't any better."

"The world needs to believe it can happen first. The more they believe, the more their faith will be shaken when it doesn't."

"What if it works?" Gordillo asked.

"It won't," Yuval said, raising an eyebrow. "Miss Eva will unfortunately succumb to the strain of her injuries—just like Mongchai."

"You are truly an evil man."

"Don't call it evil, dear Cardinal. Progress always comes with a price, does it not? You know that as well as I."

The twisted nature of Yuval's plan was still unclear to Gordillo. The scientist had earned the respect and admiration of much of the world, yet, here he was, apparently committed to sabotaging everything for his long-running feud with the divine.

"No one will trust you again, Yuval. This will be the end of your career."

Yuval squinted his eyes as if to focus on some obscure prize he couldn't quite envision. Faucett was dead. Connolly could retire at any moment. Nearly the entire world had been primed with the Bootstrap sequence. They'd all served their purpose, every piece in its proper place, just as Yuval had envisioned nearly a decade earlier.

"The end of my career?" he asked. "Perhaps. Tonight marks the beginning of the mission work I've always wanted to undertake. My true calling, you might say."

"You're going to put me out of a job."

Yuval clicked his tongue. "The Vatican may have once rested upon the faith of believers. Not anymore."

Suddenly, Gordillo realized the leverage he once felt he had was completely gone, his life now in danger. Some information was better not knowing. Yuval had just shared details so significant he wished he'd never heard them.

"What's the matter, Cardinal?" Yuval asked. "You look petrified."

"Why are you telling me these secrets? Am I the only one who knows these things?"

"It won't matter after tonight," Yuval said. "Just keep doing what you're doing, Gordillo. Secure the papacy, and we will be good friends."

CHAPTER 110

Cam bolted down the hill through flames to the metal hulk of the ruined helicopter. The tail was now flipped over, the cargo ramp underneath partially extended. Other men arrived soon after.

"Check the cockpit," Cam said as he climbed into the tail section.

An empty hospital gurney was attached to the bottom of the ramp. Sheets and ratchet straps were strewn over the floor, but there was no one inside.

"Clear," someone shouted to him from the other section of the aircraft.

"Clear here," Cam said, a tone of annoyed resignation in his voice.

"Who was it?" they asked.

"It was Thomas Finch."

"*That* was Finch we just saw?"

"I think so."

"What's he doing here? In the middle of D.C.?"

"I'm not sure. But, Ikänen called us off Gordillo. Said we had to stop Finch from getting in the cathedral."

"That Cardinal killed Gabe. I want revenge."

"Not our mission now," Cam said.

"It's *my* mission, then."

"Well, go. Find him. I'm not going to stop you."

The man looked towards the others for support. "Anyone else?"

The two remaining men nodded their heads and stepped forward.

"Alright, then," Cam said. "All of you, huh?"

"Gabe was like a brother to us. We don't even know Finch. Why should we care about him?"

"Ikänen has his reasoning, I'm sure."

"And we've got ours."

Cam affirmed their conviction. "You do. I know that."

One by one, each man stepped up and gave Cam a light hug and a pat on the back.

"Gordillo's dangerous," he said, grabbing three magazines of ammunition from his vest. "Take these. You might need them."

* * *

Brinkley leaned against Finch as they struggled through the dark, walking past hundreds of people to a more poorly guarded area of the cathedral.

"You think they'll recognize me?" Finch asked, holding his head down.

"I can't imagine they will. Not with you looking like you do."

"Hey," Finch replied, pretending to be offended.

"That mop of yours is doing the Lord's work. Trust me, they won't recognize you."

They wheeled around to the opposite side of the building where the explosion occurred. Even here, protestors were packed in hard together, pressed against the chain-link fencing being erected.

"There's hundreds of them," Brinkley said.

"They just keep coming."

"I thought you were dead," Finch said.

"Me too," Brinkley replied, his eyes watering and red from smoke. "Glad that mask still had oxygen."

"How'd you get stuck in there?"

Brinkley realized he'd said nothing about what had happened.

"Jesus, Finch. I didn't tell you. Yuval trapped me in there. He's got your daughter."

Finch turned white. "Was she alive?"

"She is. I pulled her out of the gurney."

"What happened? Why'd you let him take her?"

"I put her down on the ground to get him out."

"Why? Why'd you help him?"

"I don't know. It was on fire. He was stuck. I just reacted. My instincts aren't to let people burn to death in fires. Evidently, his are."

Finch looked up at the silhouette of the giant building looming over them. Somewhere, his daughter was inside—alive. In front of them, sections of a six-foot high chain-link fence were joined together. Behind it stood a menacing array of soldiers with helmets and riot shields.

"I need to get in there," Finch said.

"There's too many. We'll never get past them."

Brinkley opened a large bag he'd taken from the helicopter and looked inside.

"Unless..." he said, rifling through its contents.

"Unless?"

"Unless we could create some kind of diversion."

"It'd need to be big."

"Okay. Give me a few minutes. Just be ready."

"How will I know?"

Brinkley slung the bag over his shoulder and began to stagger away.

"You'll know."

CHAPTER 111

It had been days since the party and, still, Natalie hadn't heard from Yuval. The awkward exit, the way she had disappointed him, the pitiful look on his face as she left—it all made for a mortifying cloud of dread that hung over her every thought. The fact she'd left evidence of her snooping with nothing to show for it—save the cringe of reading a stilted profession of love from Yuval—made things even worse.

Anything?

Another text showed up on her phone. Another unidentified number. Another cryptic message from an unknown person, eager to hear if she'd been able to find some strange three-hundred-digit code within Yuval's research facility.

"Nothing," she responded. "Sorry."

Nothing at all?

"Nothing at all. Just made a new enemy, that's all."

How's that?

Unsure of who was texting her, Natalie wasn't comfortable discussing what had happened—how she had manipulated Yuval to gain access to his office. Something about the way he had suffered silently disturbed her. A furious outburst, despite the menace, would have been better. As it was, she was left to wonder. Did he realize she had rifled through his entire office? Of course he'd noticed the card house had fallen. He was sure to have known she had read his message.

You have my heart, Queen Natalie. I love you. Yuval.

The note he'd left made her shiver. There wasn't enough loneliness in the entire world that would have made her grant him a single night of companionship.

"I don't want to talk about it," she texted to the unknown number.

It must be at his home.

Natalie flared with indignation.

"Not doing that again. Sorry, mystery guy. I tried. Find your own code."

Days later, Natalie received a message she was dreading—a text from Yuval himself. Curiously, it mentioned nothing of her snub.

Did you touch my books?

Natalie sat down, one arm wrapped tightly over her head. *Why would he ask that?* she thought. *Did he have cameras?* If so, it would have been obvious what she'd done.

"Which books?" she responded, trying to buy a few minutes to decide how best to answer.

The only books I have. The ones in my office.

DID YOU TOUCH THEM?

Natalie didn't need the caps to realize Yuval was furious. The fact he hadn't mentioned her departure—or the note he'd left her to find—made it crystal clear.

"I didn't," she replied. "I peeked in your office. Thought it was the bathroom. Left right away."

DON'T LIE TO ME.

Natalie felt herself beginning to tremble. Perhaps someone stole one of his books, a rare antique worth millions? After unlocking her phone, she flicked through the photo library and found the picture she'd taken of the bookshelf—each section stuffed with books. One segment stood out due to its more colorful spines. Natalie zoomed in and could just barely make out their titles, some of which included children's books—an odd choice for someone like Yuval.

Intrigued, Natalie counted the particular books in that section and was amazed to find they numbered exactly three hundred and nine. She found a piece of paper and began writing down their titles.

Heart of Darkness.
Prey.
~~The~~ Indian in the Cupboard.
Three Little Pigs.
One of Us Is Lying.
~~The~~ Romanov Prophecy.
Principia Mathematica.
Four Dead Queens.
Three Little Pigs.
The Zookeeper's Wife

Natalie stopped after the first row, some thirty books later. Two things immediately appeared to her as odd. Multiple books had the same word struck through: *The*. Looking over the shelves below, she saw this same phenomenon repeated many times.

~~The~~ Golden Bough.
~~The~~ City in History.
~~The~~ Zookeeper's Wife

It wasn't a significant mark, but, despite the graininess of the zoomed-in image she was working with, it was still visible. The other oddity involved repeated books. With its distinctive spine, *Four Dead Queens* was clearly visible several times, as were other books with numbers in their titles.

Natalie sensed there was something peculiar about their arrangement and began to annotate her list.

Heart of Darkness.	*H*
Prey.	*P*
~~The~~ Indian in the Cupboard.	*I*
Three Little Pigs.	*3*
One of Us Is Lying.	*1*
~~The~~ Romanov Prophecy.	*R*
Principia Mathematica.	*P*
Four Dead Queens.	*4*
Three Little Pigs.	*3*
The Zookeeper's Wife	*Z*

Her heart began to flutter when she realized some of the titles had a tiny mark underneath their first letter, none of them ones with numbers in them.

Prey.
~~The~~ Romanov Prophecy.

"Lower case?" she asked herself, recomposing the string of characters assuming this notation.

HpI31rP43Zdu76Ai208cd592cEn02f.

Natalie stopped writing and counted the books again.

309.

Her mind full of fear, Natalie took the paper into the kitchen and lit it on fire. She found the strange number in her chat history and sent the picture of the bookcase.

"Found it," she sent. "You always said I was the smarter one. Guessing you can still figure this one out."

Natalie thought of answering Yuval but decided instead to send the mystery man one last message.

"I have faith."

CHAPTER 112

Inside the cathedral, pews slowly began to fill with guests. The first three rows were mostly reserved for religious figures, their attendance paramount to communicate what Yuval had planned. Other dignitaries filled the rows around them —political representatives, scientific luminaries, and other notable celebrities. The sounds of workers outside continued to drift in through the opening, despite Yuval's attempts to have it covered.

The cathedral's relics were set aside to make room for a stage that spanned across the width of the sanctuary. Pieces of Yuval's equipment dotted the stage, covered—for the time being—in thick black cloth. An enormous screen hung above, an abstract animation of molecules flocking like starlings projected onto it. In one moment, they'd cluster together, forming the shape of an angel, a crucifix, and other religious icons. After breaking apart, they would turn into doves and assemble again somewhere else as strands of DNA, amino acids, or the human circulatory system. Text was superimposed on top, two separate lines of type which morphed back and forth between one another.

The Science of Faith.
The Faith of Science.

"Where is Gordillo?" Yuval asked anyone near him but was unable to get a satisfactory answer.

The Cardinal had gone missing, another stumbling block Yuval did not want to deal with. With Connolly absent, he was counting on Gordillo's bombastic delivery to help kick things off. As it was, it was looking as if Yuval himself might have to carry the entire show.

Chandeliers suspended from the ceiling flashed several times, letting guests loitering outside the sanctuary know the event was about to start. Musicians began to fill the arc of chairs and bleachers at the back of the stage as Yuval checked his watch again.

Where are you, Finch? he said to himself, methodically scanning each pew, looking for any sign of the man he needed more than any other.

CHAPTER 113

The silhouette of the cathedral emerged from the darkness as Natalie drew closer. Mobs of people surrounded her every step, curious onlookers now numbering amongst the protestors.

Eva, I'm coming, she thought to herself, a projection she prayed would reach her daughter.

Eventually, Natalie could continue no further. Chain-link fences, held in place by bags of cement, surrounded the structure. Wherever the crowd threatened to break through, pepper spray filled the air, sending them crashing backwards in agony.

Nearby, a news crew interviewed a distraught-looking man wearing a *Finch Saves* shirt.

"What is your name, sir?"

"Thomas Finch."

"And your real name?"

"That's it."

"Okay, Mr. Finch," the reporter said, rolling her eyes. "Where have you been the past few days? The world has been looking for you."

"I've been hiding," he said, rubbing his hands over his eyes as if he hadn't slept in weeks. "Waiting for tonight."

"I assume you're here to stop this event from happening?"

"I am."

"What's the plan? Do you have an invitation? If not, it would appear you've got about four hundred National Guard you're going to have to try and make it past."

Natalie had a thought and pulled the binder of Yuval's research from her purse.

"Don't worry," the man said, crouching as if readying himself to spring over the fence. "I never give up. Not for my daughter."

Eva.

For the first time, she pictured her daughter not lying still in a gurney, but squirming around on the floor, laughing, her eyes closed in delight as her father tickled her belly. In a moment of clarity, Natalie felt confident no one was going to be getting healed.

Eva's just the bait.

Wresting the binder open, Natalie thumbed through its contents, looking for a paper that had caught her attention back at the mansion. Tossing the others to the ground, she finally stopped on what she was searching for.

Hijacking the Immune System: Active Transmitters and the Beautiful Weapon.

Natalie felt the valves in her heart begin to thump as they opened and closed, forcing blood through her body as it readied itself for a threat she couldn't believe was possible. She flipped through several pages of research and graphs to get to the paper's summary.

CONCLUSION

It is conceivable then, if not inevitable, that viruses will be engineered to take advantage of the idiosyncrasies of certain people's immune systems, weaknesses that prevent them from ever fully developing resistance. Given their specialization, such viruses are unlikely to be highly transmissible in normal populations. Certain people, however, will continue to actively transmit the virus, long after the infection may have seemed to clear.

* * *

On the other side of the cathedral, Finch crouched to the ground as the crack of shots rang out—heavy gunfire, the sound of machine guns. Beyond the fence, the National Guardsmen turned and looked far behind the rear of the cathedral in an attempt to pinpoint the threat.

"Stay your posts," a captain barked at the soldiers around him. "Not our problem, whatever it is."

People began to flee in panic, tripping over each other as no one could locate which direction the shots were coming from. Suddenly, sparks lit up the woods as streaks of burning white flares shot into the sky. Smoke poured out of the top of a building just visible above the tree line. Another string of gunfire ripped through the air, sending everyone hurtling into each other. Again, a shower of white embers blasted into the air, illuminating the chaos unfolding below.

Brinkley, Finch thought as he crept towards the fence. *I hope that's you.*

Unable to contain their fighting instinct, soldiers began jogging towards the source of the disturbance.

"Stay your posts!" the captain screamed again, an order entirely ignored.

Gunfire continued to erupt and other soldiers from the front of the cathedral began to pass by, intent on mounting an all-out assault on what some assumed to be a terrorist attack. Out of the corner of his eye, Finch caught a flash of movement as someone rushed directly toward him, against the movement of the crowd. Instinctively, he turned to run but stumbled over a fleeing protestor, crashing to the ground.

He scrambled to his feet, attempting to flee again, but his pursuer was too fast. They wrapped their arms around his legs, tackling him onto the cold earth. In the chaos of his struggle, Finch glanced behind him and could see nothing but someone preventing his escape, their body hidden with the folds of a thick scarlet cape.

CHAPTER 114

With just a few seats waiting to be filled, a conductor, dressed in black, walked onto the center of the stage as two dozen musicians began tuning their instruments. Arranged on risers behind them stood another sixteen people—vocalists from a small choir. The lights flashed again in earnest, beckoning any remaining stragglers to their seats. Out of habit, ushers closed the rear doors leading into the vestibule, a futile effort of quietude given the clamor of noise pouring in from outside.

Once the instrumentalists finished their adjustments, the conductor stepped away from the podium as chandeliers dimmed, and the projection screen faded to black. A film began to play, a cinematic black-and-white shot of the surface of an angry sea, frothy white foam exploding into the air as waves collided into each other. There was no music, just the din of wind and an approaching storm. Occasionally, the water would rise high enough to submerge the camera, completely changing the nature of the sound into one of frothing bubbles and the distorted welts of crashing waves.

After a few trips between the surface of the ocean, the camera bobbed further underneath as time slowed to a crawl. Imperceptibly, the sound underneath the ocean changed to a muffled throb, the unmistakable sound of the human heart beating. Something crashed into the water, then another—sending hundreds of bubbles first downward through the ocean, rebounding upwards as they shimmied toward the surface.

Once the water had cleared, it became obvious what had caused the disturbance: two feet, bound in leather sandals. A wave passed, and the water level dropped again, revealing the legs of a robed man, standing on top of the water. He began walking forward as waves struck against him. The camera stayed level with his feet as he took step after step, crashing in and out of the water as waves surged past.

After several steps, the camera spun around the front, pointing behind, the man's legs still taking up the entire frame. Beyond him, a small fishing vessel rolled in the ocean, pitching precariously back and forth. Other robed men within the boat kneeled and clung to its side, leaning out over the edge, reaching for the man in the water, their faces furled in distress.

Handwriting began to appear in bright white to the side of the man—mathematical equations with animated number and lines pointing to his feet, his body, and the demarcation between water and air. The calculations became more complex as time continued to slow down, eventually filling the screen with scribbles and formulas that no one could possibly understand.

A low drone, a single musical note, began to play as the gurgles and thumps from underwater continued to sound. The camera began to rise, out of the water and into the air, looking down on the scene, nearly frozen in time below. Portions of the handwriting were erased from the screen, the negative space it created spelling out a phrase attendees had already seen: *The Science of Faith.*

At this moment, the conductor stepped back onto the podium as the vocalists stood up on risers that arched around the back of the stage. With his baton held in the air, the conductor swung his hand, and the strains of Mozart's *Ave Verum Corpus* began to fill the sanctuary.

Ave verum corpus, natum	*Hail, true Body, born*
de Maria Virgine,	*of the Virgin Mary,*
vere passum, immolatum	*having truly suffered, sacrificed*
in cruce pro homine	*on the cross for mankind,*

Guests followed the Latin and English translations in programs they'd been provided. Initially, the first stanza of the song soared to the ceiling, suggesting great hope and beauty, a combination of melody and harmony unequaled since it had been written over two hundred and thirty years earlier. Rays of sunlight began to oscillate off the ocean's surface towards the camera as it peered down at the tiny boat bobbing in the storm below. With extreme cunning, the arrangement changed into a melancholy cry, perfectly echoing the bleakness of the text.

cuius latus perforatum	*from whose pierced side*
fluxit aqua et sanguine:	*water and blood flowed:*
esto nobis praegustatum	*Be for us a foretaste of the Heavenly banquet*
in mortis examine.	*in the trial of death!*

Sunlight disappeared into the clouds as the song turned into extreme sorrow, the singers following one another in a crescendo of rising sadness. Then, as magically as it had first transformed, the chords turned once again to joy as the camera continued to rise in the air, just high enough that pieces of land began to appear in the corners.

O Iesu dulcis, O Iesu pie,	*O sweet Jesus, O holy Jesus,*
O Iesu, fili Mariae.	*O Jesus, son of Mary,*
Miserere mei. Amen	*have mercy on me. Amen.*

The song ended without the singers—just the orchestra closing with the exact chord it began with. Not a single person clapped as the conductor held his baton in the air. The rumble of approaching thunder began to sound throughout the building as clouds moved past the camera. Without warning, it fell towards the ocean, zoomed past the boat into the water, enclosed within the darkness below.

CHAPTER 115

Gunfire continued to ring out behind the cathedral as Finch struggled to break free from his attacker. Pressed up against the fence, Finch hooked his free leg underneath and slammed his knee into the man's rib cage with such force he twisted away, gasping for air.

The man wore the unmistakable vestments of a Cardinal, his red hat resting several feet away. Finch stood up, ready to inflict more pain when he recognized who it was.

"Dr. Ikänen?" he asked. "What are you doing? Why are you wearing that?"

The vigorous scientist had transformed into a wizened clergy, his wrinkled face creased with worry. Ikänen tried to sit up, but it was too painful.

"Help me up," he said.

"I'll push you right back down," Finch said, extending his hand to him. "And I won't be nice this time."

"No funny business. Promise."

Ikänen winced in pain as he coughed, trying to catch his breath.

"What's with the costume? Are you trying to sneak in? I thought you had an invitation."

"Oh, this isn't a costume."

"You're a Cardinal?" Finch asked.

"I *was*. But, it's a lifetime appointment. I retired, so to speak, but they won't let you go that easily."

Finch was still completely baffled as to what had just happened.

"Science was always my passion," Ikänen continued, coughing mid-sentence. "I am a man of faith, of course. That never wavered, thankfully. But my intellectual curiosity was just too much for the church, I suppose. So, I 'hung up the cleats,' as they say."

"I had no idea."

"Most don't. Not in research, at least."

Ikänen turned over and coughed hard, splattering blood onto the ground.

"Oh," Finch said. "I'm sorry. I didn't mean to...."

Ikänen held up a hand, intent upon stopping the apology. "I'm old and frail now. You play with the big boys, you're going to get burned. Or am I mixing my metaphors?"

"Why?" Finch asked, still confused. "Why did you attack me?"

"That was my pitiful attempt at trying to stop you."

"From what?"

"Going any further. You have to leave now Finch. You can't do this."

"What happened? You know the mission. I came here to stop him. To stop this whole thing. You know what's at stake here."

"The stakes have changed."

"How? Everyone in there's at risk if Yuval's able to infect them somehow. You know that."

Ikänen reached his hand out in an effort to calm Finch. "Son."

"It could spread from there. To anyone."

"Finch."

"We have to stop him. We have to go now."

"Finch. Listen to me. I don't know how to tell you this. *You're* the threat."

Ikänen grabbed Finch with both of his hands. "*You're* the threat. *You're* the virus. Do you hear me? *You* are Yuval's master plan—the way he plans on infecting everyone."

Finch's head spun in opposite directions, a dizziness he'd never experienced. His heart ramped into the stratosphere as he tried to slow his breathing.

"You thought they were giving you vaccines in prison," Ikänen said. "They were infecting you."

"I don't understand."

"With a virus that could activate the Bootstrap sequence."

Finch had trouble speaking. "I...I can't...."

"You know there are some viruses people never really develop immunity to, right?"

"Engineered viruses."

"That's right. I'm sure they had to get your blood samples to work with. A few months later, once they'd developed what they needed, they infected you. Probably tested you to make sure it was working the way they wanted."

"But I'm not sick," Finch said.

"You don't *feel* sick. But, you're carrying a virus, spreading it everywhere you go."

"Active transmitter," Finch said, quietly.

"Super spreader," Ikänen confirmed. "Yes."

Finch recalled the men who had chased him through the woods earlier that morning. The strange gear they'd worn over their faces. The way in which they were so careful not to harm him. He collapsed to the ground as tumblers began to click into place.

"That's why he's been trying to get me here."

Ikänen nodded his head. "I'm sure was his plan. From the beginning."

"That's why his men didn't kill me."

"No—they definitely wouldn't kill you. You're the most valuable thing in the world to Yuval."

"Alive, I am," Finch said, considering his options.

"Alive?" Ikänen asked. "Yes."

CHAPTER 116

Inside the cathedral, the projection screen went dark as stagehands moved the conductor's podium aside and set four speakers in the center on the floor, facing upwards. Cables were lowered from the ceiling, a microphone hanging on each end directly above the four speakers.

Two performers in black approached from the left-hand side of the stage, while two others entered from the right. They stopped just short of the speakers, grabbed a microphone and pulled it back, away from its natural resting place. Directly after the lyrics to *Ave Verum Corpus*, the program listed the next piece of music, a song with no words, no melody, no chords, and no printed sheet music at all.

PENDULUM MUSIC
For Microphones, Amplifiers, Speakers, And Performers

White text appeared on the screen reading *The Faith of Science*, an inversion of the previous title. The video faded in, revealing the camera still underneath the fishing boat, pointed upwards. Above, the vague figure of a man still stood in the water as waves continued to rage around him.

The performers released their microphones, which began to swing back and forth above the speakers. Each time they passed the speaker, a short burst of feedback pulsed out loud, resembling the whoosh of someone swinging an electric sword of light through the air. Every speaker produced a slightly different tone, their rush of sound occurring at different intervals as the phase of the swinging microphones changed in relation to each other.

The effect was something much different than the choral piece that just finished. This was the work of chance—random notes and tones whose duration in pitch were set in motion when the microphones were initially released. The performers themselves sat down, their work nearly done, despite the song continuing.

For those paying attention, it became apparent the video playing on the screen was not recorded in advance, but was somehow generated in real-time, derived from the sound of the performance. Sunlight sparkled into the water, sending rays of light in different directions and intensities, depending upon the noise each speaker made.

Again, text began to fill the screen. Before were scribbles and notations of mathematical equations. In the ocean around the fishing vessel, there was now beautiful handwriting, the scribe work of important religious documents, written within the beams of light that danced around the screen, many in archaic languages most could not understand.

The scattered offsets of feedback grew closer together as the motion of the microphones slowed—the result, a grating howl that nauseated nearly everyone who listened. As the sound became nearly unbearable, rays of sunlight burst from above into the water below, illuminating the sanctuary in bright, white light. Slowly, an enormous transparent cube descended from the ceiling, a twenty-five foot terrarium covering the entire orchestra and choir within a sound-proof cloche. The conductor returned to the stage and held his arms in the air.

The performers pulled their microphones away from the speakers, plunging the cathedral into deafening silence. At the same time, the sunlight on the projection screen was extinguished, the silhouette of the boat above barely visible.

With the faint gurgle of the ocean deep, the only sound, the camera began to move back up towards the boat, but stopped just at the surface, the screen divided in half by a cloudy sky above, the murky ocean below. The conductor gave a signal, and the performers released their microphones, allowing them to swing freely again. At the same time, the musicians and singers began another rendition of *Ave Verum Corpus*, this time, the natural sound of their performance made inaudible by the clear covering they sat within. Instead, a digitized version of their performance pulsed through the speakers each time a swinging microphone passed over.

The camera zoomed into the thin layer of water separating the sky from the sea, a man's legs visible in the background. Mathematical equations appeared above, while hand-written scripture appeared below. The camera continued to focus on the undulating layer of water that formed the surface between the two worlds. Slowly, the scripture and mathematical equations began to converge, portions of each moving into the other side, connecting back to the other with lines, arrows, and curves.

Other microphones descended from the ceiling and were flung into motion—its effect, an increasingly frenetic dance of sight and sound. The faint grid of graph paper emerged behind the water's surface, its curvature calculated and annotated by the animated equations and notations that filled the screen. On the stage, the cube rose into the air, allowing the unfettered beauty of the song to ring out fully. The camera began to zoom back as the last strains of the song played through the hypnotic oscillation of the microphones passing over the speakers.

Others who had remained in the boat stepped out onto the water, their buoyancy maintained by a steady flow of equations and scripture that floated around them—some pushing them up from below, others suspending them from above. More people began to pour out of the vessel as the angle continued to widen, eventually filling the ocean with hundreds of people walking across the turbulent water in every direction.

The camera eventually pulled back far enough that spits of land became visible on the left and right sides of the screen, the boat and people on the water nearly indiscernible as the last chords of the song were played. All movement appeared to stop as the two titles appeared above and below the horizon.

The Science of Faith

The Faith of Science

Again, the conductor held his baton in the air for a dramatic few seconds before letting it fall to the ground. The cathedral erupted into applause, stunned at the beautiful display of tension they had just witnessed, the perfect start to an evening they were promised would change the course of the world.

For many of the religious clergy in attendance, the spectacle registered differently. The final rendering of the music was odd, particularly the combination of swinging microphones and digitized musicians and singers. But, something else bothered them—the presentation's focus on science and a growing sense their faith was about to be tested in an entirely new way.

CHAPTER 117

"Why me?" Finch asked. "Why'd he pick me? Can't he just make another virus? Do it again to whoever else?"

Ikänen dropped his chin to his chest. "I'm afraid I might have had something to do with that."

"Seems unlikely."

"The Bootstrap sequence was protected by a three-party code. It was a security measure they put in place to keep it from being used by a lone rogue actor."

"Let me guess—Yuval got it somehow?"

"Yes, he did. Yuval held one of keys. Faucett was the other—which I'm sure they shared with each other. I'm fairly certain another Cardinal—a Cardinal Gordillo—held the third. I'm guessing some deal-making went on and Gordillo gave up his key."

"So where do *you* come in?" Finch asked.

"We stole it from him."

"Gordillo?"

"No, Yuval. Somehow, he got the whole thing. Not just a part of it."

"How? I can't imagine the security he must have had around it?"

"We convinced someone he cared about deeply to take it."

"A honey trap?"

"Yes."

"Who?"

"Your wife."

Natalie? Finch thought, his soul crushed with gloom. Despite their separation, Finch couldn't imagine his wife with anyone else. Particularly Yuval Naftali.

"Natalie?" he asked.

"Yes, Natalie."

"Yuval?" Finch asked, still incredulous. "He cared deeply for Natalie?"

"*Cares*—present tense, I would guess—given the fact he hasn't killed her."

"He found out she stole it?"

"We think so—given the fact he targeted *you* with the virus."

"You think he did this because he *hates* me. Personally?"

"Hell may have no fury like a woman scorned, but an insecure man spurned is much worse."

At least he was spurned, Finch thought. If Natalie had abandoned him for Yuval, it would have stung more than nearly anything he could think of.

"But how? If she stole it, how did he do anything without the code?"

"I'm not sure, but I think something was already being developed. Possibly a prototype. The code is gone now. I've made sure of that. I don't think he can do any more harm."

"Besides what I'm able to accomplish," Finch said, sarcastically.

Ikänen compressed his lips. "That's one way of putting it."

Finch held his hands to the back of his head and pulled forward, groaning in dread at the question he was about to ask.

"What kind of virus is it? Do we know what it does?"

"This is the part where I tell you to leave. Go. Live alone, like you've been doing. Enjoy your life as much as you can."

"Connolly said the same thing."

Ikänen ventured a tiny smile. "He must have known."

"Tell me," Finch said. "Just tell me what it is."

"This is going to be very difficult."

"I can handle it."

"Difficult for the *both* of us."

Finch felt a pit sink into the bottom of his stomach. "Oh God, Dr. Ikänen—I… You got the shots. You… I've infected you by now, I'm sure."

"Probably, yes."

"And Connolly, too," Finch said, his head reeling again. "That's why he jumped."

"I'm afraid that's a possibility."

Finch thought back to Garcia, just before he killed himself—the crazed look in his eyes, the voices he was apparently hearing. He then remembered the man in the cabin who'd gone on a killing spree before taking his own life. And the little girl Brinkley spoke of—the horrible way she had ended things. Perhaps it was a chance encounter at a grocery store? A house he had broken into? Finch was overcome at the thought of all the lives he'd possibly ended just through his mere existence.

Finch struggled to speak. "Connolly said his 'life had been full of faith' and that 'he wouldn't die without it.' Is that what the virus does? Destroys people's faith?"

Ikänen's face turned white as he contemplated the next few hours of his life. "Yuval has always had an interesting relationship with religion. I suppose you know that."

"He hates it. He'd end it if he could."

"I think he figured out a way."

"Through me."

"Possibly."

"I don't understand how a virus could ruin people's faith."

"I have an idea, but I fear Yuval's created something that goes even beyond."

"On purpose?"

"Purpose or not—it doesn't matter at this point."

What little hope Finch had for Eva evaporated. "I'm guessing the healing technology doesn't work at all."

"Probably not," Ikänen said. "Just a ruse to gather the world's most faithful and humiliate them in front of everyone else."

"What a sick bastard."

"Sick doesn't begin to describe him."

With few soldiers left to man the border, crowds around them begin to shove on sections of the fence, hoping to pull them apart. Ikänen crawled away to avoid being crushed. Finch looked at the cathedral, trying to decide what do.

"Finch, your daughter is in there. Possibly your wife, too. I know you want to save them, but you can't. You need to let them live their lives as best they can."

"I'm going to save them."

"No," Ikänen said, his voice suddenly shifting to anger. "You can't. There's hundreds of people in there—many of them faith leaders. They were picked specifically by Yuval in hopes you would destroy them."

"I'm going to go in there."

"It's not just your family, Finch. You infect those people in there, you may cause a tidal wave of infections that spread throughout the most important religious leaders in the world. That's exactly what he wants to happen."

Finch stood up and started walking towards the fence.

"Don't do it, Finch. I am warning you."

Finch turned and realized Ikänen had also stood up. In his hand, he held a small gun, pointed directly at Finch.

"You would kill me? For trying to stop him?"

"Listen to yourself, Finch. You can't save anyone in there, especially your family."

"You're just going to let him win? Walk away, and he wins everything?"

"He *wins* if you go in there. Walk away, and he loses."

"*Kill me*, and he loses," Finch said. "Isn't that the real solution? This ends with me. Isn't that right?"

"It doesn't have to. You can live alone. You know how to do it. You can make it like that."

"Sorry. I can't, Ikänen." Finch grabbed the top of the fence and pulled himself up. "Yuval is evil, and I'm going to stop him. Come what may."

Ikänen fired a shot into the air, warning Finch of his intentions. "I'll kill you before you go in there. Don't test me."

Finch paused at the top of the fence, concerned the scientist might follow through on his threat. Ikänen stepped closer and, with his free hand, reached into a pocket.

"I have something that can end this. Quickly, I'm guessing."

"What is it?"

Ikänen pulled out a small vial and a syringe. "You can do it yourself."

"What is that? Pavulon? Potassium chloride?"

"It's not medicine."

"What is it?"

"It's the vaccine, Finch. Run away from here. Give yourself the Bootstrap sequence. It'd be over in minutes."

Finch looked at what Ikänen held, in horror. Just hours before, he thought he was doomed to an early death. Less than an hour earlier, he'd found out he wasn't. Now Ikänen suggested he take the shot anyway, to protect him from killing anyone else.

"Please," Ikänen said, pushing his hand towards Finch. "It's the only way."

"You want me to kill myself?"

Ikänen straightened his back. "I'm not sure what exactly your virus does, but I'm going to fight it. I'm not going to jeopardize my salvation like Connolly. I'll go out fighting whatever demons come my way."

He held out the vial and syringe in an open hand. "Please, Finch. Don't make me add murder to my list of sins. Take it. Please."

Finch looked at the crowds of people beginning to breach the perimeter and leapt from the fence, pushing the gun out of the way as he fell directly on top of the scientist. Ikänen's liver was crushed, sending him into a fit of coughing.

"I'll take it," Finch said, "but, I'm sorry. I need to see my family one more time, first. I can save them."

He gathered Ikänen's belongings, scaled the fence, then jumped over the top and began sprinting with hundreds of other people towards the cathedral.

CHAPTER 118

Vickers and Brooke continued their trek to the cathedral. Abandoned cars clogged the streets. Even pedestrian traffic slowed as more people decided their vehicles were going nowhere.

Brooke checked her watch. "It's 7:20. They've probably already started by now."

"Probably," Vickers said. "But they'll wait for us."

"I'm that important?"

"Almost."

Brooke stopped to retie a loose shoelace. "This isn't what I was planning on wearing tonight. I hope I don't embarrass Dr. Naftali."

"I thought you and him were on a first name basis."

Again, Vickers caught Brooke off guard. "Privately, yes. Publicly, it's all business."

"You texted your husband and told him not to come. You said it was a trap."

"Yes," Brooke said, confident her ruse pretending to be Finch's wife was nearly up.

"What did you mean?"

Brooke realized Vickers knew less than he let on. "I thought you knew the plan."

"I do."

"What is the plan, then?"

"I'm not telling you."

"Let me ask you something. You think you're working for the good guys or the bad guys?"

"No such thing."

"They're all the same, right? All corrupt. All in it for themselves?"

"Definitely."

"Whoever's got the bigger paycheck is your boss, then?"

"That and better guns."

"Are you married?"

"Sorry. I'm taken," Vickers said with a wry smile.

"*Married*, I asked. As in something committed beyond fighting over the dog when you break up."

"No, I'm not. Why do you ask?"

"I hope one day you learn what it's like to truly give yourself to someone."

"I wouldn't say that to *Dr. Naftali*, as you call him. From what I hear, sounds like he gave himself to you before you humiliated him."

Brooke had no idea what he was talking about. "Is that why you said we're going to meet my new boyfriend?"

"I suppose."

The spired towers of the cathedral emerged as they walked closer, the media helicopters circling above clearly visible.

"What's about to happen?" Brooke asked, her apprehension growing by the second. "I really wish I'd worn something different."

"I don't think the clothes matter. Sounds like Yuval is giving you a second chance. I'd advise you to *not* humiliate him this time."

* * *

In a hallway just off the stage, Yuval swelled with pride as he heard the booming applause, which marked the ending of the introduction. The last stage of a lifelong ambition was about to begin—something many of his intellectual heroes had only dreamed of accomplishing.

Thou has conquered, O pale Galilean; the world has grown grey from thy breath;
We have drunken of things Lethean, and fed on the fullness of death.

It was a poem Yuval once memorized, nearly the only collection of verse that had ever impressed him. As a rebellious youth, the lines struck him deeply, eager to cast aside the religious trappings he felt had fettered the human race for so long.

O Gods dethroned and deceased, cast forth, wiped out in a day.

In just a few moments, millions across the world would come together in prayer that God—or their gods—would heal the frail little girl laying in the gurney beside him. Finch's appearance alongside many of the most significant men of faith would set in motion a vector of doubt that—with luck—might infect the entire planet. Despite the promise of the evening, the prayers of those who prayed for Eva would fail. Yuval would make sure of that.

An assistant brought him a small silver tray and handed it to him.

"Thank you," Yuval whispered, inspecting the contents. "Potassium chloride?"

"It is," they replied.

"How long will it take?"

"Thirty seconds. Her heart will completely stop before then."

"You're sure."

"Quite sure."

Yuval turned towards Eva. "Are you ready for your big night?"

Water pooled in her eyes. "Is he coming?"

"Your father? He's already here."

"He'll kill you."

"Perhaps," he said, rolling up the sleeve on her gown. "Perhaps he will. But, he will save us all first. And that is a promise."

"From what?"

"Ignorance."

Yuval removed a needle and IV line from the tray, then wrapped a rubber band around Eva's arm, just above her elbow.

"What are you doing?" she asked.

"Just relax," he said, unable to control his face from twitching. "This won't hurt a bit."

CHAPTER 119

Gordillo climbed the wooden stairs that lined the inside of one of the cathedral towers, stopping every flight to allow his heart to recover. There were too many people outside for him to have any hope of finding the last person standing between him and the papacy—Cardinal Vallcorba. Unable to see more than a few feet in front of him, he decided a higher vantage point might allow him to spot the distinctive vermilion robe they both wore.

As Gordillo neared the top platform, someone called out to him from above.

"Halt," they said in a commanding voice. "You are unauthorized to be here. Turn around now."

"You halt," Gordillo said, his booming voice twice as loud. "You are unauthorized, whoever you are. This is my house, not yours."

He continued up the last flight of steps. On the platform, a soldier set atop a pile of discarded hymnals, binoculars in his hand. A rifle set across his lap, its enormous scope clearly the instrument of a sniper.

"What are you doing here?" Gordillo asked, his face full of scorn. "Who authorized you to be here?"

"I'm not supposed to say. It's official business. I'll say that much."

"Who are you?"

"I'm not a terrorist," the soldier said, growing defensive.

"I know you're not a terrorist. Are you with Yuval? Military? I don't care who it is, just tell me."

"Capitol police."

"Oh," Gordillo said, sensing an opportunity. "You're the good guys, then."

"Yes, we are."

"Okay, good. I may need your help. Give me those binoculars. I need to find someone."

* * *

With few Guardsmen remaining, protestors began to tear down the fencing that surrounded the security perimeter. A surge of people rushed over the line, crushing Natalie within them as they jogged toward the building.

"Stop," Natalie yelled, trying to turn them away. "Don't go in there!"

Unable to thwart the crowd, she fell to the ground, causing others to trip over her. She tried to stand, but a river of humanity flowed around her, occasionally stepping directly onto her. Another woman fell onto Natalie's torso and began to scream.

So this is how I die, she thought as she sensed she wasn't getting enough oxygen.

Without even realizing what was happening, a burly man reached down and yanked her to her feet, pulling her along with him.

"Hey," he said to her, his face in shock. "You're Finch's wife, aren't you? Natalie?"

Still in a daze, Natalie answered honestly. "Yes. I am."

"He's here!" the man said, his eyes full of excitement. "People have seen him. He tried to blow the whole thing up."

Natalie couldn't think of a coherent answer.

"Are you on our side now?" he asked.

"I think so," Natalie said, gathering her wits. "But we can't go in there. We have to stop."

"Why not? They've got your daughter in there. Who knows what they're going to do to her."

Many of the protestors were probably safe from harm, but many others were not—a distinction impossible to communicate given the chaos unfolding around them.

Natalie grabbed his arm and forced him to look directly at her. "Listen to me. Did you get any of the shots?"

"Why do you care?" the man responded, offended. "*You* got them."

"Don't go in there if you did. That's all I can say. Everyone needs to know that. Especially Finch."

CHAPTER 120

Dressed in a fitted black suit, Yuval walked onto the stage as the crowd broke into claps and cheers, his face radiant with their adoration. After what felt like minutes of applause, he held his hands in front of him, asking for calm. Undeterred, they started into a new round of whistles and calls, his appearance of humility sending them into fits of joy.

"Please," Yuval said, barely audible over the roar of the crowd. "Please."

Throughout the sanctuary, dozens of cameras were set up to broadcast the feed in perfect clarity around the world, the international cooperation required to pull off such a feat, nearly unheard of. Two sign-language interpreters sat near the front, relaying what was happening to any who could not hear. At the back, interpreters sat ready to translate the words of Dr. Naftali into over twenty different languages.

"Please," he said again, emphatically pressing his hands in front of him as he begged for quiet.

Eventually, the screams died down, and Yuval was able to speak normally.

"I thought we were going to have to reschedule this thing, but I knew you'd be anxious for it go on anyway. Was I right?"

Again, the crowd began their wild applause.

"Okay," Yuval said, smiling. "Save that energy. Save it. I want to demonstrate something really interesting to you in a moment. But, first, I need to thank a couple of people for making this event—and everything it entails—possible."

Yuval walked to a podium, where the faint glow of a digital device illuminated his face. "Always dangerous to thank people, of course, because I know we'll leave someone important out but let's try anyway. My team of researchers, who've worked with me for the past few years—some of them for over a decade—I want to thank them for their tireless service in our quest. They know who they are. Over a dozen of them, actually. Two are no longer with us, and I want to give them a special moment of remembrance here for their sacrifice."

The screen lit up with the pictures of two scientists, their names, and the years that marked the beginning and ending of their lives.

"My team at the World Health Alliance has also been invaluable, of course. Helping us to secure funding. Partnerships. Permissions."

Yuval tilted his head down and peered over his glasses in a look of contempt. "Helping us to secure *forgiveness*, in some cases."

The mass of people laughed at his joke, fully aware of the cost of cutting-edge research.

"But only a few times," he continued. "As far as you know."

Again, a roll of laughter throughout the sanctuary. It was a display of humor they had rarely seen from him, a bit of comedy they enjoyed every second of.

"Albert Connolly, my partner in crime, my main squeeze—scientifically speaking of course—is the man of the hour."

Loud applause, followed by whistles of appreciation.

"Interestingly, we cannot find Dr. Connolly at this time. He is supposed to have been standing here, saying what I am saying—which would have been awkward, saying these nice things about himself—but I am sure he is okay. Feeling under the weather or something."

Yuval raised his eyebrows and scratched his head.

"And I would be remiss if I didn't mention our beloved Walter Faucett."

Silence overtook the sanctuary as a slide of his picture showed on the screen. "Taken from us too soon. He could have been *one-hundred*-and-seventy-years-old and it *still* would have been too soon. Regardless, much of what you will see tonight we owe directly to his efforts, and I want to dedicate tonight to Walter's memory. I'm sure you will, as well."

Nods of reverent approval punctuated the hundreds of people that sat within the rapt audience, their attention focused on his every word. Cameras panned around the sanctuary, trying to give an accurate representation of the admiration those who filled the pews had for Faucett.

"We should applaud him," Yuval started as a few claps sounded.

"But not yet," he said, extending his arm to stay their appreciation. "Not yet. We can applaud him as part of that demonstration I just mentioned."

The lighting changed in tone as Yuval walked from his lecturn to the center of the state.

"Tonight," he began, "is about the relationship between science and faith. No secret there. Many of you here are researchers, physicians—Nobel prize winners in some cases—many of you, thought of as the leaders in your field. Advancing the cause of humanity through reason and knowledge. A noble quest, obviously."

The projection screen displayed the headshots of several scientists invited to attend.

"Look at these men and women. Heroes to our cause. And yet...and yet, there is another group of people that are heroes to another cause. Many *others* of you here are great leaders within your faith."

The screen changed to an animation of the names and photographs of pastors, priests, clerics, and other religious thinkers in attendance

"Look at all of these wonderful, beautiful men and women," Yuval said. "Heroes to a different cause."

Scattered applause sprinkled across the room.

"That's right," Yuval said, trying to encourage them. "These are heroes to a different cause, but one that is just as important as the cause of science. We tend to think of these things in opposition to each other, but tonight, I am hoping we can begin to see things differently. It is my hope that by the end of this evening, you will see that faith and science can work together in such a way that things you don't currently believe are possible you will think of as possible by the end. Inevitable, in some way."

Yuval raised his eyebrows as he continued his speech. "The first of many reconciliations this evening, I hope."

Two stagehands brought microphone stands onto the left and right sides of the platform, pointed them at the crowd, then raised them high into the air. Yuval took off his jacket and handed it to one of the stagehands as they left.

"Are you ready?" he asked, as he rolled up his sleeves, a symbolic gesture he was told would make for more riveting press photos of the event.

The crowd nodded in approval as the lights changed again, this time illuminating portions of those sitting in the sanctuary.

"This is going to be fun."

Yuval felt in his pockets for something he apparently couldn't locate.

"Where is my sound meter?" he asked, looking on the lecturn. "Oh, it's in my jacket pocket."

He pointed to someone off stage. "Can you bring me my jacket?"

The stagehand returned his black jacket and waited while Yuval fumbled around the pockets until he produced a small silver device. Still bubbling with excitement, the crowd cheered at his discovery.

"That was not the amazing part, I assure you," he said, smiling as he handed his jacket back to the stagehand.

Yuval raised the object he held into the air. "This is a sound meter. It measures how loud sound is. We don't need the meter to know that you are loud, obviously. But, *how* loud are you? If we wanted to quantify it, we'd need something like this. It measures *how* loud you are in decibels. You remember Alexander Graham Bell, I'm sure? Well, we can measure how loud things are using a sound meter like this, and it gives us a number—in deci*bels*."

Switching the device to his other hand, Yuval walked to the other side of the stage so others could see it. "On the count of three, I want you to cheer as loud as you can. Okay?"

Yuval returned to the center of the stage and pointed the meter towards the crowd. "Are you ready? One! Two! Three!"

The crowd produced an ear-splitting clamor as Yuval stared at the readout on his display.

"Okay, stop! Stop!" he said, dragging his finger across his throat to drive the message home.

"That was pretty good, I think. That was 118 decibels. Anyone know what a jet airplane is?"

"One hundred and thirty," a British-voiced person yelled out.

"One hundred and thirty?" Yuval asked. "Okay. American airplanes are louder, I'm sure, but we can do better then, can't we? Let's try again. We're already at 118. But, this time, let's do it for Walter. We want to thank him for all he did. Maybe he can hear us—wherever he is...."

Yuval looked up, shading his eyes from the lights, before looking down over the front of the stage, drawing wild peals of laughter from some. The consultants he had hired to write his script had come through, insisting people would laugh at certain points during the evening despite Yuval's unbelief.

"Okay, I'm going to count to three again. And let's see if we can hit 130 decibels."

Yuval returned to the center of the stage, but this time held the meter out past the edge, trying to get as close to their mouths as possible.

"One! Two!"

Just as they were about to scream, he stopped and held his hand up in the air.

"Wait, wait, wait! Just a minute. For Walter. And we don't need a *long* round of applause, just an instantaneous sound. As loud as you can."

He adjusted his stance, held out the meter and cover his eyes with his free hand, as if to shield himself from what they were about to do.

"One! Two! Three!"

In one second, the sanctuary went from near silence to a deafening roar, its reverberation taking nearly ten seconds to evaporate. Yuval looked at the sound meter as his shoulders sunk in pretend disappointment. He shook his head, exaggerating the overall effect.

"For *Walter*?" he asked. "That was the best you could do for Walter Faucett?"

"What was it?" someone asked out loud.

"What did we get?" another asked.

"You want to know what it was?" Yuval asked, a question to which everyone in the audience nodded their head emphatically.

"The number was...."

Again Yuval stopped mid-sentence to increase the dramatic tension of not knowing.

"The first measurement was 118, I believe? This time...you got 123 decibels."

Groans emerged from the audience, frustrated they couldn't reach the goal Yuval had set out before them.

"Are you positive that's the loudest you can get?"

He waited for answers from the audience. Some pleaded with him to let them try again. Others felt pain in their throats from overexertion.

"Many of you are convinced that's the loudest you can get. Who of you are like that?"

Yuval gestured for a show of hands in the audience as cameras cut to the hundreds of people raising their arms from their seats.

"What is that? Maybe 70 percent? 80 percent of you think you can't get any louder? You're positive, right?"

After placing the sound meter back in his pocket, Yuval returned to the lecturn to get a sip of water. "Ye of little faith," he said, a phrase that drew more laughter from the religious leaders than anyone else.

"Now, I'm sure you're asking—what does *this* have to do with science and faith?"

He left the lecturn and stood in front of one of the microphones that had been placed on the stage.

"Now for something really interesting," he said. "Let's turn on a sound meter so that *everyone* can see it. Not just me."

The screen lit up with an animated green bar that ran from left to right. Underneath it were numerical markings indicating the value of sound the microphones detected.

"Whoo!" someone yelled out loud, triggering the meter to scale leftwards.

A number on the screen captured the peak for all to see—*Peak Hold: 54db.*

Yuval smiled and pointed to the person in the audience who had yelled.

"Not bad. For just one person."

He clapped his hand in front of the microphone, showing it clearly moving with the sound he created.

"As I talk," he said, you will see the sound of my voice moving on the meter. The loudest part of what I say will stay up on the screen for a few seconds."

Yuval grabbed a stool and climbed on top so that he stood directly before the microphone. With a laser pointer, he highlighted the decibel readout.

"Welcome, everyone!" he yelled directly into the microphone, distorting the sound badly.

The screen read the result—*Peak Hold: 103dB.*

"Okay your loudest reading was 123db. You swore to me—at least he did," Yuval said, pointing to a man laughing in the front row, "that this was as loud as you could get."

Yuval jumped down from the stool and pointed both hands at the two microphones on either side of the stage. "Now let's see what happens. Let's see what happens when you have a little feedback on how you're doing. Everyone ready?"

Groans could be heard from the audience members, convinced they could do no better.

"This will be amazing. I promise. Okay, everyone ready? One! Two! Three!"

CHAPTER 121

Finch tried to distance himself from the mass of humanity that swelled around him but there were simply too many. Rather than heading straight at the cathedral, the crowd was swirling around the front towards the other side, intent upon gaining entry through the yawning hole in the building's side.

An incredible roar of noise poured out from within the cathedral, the haunting sound of a thousand screams.

"It's already started," someone yelled at him. "Shouldn't you be in there by now?"

Convinced they had recognized him, Finch glanced down and steered himself away from the main channel of movement, looking behind to see if anyone was following.

Ikänen's suggestion played over and over in his mind. Walk away. Leave his family forever—or end his life. Those were his two choices. There was no other. Finch looked away from the cathedral, down the streets where thousands of people and hundreds of cars lay stranded. It was the most people he'd seen in years, a reminder of the isolation he would have to endure forever.

A group of people walked by, all wearing the same T-shirt: *Save Mongchai.* Still intent upon saving the Asian boy who nearly drowned, despite his reported death, they hoped beyond hope Yuval's technology might do what seemed impossible. As they passed by, a thought occurred to Finch.

You're the most valuable thing in the world to Yuval, Ikänen had told him. *Alive.*

Ikänen had told him he could either leave or kill himself. Finch took a deep breath, turned back with the crowd and began walking toward the cathedral. He'd just thought of a third option—one Mongchai would have been proud of.

* * *

"How do you focus these things?" Gordillo asked the sniper sitting beside him.

"There's a ring in the middle. Turn it with your finger."

Gordillo peered through the binoculars as he adjusted the black knob back and forth. With no windows, the top of the tower was frigid. Regardless, it afforded a clear view of the pandemonium playing outside.

"Who are you looking for?"

"A good friend," Gordillo said. "We were supposed to meet a half an hour ago, but I haven't been able to find him."

As far as he could see, the fencing was completely toppled over, the National Guardsmen charged with security drawn away elsewhere. A throng of people walked towards the side of the cathedral, the crowds behind them growing by the second.

Someone moving in a slightly different direction caught Gordillo's eye, someone appeared to be dressed in red. The portable light towers provided some illumination, but it was still nearly impossible to tell for certain.

"What's the magnification on your scope?" he asked the soldier.

"Fifty-six millimeters."

"What does that mean? Is that any better than these binoculars?"

"You can look farther out. But, it'll be darker. You'll have better luck with those."

Gordillo turned around and held his hand out. "Give me that."

"My rifle?"

"Yes. Give it to me. I'm not going to shoot anyone."

Reluctantly, the soldier handed the firearm over to Gordillo, who immediately held it to his cheek and looked down the barrel. Through the glass, he panned around until he spotted the man again.

"Keep your finger off the trigger, if you don't mind," the soldier said.

Within the scope, Gordillo saw what he was hoping for—the ruby-red figure of a Cardinal, walking towards the cathedral.

"Is this thing loaded?" Gordillo asked, his face pressed against the eyepiece.

"Of course. Why do you ask?"

Gordillo looked behind him and, with both hands, slammed the butt of the thirty-pound rifle into the soldier's face, breaking his skull in half.

"I'm doing God's work," he said, returning his eye to the scope. "That's why."

CHAPTER 122

Inside the cathedral, the meter had shot to 118db—their original starting point. Slowly, it crept up, two decibels at a time. The crowd roared as it crossed 123db, their previous record, sending it momentarily up to 128db. Aware of their newfound power, the crowd doubled their efforts until the meter hit 128db again.

"Can we do 130?" Yuval screamed into the microphone. "Can we do it?"

Some in the crowd stood up, cupping their hands to their mouths to focus the sound of their voices towards the microphone. The meter oscillated up and down, but wouldn't budge past 129db.

"That's it!" Yuval screamed. "Stand up! Stand up! Let's hit 130!"

The crowd stood up, their backs arching with effort as they inhaled as much air as possible, screaming until their throats hurt. Yuval dashed to the lecturn and tapped on a digital screen. Immediately, the display added a decimal point to the readout, its meter now flickering between 129.7db and 129.8db.

Realizing how close they were, the crowd went into a wild frenzy, the pitches of their voice rising into screams as their vocal chords burned with pain. As soon as the meter hit 129.9db, Yuval held his arms up like a conductor, circling his arms as he beckoned more energy from them.

"Are you ready? People are watching you at home on their televisions! On their phones! On their laptops! On the count of three give it everything you've got. Okay? Ready? One... two... three!"

Everyone in attendance screamed with abandon—even the security, the media, and musicians—all delighted to see the meter surge past 130, registering an incredible 132.4db before they stopped. Many in the crowd were doubled over in exhaustion, their faces full of laughter and unbelief. Others held their throats in pain.

"You did it!" Yuval exclaimed. "I didn't think you could. Did you?"

The crowd had still not settled down, the roar of their murmur loud enough for Yuval to be nearly inaudible.

"I didn't think you could do it? Did you?" Yuval asked again, this time more loudly. "Look at that. One hundred and thirty-two point four decibels. From you guys, no less."

Laughter filled the room. Whatever Yuval had planned for them, they couldn't imagine. If it was as good as their entertainment, they wouldn't be able to stop talking about it.

"Take a picture of that screen," Yuval told them. "Get out your phone and take a picture of that screen. Never forget what happened here tonight. One hundred and thirty-two point four decibels. Incredible."

Many did as he asked, taking group pictures of themselves with others standing next to them, the giant display visible behind them.

"We are bonded now," he started, the crowd still rumbling from their experience. "Okay, sit down. Let's sit down, and everybody calm down."

Yuval returned to the lecturn for a moment and drank a glass of water, purely an attempt to buy some time for the crowd to settle. "Calm down, everyone. Lots more to talk about here," the scientist said. "If you think that was amazing, you're not going to believe what comes later."

Yuval grabbed a stool and returned to the center of the stage, collecting himself before he spoke again.

"Why did that just work?" he asked, as he sat and buttoned his sleeves back to their more formal setting. "Think about what just happened. Before, you could only reach 123 decibels, a significantly quieter sound. And yet, something changed that caused you to be able to create much more sound than you thought possible. How did it happen? Why was it not possible to begin with?"

He paused to let the millions watching around the world think about what they had just witnessed. After taking another sip of water, he continued.

"You didn't believe you could—because you had no *idea* if you could. You had no *reference point*. There was nothing for you to gauge how close or far you were away from the goal. But, there was something more important—there was no feedback mechanism. Nothing to tell you were doing the right thing. Nothing to give you hope."

A black and white image appeared on the screen. Glasses of water sat on a table, each containing a rat.

"Many of you are, no doubt, familiar with this experiment. In 1954, Albert Lambing wanted to see how long rats would survive in the water before they drowned. For most of them, it was two minutes. A few others were able to last much longer. What was the difference? *They'd been previously rescued*. They had already been put in the water once before, but just before they were about to die, they were rescued by the scientist."

The slide advanced to the next image, showing a scientist holding a rat above the jar, their fur dripping with water.

"The first-timers lasted two minutes. The ones who learned that rescue might come—guess how long they lasted. Five minutes? Twenty minutes? An hour?"

Yuval advanced the slide again. Two rats were floating in their jars, apparently dead. Another was still alive, grasping for the top of its jar.

"This is almost three days later. Sixty-five hours and this rat was still alive, all because of the *hope* it had of being rescued."

Like many scientific experiments, the story made some uncomfortable. The thought of purposefully being subjected to such torture—facing drowning for nearly three days—sickened many.

"Dr. Lambing showed us how certain behaviors are pre-programmed in our mind, from the moment we are born, just waiting to be triggered when the right hormone comes along. Dr. Lambing's daughter, Ruby is here tonight with her family. Stand up Ruby so we can honor your father's legacy."

The crowd applauded as a family of three stood up and waved to those around them.

"Just a few minutes ago, you were convinced you had yelled as loud as you could. We now know you weren't even close to your maximum potential. All it took was some belief you could push yourself a bit further. Some feedback that what you were doing was working."

The screens turned black, darkening the entire cathedral.

"If some of us were placed in giant jars, on the verge of drowning, we might place a timer on the wall—a countdown of sorts—for when we would be rescued. How much further could we push ourselves if there were some visible indication our rescuer was near? Our savior?"

Yuval was clearly making a turn towards the spiritual. For those who knew him, it was entirely awkward. For those watching him for the first time, it felt like an authentic display of belief.

An image appeared on the screen—a classic painting, a depiction of the ninth chapter of the Gospel of Mark. Jesus was packing mud onto the eyes of a man blind since birth.

"Jesus heals a man born blind," Yuval said. "One of the great miracles from the Bible. Many of you here tonight don't believe this actually happened. You don't think it's possible. Are any of you brave enough to admit it?"

Several in the crowd raised their hands.

"Yes, okay—a few. Why do you think this isn't possible? Is it because there's no plausible scientific explanation for it? Or do you just have faith—blind faith, we might call it—that miracles *cannot* happen?"

Cameras panned around the sanctuary over the hundreds watching, trying to depict the emotion of those in attendance. Most were clearly enthralled, hanging on Yuval's every word.

"You do not believe. You do not have faith. You may not believe Jesus even existed. Even if you were to see someone healed before your very eyes, your mind would tell you it's not possible. Your mind would say, 'What I just witnessed didn't happen because I don't believe it can happen.'"

Yuval stood and walked to the left side of the stage. "How have we come to this point? How have we lost so much of our faith? Is science our problem? Has science robbed us of any faith we might otherwise have?"

Again, Yuval took a long sip of water from the glass that sat on the floor beside him. He thought for a moment, then held up his finger as if he had just stumbled upon something incredibly profound.

"What if there was a way for us to visualize our belief? What if there was a way to see our faith?"

He paused to let the question resonate more fully.

"A few minutes ago, I asked you to yell as loud as you could, but until you had that feedback mechanism to show you, you thought you had reached your maximum. If I asked you how much faith you have that a blind man can be healed—if I asked you that right now—most of you would probably have very little."

Yuval advanced the slide. It showed another painting from Mark. A crowd was gathered around Jesus, his arm wrapped around the blind man—except the man can now see. The man, blind since birth, appears ecstatic with joy at being able to visualize the world before him.

"If this man were here today, and we were to pray for him—if we were to pray our God or gods would heal him—for most of us, we'd have very little faith it would actually happen. This is why we are here tonight. This is what is about to change.

"We are going to do another experiment. Just like before, but this time everyone here—and everyone watching on television, online, wherever you are—this time all of you will be able to participate. We are going to pray for our special guest, Miss Eva Connolly. We are going to pray that she would be healed… but with a special twist. A new bit of technology is going to help us *see* our faith. Just like the sound meter showed us how loud we were, tonight—for the first time in the history of humankind—you are going to be able to *see*, in real-time, a measurement of our faith."

Another slide. An image from the introductory video at the beginning. Underneath a fishing vessel, the camera was angled up at a lone pair of feet floating just below the water level. As before, white, handwritten equations filled much of the negative space around the boat.

"Scientists, this is where your faith—in science—will likely fall short. You do not believe this is even possible. Billions have been spent developing this approach. I've been ridiculed for years at all the wasted funding, but I'm here to tell you it works. If this girl is healed tonight, your worlds will be shaken. Those of faith in the audience already believe in miracles. They may assume they don't happen today, but they accept that miraculous things *did* occur at some point in time. You—scientists—you reject this. You don't believe in God, or gods, and don't believe they have the powers to perform miracles even if they did exist. And… and you likely don't believe in this technology either.

"So, what happens if this girl is healed?" Yuval laughed. "Those of faith will confirm what they already believe. Their belief in science, however, may be renewed. And that is a good thing, is it not?"

Yuval paused to take another sip of water as murmurs filled the room.

"Those of science—those of you with absolutely no faith—you will go for quite a ride, won't you? How is it possible? How were the miracles possible? We don't understand them. We can't replicate them in our labs. They just don't make any sense."

"But that is not why we are here," Yuval said, walking to the other side of the stage. "We are not here to explain miracles. We are here to perform them!"

The crowd, hanging on his every word, burst into wild screams and applause.

"That's right, we are here to perform miracles! The faith of the world will be on full display, in such a way no one can deny it!"

The crowd stood up to thunderous applause. Yuval felt as though he were floating, his feet dragging along the floor as he willed himself back towards the center of the stage.

"I know you want to see this right now, but I need to explain something. There was a lot of money, from many different countries, that went into this. I may be up here on the stage directing things, but this is, in a sense, a gift to the world—*from* the world. This will not be patented. This will not be sold or licensed. It will be available for anyone, anywhere, to use."

Again, deafening roars from the audience exploded into the rafters.

"Before we can begin, we need to meet little Miss Eva first, do we not? Anyone want to give her a warm welcome? Let's bring her out so we can all have a look at her beautiful face."

Yuval gestured to the side of the stage, where a bright spotlight shined into the darkness. After an awkward few seconds, the crowd jumped to their feet again, screaming for joy as Yuval's assistant rolled Eva out onto the stage, a tiny camera mounted to the gurney's railing beaming her terrified expression onto the screen above for everyone to see.

CHAPTER 123

Natalie ran around the back of the cathedral towards an entrance she'd been using throughout the week. The grounds were crawling with activity as hundreds of National Guardsmen tried to locate the source of the attack that originated from the top of the nearby library.

Unfortunately, the door was still guarded, two security personnel standing by to check the credentials of anyone who tried to enter. Natalie moved to retrieve the pass her father had given, but realized her purse and everything in it was gone, dropped somewhere along the way as she fought for her life amongst the stampede of people.

Still some fifty feet away, she looked up and was horrified by what she saw—Brooke being escorted through the doorway by the same man she'd seen on the mansion security cameras.

"Brooke," she screamed. "Don't go, Brooke! You will die!"

The figure turned around, his attention drawn to Natalie's hysterical cries. He said something to Brooke, who didn't respond. After looking back one more time, he grabbed her arm and pushed her through the door.

Natalie ran towards the door, hoping the guards would recognize her. "Hello," she said, barely able to speak. "I'm Natalie Connolly—Albert Connolly's daughter. I've been working here all week. I need to get in to see my daughter."

The guards were unimpressed. "I haven't seen you before. Sorry."

"I just need to see my daughter. Yuval and I are kind of a thing. He's got her in there—I'm sure you've probably seen her."

"He didn't come through here," one of the guards said. "If you've got a security badge, we could let you in. As it is, you're not getting through."

Her patience completely spent, Natalie ran at the door and tried to open it. The guards blocked her path and shoved her to the ground.

"Please let me get her," Natalie cried, pulling on the soldier's pants legs. "She will die in there. Please! I don't want her to die."

A half-dressed elderly man staggered towards them from the darkness, his body bent nearly in half from age. "What seems to be the problem?" he asked.

Natalie looked up, her eyes unable to blink.

"You're Dr. Connolly's daughter," he said, his face brimming with shock.

"I am," she answered.

"You can't go in there. You'll die."

"Yuval has my daughter. I don't want her to die."

The man sighed, then spent a moment considering what he should do. He reached into a pocket and pulled out a laminated card—a security badge with his picture on it—and presented it to the bewildered security guards.

"She's with me," he said. "Now let us through."

* * *

Gordillo scanned the courtyard below him looking for the Cardinal. Through the rifle scope, colors were so muted it might as well have been a black and white image. Hundreds of people walked around, stopping to talk, changing directions. There was nothing discernibly red he could see.

After lowering the rifle, Gordillo again held the binoculars to his face, waving them around the crowd in hopes of catching a dash of red. Just when he thought of giving up, someone emerged from the mob, jogging up the stairs directly at the entrance below him.

Taking the heavy rifle with him, Gordillo raced down a flight of stairs where interior windows in the tower opened into the vestibule below. The floor was full of participants, crowded into makeshift seating, content to sit in attendance though they could only hear—and not see—the proceedings inside the sanctuary. Gordillo slid the barrel through the opening, pressed the gun to his cheek, and waited for the Cardinal to appear.

CHAPTER 124

The audience didn't return to their seats until Eva's gurney was rolled into the center of the stage, its wheels locked in place to keep it from moving. Stagehands took away the two microphones and began removing black cloth that covered strange metallic arrays dotting the platform.

"Do you see these things?" Yuval asked, pointing to the some of the equipment. "These are essentially antennas—not for detecting radio waves. Not for detecting any kind of electromagnetic frequencies at all, really. These detect something much different: the waves—if we can call them that—of faith. Of prayer. Of belief."

Yuval walked to the lecturn and tapped on a glass display. The screen above the stage changed to something entirely new. A grid of dark gray lines formed a measurement graph, the meaning of the numbers located on each side unknown to everyone. Two thicker lines—one vertical, the other, horizontal—crossed in the center.

"This look familiar?" Yuval asked. "Remember your math classes? X and Y coordinates and that sort of thing? This may look the same, but I can assure you it's much different."

Yuval motioned to the crowd for someone to come onto the stage. A man dressed in a clerical collar walked around to the side and jogged up the small set of stairs.

"This is Father Devin Spinney, from...."

Yuval covered his microphone, asked the man a question, then lowered his ear close to the man's mouth to hear his answer.

"Father Devin Spinney from Ainsworth, Massachusetts. Everybody give him a hand."

Unsure what was about to happen, scattered claps dotted the sanctuary. Yuval put his arm on the man's shoulder to encourage him.

"Father Spinney has agreed to help us do a little demonstration. I asked him this beforehand—just so you know. I'm not putting him on the spot. I asked him to say a little prayer for Eva. Nothing big. Just something small—for now."

The priest nodded his head in agreement, showing the audience he wasn't opposed to the spectacle.

"Now what's going to happen is you're going to see movement on the screen as he prays. It's really hard for me to describe, so I'll just let you see it as it happens."

Yuval gestured for the priest to move closer to Eva's gurney.

"So before we begin, Father Spinney, ask Miss Eva if there's anything you can pray about for her. A prayer *request*—isn't that what we call these things?"

The man leaned beside Eva's head and spoke to her quietly. He listened for a few moments then stood up, indicating he was ready to start.

"Are you ready, Father?" Yuval asked. "Can we listen to you pray? Can someone get this man a microphone?"

The priest dismissed the request with his hand, apparently preferring to pray in silence.

"Okay, never mind. We will let him pray silently. So, whenever you're ready, Father Spinney, please—go ahead and pray for little Miss Eva. Everyone else, be quiet—*please* be quiet—and watch the screen above."

Yuval stepped back as the sanctuary dimmed, and a fake splatter of stained-glass light illuminated the stage. The priest lowered his head and closed his eyes.

At first, the graph appeared unchanged. As the audience grew accustomed to the light, they could begin to see tiny blue dots appear on the graph, floating around aimlessly. Eventually, a few of the dots floated close to the center and began to circle—some clockwise, others counter-clockwise—until they gathered on top of each other towards the middle.

Protestors from outside the cathedral began to push their way in—not only through the vestibule, but over the rubble that covered the floor on the right side of the sanctuary. Transfixed by the lighting and the image of the man on the stage, his head lowered in solemn prayer, they kept largely silent.

As the priest continued to pray, the center of the graph accumulated enough particles that the darkened sanctuary filled with a pale cobalt glow. Whispers of conversations penetrated the silence as the audience tried to make sense of what they were witnessing.

Yuval realized the sanctuary was beginning to fill with protestors from outside and thought of stopping the priest, but couldn't bring himself to interrupt the magic everyone was watching. He quietly walked to Eva's gurney and waved his hand over her bed, an act which caused a visible disturbance within the swarm of particles on the screen. Some began to weep. Others grabbed the arm of someone beside them, their mouths held open with awe.

After another minute of silence, the priest raised his head and opened his eyes. Instantly the blue glow of light on the screen disappeared, plunging the sanctuary into near darkness again. The audience was stunned, their complete silence a clear sign they were overwhelmed with wonder.

"Okay," Yuval whispered quietly, reluctant to break the spell that had been cast. "Okay, Father Spinney, thank you. Come over here if you don't mind."

Yuval held out his hand as the priest joined him towards the lecturn.

"Ladies and gentlemen, what you have just witnessed for the first time is a scientific recording of prayer. If you thought closing your eyes and petitioning our creator was for nothing, well then, maybe this will cause you to think again. Something was going on, right? You saw it, right?"

Nods of agreement spread throughout the pews, even the protestors enraptured by what they had just seen.

"What is faith?" Yuval asked. "What is belief? We still don't know for sure, but we're getting closer. We're getting *real* close, actually. I don't know about you, but I'll take this as an improvement. Now, we can *see* faith. We can even *measure* it. And just like with the sound meter, if you have some feedback your prayers are working, I'm guessing that miracles may actually happen."

More protestors climbed through the opening, their frothing anger from outside immediately squelched by the reverent silence that greeted them once they entered. Yuval sensed the tone shifting and improvised.

"Come in," he said, beckoning the protestors from outside. "Come in. Everyone needs to see this. Please."

Unaware what was happening, those in the front turned around, staring in wonder at the hundreds of people packed into the sanctuary behind them.

"Everyone is welcome here. We are all friends in here."

Yuval waved his arm from side to side. "Please try to make room for everyone. We can all fit in here. We might see a miracle happen if we do."

Father Spinney took a sip of water offered to him by Yuval.

"Were you aware of what was just going on?" Yuval asked.

"I wasn't, no."

"But you were praying that whole time."

"Yes."

"What were you praying for? Did you ask Miss Eva what you could pray about for her?"

"I did," the priest said. "She prayed that she could see her father."

Audible gasps broke out across aisles, just the effect Yuval had hoped for.

"And you prayed she could? That God would bring her father here tonight?"

"I did."

CHAPTER 125

Gordillo held his breath as, three floors below, the exterior door opened, a shock of red clearly visible. He closed his eyes and pulled the trigger. It wouldn't move. He looked on the right side for a safety but couldn't see anything meaningful. Just as he flipped the rifle over, someone behind him grabbed the weapon with both hands and pulled the barrel against his throat.

"This is for Gabriel," the voice whispered in his ear as Gordillo felt his windpipe being crushed in half. Blindly, the Cardinal reached behind him, trying to find anything to grab onto. Unable to grasp his attacker, Gordillo kicked off the railing that lined the interior of the stairwell and slammed himself backwards against the wall, crushing the man underneath him on the stairs.

The man let go of the rifle, gasping for air as he tried to push Gordillo's massive body from on top of him. Able to move more freely, Gordillo slammed his elbow behind him, smashing into the side of his assailant's face. He prepared to strike him again but felt a searing pain in his side, forcing him to roll away and, for the first time, confront his knife-wielding attacker—someone he recognized from the tunnels.

"Cam," Gordillo said, his hand covered in blood from where he'd been stabbed. "Ikänen sent you?"

"God sent me," Cam said, trying to catch his breath. "To avenge Gabriel."

Gordillo grabbed the rifle by the barrel and swung it like an axe, nearly crushing his skull. Cam rolled away, slashing the knife through the air as the Cardinal spun the rifle around.

"God is not on your side," Gordillo said, slamming the heel of his foot into Cam's lower back.

Screaming in pain, Cam rolled down the stairs and crashed at the bottom of the landing. Gordillo held the rifle behind his head like a javelin as he struggled across the steps.

"God is not on your side," he said again, as Cam tried to crawl away.

Gordillo slammed the rifle into Cam's chest, its bloodied barrel catching in the wood beneath him as the Cardinal pushed it all the way through his body.

"And neither is the devil."

CHAPTER 126

The cathedral was now packed with bodies, a state of affairs Yuval couldn't have been more happy with. Father Spinney had played his role perfectly with the suggestion Eva wanted nothing more than the appearance of her father.

Yuval gestured for the priest to return to his seat. "Thank you, Father Spinney. And thank *you*, Miss Eva. I think you might get your wish."

Returning to the stool, Yuval sat and smiled in silence as he looked over the horde of people sitting and standing before him.

"This is just the start. This is just the beginning of what may be possible. Do you see why I have been pushing so hard on this for so many years? The *marriage* of science and faith, right? We don't have to be at war with each other. We can all be friends, can't we? We can all get along and play nice together."

Still recovering from the demonstration, the crowd hung on his every word, eager to push the technology even further. Eager to push themselves even further. Their *own* faith. Their *own* prayers.

"Maybe this is what happened to miracles," Yuval continued. "Maybe we just don't believe in them anymore. Maybe *this* is why they don't happen anymore. Simply because we lost our ability to believe. With all our medicines and internal combustion engines and computers and internet, maybe we just lost our ability to believe."

Above them, the screen changed to a black and white image—a cross-section of a toddler's upper body.

"This is an MRI of our special guest's spine."

Yuval got out a laser pointer and aimed it at the screen. "If you look closely right here—*C4* as we call it—this is Miss Eva's problem. Her *C4* vertebra was shattered, cutting through much of her spinal chord. We all know *how* this happened and I'm not going to belabor the point any more than has already been done."

The crowd grew restless at the cavalier way Yuval described her injuries with her lying right there in front of them. He clicked off the laser pointer and continued speaking.

"What's important is...this is what science alone cannot fix. Millions of dollars were spent trying to, and Miss Eva is still unable to move. Thankfully, she can breathe on her own—a miracle in its own right, considering the nature of her injury—but she cannot move anything below her neck. And that is why we are here. We are here because science has done all it can do—for now."

Yuval walked confidently towards the center of the platform and squarely faced the audience. "But faith—the power of faith...it's just getting started."

The screen changed to a picture of a happy family. A mother and father, each holding a hand of their daughter walking between them. Some didn't recognize them at first, but many of the protestors filling the back and sides did. It was Thomas and Natalie Finch, with a smiling, perfectly healthy three-year-old Eva suspended in mid-air as they held her aloft.

"Miss Eva prayed that her father would show up tonight. I have prayed that, as well. If we're going to take this quest to unite faith and science seriously, we have to be able to bury the hatchet between us, no matter how difficult that may be. That's why I've worked so hard for amnesty. Forgiveness—an important part of faith, right? Forgiveness?"

Having spent the last hours raging through downtown Washington, D.C., the protestors' turn was nothing short of amazing. Before them spoke someone they felt was the most evil man on the planet—and he was making sense. Earlier that day, many would have stormed the stage, hoping for the chance at ending his life. Now, they listened intently to what he was saying, a situation they would've never imagined possible—peace between two sides that would otherwise be eternally at war with each other.

Yuval stood up. "I feel certain Mr. Finch is here with us tonight. Possibly, already in the room right now."

Everyone immediately looked to their left and right, confirming they weren't sitting beside the world's most wanted man. Yuval glanced at the picture of the Finch family as a dark vein of hatred pulsed within his chest.

"Before we ask Mr. Finch to make his presence known, let us speak with Eva's mother. Natalie, could you come out and say hello to everyone?"

As before, a spotlight focused on the side of the stage. After several moments, a young woman was pushed out into the light, her light brown curls a much different image than who they saw pictured on the screen above them. She walked across the platform, her hands clutched to her stomach as if in pain.

Yuval immediately recognized it was Dr. Connolly's assistant, Brooke. His body went numb, unable to stop her from reaching Eva.

"I'm sorry," Yuval said. "Someone is playing a joke on me."

After realizing it wasn't the woman from the picture, others in the audience began to laugh.

"Grab her," Yuval hissed, before composing himself. "Can someone remove her, please?"

Brooke ran towards Eva and pulled her from the gurney, a large syringe dangling from an IV that ran into her arm. Two security team members rushed the stage and fought to pull the girl from Brooke's arms.

"He's going to kill her," Brooke screamed, her voice blasting out of the PA system before an engineer could mute the microphones.

The spectators were completely confused, unsure as to whether Brooke's appearance was part of the incredible show. Eventually, one of the men was able to wrestle Eva out of Brooke's arms while the other dragged Connolly's assistant away.

"He's going to kill you all," some of those in the front rows could hear her shouting as she disappeared off the stage.

Yuval said something to calm the situation, but like the others, his microphone was turned off. He pointed to it, trying to get it working again. Unsure of what to do, the security guard handed Eva to Yuval, assuming he'd want to hold her.

"Don't give her to me," he boomed across the sanctuary, unaware his microphone had just been turned back on.

The security guard took Eva and placed her back in her gurney, her syringe hanging conspicuously over the side.

"Well, that was interesting," Yuval said, setting his glasses back on his head. "That wasn't part of the show, in case you were wondering. That was our beloved Albert Connolly's assistant, and I'm not exactly sure what is going on with her. Not feeling well, I suppose."

Yuval tried to improvise, a skill he'd never been good at. "Perhaps we should pray for her."

He returned to the podium and swiped his finger across a digital display, trying to find his place.

"Where were we?" he asked, completely flustered at the break from the script. "Oh yes, I was expecting Natalie—Eva's mother—to come on stage as we prepared to pray for her daughter, but I suppose that's not going to happen, obviously."

Yuval scratched the side of his face as he tried to figure out what to do.

Where is she? he asked himself.

"Okay, well we will move on without her, then. Can we get the clergy up here? All of you who I've already asked to pray for her—could you come up here now? Either side is fine."

Members of the audience shuffled down the pews and made their way to the stage, circling behind Eva's gurney. Some were dressed in what were obviously liturgical garments, while others wore more secular formal attire. Stagehands moved the antennas farther away to accommodate the crowd that formed, the cords that connected them together quickly re-taped to the ground so no one would trip. Eventually, nearly one hundred of the world's most influential men and women of faith stood, ready to make their petitions Eva would be healed.

"Nobody pray yet," Yuval said, a line he hoped would generate a few laughs. "Just a few more words before we get started."

A few stragglers made their way onto the stage, crowding in close around Eva's gurney. Someone pushed through the rows of people directly behind her, causing a disturbance as they made their way to the front. Some stepped backwards, others leaned away to allow them through.

Two people directly behind Eva moved aside as a woman emerged from between them. Her mouth was closed, her nostrils flared in anger. Quivering, she placed her hands on Eva's head and stared directly at Yuval.

CHAPTER 127

Brinkley crept through the darkness between the library and the cathedral. National Guardsmen had stormed the building as they sought to discover the source of what they felt to be an enormous attack. Just as they approached the building, Brinkley had jumped from the roof onto a nearby tree and climbed down, running far away into a nearby neighborhood.

What they would find was everything Brinkley had grabbed from Yuval's helicopter: decoy flares, smoke grenades, and hundreds of shells of ammunition he had fired into the air from a small machine gun.

It was a diversion he realized had worked as the security perimeter that lined the cathedral appeared to be completely gone. Hundreds of people once pressed against the fence were nowhere to be seen, likely wrapped around the front of the building—possibly inside, if they were lucky.

Where are you, Finch? he asked himself as he studied the back of the cathedral, looking for a way in.

Feeling he was far enough away not to be spotted, Brinkley stood up and began walking toward a rear door, a single security officer standing beside it.

Someone yelled out from behind him. "Hey! You there. Freeze. Don't move!"

Brinkley circled around and saw a soldier a hundred feet away, standing with a rifle raised to his shoulder. Other soldiers were jogging up behind him. The officer guarding the cathedral door heard the clamor and instinctively crouched, drawing his own pistol.

Surrounded, Brinkley ran directly towards the security officer with his hands in the air then dropped to the ground. Within seconds, a plume of smoke began to surround him, slowly drifting into the surrounding trees.

Screams and commands issued forth from both the Guardsmen and the security officer until they were finally able to see each other in the smoke.

Brinkley, however, had disappeared.

* * *

Bodies were pressed together tightly, and Finch found it nearly impossible to get into the cathedral. Whether they recognized who he was or not, he was unsure. Regardless, something about the demeanor in which he carried himself seemed to give them reason to allow him to pass.

"Excuse me," someone said, stepping aside out of his way.

"I'm sorry," another person muttered, holding their hand out in front of them.

He paused for a moment and removed the vial and syringe Ikänen gave him. Carefully, he stuck the needle through the rubber membrane on top of the vial, loaded the syringe, and replaced the cap. Trying to conserve his energy, he walked forward slowly, turning sideways where necessary to fit, speaking nothing, focused on entering the sanctuary and reaching his daughter before it was too late.

CHAPTER 128

Natalie, Yuval thought to himself.

Standing behind her daughter, Natalie met Yuval's gaze with as much hatred for him as he had for her.

One more piece, he thought to himself. *One more piece, and it will be done.*

Yuval turned to the audience and smiled broadly enough for everyone in the room to see. "Eva's mother—Miss Natalie Connolly—has decided to join us as we pray for her daughter's recovery. Isn't that wonderful?"

The projection screen cut to a close-up of Natalie, her icy stare impossible to miss.

"I almost forgot," Yuval said. "Before we begin, we should acknowledge someone we lost this morning, someone for whom this technology might have been able to save, had we been a day earlier. I'm talking about Mongchai, of course."

An image of the boy before his drowning appeared on the screen. Surrounded by his friends, his face full of joy, he looked directly at the camera, the others apparently unaware they were being photographed.

"Many of you are here, no doubt, for him. To see *him* healed. To get back some of what he sacrificed for his friends. I grieve with you for his passing."

Yuval stole another glance at Natalie, her frigid stare unmoved. He looked down towards the floor and counted to ten, the only sound, generators running the light towers outside. After he was finished, Yuval looked up toward the audience and pressed his fingers together.

The screen switched back to the graph, a speckle of blue dots already swirling around the center.

"I told you not to start praying yet," Yuval said as many in the audience laughed, amazed once again at what was apparently happening. "Maybe it's the people at home. Wouldn't that be something?"

Yuval held a finger to his mouth and paced across the stage, consumed with thought. "I have an idea. Let's try something interesting. How many people are watching this now? Do we have any idea? Anyone out there see a number?"

He shielded his eyes from the bright lights aimed at the stage and peered out into the audience for someone to come up with an answer. At the very back of the sanctuary, shrouded in near darkness, the center door opened quietly as a Cardinal—covered in a scarlet robe—walked slowly through the opening.

"Thirteen million," someone said.

"Five point seven million," another shouted several rows back.

Yuval nodded his head. "Okay, thirteen million. Five million. I'm sure there's other services streaming this. Let's say twenty million people watching this at home. At work. Listening maybe in their cars. All of you, wanting to know the answer—are miracles real? Can faith really heal?

"If you're at home. At work. In your car. Wherever you are, I want you to start praying for Miss Eva here. Pray that she could be healed."

The screen began to fill with the faint blue speckle of a thousand tiny points of light—some hovering in place, others swirling around the edge of graph. In the audience, people felt the back of their neck tingle as their hair stiffened. Others shivered as chills overtook their bodies, the skin on their arms raised up into prickles.

"Wow," Yuval said. "Look at that. I don't know if you can see this at home, but we can see it here. We can see your prayers come in. Eva can feel them."

Now halfway up the aisle, the Cardinal continued walking slowly towards the stage, his progress beginning to be noticed by more people.

"Before everyone here starts to pray—before the real fireworks—I want to make one more plea, one more appeal to Eva's father. I know he's here somewhere. Your family is here, Finch. Your daughter. Your wife."

Natalie wanted to scream, but with millions of eyes looking upon her daughter, praying for her recovery, she couldn't summon the will to move a muscle.

"Eva was in a very bad helicopter crash," Yuval said, scanning the room. "Just an hour ago. She is in a very frail condition. She needs you, Finch. She needs *your* prayers as much as anyone."

The Cardinal was now just twenty rows from the front, his stilted movement slowing his progress. Yuval spotted the priest and beckoned him toward the stairs.

"Come up, Cardinal. Come around here to the side and join us."

As hundreds watched his red robe flow by, the Cardinal walked slowly to the edge of the stage, bowed his head, and began to climb the stairs.

"There are many faiths represented here," Yuval said. "Many others watching throughout the world. They all want your daughter to recover from her devastating injuries. They're all ready to forgive you."

With his head still bowed, the Cardinal walked behind Eva's gurney and stood beside her mother.

His face fraught with frustration, Yuval had run out of ideas. If Finch was in the room, he wouldn't show himself. He bowed his head before lifting it up again. "Let us now pray that God would heal Eva Connolly."

The people standing behind her closed their eyes and bowed their heads. The screen above them instantly filled with bright blue dots, whirling towards and away from the center of the graph. Some of them flocked together, as if joined by a common force, while others bounced around with no apparent logic.

"Look at that," Yuval said, pointing toward the screen. "Look at your faith. Don't close your eyes—see your faith right now."

In the audience and on the stage, those praying for Eva opened their eyes and were struck with wonder as the particles flocked closer together in a more distinct pattern, spiraling through and around the center in a beautiful geometric pattern.

"That's it," Yuval said, the pitch of his voice raising in intensity. "You see it now. And you *believe* in it, don't you?"

The frequency of shapes surrounding the graph doubled in intensity, bathing the sanctuary in a bright light from the screen. They began to spin faster through the pattern, splitting off into two separate shapes—one that spun clockwise, the other spinning against it.

"God will heal her!" Yuval screamed, his voice cracking under the strain. "I know he will."

The dots began to change color wherever the two spinning shapes overlapped, a shower of purple and red particles that exploded outward and rejoined the others, illuminating the sanctuary in flashes of light.

"Keep it up," Yuval said. "Keep praying."

Beside her, Natalie could sense the Cardinal beginning to shake.

Yuval stepped towards the very edge of the stage. "Let's pray something together, shall we? What will our faith look like then?"

A stagehand placed a wireless microphone in Yuval's hand before he returned to Eva's gurney, joining the group of people that circled around her.

"Cardinal," he said, handing the microphone to the man in red. "Would you lead us in prayer? For Eva?"

The man continued to tremble but wouldn't move.

"Cardinal?" Yuval asked. "Take the microphone. Show us how to pray for Eva."

He extended the microphone even closer to the man, but his quivering had turned into visible shaking.

"Cardinal, are you okay? Do you need to sit down?"

The man began to teeter. Natalie grabbed the sleeve of his arm and steadied him to prevent him from falling. She looked directly at him to ask a question but screamed at what she saw.

A face from the past. The face of her husband, his skin mottled blue from lack of oxygen.

At that same moment, the blast of a gun shattered the reverent prayers of everyone in attendance as Thomas Finch, standing behind his daughter and beside his wife, crumpled to the ground.

CHAPTER 129

The echo of the gunshot evaporated, but the lone scream of a woman on the stage continued to ring out. Ducking along the left side of the aisle, Gordillo looked behind him, trying to locate the shooter. It sounded like the crack had come from the rear of the sanctuary but, given the building's acoustics, was impossible to tell.

Those who were able crouched beneath their pews, expecting more gunfire might follow. Others ran for the exits, a stampede of humanity climbing on top of each other to escape. Gordillo continued to stare as hundreds of people scrambled past him. On the stage, Eva's gurney was rolled to the side as some of those praying for her knelt beside someone lying on the ground.

"Don't leave," Yuval said into the microphone, his voice in a panic. "No one leave! Close the doors. Security—don't let anyone leave."

Armed guards tried to block the exits, brandishing their rifles as a threat, but it was too late. Swarms of people pushed them out of the way. Others clawed over the rubble and through the hole in the side of the building. Yuval's plan was quickly coming apart. Gordillo calmly walked toward the risers where the audio and lighting controls were located, curious as to how the enormous cube was operated.

* * *

Brinkley ran down the right aisle, his eyes locked on a man still holding a gun in his hand. He had just made it into the sanctuary when the stooped figure emerged from the shadows, drew his gun, and fired at the stage. Incredibly, mobs of people ran directly by him, oblivious to any danger.

"Freeze," Brinkley yelled at the man, before realizing he had no weapon to challenge him with.

The man looked up, his vacant stare reaching straight through Brinkley.

"I killed him," he said. "I killed him."

He dropped the gun, collapsed to his knees, and began to weep as he felt his faith beginning to waver. "Father, forgive me. Father forgive me, for I know not what I do."

Brinkley kicked the gun away and yanked him from the aisle onto a pew.

"Killed who?" Brinkley asked. "Who did you kill?"

Pointing at the stage, the man coughed up blood as he tried to speak. "Finch," he said, his brows creasing into anger. "God made me do it. I didn't want to."

Brinkley looked at the stage and saw Yuval walking towards the injured man.

"He was a hero. To all of us."

"Who are you?" Brinkley asked, standing up.

The man smiled, his teeth stained red.

"My name is Arvo Ikänen," he said. "Please kill me. Before I do."

CHAPTER 130

Yuval looked in horror as he realized Finch was lying wounded on the ground, his face stained an unnatural shade of blue. Around them, the pastors and priests that were praying for Eva panicked. Some fell to the ground while others scampered toward the nearest exit.

"Save him," Yuval shouted. "Save him. Don't let him die. Someone help me."

Finch rolled over, trying to crawl away. His vision began to fade as he clutched at cables running along the floor, pulling one of the antennas to the ground. Natalie wrapped her arms around Eva and lifted her from the gurney.

"Don't let him die," Yuval said as the rest of the petitioners cleared the stage.

Finch ripped a long strip of tape from the floor and wrapped it around his own head several times, completely covering his lower face. Silently, the clear cube hanging above them started to descend.

"Get back!" Natalie said to others near the stage, looking up at the transparent block. "Get away. Let him handle this."

Yuval jumped on top of him and tried to claw the tape away. Finch's eyes began to bulge as his body screamed for oxygen he no longer had.

"Someone help me," Yuval shrieked. "He's trying to kill himself."

Their hands locked together as Yuval continued to rake at the layers of tape covering Finch's nose and mouth. Finch tried to buck Yuval from his chest, but his muscles were nearly useless. From the side of the sanctuary, Vickers ran onto the stage just as the clear cube neared the floor. Inside, Yuval and Finch continued to grapple with each other.

"Shoot it," Yuval shrieked. "Destroy it."

Vickers raised an assault rifle and fired his entire magazine into the side of the glass, each shot leaving a half-inch pock mark.

"Shoot it again," Yuval cried out, his voice barely audible as Vickers loaded another magazine and aimed at a single spot, trying to shatter the cube.

With Yuval distracted, Finch reached into his pocket and uncapped the syringe. He tried to stand but immediately blacked out and crashed to the ground. Incapacitated, Yuval wrapped his fingers around the edge of the tape covering Finch's face and pulled hard, ripping clumps of his beard from his skin.

Finch tried to scream in pain, but nothing came out. Realizing his mouth was free, he drew in a cold breath of air and exhaled, his chest heaving as his body struggled for more oxygen.

"That's it," Yuval said, nearly in tears as he held Finch in his arms. "Breathe it out. Breathe it out as much as you can."

Yuval began to pull the folds of Finch's red robe away.

"Where are you shot?" he asked. "How bad is it?"

Finch slammed his hand onto Yuval's leg, thrusting the syringe through his pants and deep within his muscle. Before he could squeeze the plunger, Yuval spun away, removed the syringe, and squeezed the contents onto the ground.

"What's this?" Yuval asked, sniffing the tip of the needle. "You don't think I got the shot already?"

"You're too smart for that," Finch said, still trying to catch his breath. "I know you didn't."

Raging with anger, Yuval looked outside the cube at Vickers and pointed towards Eva, still held in her mother's arms.

"Kill her!" he said.

Vickers lifted his empty rifle, showing he was out of ammunition.

"Use the syringe!"

Natalie looked down and saw the IV hanging from Eva's arm. Just as she spun, Vickers dove and tackled her onto the floor, the clear syringe sliding inches from his hand. Natalie twisted Eva from him, flinging the IV over her face. Using her teeth, Natalie bit into the plastic tubing, trying to severe it in half.

"I'm sorry, Eva," Natalie said, as she wrapped the IV around her hand.

Vickers grabbed the syringe with one hand and pressed down hard the moment Natalie ripped the tubing from Eva's arm, its contents spraying onto the side of the glass cube.

Yuval beat on the transparent wall in frustration. His strength returning, Finch was able to stand. He hurled his body into Yuval, smashing him into the glass, sending the needle skittering across the stage. Falling to the floor, Yuval saw a steady current of blood dripping beneath where Finch stood.

"We need to get you patched up," Yuval said, struggling to breathe. "You're losing a lot of blood."

"I'm going to kill you before I die."

"Your daughter is going to die, Finch. Natalie thought you could save her."

"Everyone dies."

"There'll be no rescue. No healing. It was all trickery."

"I prayed for her, Yuval. While I was standing behind her, I prayed for her. For the first time in my life."

"Faith is a scourge upon the earth," Yuval said.

"You're probably the only one who could have made that happen."

"A blot upon humanity."

Finch could feel himself begin to wobble. "I want to thank you. You've given me faith—something Natalie always wanted for me."

"You'll never have her again, Finch. How does that feel?"

Finch stumbled to his knees, fighting the urge to close his eyes.

"You'll never hug your daughter again."

"Perhaps."

"She will never, ever hug you."

"We will see."

"I want you alive, Finch. They want you dead."

"Nothing you wanted is going to happen."

"It's not too late. I can save you. No one else will."

Finch began to mumble as consciousness slipped away. "You lose. At everything."

Yuval stepped closer as Finch fell to the floor. He stopped to check for a pulse, but could feel nothing other than a stabbing pain in his upper chest. In horror, Yuval turned his head to see an empty syringe hanging underneath his collarbone. Finch had injected him with a bubble of air that moved inches towards his brain before lodging in place, blocking the flow of blood.

Beating on his chest, Yuval tried to dislodge the embolism that had formed. He grasped at the needle hanging from his body, but it was too late. His vision began to fade and Yuval fell backwards, looking toward the screen above him, blue particles still swirling around the center.

CHAPTER 131

Brinkley heard something click as the lights flickered off, plunging the cathedral into darkness.

"What happened?" Vickers asked, waiting for his eyes to adjust.

"Someone turned the power off."

The last of Ikänen's mercenaries—unaware that not only had Gabriel been killed, but Cam as well—groped their way onto the stage, still searching for Gordillo. Brinkley followed close behind.

Vickers fumbled across the floor until he ran into a side of the cube.

"Who's here?" Vickers asked. "What happened to Yuval?"

He beat on the glass and listened for some sort of response from inside.

Hearing nothing, a soldier turned on his flashlight and swept it around the stage within the box.

Natalie gasped when she saw Finch laying on his side, a pool of blood gathering beneath him.

"Get him out of there," she said, as she noticed the slight rise and fall of his lungs. "He's going to bleed to death."

Certain she was speaking of Yuval, Vickers began to bark directions to everyone else.

"We have to lift it. This side. Everyone over here. We can lift it up."

Brinkley and Ikänen's men felt their way around the cube until they were all lined up along the same side.

"On the count of three, everyone lift."

They wrapped their fingers around the bottom of the glass and tightened their backs.

"One," Vickers said. "Two. Three!"

The edge moved just enough they were able to wrap their hands underneath it.

"Lift!" Vickers shouted, as the bottom of the cube reached their waist.

Suddenly, something grabbed Vickers' legs from within the cube and yanked him halfway inside. The enormous block crashed downwards, crushing his abdomen beneath thousands of pounds of glass.

"What happened?" Brinkley asked. "Why'd we drop it?"

A soldier flashed his light around the darkness inside the cube again, stopping when he reached Finch's body. Looming behind him stood the stilted figure of Ikänen.

Natalie screamed in fright.

"What in the hell?" Brinkley said. "How'd he get in there?"

"Stop him!" Natalie cried out. "He'll kill him!"

Ikänen knelt beside Finch and put his hand on his neck. Brinkley moved to the back of the cube and began to push it towards the front of the stage.

"Help me," he howled at the other men. "Push it over the edge."

"Don't," one of the mercenaries yelled. "Ikänen knows what he's doing."

Without warning, the cube slid sideways, pushed from within by a powerful force.

"He's possessed," Natalie screamed. "He'll kill everyone of us if you don't stop him."

Ikänen's men ran behind the cube and pushed with Brinkley, sliding it until it hung on the body of Yuval.

"Harder," Brinkley called out. "All the way over."

They doubled their efforts until the back of the block hit Ikänen and knocked him on top of Finch. With three men trapped inside, the cube was nearly impossible to move. Ikänen recovered his balance and tried to sit up.

"Help us," Brinkley called out. "Push!"

Cradling Eva in her arms, Natalie leaned her back against the cube and extended her legs, pushing with every muscle. Suddenly, the block broke away and slid freely across the stage.

"All the way," Brinkley screamed. "Don't stop."

Ikänen fell to the floor and slid alongside Finch as the front of the block extended past the stage and began to tip downwards. Brinkley grabbed underneath the cube and lifted it up into the air, exposing Finch to his grasp.

"Grab him" he said. "Pull him out."

One of the mercenaries grabbed Finch's red robe to wrestle him free, but Ikänen took hold of Finch's leg, preventing him from being pulled to safety. Brinkley let go, and the block crashed onto Ikänen's arms, splitting both muscle and bone apart. Incredibly, Ikänen stood up, ripping himself from beneath the cube.

Terrified by the sight of his bloody stumps pressing against the glass, they drove the block off of the stage, sending Ikänen and Yuval down with it. The cube shattered as it hit the ground, splitting into a thousand fifty-pound daggers, one of which pierced Ikänen's throat as he dropped, pinning him to the wooden floor beneath.

EPILOGUE

Cardinal Gordillo walked across the tarmac toward his airplane, its jet engines already spooling up. A female attendant reached out to help as he hobbled up the stairs leading inside.

"Get me some more clothes," he said. "These are ruined."

"What happened?"

"Where is he?" Gordillo asked, ignoring her question.

"He's on his way."

Gordillo shouted loud enough for the pilots to hear. "We need to be in the air as soon as possible. Be ready to leave as soon as he's on."

The attendant left for the back of the plane and returned with several hangers of clothing. She held them up for Gordillo to consider.

"Don't we have anything white?" he asked.

"I don't think so. But, I'll look."

She hurried down the aisle to the closet outside his private chamber.

"Who's my security now?" Gordillo asked to no one in particular. "Or are they all dead?"

Outside the plane, an ambulance slowly pulled to a stop. The rear door opened and two EMTs lowered a wheelchair to the ground, the man sitting within covered with bandages.

"He's here," Gordillo said. "Somebody's going to need to help get him on."

The Cardinal sat in a leather seat and took a sip from the glass of wine already prepared for him. A pilot stepped out of the cockpit and grabbed the wheelchair's footrest, guiding it up the stairs as the EMTs pushed it from behind. After considerable struggle, they were able to get the man aboard.

"Don't forget this," an EMT said, handing the pilot a bag of medicine. "Instructions are inside."

The pilot wheeled the man down the aisle and parked him across from Gordillo.

"Thank you for offering me a ride," the man said, a bolt of red cloth visible under his seat. "Flying commercial is a nightmare in a wheelchair."

Gordillo raised his eyebrows and took another dram of wine. "It's the least I can do. We Cardinals—we have to help each other, do we not?"

"We do. And I appreciate it. How long is the flight?"

"Not long," Gordillo said, his eyes lighting up. "Not long at all. I'm sure you'll be home soon."

* * *

Finch tried to open his eyes to force himself back into consciousness. What will power alone couldn't do, the throbbing pain in the side of his abdomen was able to accomplish. He shifted to his other side, trying to alleviate the stabs that kept him from rest.

"Tom?" someone said, stroking the hair from his face. "Tom, are you awake?"

Focusing every ounce of energy on his eyelids, Finch lifted them just far enough to see his daughter near, lying on her side, looking directly at him.

"Eva," he said, reaching out to touch her.

"Hi, Daddy," she replied, smiling.

"I'm so glad to see you."

"Me, too."

Without moving his head, Finch glanced around the room. "Where's Mommy? Where's Natalie?"

"I'm right here," Natalie said, rubbing her hand on his face.

Finch tried to twist towards her, but it was too painful.

"Let me see you. Where are you?"

Natalie walked to the side of the bed behind Eva where he could see them both.

Finch began to tear up. "I've missed you. So much."

"We have a lot of catching up to do."

The fog that clouded his thoughts began to lift as Finch realized they were in a hospital room.

"Where are we?" he asked.

"Prince George State Hospital. It didn't all burn down, if you're wondering what that smell is."

Finch sniffed, the air loaded with the pungent smell of charred wood.

"Why am I here?"

His memory clearly fragmented, Natalie was unsure how to answer. "You were shot."

"By who?"

"Someone who thought they were doing the right thing."

Finch shook his head, trying to clear the haze of the last twenty four hours. The door opened and someone rolled a cart of food into the room.

"Thank you, Brinkley," Natalie said.

"Brinkley?" Finch asked, craning his neck to see him. The moment he saw his face, scenes from the previous evening began to coalesce in his mind.

"Yuval? What happened to him?"

Natalie paused, hesitant to expose Eva to any more drama than she had already experienced. Sensing her reluctance, Eva tried to comfort her.

"It's okay, Mommy. Just tell him everything."

"Yuval is dead," Natalie said. "You were trapped under the glass cube with him."

"He tried to save me," Finch said, his memory beginning to return. "He wanted me alive."

Suddenly, an intense pang of fear scorched through Finch's body.

"Get away from me!" Finch shouted. "What are you doing in here?"

Natalie put her hand on his arm, trying to comfort him. "Tom, it's okay."

Finch twisted away violently as waves of pain shot down his side. "Get away! I'll kill you! What are you doing? I don't want to hurt you!"

Natalie gripped his arm tightly. "Tom, listen to me. I think we're going to be okay."

"What are you talking about?"

Natalie looked at Eva. "Go ahead, Eva. Tell him what Papa told you."

"About the shots?"

"Yes."

"When Mommy and me went to get the shots—where Papa works—I was really scared. He said 'Don't worry, Eva. You and Mommy are getting the sugar shots. I made sure.'"

Natalie began to sob. "We would have known something by now, Finch. We feel fine. I think we're going to be fine."

Tears ran down Finch's face. "He was scared for you, wasn't he?"

"He was. He made sure we were in the placebo group."

"You didn't get the real ones?"

"We must not have."

Another memory came into focus—Finch reaching out for Connolly as he fell backwards from the balcony.

"Oh God, Natalie. I'm sorry. He...."

Natalie held out her hand to stop him. "I know. I know. We can talk about it later."

The emotional toll of the previous day—the past few years—converged all at once as Finch began to weep.

"I thought I'd never see either of you again."

"I am so sorry."

"I thought it would kill you if I did."

"I don't think we have to worry about that any more."

"I didn't want to live like that."

Natalie bent down over the bed and hugged Finch tightly. "You don't. *We* don't. We don't have to live like that anymore."

"But the hospital?" Finch asked. "What about all the other people here?"

"Relax, Tom. This wing was already abandoned—before the fire. This is the only room left standing. We found a surgeon who was safe to be around you. Everything is fine."

Brinkley walked beside Natalie, a plate in his hand, his mouth full of food.

Finch couldn't help but to consider what the future might look like. "Where will we live? I'm cursed."

"We'll figure that out," Natalie said. "Don't worry."

Brinkley spoke up. "I know a nice cabin in the woods where I think you'll feel right at home."

"Garcia," Finch said, remembering the man's haunting last words before he killed himself.

Brinkley held his hand up. "Enough of that for now. Let's be happy for ten minutes. We can cry all we want later."

"Get me some coffee, then. I'm dying."

Brinkley rolled the cart closer, a steaming mug surrounded by packs of sugar, cinnamon, and an assortment of flavored creamers. "Hope this works for you."

Finch laughed tears of joy, still unbelieving his family, against all odds, was reunited.

"I have a question for you, Daddy," Eva said.

"What is it?"

"Did you pray for me? While you were up on the stage?"

"Everyone in the whole word was praying for you, Eva."

"Did *you*?"

Wearing Ikänen's red robe, Finch had wobbled onto the stage after holding his breath for nearly two minutes. Losing consciousness, confident he had breathed his last, Finch finally found the humility to ask for help.

Not for himself. For Eva—his daughter, who he felt he'd never be able to see again.

"I did pray for you. It wasn't very good, I'm sure. But, I did. Why do you ask?"

"I have a new trick. I want to show you and Mommy something."

Natalie moved closer and placed Eva's hand in hers.

"Ready?"

"Yes."

Natalie flinched.

"Did you feel that, Mommy?"

"I did," Natalie said, her eyes filling with tears. "Do it again."

Startled, Natalie gasped a second time. "I felt it again. Grab her hand, Tom."

Eva's father rolled closer and latched onto her other hand. "Come on, Eva. Give us all you got."

Finch closed his eyes and felt a surge of joy explode within him as Eva's tiny fingers contracted around his.

Other popular books by Forrest Maready:

The Moth In The Iron Lung:
The story of polio that explains everything.

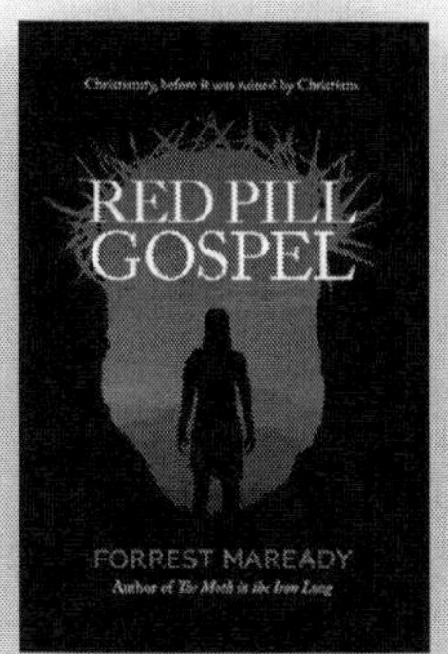

Red Pill Gospel
Christianity, before it was ruined by Christians.

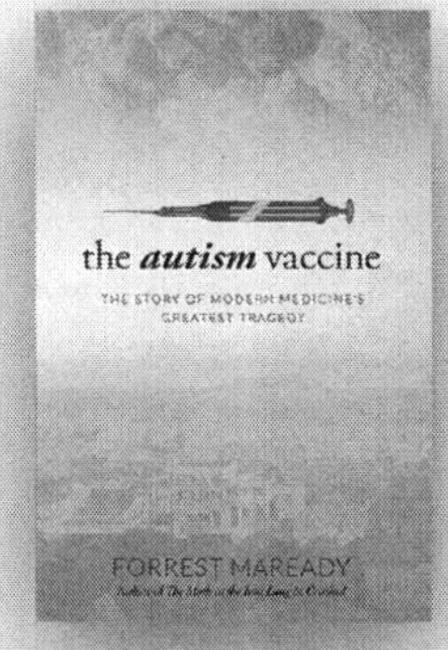

The Autism Vaccine:
The Story of Modern Medicine's Greatest Tragedy.

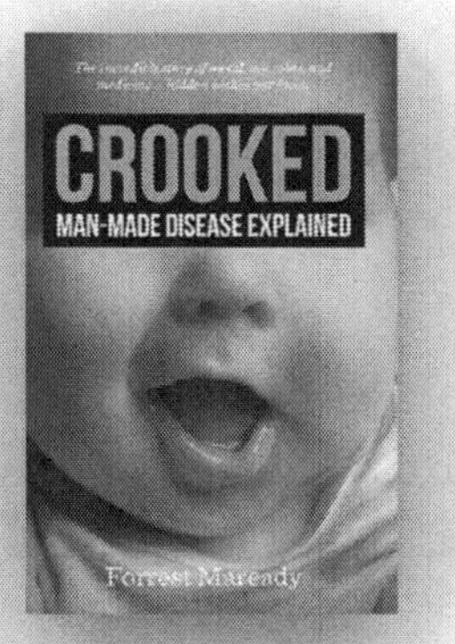

Crooked:
The incredible story of metal, microbes, and medicine—hidden within our faces.

Available at select retailers and:

www.**forrestmaready**.com

ABOUT THE AUTHOR

Rarely does an author have the gift for spanning the divide between faith, science and storytelling, but Forrest Maready has found his voice within this exploding genre. A masterful storyteller, Maready is able to explain complex medical and scientific phenomenon simply, often woven within the fabric of a human-sized account. Like Erik Larson or Candice Millard, Maready dives deep into historical literature in search of the interesting, the obscure, and the frightening–all in an attempt to inform and educate the reader. Maready's works read more like detective thrillers—short chapters, fast-paced action, often with a stunning conclusion that will surprise the most astute student.

But that is not all. Maready employs his prescient scientific mind to propose the answers to many of medicine's greatest riddles. Why did epidemic polio suddenly appear in the 1890s and disappear in the early 1950s? Why are people with neurological injuries so often left-handed? Why did food allergies suddenly appear in the 1930s? On and on his inquisitive mind takes the reader—a journey full of possibilities and answers to questions that have stumped the greatest scientific minds for decades. If you have a weekend to spare, grab a Maready book and prepare to be entertained and enlightened!

Forrest Maready is a native of North Carolina and graduate of Wake Forest University, where he studied religion and music. He spent the early part of his career working in the film, television, and advertising industries as a sound engineer, composer, animator, and editor. He is the author of over a dozen books, many of them stemming from years of medical research. *The Moth in the Iron Lung*, his most popular, tells the true story of polio—a tale much different than most were taught as children. More recently, he founded Protarianism, a Christian denomination focused on restoring both tribes and an understanding of the faith before it was taken over by pagans, polytheists, and philosophers. His book *Red Pill Gospel: Christianity, Before it was Ruined by Christians*, documents the takeover. Maready still lives in North Carolina with his family and is an avid musician, tennis player, and competitive shooter.

Made in the USA
Middletown, DE
11 June 2024

55597086R00246